HARD CORE

R. Michael Bullotta

MILVERSTEAD PUBLISHING

Philadelphia

ISBN-13: 978-0-9842847-9-5

ISBN-10: 0-9842847-9-5

Cover and interior designed by Joel Friedlander
www.TheBookDesigner.com

Milverstead Publishing LLC
31 Rampart Drive
Wayne, PA 19087

Visit us on the web!

http://www.milversteadpublishing.com

One

It was early morning in the Santa Ana Canyons when the tattered, pale-blue 1978 Buick Regal reached the pinnacle of the steep incline of Via De Lomas Road and rested near the gray rocks at the dead end. The car and its driver were in unfamiliar territory, worlds away from the unforgiving streets of South Central Los Angeles and the bloody crack alleys of Compton. In the distance, Orange County and two of its less urban cities – Yorba Linda and Anaheim Hills – were featured in a spectacular bird's-eye view. Though it was 6:45 a.m., the Riverside freeway was already packed with commuters bound for downtown L.A., and the cars became a giant centipede inching westward, emitting an anti-atmospheric gas as if to stave off potential attackers.

The orange sun was rising slowly in the cloudless sky, just over the shoulder of the 17-year-old boy as he exited his car. He followed the directions he had been given to a T, but still felt he made a wrong turn somewhere.

He stood on the dirt road, staring into the dead canyon directly in front of him, and his mind flashed him bits and pieces of his young life. Images were shown him, one after the other, as if paging through *Life* magazine's photo year in review. His enemies were kids just like him, born in wrong neighborhoods. He saw himself asking the question he'd always asked his young victims. "Where you from?" he'd say, as a matter of rhetoric only. Then he pulled the trigger. He had never shown a sign of weakness, especially when pulling the trigger.

He could not remember the faces of the strangers he had jacked. They all melded together into a vague memory that brought a feeling he had never known as remorse. But something was living inside him, and was gnawing at his innards.

The horror was slowly killing him. He wished that his mother had hit him, or at least battered his soul. Maybe then he wouldn't feel like this. He'd be just another young Latino fallen victim to L.A.'s violent urban culture. He too could claim that he had resorted to gang banging in order to survive in a jungle of lovelessness and death. But at every wrong turn, she was there, giving a seemingly endless supply of herself. She would never be ashamed of her only son.

He thought he was going back to juvenile camp when his homeboy told him that the cops were at his house. When he got there and saw them carrying her body out, he hoped that she had suffered a heart attack. But he knew that it was all too common for the rival hood to pull a drive-by without checking to see if the target was home. To them, it's a win-win, as there was satisfaction in taking down loved ones of ones hated.

It was clear to him as he looked straight through the grassy canyon that it was time to make it up to her. He was going to "flip and cooperate," as his friend the detective put it. His homies would call him a "buster," or coward, and it would be a matter of neighborhood pride to smoke him for disrespecting his set. But he truly believed that going legit was the only thing that would make her proud.

As he waited, he thought about the shocked look that would surely find the detective's face when he learned the truth, the whole ugly and confusing truth, parts of which still puzzled this boy-man. His heart, what was left of it, yearned for his mother to be there when he fingered the murderers, all of them. He hoped that she would smile down on him from heaven, just before he was taken down to hell.

After an hour he was no longer introspective. He figured that either he was in the wrong place, or the man was not coming. "Damn it homes, you're supposed to be here," he thought. The detective, his friend, had always kept his promises.

He got back into his car to wait five more minutes. He would only wait one. The first "pop!" was quickly followed by three more. He saw blurry people looking at him from outside his car. He saw a gun. His entire body tingled with pain. Overwhelmed, he leaned back in the driver's seat and felt his mother's loving arms around him. He would swear that he saw her smile at him.

Two

The first boarding call for Jordan Stowic's plane was announced. Jordan and Kendall focused eyes and thoughts on each other at gate F-11 of Chicago's O'Hare airport. They had been together since a love scene four years ago at Northwestern. The class was Advanced Principles in Drama. That's where it started. Now it was ending. Kendall recalled the confidence that overflowed from Jordan the day they met and said their lines, both real and fictional. She still carried with her the charm of their first date and the moonlit walk along the beach, looking miles out into Lake Michigan between kisses. Lost forever in the recesses of her mind was Lee Strasbourg's Acting Method.

"We'll be together before you know it," lied Jordan. It was his role to be the rock. He smiled into her emerald greens. "Come with me to L.A. Cupcake, and I promise to keep you in the style to which you're accustomed."

She grinned with teary eyes (and her eyes were unusually large, green and beautiful).

"If you stay in Chicago, I'll do you the honor of living with you and making you my love slave, despite the fact that Joe and Barb will immediately disinherit me."

"Yeah, they'd probably try to have your birth annulled," he retorted, agreeing with her assessment. Joseph and Barbara Wright, as Catholic as the scapula that shrouds Joseph Wright's Catholic neck, would become rather unglued at the very thought of their daughter, their baby girl, giving serious consideration to the aforementioned premarital evils of the flesh. "Living in sin" would be their battle cry for the foreseeable future.

As they sat in a row of waiting seats, Kendall rested her head and neck on Jordan's shoulder, and he reeled her body closer. She talked silently in her mind. Being apart during Jordan's three years at

Georgetown law school was formidable, but there was always a re-union around the corner. Their separation took on a new quality now. It was an attribute that, at one time or another, has frightened every human being -- the fear of the unknown.

Jordan's goodbye Kendall blues were suddenly washed away by a tidal wave of excitement. He focused on why he was at the airport. The thought of moving to California to pursue his dream had com-pletely revived him. Being a Deputy District Attorney in the City of Angels. Very cool.

"This will serve as the final boarding call for flight 557, non-stop to Los Angeles," said a male Chicagoan over a too loud speaker. It was time.

"I love you K," he reiterated.

"You too," she sighed from her heart.

As he shuffled down the airport gang plank, he turned. She was staring and waving. "Don't forget about me!" she belted.

He shook his head. "Like I could." She strained to hear him, and then smiled when it registered.

The plane took off twenty minutes after its scheduled departure. The hum of the engine drew Jordan into a light sleep, exhausted from the previous night's farewell partying at his and Kendall's favorite Lincoln Park pubs. There is no shortage of neighborhood bars in Chicago, whether it's North side, South side, or West side. The only things more popular than neighborhood bars in Chicago are local sports teams. And maybe pizza with the sauce on top and cheese underneath.

When his plane touched down at LAX, Jordan wondered about Stan and how he was coping. Stanley Reid had recently under-gone extreme emotional trauma. And Stanley Reid was Jordan's best friend since seventh grade when they met in a Michigan junior high. Back when Jimmy Carter was president and there were American hostages in Iran. Jordan and Stan, too, were being held hostage when they met. Their captor was one Mr. Stewart, their seventh grade science teacher. He did not carry an Uzi. His weapons included extreme boredom and projectile saliva, as Mr. Stewart had a penchant for spitting when he spoke. Stan had warned Jordan to move to the back row to avoid the spray when words like "Paramecium" were formed. Strangely, the two became friends when Stan brought Jordan's world to a crashing halt. He handed him a note from Tracey Forehand, a peppy, blue-eyed, blonde cheerleader that Jordan had been "going with" for two weeks. Of course, in seventh grade, no one was quite sure where they were "going" in such a relationship. It was important only whose mom was driving and whose mom was picking up. The note from Tracey informed Jordan that she did not want to "go with" him anymore. Mercifully, Stan allowed Jordan a good three minutes to recover before handing him a second note. It informed him that Stan had asked Tracey to "go with" him in second hour, and she said 'yes.' Stan hoped Jordan didn't mind. Out of tragedy and controversy, a best-friendship was born.

They had glory days in every category: girls, school, and sports. Especially sports. They played basketball together from seventh grade through all of high school. Jordan's point guard performance was respectable, but it was Stan who was the all-state standout at the center position. Tall as a sycamore, Stan could jump like a Frisbee dog. And Stan-man had a skyhook that Kareem wanabees lusted. But today Stan was no athlete. The police determined that it wasn't Jordan's fault. It was dark and rainy, and, more importantly, the other driver crossed to Jordan's side of the road. Still, he felt he owed Stan, whose knees would never be the same, even after three painful surgeries. Within a tiny tick on Jordan's watch, Stanley Reid was deprived of the opportunities for which he had worked much of his young life, opportunities he had been born to seize. Though a measure of guilt remained, especially when face-to-face with the would-be Kareem, it was indeed comforting to him that he was moving to this city, this crazy, crazy, strung-out and stuck-up La La Land, home of the weirdest of the weird, the freakiest of the freak, the 'it's not how you feel but how you look' population of nine million, replete with his personal anchor in sanity, his best friend from home, Stan the Man.

As the plane pulled up to greet its gate, Jordan said a polite goodbye to the blue-haired lady sitting next to him, but not before graciously accepting the telephone number of her granddaughter who, he was assured, was 'a very dear girl, beautiful too,' and who would love to meet such a handsome and successful boy. 'Successful' was accurate. He was 25 years old. He had a diploma from Georgetown Law Center, and the ink was still wet (he had just graduated in May). Jordan felt successful but unfulfilled. He graduated in the top 2% of his class of 600 at Georgetown, but felt that one of his greatest accomplishments was helping one of his clients in the Criminal Justice Clinic get into a court-ordered detoxification program, stay out of jail, and get back with his wife.

He walked off the plane and entered the vast terminal that was littered with bars and souvenir shops. Jordan Stowic scoured the area suspiciously for any sign of The Man. The fact that Stanley Reid was nowhere in sight was to be expected. It was tradition for the greeter to come out of the clear blue to surprise the traveler whenever a visit was made. On one visit Jordan made to San Diego, Stan went to the lengths of cross-dressing, complete with wig, heels, dress, cheap fur and falsies, all borrowed from his theater's prop department, all for the sake of the sacred surprise hello. Stan was no longer a thespian. After graduating from San Diego State, he obtained a graduate degree in forensic chemistry, and was the last person hired to work in the Los Angeles County Sheriff's crime laboratory before the county-wide hiring freeze went into effect. Despite his love of drama, Stan always had a knack for science, and he reveled in the reality of a monthly paycheck. Though he was now a police chemist, a "criminalist," as he was referred to by his colleagues and the Deputy District Attorneys who elicited his credentials on the stand, Stan's flair for the dramatic remained.

Jordan was starting to believe that Stan spaced on his obligatory airport run. He ambled through the giant hallway and rode the escalator down toward the baggage claim, looking all ways and over his shoulders for clues. In addition to California's yearly drought, he thought, there was a shortage of Stan. Jordan surveyed the folks waiting in the baggage area, many of them looking lonely and sullen. Lost souls. He concluded that even when their bags were returned to them they would still look the same. Then he caught a far-away smile from someone he recognized. She sat diagonally across from him on the plane. What a stunning human being! Her olive skin and dark eyes made her mysterious and seductive, and her straight velvet black hair that fell to her waist completed a dreamy vision. He smiled back (there's no harm in a smile, he thought), and the baggage claim began to spill luggage as if to mark the connection made. Jordan turned to see if he recognized any of the leather or vinyl passengers on the carousel, and saw the unmistakable green, plaid Ralph Lauren steamer trunk his parents bought him as a high school graduation present. As he reached for the trunk, he felt and saw arms and hands reach around him and beat him to the trunk. The arms, to which legs were eventually attached, ran towards the exit with his luggage! Jordan, in a frenzy, chased the perpetrator to the door where the thief was stopped by a middle-aged, overweight black woman in uniform. The thief could not make his Butch Cassidy getaway because he had no claim check. Jordan was amazed at how short a time it took for crime to find him in L.A.. As Jordan approached to reclaim his property, the criminal in the trench coat turned to face his accuser.

"Welcome to L.A. Stow!" he bellowed, triumphantly.

"Stan-man, you bastard! By the power vested in me as a Deputy District Attorney, I hereby place your ass under arrest!"

Stan let out a hearty Stan-Man laugh. They hugged. The security woman rolled her eyes.

It was a short walk to Stan's beat up old Chevy Impala convertible resting illegally at the curb.

"Stan-man, you best be cleaning up your act now that you have a roommate who's a D.A."

"Actually, the way I see it, it's the opposite. Now that I have the law on my side and living in my apartment, I can get away with about anything short of murder."

"Stan, you promised you'd stop your serial killing before I moved in with you."

"Yeah, I know. But once in a while I see a helpless old lady or a kitten with a bad leg, and I can't help myself."

Jordan smiled, enjoying the dry humor they shared.

"So are you excited to be here Stow, you stud L.A. prosecutor?"

"Seriously Stan-man," and Jordan *was* getting serious, "As totally naive as it may sound to you, I really wanna make a difference."

Stan raised his cynical left eyebrow, like only he could.

Jordan continued, "Law school contains some of the most selfish people you never want to meet. I guess you have to be selfish to get by. But now that's over. I just want to make it all mean something."

"You're a good man Charlie Brown," said The Man, with a pat and a wink. "And you won't last a minute here in L.A. with the gangs, the killer drug dealers, the anarchy in the streets. Did you know that we had twenty-eight murders in L.A. last weekend?"

Jordan, with his characteristic confidence, stared down The Man. "That's why something has to be done. And I came here to do something."

It was the classic battle, and one that had been waged all through their friendship – a battle between idealism and realism, and the search for the point where the two came together. The subject was soon dropped, as both sides saw the other beyond persuasion.

As they winded North on the 405 freeway (if you're not on a freeway in L.A., you're not in a car), the open air blew across Jordan, and his lust for the dark beauty from the plane was blown out into the cool L.A. night. In no time, the Impala navigated Stan's alley and braked in a garage with no door. The garage was too narrow to open car doors, so the two mountain-climbed out of the convertible. Though the back alley area reminded Jordan of recent footage from war-torn Bosnia, the front of Stan's apartment building was old

Spanish styled stucco, well-kept and surrounded by landscaping that included queen, king, and pineapple palms. Stan and Jordan walked up the brown-carpeted stairs to the second floor. On their way up, they passed a large oil painting on canvass that Jordan could not pass without comment.

"Let me guess, this symbolizes man's inhumanity toward man?"

"No. It's the night of the Last Supper, and the black splotch is Christ and that red line through it symbolizes Judas."

"You are a weird guy Stan-man," he said, reveling in Stan's analysis.

When they were inside the apartment, Jordan realized that Stan had, in fact, spent some of his inheritance. The floors were shining hard wood, the furniture was modern and appeared very expensive, and the place was smartly decorated with an eclectic mix of treasures from South America and the Orient.

After catching up with Michigan gossip (which of their old friends and acquaintances had been married, were cheating, were living at home, were fired from their jobs, were back in school, had children, had abortions, appendectomies, vasectomies, tracheotomies, etc.), the pair adjourned to the fresh air. The new roommates sat on the balcony, staring off into the night toward the Hollywood hills.

Three

The Lieutenant burst into the Detective's office with great urgency. "Sorry to interrupt your dinner JJ, but Sniper's been taken out." The detective almost choked on the hot dog with everything he had just obtained from the roach coach on Temple Street.

"Jesus Christ" he said through his food. "What happened?"

"They think some Compton gangsters led him to a canyon in Orange County where they shot him."

"Jesus. When?"

"Jogger found the body early this morning. I guess there were several shots to the boy's chest. A nine millimeter, I hear."

"Who's working it?"

"Orange County Sheriff."

"Any reports yet?"

"I called and they said they'd fax a draft over before it's signed off. Looks like you're back to square one on Snow."

Roosevelt High School in Compton had been the scene of one of Los Angeles's latest and most brutal gang homicides. Five people were gunned down in the schoolyard by an AK-47 assault rifle. The fact that at least two of the victims were innocent bystanders, one a beautiful three-year-old girl named Leticia Snow, made this one gang shooting that even an L.A. press that had long ago grown numb to gang violence could not ignore. Detective Juan Jose Ramirez was a senior detective in the Los Angeles County Sheriff's gang unit called O.S.S. (an acronym for Operation Safe Streets), and the Snow case was top on his stack of gang-related homicides in need of solving. What made this more challenging than most was that there were no witnesses. Everyone who could have seen the perpetrators was killed. And nobody on the streets was talking. Except one gang banger. But now he was gone too.

"Hey, wasn't Sniper supposed to come downtown to talk to you today?"

"Yes he was."

"What are you gonna do now?" asked the Lieutenant, as if JJ had an easy answer to how to proceed with a murder investigation without any leads.

"I'm gonna have a drink. You want one?"

"No. Thanks anyway. It's my turn to work the shooting range at the academy. Guess what the cadets are getting tonight?"

"I give up," said the detective, unscrewing the cap on his week-old bottle of Jack Daniels and pouring himself a much needed friend.

"Their service nine millimeters," smiled the Lieutenant. "Kinda scary for this group."

Seeing that JJ was in no mood for conversation, Lieutenant Flores left the detective alone to ponder Snow. As he shut the door, he looked back. He claims to this day to be the only living person to have ever seen Detective JJ Ramirez shed a tear.

Four

At 7:38 a.m., Jordan's hunter green Jeep Wrangler catapulted into the parking lot just blocks away from the Los Angeles County Criminal Courts Building, or 'CCB,' as it is affectionately referred to by all who make a living within its walls and complain about its elevators. This day had been on Jordan's mind for the last six months, ever since Marlene Matsomita, the hiring D.A., informed him of his start date, his first day as a Deputy District Attorney. It was August 17, 1992. After seven years of college and law school, he was going to make it all mean something. During the scenic drive from West L.A. down Olympic Boulevard through graffiti-covered Korea town, he practiced.

"I, Jordan Andrew Stowic, promise to support and defend the Constitution of the United States and the State of California." He was ready to be sworn in.

Jordan dressed sharply in a dark olive, almost brown, suit that he bought on a lazy Chicago afternoon a few months ago while perusing Michigan Avenue. His black leather suspenders picked up the faint pattern in the suit, and his tie was his favorite conservative striped one. He managed the look of a serious but stylish prosecutor.

As he walked from the parking lot to CCB, he started across a bridge that overtook the Hollywood freeway (at this hour the Hollywood parking lot), and saw an old man with coal-black skin and a scruffy gray beard. He was greeting cars as they came off the freeway with a sign that read 'HELP ME I AM HOMELES. GOD BLESS YOU!' As he came closer to the inevitable confrontation, Jordan had a familiar debate within himself, one that he had many times in Washington D.C. as he passed the beggars on Massachusetts Avenue. He felt the need to place blame. Was it the man's own fault that he was destitute on the street with a misspelled cardboard sign? Or was society or even Jordan Stowic somehow responsible for him and the hundreds of thousands like him who sleep on the asphalt beds of the nation's cities? He still had no answer. He could rationalize away any obligations to this man, a man who was able-bodied and prone to beg because all of his life he was taught that he was a victim, a dependent of the state. He was taught that if something in his life was messed up, it couldn't possibly be his own fault because he had no control. Jordan's handout would only confirm the man's fatalistic philosophy. Jordan saw a black Mercedes 450 SL convertible roar up the exit ramp onto Broadway. As he passed the man, the driver yelled, "Get a job asshole!" So much for Jordan's theory. He promptly removed his wallet and pulled out a dollar bill to be forked over in the name of compassion, fatalism be damned.

Jordan entered the lobby of CCB and went to the end of a long line of people waiting to file through a machine that was designed to detect guns and knives but which, more often, exposed keys, jewelry, belt buckles and loose change. He made it into a crowded elevator that serviced the higher levels, and pushed the button for the 18th floor. On his way up he made cameo appearances on floors nine through seventeen. When the claustrophobic's torture chamber made it to the top floor, Jordan stepped off briskly, checking his watch. Happily, he was five minutes early.

The seal of the Los Angeles County District Attorney's Office loomed above the heavy oak door that led into the main corridor. Below the seal it read, 'Steven H. Salsman District Attorney.' Jordan knew he would soon be shaking the hand of Steve Salsman, the District Attorney presiding over the largest single prosecutor's office in the country. At a cheap metal desk outside the door sat an armed Los Angeles County Marshal.

He approached her and said cheerfully, "I'm Jordan Stowic, one of the new Deputy D.A.s." She checked his name off on a list which she had to locate on her desk, then told him to "Go ahead on in to the first room on your left," with a half-smile but without a hint of friendliness. 'They ought to work on their welcoming committee,' thought Jordan as he opened the hefty door during the sounding buzzer. He entered the spacious conference room through an open doorway and saw a large oval table with 14 young lawyers, some standing, some sitting, all engaging in the foreplay to comradely. At the end of the table, there was a podium with the D.A.'s Office seal, which was used for the press conferences called by Salsman whenever there was a juicy case fueling the media's interest.

Jordan approached a very attractive blond who looked like she was in her early twenties.

"Hi, I'm Jordan Stowic."

"Vaughn Reynolds. I went to UCLA law, where'd you go?"

"I went to school in D.C.," he answered as he subtly soaked up her quite obvious curves, "Georgetown."

"Did you see all these forms we have to fill out?" she queried, holding up a stack of papers in several different colors.

"Looks like they killed off a small rain forest."

"Forest?" she asked with puzzled look.

"Nothing. Just a dumb joke."

"Oh. Aren't you totally stoked about becoming a D.A.?" she asked with a combination lights-on-nobody's-home and deer–in–the–headlights look.

"Yeah. I'm stoked," he said, wondering who her father was. Probably Salsman's biggest campaign contributor.

Before Vaughn could speak again, to ask Jordan which beach he goes to, Marlene began her brief welcoming remarks from behind the podium.

"I'm Marlene Matsomita, the one who's been talking with you on the telephone for the last few months. It's nice to see all of the faces behind the voices. I want to welcome you to the best job you will ever have. In about twenty minutes Mr. Salsman will meet you in court and you'll become Deputy District Attorneys. Until then you can fill out some paperwork for us, then just relax and get to know your colleagues."

When his forms were complete, Jordan began speaking to a diminutive man who sported a curly patch of hair and spoke with a twang about having attended the University of Texas law school. After a short conversation with Manny Gonzalez from U of T, Jordan moved on. He walked around the room, introduced himself, and socialized with his new brothers and sisters in prosecution. He remarked at the diversity of the bunch. The fifteen new Deputy D.A.s were men and women of every race, spanning top law schools from Yale to Berkeley.

After thirty minutes, Marlene reappeared and collected the colorful forms. She ushered the group out of the conference room, onto an elevator, then to a Superior Court room on the 11th floor where they would take the oath of office. There was a video camerawoman, tripod in place, waiting for them in the courtroom to capture the ceremony. Steve Salsman was near the judge's bench talking to his public relations director. There were a few family members of the new D.A.s sitting in the uncomfortable courtroom pews. Jordan wished his parents could be there, and more so Kendall. She would really savor the pomp. He would send a copy of the video.

Steve Salsman began speaking, reading from a stack of index cards. The D.A. announced fifteen names, states of origin, and summaries of academic credentials. Applause followed for each of them. Then they took the oath. Jordan felt and meant every word, and was intoxicated by the gravity of the moment. He now represented the People of the State of California.

The District Attorney congratulated them, and they cued up to take advantage of a rare photo opportunity to pose with their ultimate boss, whom they would never see in their daily work. When it was Jordan's turn, he shook the D.A.'s hand and said "It's an honor to meet you Mr. Salsman. I can't tell you how happy I am to be here. This is what I've always wanted to do."

"Congratulations Eric," he responded, flashing a Capital Hill smile to accompany his vice-grip shake, with left hand on top, like the politician's manual suggests. The camera loved it.

When everyone had their moment in the sun with Salsman, Marlene addressed the new DDAs. "Congratulations. I know that each of you will serve the people of Los Angeles County well. Please don't leave until I give you your assignments."

It seemed like hours before Marlene approached an anxious Jordan Stowic. Vaughn Reynolds was about to introduce her parents to Jordan, when Marlene interrupted again. "Jordan, you're going to Compton. I've lined up a ride-along for you tonight with Compton P.D."

Jordan had heard of Compton. He saw "Colors" and "Boyz in the Hood." Unlike some of the other assignments, like Malibu or Beverly Hills, where Jordan envisioned prosecuting 'criminals' for surfing without a permit or crossing Rodeo with too many shopping bags, to Jordan, Compton was the best available assignment. As he reacted to the news, he thought of the gang movies and his heart pounded.

"Excellent Marlene. I can't wait to start," said Jordan Stowic, to his fellow Deputy District Attorney.

Five

When the fax machine sprang to life, it awakened JJ from a deep sleep. Nine-thirty being late morning for cops, telephones were ringing off their hooks, and officers, detectives, sergeants, and lieutenants were bantering about wives, other women, promotions, movies, food, and, occasionally, their cases. While JJ had long ago become impervious to this familiar buzz, the fax was a new addition to his office and its alien sound jarred him from a better place. He was with his first wife Rachel, reliving a November weekend that they had spent in a bed and breakfast in Monterey, her favorite city. Only in the dream, Rachel hadn't yet fallen out of love with him; and he hadn't yet lost sight of what it meant to have her at his side.

It was not unusual for JJ to spend the night on the narrow green 1970s couch that looked like it had the stuffing beat out of it in an interrogation. The cops and secretaries at OSS knew it was too early to bother JJ. Nobody minded his strange hours or his occasionally sleeping in his office, given how hard he worked.

JJ wished he could go back to sleep. Back to Monterey and back to Rachel. But there were gang bangers and a crime-drenched County to grapple with, not to mention Snow, and, unbelievably, Alex's murder.

When the eighth and final page of the Orange County Sheriff's report was spat out of the fax machine, JJ got up off the couch and pushed the button on the Black & Decker coffee machine that his second wife Ariola bought him on their first and last wedding anniversary. Somehow JJ wasn't amazed that the coffee maker outlasted their marriage which never quite percolated. He thought he could be happy with a dark-eyed Mexican beauty whom his parents would have adored had they lived long enough. But Ariola would never be Rachel. And his love for Rachel was ageless. Though

Rachel's love had been extinct for almost two decades, JJ always acted as if they had recently divorced, only to be corrected by those who knew him back in the Rachelzoic era.

JJ grabbed all eight pages from the fax, descended comfortably into his creaky wood desk chair on wheels and reclined for a serious read, first time quickly skimming, second time slowly and deliberately devouring. The cover page was a hand-written note from Orange County Sheriff's Detective Harkin, stating that the coroner's autopsy report wasn't ready yet. Harkin's report provided JJ the gist of what Detectives Harkin and Moore saw the day before inside the yellow-taped perimeter at the end of Via de Lomas Road. The report repeatedly referred to "V-1," which is how cops refer to victims, by number.

"V-1 in seated position in driver's seat of V-1's vehicle," JJ read out loud to the coffee machine, as it signaled him to claim his morning elixir. The faxed copies of photographs of the body and car were barely discernable due to poor copying. It was just as well. JJ hit an emotional snag as he read the box entitled "Victim Data."

It read, "Alejandro Garcia Sandoval. 3452 Alameda Street, Compton, CA 90220. D/0/B 4-15-75." In the column for describing the injury, it was written in "deceased." He swallowed hard. He thought of the meals that he had shared with Alex and Maria at their home on Alameda Street. His eyes became watery, adding insult to their already bloodshot state. A razor sharp pain cut him in the back of his throat. "What the hell is *this?*" he thought. He was surprised he still had it in him.

An ugly cynicism had been building up for the last 21 years in Detective JJ Ramirez, since first dealing with the dregs of society as an L.A. County Deputy Sheriff, and it firmly encased his heart like the bullet proof vest worn when so many search and arrest warrants were executed. But over the last two years, by chance, he had come to know and grow very fond of a boy and his mother. It was not uncommon for JJ to be in Compton mixing with gang member informants or the brown-bag-drinking locals, gathering information, then to stop by to break bread with Alex and Maria. Alex had reminded JJ of himself when he was growing up in Compton. JJ was well aware that Alex had chosen the life of a gang member, a gangster who signed up out of a need for self-esteem, who committed crimes, even violent crimes, to gain respect from his peers. But JJ saw something in the eyes of this teen-aged boy, a spark of intelligence and, most importantly, a sense of loyalty and honor. JJ resolved to save him. With every meal they shared, every talk, whether at the Sandoval home or when JJ would occasionally see him on the street absent his homeboys, he encouraged him to take a new direction. Alex had been accepted back into school, and appeared to be questioning the gang life he'd chosen. A life that, for a large majority of L.A.'s gangbanging population ends in a bloody fizzle or long-term incarceration by age 19.

JJ hoped that Alex would see by his example that you could grow up Mexican and poor in Compton, with all of its pressures to belong to the underworld of the gang culture, and make it out. Alex respected JJ because he was from Compton and knew what it meant to struggle for an identity and self-worth in a city that, to many who don't know its people, see it as a human trash dumpster.

To Alex's Kansas Street Crip homies, JJ was just another cop. And Alex, or "Sniper," as he was known to his set, was a new vato, still earning his stripes. Therefore, all meetings between JJ and Alex had been secret. They first met when Alex was 14, shortly after Alex had been 'jumped in' to the gang, which included the ceremonial pummeling by all of the other members. Alex had been one of the few people on the street who was willing to talk about a drive-by shooting that happened in unincorporated Los Angeles County, part of the Sheriff's jurisdiction. The shooting left a young girl paralyzed from the waist down. Alex was at a party at the house where the shooting happened, and was able to provide a description of the shooter's car and relay the street rumors about who was responsible. As JJ and all gang officers know, street rumors are the cops' best friend when it comes to solving crimes, especially gang-related homicides. Thankfully, human nature's urge to brag about one's deeds, as well as the equally powerful desire to gossip about those of others, has landed countless violent gang members behind bars who otherwise would be free to sin some more.

As JJ read the report a third time, he leaned way back in his chair and sipped his coffee. Then, after clearing his desk of several stacks of phone messages, including unreturned calls from the District Attorney and the *Los Angeles Times*, he set the report down and plunged deep into thought. Something about the report was wrong, but he couldn't say what. He picked up the phone and dialed the Sheriff of Orange County, a personal friend from when they rolled together in a joint gang task force in the early 1980's.

"Hi Rich, its JJ."

"JJ, how goes the struggle?"

"It's going. How's life at the top of the heap?"

"Fine, but lately I've been feeling like that heap is on top of me. What about you, are you still sleeping at the office?"

"No, I'm takin' life easy, kicking back. You know how it is."

"Sure you are. With all the press I'm reading about that Leticia Snow caper, I'd bet the farm that you have insomnia and won't get a nap until some guys are stamping license plates at Pelican Bay."

"That may be true. Listen, the reason I'm calling is that there was a 187 yesterday that your detectives are handling."

"You talking about the boy found in Yorba Linda?"

"Yeah."

"I've been briefed. Looks like he was a gang member from Compton."

"Yes, he was. But he was also an informant who was providing information to me. He was supposed to meet me yesterday. He said he had something major to tell me. I think it had something to do with the Leticia Snow investigation."

"Then he was killed, and you never found out what he had."

"That's right. So, I'm going to ask you a favor. A big one."

"Anything."

"I need you to let OSS work this boy's murder. I think it ties directly into Snow, and I just don't want too many hands stirring the pot, you know what I mean?"

"I'll tell you what I'll do. I'll make it a joint investigation. OSS can do the leg work. We'll help when you want us to. But when you're close to making an arrest, let me know. My guys will be there. We get credit. I know you don't give a shit about getting credit."

"You know me well old buddy. And I can play by those rules."

"After this favor, we're even, right?"

"We were always even. Thank you Rich."

"No problem."

"And Rich, I want to come to Santa Ana in a couple hours to look at the evidence your guys picked up from the scene."

"Great. Why don't we go for some barbecue around one? We'll talk about your murders, I can complain about the County Council, and you help me figure out who I have to show my tits to around here to get a decent budget."

"It's a plan."

JJ Ramirez threw on his old Nikes, dabbed on some Old Spice deodorant and headed for the basement floor where his 'unmarked' white 1992 Chevy Caprice Classic, with multiple antennas and black wall tires, awaited. It was time to hear what the streets had to say.

Six

"Yo homey, what up G?" said the 16-year-old to his 21-year-old companion. They had rendezvoused at Kim's Pizza on Compton Boulevard at lunch time to split the morning's profits. Li Lan Kim, the restaurant's proprietor, watched with suspicion from across the counter (over which he maintained only a slight height advantage) as the two black males in gang attire sat at a table next to a video machine that simulated martial arts fighting.

"Business good, Lil' T?" asked G-Dog, referring without reservation to the sale of crack, or rock, cocaine. Their 'clients' were mostly addicts living on the streets or in abandoned buildings, whom they often referred to affectionately as "cluck heads."

"Yeah, but some fool crack-bitch tried to short my ass with some funny money, so I cut her up a little. She ok, ain't no thing, but she ain't try that shit again with no 8th Street Piru."

"That's my boy!" exclaimed G-Dog, as he reached out and showed his affinity by bumping clenched fists with his young homey. G-Dog's respect for Lil' T was growing. Lil' T was short for little thief, a name that was earned when he became proficient at stealing cars by age thirteen. This talent also earned Lil' T three months in Camp Scooby, one of several county boot camps where juveniles are sent for committing less serious felonies. The night of his release from camp, he was jumped into the 8th Street Pirus.

"Can I taka you orda?" asked Li Lan.

"Yo man, give me and my homey a large pizza with everything but anchovies. And two large Cokes." G-Dog was speaking in his take-charge tone.

"You wanna salsa?"

"Naw man. What do I look like, a damn Mexican?"

Li Lan left intimidated and without another word to get the Cokes.

It was apparent from their dress that G-Dog and Lil' T were Blood gang members, whose heritage of terror goes back several decades. It is widely believed that the Bloods originated in Compton in the late 1960's. The reason the gang formed was to provide protection for its members from another gang - the Crips, who were based, primarily, in the City of Los Angeles. The Crips would come into Compton, especially to the high schools, and terrorize campuses and neighborhoods by extorting money and committing robberies and assaults. In reaction to this, Piru Street in Compton organized the first Blood gang. The color red was adopted because the school colors of Centennial High School in Compton were red and white. Similarly, the Crips, many of whom hailed from Washington High School in Southwest Los Angeles, donned their blue and white school colors.

G-Dog and Lil'T adorned themselves in Blood red. Lil'T sported red leather converse high tops, baggy jeans that could fit his obese mother, a red cloth belt with a metal buckle that had a 'P' for Piru, a white t-shirt, and a red St. Louis Cardinals baseball cap. G-Dog's attire was slightly more subtle: a black nylon warm-up with a red Nike swish and black leather high tops with red laces. The piece de resistance was a red tattoo of a tear under his left eye to mark the year he spent in state prison for violating Section 245(a)(2) of the California Penal Code- assault with a firearm. G-Dog lectured all of his homeboys that the D.A. wanted to charge him with attempted murder for the shooting, but he couldn't prove G-Dog intended to kill anyone, since G-Dog was smart enough to invoke his right to remain silent after his arrest. "Let that be lesson to y'all," he'd say, "If you get busted, act like yo' mouth busted too."

G-Dog got up from the table and pumped two quarters into the video game, "Street Fighter II." Lil'T followed and watched, but kept the front door in the corner of his eye. G-Dog completed the ambiance by turning on his portable compact disc player, with Ice Cube demanding notice in his prosaic bass-thumping gangster rap:

"No helicopter looking for a murder
Two in the morning got the Fatburger
Even saw the lights of the Goodyear blimp
And it read 'Ice Cube's a pimp.'
Drunk as hell but no throwin' up
Halfway home and my pager's still blowin' up
Today I didn't even have to use my A.K.
I gotta say it was a good day."

Suddenly the music stopped and the video screen went dark.

"Hey, what the fuck!" barked G-Dog, as if someone had ripped off his dope.

"Yo man, we 'gonna kick your mothafuckin' ass," said Lil'T, mostly to impress G-Dog.

"Chill, T. This here's detective JJ Ramirez. He a cop. Fact, he a gang cop, but he's cool. This Mexican brother cut me some slack last time he caught me slingin." G-Dog was referring to an incident three weeks ago when JJ busted him selling rock cocaine on a street corner in Compton.

"G-dog, we got some business."

"Yo, man, I told ya the otha day that I ain't heard who did no Roosevelt High drive-by."

"No, it's not about that. It's a Kansas Street homeboy who was a personal friend of mine. He was shot and killed yesterday. Did you hear anything about this?"

"Naw, man. I ain't heard nothin' 'bout that."

"You sure?"

"Hell yeah, I'm sure."

"Are you sure you and your little homey feel like getting locked up over the rock I know you have on you?"

"JJ, I'm clean man. I don't sling anymore."

"Then you don't mind if I search you, now that you've cleaned up your act."

"Wait, let's not get hasty. I maybe heard someone from Kansas got capped. But what you want with some crab fool anyway?" G-Dog and other Bloods called Crips "crabs." Crips returned the favor whenever possible, substituting "slob" for "Blood."

"I told you. He was a friend of mine."

"Well, I can tell you this: 8th Street didn't smoke no crab from Kansas. We ain't even at war with them fools right now. But word is that they feudin' with Southside. Why don't you go talk to they ass?" G-Dog was referring to the Southside Playboys, an Hispanic gang that historically has been the enemy of all Crip sets, including the Kansas Street Crips.

"Fine. But if I find out you lied to me, I will put you away for a long, long time."

"I ain't lying."

"If you hear anything on the street, you drop a coin in the pay-phone and call me. I'll even owe you one."

"That's cool."

JJ handed G-Dog a business card after he wrote his home number on the back.

"I'll add this to my collection. Hey, this one got a new look. How come you changed your star to a different color?"

"I like all colors. I don't discriminate."

"I always knew you ain't down with no Larry Powell or Stacey Koon. That's 'cause you ain't white."

"Hey, who is this little guy?" asked JJ, motioning toward Lil'T.

"I ain't no 'little guy.' I'm old school 8th Street," defended Lil'T, as he threw his gang sign, which consisted of the number 8, accomplished by forming circles with the index finger and thumb of each hand and putting the left hand on top of the right.

"Oh yeah, this my homeboy, T. He gonna be an O.G. like me."

"You really wanna be like G-Dog here?"

"Hell, yeah!"

"It's not too late to apply yourself in school and go to college," said JJ with more than a hint of sarcasm that was completely lost on the boy.

"Fuck that shit. I make more money on the street in one morning than one of them snob-assed college boys make in a month."

"Ok but if you hear anything about who shot that Kansas Streeter, tell your friend G-Dog to call me. I'm a good cop to know the next time you need a friend, and you *will* need one."

Li Lan had recognized JJ when he came in, and now he walked over with a hot slice of pepperoni pizza and a Coke. Li Lan always gave JJ the law enforcement discount, which, no matter what was ordered, totaled one dollar.

"Thanks Li, but I don't have much time, so I'll take this to go." He handed Li Lan a dollar.

"You go catching criminals JJ?"

"That's right Li, I'm gonna catch me some criminals." JJ dropped a second dollar on the video machine in payment for the game he cut short, and headed out the door.

Seven

It was a sweltering August night in Compton. Though darkness was fast

approaching, the thermometer hadn't yet subsided. It seemed like all of Compton's 100,000 residents were outside, in their yards, on their porches, in the street, many with their favorite drink in hand. Some were concealed in brown paper, others openly exposed. Every single one of the 100 grand old enough to know the crime problem knew that the police had better things to do on a Friday night than cite folks for drinking a 40-ounce on a public sidewalk. This was the kind of night on which the citizenry and their police were certain someone would be shot.

The patrol car skidded and slammed over a curb, onto a bumpy, trash-covered alley, behind a deteriorating two-story building. A beautiful, old pineapple palm was glaringly out of place in the seedy alley. The car sped down the narrow path and the cop in the passenger's seat, eyeing a group of male Mexicans, called out "Gun! Red shirt's got a sawed-off behind his back."

The car screeched to a standstill. Both driver and passenger doors flung open and the Kevlar-clad officers exploded out, hands on auto pilot, grabbing and pointing Barretta 9mm handguns at the suspect. The younger officer aimed a red laser beam directly at the head of the man with the gun. The laser brightly dotted the suspect's forehead, foreshadowing the end of a bullet's trip. The suspect's buddies scattered in every direction.

"Put the gun down and put your hands up," the cop demanded. The older cop added, "That dot on your head is where the bullet's going if you don't drop your weapon." The younger officer repeated the commands in Spanish for the man to drop his gun and put his hands up.

The man stood next to a motorcycle with a missing wheel and his body shook. His forehead gushed with perspiration. He did not drop the shotgun he held behind his back.

Jordan Stowic slumped down in the back seat of the police car, bracing for gunshots, wishing he had a Kevlar vest, and wondering if a ride-along was really the best way to prepare for his work in Compton.

Finally, after the stalemate lingered on too long, the veteran officer told his partner he was going to give the man a "wake up call." He fired a shot over the head of the man with the shotgun. The pellets dug into the roof of a detached garage. The man dropped his gun and ran to a brown Chevy Camaro parked in the alley, fired it up, and burned rubber onto Rosecrans Avenue. The officers glided back into their patrol car. Then Officers Stevie Ladd and Grant Punderson of Compton P.D. began a Code 3 pursuit of a fleeing suspect, something every cop will tell you is the ultimate adrenaline cocktail.

"Whadda ya think Jordan?" asked young Officer Punderson of the younger DDA in the back seat. Jordan was putting on his seatbelt as the patrol car whisked through a solid red light, sirens blaring, lights flashing.

"So this is the chase scene?" he said, needing to scream to be heard over the roar of the engine and whine of the siren, "It almost seems real."

"Hold onto your gonads Mr. DA!" yelled Ladd from the driver's seat with a smile and a tone that said, "I love being a cop."

Punderson operated the radio. "Dispatch, this is Compton 2. We are pursuing a suspect fleeing in a brown Chevrolet Camaro Westbound Rosecrans at Alameda. Request backup."

"Roger that Compton 2. Compton 3, Compton 6 please respond."

After radioing in the license plate on the Camaro and having the dispatcher run its registered owner, the Officers learned why the man was running. They had stumbled upon the proud owner of a felony robbery warrant, and, despite the nervous sightseer in the back seat, they weren't about to lose him.

Rosecrans Avenue, a four lane road, was crowded with cars. It seemed that everyone who wasn't hanging out in their yard was cruising the street. Suddenly, the Camaro slowed sightly, then made a dangerous 180 degree turn from the center lane. The rear end of the car skidded to kiss the curb, then the tires screamed as the bad guy punched his accelerator, launching himself eastward. Several civilian cars were affected, and they swerved and screeched.

Stevie Ladd was only three car lengths behind his suspect. At this point he was joined by another patrol car, lights and sirens in stereo, Code 3 all the way. The Camaro turned South-bound on Alameda. When it got within range of the 91 freeway, Officer Punderson grabbed the radio again.

"Dispatch, this is Compton 2, notify CHP of possible Code 3 pursuit, Riverside Freeway at Alameda, direction unknown."

"Roger Compton 2. CHP will be notified."

As it neared the West-bound entrance ramp to the 91, the Camaro slowed again. This time it stopped dead in the road.

Jordan didn't slump down in his seat. From the loud speaker in the patrol car, Punderson ordered the suspect out of his vehicle. He complied. The four officers approached from different directions with guns drawn. The man was laying face down on the asphalt like an old pro. He knew the procedure well.

"The idiot ran out of gas!" yelled one of the other cops who was searching the suspect's car for weapons and drugs.

"Get yourself a Honda. They get better mileage," advised Officer Ladd, as he body-searched the wanted man.

By this time, Jordan was out of the car, observing the searches of the car and suspect, whom he was already thinking of as "the defendant." As he watched, he thought about the Fourth Amendment search and seizure law that he learned in law school. The searches seemed a lot more reasonable and necessary on the streets than they did in the classroom when complained about by liberal criminal procedure professors.

The defendant was taken to the Compton Police station on Willowbrook by the other patrol officers. Jordan's duo resumed their nightly routine.

"You do realize that we would've kicked the shit out of that guy if you weren't here."

Jordan wasn't sure if Ladd was serious or not, so he decided to clear up the record.

"Hey, I didn't come out here to check up on you guys. I came to see what really happens, so when I call you to the stand in my cases, I know what the hell you're talking about. Not that I want to see you beat somebody."

Punderson and Ladd chuckled at Jordan's defensive response to the joke, then went back to playing their game. As they drove the perilous streets of Compton, they listened to a classic rock station and tried to be the first to name the artist as the guitars began to wail. This appeared to Jordan to be a stress-reduction device, and prompted him to ask:

"How do you deal with the fact that any of these guys you pull up to or stop could just blow you away?"

Grant Punderson fielded the question.

"I think we're beyond stressed. We're numb to it. Don't even think about it anymore."

Jordan was going to follow up his line of questioning when Stevie Ladd screamed: "AC/DC, Back in Black!" within seconds of a robust guitar riff. Before Punderson could congratulate him on evening the score, a carload of gang bangers, heads shaved, blew through a stop sign, right under the noses of two, make that three, of Compton's finest. The red and blue lights were ablaze once more.

Eight

JJ read his watch. It was 8:42 p.m. He meant to call the Sheriff and cancel their lunch but was so focused on coming up with something on the street that he had forgotten. The Sheriff would understand. JJ had spoken to at least one member of each of Compton's 100 gangs. He talked to gang members in sets that might have a score to settle with Alex's gang. Still, he got nowhere.

In one possible scenario, Alex's own homeboys took him out after they learned he was going to snitch on them about the Snow shootings at Roosevelt High School. JJ was desperate to talk to members of the Kansas Street Crips, but they were laying unusually low. A fact that seemed to corroborate JJ's Kansas Street theory. The only Kansas Street Crip he found actually found him. JJ was stopped at a red light when a 25-year-old heroin addict named Lucky tried to wash his windows. Lucky hadn't been active in the gang since he'd become an addict in 1991, shortly after he was shot in the groin because he sold a customer "rock cocaine," that consisted, in fact, of rocks. The customer had a temper and didn't take his purchase of the bunk very well. Lucky claimed he used heroin to deal with the pain, but it eventually became a recreational activity.

JJ told Lucky that he wouldn't arrest him for being under the influence of heroin if he would tell him any rumors he heard about Alex's murder. Lucky agreed, but was not particularly helpful. In fact, he was so out of it that he promised that when he was no longer high he'd come to the Sheriff's station to talk to JJ about the Southside Playboys who were stealing cars for Miguel Menendez. Though a nice gesture, the Menendez chop shop had been put out of business permanently six months ago, and Lucky, if in a rare state of sobriety, knew that. Lucky did say something that troubled JJ, though. He claimed that the whole Kansas Street gang was up in Oakland. He said they drove there a few days ago for a concert, and stayed there to visit some friends. JJ was understandably skeptical because Lucky said the artist giving the concert was "Marvin Gaye or some shit."

It was too late to drive to Santa Ana to examine the evidence at the Orange County Sheriff's Station. Nobody would be on duty working the property room, and JJ didn't feel like using another favor to make it happen. It would all be there in the morning. So he grabbed a drive-through In-n-Out burger, and then ate it as his car instinctively drove him to the Aftershock, a blue collar dive of dive bars in Long Beach. It was a sanctuary where there were more McDonnell Douglas line workers than cops. It was the detective's other home.

When he arrived at the Aftershock, he blocked a fire hydrant because there were no parking spaces. When he entered, he sat down to a double Jack Daniels and Coke. There was no sign of the ice cubes that once floated in the slightly chipped glass.

"You're late JJ," said a husky female voice from the well-stocked side of the bar.

"Better get me one on deck Loni. I got a lot of thinking to do."

Loni nodded in agreement. She had always propounded the belief that JJ solved all of his toughest cases right there at her bar, over many a Jack and Coke.

Nine

Jordan spent much of the morning unpacking and arranging his personal effects in one of the two bedrooms of the apartment he could now call home. He felt not the least bit exhausted, though he had only slept about five hours. He was amazed he slept that long after taking last night's adrenaline to bed with him. The first two days in Los Angeles had been hectic, and he hadn't been able to get to his errands. He had to open a bank account, get sheets for his bed, study California criminal procedure, buy groceries, and call Kendall, though not necessarily in that order. He needed to get the errands out of the way over the weekend so that he'd be ready for his first full week as a Deputy District Attorney. As he unpacked, he could actually feel the chemical electricity traveling from his brain through his body. He was ecstatic that he was in L.A., unpacking, living with his best friend in the world, starting the career he had dreamed of.

"Top of the mornin' Stow," said a friendly voice, as an appendage reached through the opening in the bedroom doorway and handed out a cold Diet Coke. Stan knew that Jordan didn't share his love for java, but instead had a morning lust for its cold caffeine-bearing counterpart.

"Thanks Stan-man. Who woke you up this early on a Saturday morning?"

Jordan was making an obscure reference to Stan's childhood. Stan's father invited all of the neighborhood kids and Jordan into Stan's bedroom on a Sunday that found Stan slumbering into the early afternoon. Mr. Reed had the kids sing the national anthem while he said "good morning" with ice water. The following weekend, Mr. Reid followed up by moving his sleeping son, mattress included, on to the front yard. Only when Mr. Reid pull-started the lawnmower did Stan's own pistons start pumping.

"I gotta go in to work. I have a bunch of reports to write up. I wouldn't care, but they're all due to my supervisor on Monday."

"Sucks to be you, Stan-man."

"Yeah, but at least I have a penis."

"I meant to talk to you about that. It's been gathering quite a bit of dust lately. Why don't you cut it off and donate it to somebody who could use it?"

The roommates and best friends smiled. They were exchanging old lines, enjoying familiar banter. Then Stan left for work, but not without exchanging 'the handshake' which they invented in 7th grade, consisting of a regular handshake, then the locking of fingers, then two high fives.

"I'll be home around 9:00 to take you to my friend's party!" screamed Stan, from his topless car, as he drove by Jordan's second floor bedroom window.

"Remind me to tell you about last night!" Jordan volleyed back, but Stan was out of earshot.

Jordan picked up the phone and began dialing Kendall's number. He figured that is was around seven in the morning in Chicago. A knock at the door kept him from placing the call.

"Are you Jewish?"

"No, I'm Jordan Stowic."

"Sorry. My name is Isaac Hoberman. I live downstairs. I have a problem. Are you Jewish?"

"No, Catholic. But I'm in the reserves."

"Could you please come with me? It will only take a second."

"What do you need?"

"Please, just come."

Jordan followed Issac into his first floor apartment, which was filled with men with dark beards resembling Issac. The entire crowd of 20 or so was watching and smiling as Issac led Jordan into the kitchen. There was an annoying buzzing sound that had to be stopped. The crowd was paralyzed. It was up to Jordan to save them.

Issac directed Jordan to the challenge at hand. Jordan grabbed the cause of the torture in his bare hand and twisted it effortlessly. HE DID IT! The crowd applauded.

Jordan was very amused. He wondered how many non-Jews were needed that day to turn off oven timers.

"I also do alarm clocks, light switches and answering machines. But I *don't* do elevator buttons." The crowd laughed. Issac said thank you.

As Jordan ascended the stairs past the Judas painting, he remarked to himself how truly interesting the Orthodox Jewish culture is, with its prohibitions against turning off oven timers on the Sabbath. He looked out of the window as the crowd from Issac's apartment set off on foot for the temple, a good mile away. Jaded by the hypocrisy he'd seen growing up with organized religion, Jordan was content to live by the motto of Thomas Paine who declared: "The world is my country, all men are my brethren, and to do good is my religion." Jordan worshiped through his everyday conduct.

When he made the call to Kendall he got her machine and hung up. He picked up paper and pen and began to write:

August 19, 1992

Dear K,

I had an amazing experience last night. I went on a ride along with the Compton Police Department. Don't worry; I'm not writing from a hospital with a bullet in my chest. I'm safe and sound. But I do have a hole in my heart left by you. I miss you dearly. Let me tell you about last night.

I arrived around 6:00 p.m., and waited in the lobby for about 30 minutes. They came and got me and took me to roll call. That consisted of a room full of cops, mostly of the very large, buff kind. I made the mistake of talking to one of the officers while the Sergeant was giving the briefing. He stopped and took me into the back room where he demanded "decorum." I complied, of course. I'm not crazy. Then I went out to the parking lot where the officers held crowd control and riot drills. They marched in wedge formations, taking half steps. There were several officers in the middle of the "wedge" who acted as "clean-up" to arrest any person who got through the wedge.

I was assigned to ride with Officers Steve Ladd and Grant Punderson, who are specially assigned to handle gangs and investigate murders and other serious crimes. They are allowed to go anywhere in the 15 patrol districts in Compton. They carry 9mm handguns and a shotgun which rests under the front seat.

As we drove away from the station, as if off to battle, Ladd greeted the folks we passed on the street. They all knew him. He was friendly to them, and then made fun of them when we drove away. He told me that he thought it was important to build a rapport with them. Punderson was a little quieter. He had a laser sight on his gun that he liked to use to scare people. Our first encounter involved a man who wouldn't put down his shotgun. We got into a car chase. Ladd admitted that he almost shot this man.

We drove through the streets, overpopulated with gangs and guns. It was Friday night around 7:30 p.m., and people were everywhere. There were people drinking in public without fear of the police. Not all people who commit crimes that night were arrested. I learned that it takes a good hour to complete the booking process. Every cop is needed on the street. For that reason, it seems that the most the police can hope to do is to keep the peace. Especially with the gangs that thrive on every corner.

As we drove along through the war zone, the officers in the front seat had flashlights that they used to illuminate every person who lined our path. Sadly, in Compton on a night like last night everyone's a suspect. On several occasions, the officers would stop and frisk groups of young black and Hispanic gang members. A few times the officers spotted furtive gestures and conducted searches that yielded German lugers or rocks of cocaine. Most of the time, you could hear the dull rotary of a helicopter in the back of your ear. A couple of times the helicopter hovered directly overhead, providing air support and lighting to the officers as they frisked the gang members for weapons and drugs.

K, the most amazing thing to me was the lack of outward fear or stress shown by these badged warriors in blue. In fact, their mannerism was so cordial you'd think they were driving to a pub to play darts. But whatever confidence they had, whatever they knew that I didn't, it rubbed off. You don't want to hear this, but by the second time they pulled their guns to confront some gang members, I found myself getting out of the car to watch them. I was the only one besides the suspects without a bullet-proof vest, but I didn't care. I felt invincible. It was an incredible feeling that became quite addicting. When we were forced to take the time to book some gang members with guns, I kept thinking, "Hurry up, let's get this over with so we can get back on the street. Back to the ACTION!" I think I can now understand some people's addiction to danger.

Another interesting incident involved a call we received of a shooting at a carnival taking place in a neutral gang zone. The area surrounding the carnival had burned down in April's riots. We pulled up and parked in the middle of the street. The ambulance was already there. We had a suspect in custody in the back seat, but Punderson and Ladd wanted me to see this, so they stopped. I got out of the car and walked up to the victim who was lying on the ground with a paramedic at his side. I had seen a bullet hole in someone on television, but never live and in person. Never a fresh bullet hole in someone's leg. Like being at some newsreel war scene. But it was a gang hit. Bloods v. Crips. We would find out later that there were three people shot at the carnival last night. We went to the hospital and interviewed these victims. We learned that one of the victims was also one of the shooters.

One of the lessons from last night was that the Police in Compton are like surrogate fathers looking after the young gang members. For example, we returned to the carnival in search of a gang member in burgundy pants and a black jacket who was reported to be brandishing a gun. We never did find him. But the officers found a 15-year-old Piru gang member who was wearing his gang colors, including a red bandana dangling from his back pocket. I learned that this was practically an invitation to be shot by a rival gang, especially in a neutral territory not claimed by any gang. So the police "arrested" him for underage drinking, as an excuse to get him off the street. They took him to the police station and called his step mother, to whom he was later delivered.

At the station, Ladd and Punderson took a picture of the young man for their Field Identification Book. They also recorded his name and gang moniker. I asked the boy if he would want his son to be a gang member. He said "no way." I then asked him why he gang banged. He looked me in the eyes and said, most sincerely, "That's me. It's who I am. Anyways, you gotta die sometime."

When my night ended at about 1:30 a.m., it was kinda scary driving back to West L.A. because my car was engulfed by fog and I almost didn't find the highway out of Compton. But I did find my way out. Most of the people I met last night I know never will.

Just a few thoughts on my mind. Can't wait to talk to you soon cupcake. I miss you desperately.

Love,

JS

P.S. Don't worry, I don't plan on any more ride alongs.

Ten

JJ left for the Sheriff's Station in Santa Ana around 11:00 in the morning. As he drove from his one-bedroom studio in Long Beach down Shoreline Drive to the freeway, he thought he might have to fold down the back seat of his Caprice to make room for his hangover. Feeling like last month's meatloaf, he pulled into a 7-11 to get a large coffee. When he was paying, he glanced down at a stack of *Los Angeles Times* newspapers. He saw the headline on the upper left side of the front page: "No Footprints in the Snow" with the subheading "Compton Murders Still Unsolved." His stomach churned from the lethal combination of stress and alcohol poisoning.

He had thought it over thoroughly at the Aftershock last night. Alex's murder had to be linked to Snow. JJ started with the assumption that what Alex was going to tell him, had he lived, was that members of his gang, the Kansas Street Crips, were responsible for the Snow murders. It made perfect sense because three of the five that were killed by the AK-47 fire in the school yard were Southside Playboys, a gang that was at war with Kansas Street. Over the last year, the two gangs had traded assaults, and even homicides, in an endless, deadly cycle of payback. Sadly, the mother and child who died at Roosevelt High were the inevitable innocent bystanders. In fact, statistics showed that more than half of the victims of gang-related gunfire were not the intended targets. This statistic is supported by common sense. First, gang members don't tend to spend much time honing their skills at the firing range. And certainly no range simulates the reality of a drive-by, that is, firing in the dark from a moving car after drinking a couple of 40-ounce beers and smoking a "sherm" (slang for a marijuana cigarette dipped in PCP). Their errant shots often killed children and other innocents. Second, gang members don't ask for gang identification cards from their victims before capping them. Looking like a rival gang member is all it takes. That's why there are always articles in the newspapers about gang-related shootings where puzzled relatives and friends say that their loved one had a good job and never belonged to a gang. What they fail to realize is that, on the streets of Los Angeles, fashion kills.

JJ resolved that his first priority would be to solve Alex's murder. Then, he figured, he'd be able to close out Snow. He was so convinced that *he* had to be the one to find Alex's killer that he was putting his job and retirement in jeopardy by investigating a case that was not even within his own jurisdiction. Though Sheriff Richard Blade of Orange County had owed him a favor and was willing to wait until JJ had the perpetrators in handcuffs to claim the credit, JJ's own bosses could have his badge for this. From all appearances, Alex's murder was a simple gang hit. And JJ planned to solve it in a matter of days, like he'd done in a hundred other cases. He'd worry about repercussions later.

He arrived at the Sheriff's Station in downtown Santa Ana, which was a white-washed, two-story building with terracotta shingles set on an immaculately-kept, landscaped lot, sprinkled with young queen palms. He drove around to the rear, and the black metal gate was opened by a deputy in a guard booth when JJ badged him.

"Nice to see a detective working on a Saturday."

"Only parts of me are working," said JJ, in a gruff, morning-after-New Year's Eve voice.

Once inside, he was directed to the watch commander, who told him that the Sheriff was in Palm Springs for a long weekend and would return on Tuesday. She handed JJ a fat manila envelope that the Sheriff had left for him. Then she showed him to the property room, which was cavernous, with rows of standing metal shelves. On each shelf was a line of numbered, black, plastic boxes containing a stranger collection of random things than most garage sales or flea markets, with all items having been promoted to the status of 'evidence' because of the context in which they were found.

The civilian employee working the room retrieved box number 239, and signed it out to JJ. The detective examined the contents in the box and jotted notes. "Blood-soaked white T. Black jean shorts. Blue and white sneakers. Pair of socks. $24.35. Calif. DL. Black belt with metal buckle. 4 coroner's bullets- from V's body in autopsy." He wrote on his note pad, "Cash?" He thought it was strange that his homies took his life but didn't take his money. It was his experience that, if given the opportunity, killers usually take the money.

JJ had seen many inhuman acts perpetrated by humans in his twenty years as a cop. His job taught him to expect the worst from people. One of the coldest acts he'd ever seen was captured on a jewelry store's surveillance video. During an attempted robbery, the suspect killed the owner of the store, and, on his way out, shot an elderly security guard at point blank range. But somehow that wasn't the most disturbing part. A woman, apparently unconnected to the robber, walked into the store after the shooting. She stepped over the dying security guard and made her way to the cash register, where she took handfuls of change, filling her pockets before stepping back over the security guard and out to the street. JJ had memorized her face, and had been looking for this woman for the last five years.

JJ opened the envelope the Sheriff had left for him. He found the coroner's autopsy report, along with pictures taken at the scene and at the County morgue. Though he'd attended hundreds of autopsies and seen countless photos of victims shot, stabbed, bludgeoned, and mutilated by weapons ranging from shotguns to ice picks to scissors to golf clubs, these photos disturbed him immensely. Not for their gore, as they were not nearly as gory as most. It was something else. In one picture, Alex sat in the car where he was murdered. His eyes were closed and his left arm stretched through the open car window. Was he trying to defend the bullets? No. He was reaching out for something. Something he would not find in this lifetime. JJ was suddenly rendered breathless by the surreal pose of the dead boy he had been trying to save. He spotted a small, metal chair in the corner of the room and took a seat to recover. He pushed all thoughts of Alex out of his head. In his mind, he sat in front of a large, blank movie screen.

When he felt better, he read the autopsy report. The stated cause of death was multiple gunshot wounds to the chest. Four entry wounds. Each one fatal in and of itself. He re-read the property report to make sure that he was seeing all the evidence that was recovered from the scene. There were no cartridge casings found. Revolvers don't eject casings, though semi-automatics like nine millimeters do. Of course, if Alex's murder happened somewhere else, there shouldn't be any casings where the body was found. Still, his cop instinct ingrained in him over twenty years told him that something did not make sense. But it didn't tell him what.

Eleven

At 4:30 p.m. Jordan returned from shopping. He carried the bags, four at a time, from his Jeep to his kitchen. He couldn't believe how much stuff he needed to buy. He had only taken the steamer trunk and a carry-on with him on the plane. Add them to the two boxes his parents sent via UPS, and his Jeep that arrived via semi truck, and that was all of Jordan's worldly possessions. Not that Jordan's family didn't have money. They did. His father owned a medium-sized manufacturing plant in Detroit that made machines that make auto parts. He sold these machines to the big three auto makers. Henry, a.k.a. Hank, Stowic had inherited the business from Jordan's grandfather. Commendably, he had tripled production during his fifteen years as the company's president and C.E.O. Jordan made it clear to his father early on that he wanted to pursue his own brand of success, apart from the loud, grinding machines of Stowic Enterprises, Inc., and its plush corporate board room.

After law school, Hank Stowic had pleaded with his son to take the sensible job with the prestigious Chicago law firm where Jordan had been a summer associate. Hank strongly advised Jordan to "go where the money is." Hank was simply dumbfounded when his son accepted half of the starting salary offered by the Chicago firm to work as a state prosecutor. The firm certainly spent enough money trying to woo Jordan and the others in his summer associate class with expensive lunches and dinners, ritzy happy hours, yacht trips on Lake Michigan, and baseball and NBA playoff games. The firm even arranged for the summer associates to play a softball game in the new Cominsky Park. The firm was able to swing that because their client was the Chicago White Sox. But Jordan was not falling for the bait and switch. He knew what lay ahead if he accepted the

43

offer. Excruciating hours, all recorded and charged to clients to the tenth of an hour, and all devoted to an unworthy cause. Jordan knew he could never be motivated only by the promise of acquiring dead presidents.

Jordan pacified his father, explaining that the best way to gain experience was to work for the D.A.'s office. A seasoned litigator could then move on to the law firms and make the big bucks. But Jordan had never planned to do anything that he did not consider "making a difference." He had to practice his religion.

The telephone rang as Jordan unpacked.

"Hello?"

"Hi darling," said a welcome voice.

"Cupcake! I've been trying to track you down. What've you been up to?"

"Missing you uncontrollably."

"As you should."

"Have you taken up surfing yet, or are you too busy cavorting with blonde bimbos in skimpy bikinis?"

"Hold on, that's my call waiting. I think it's Trixie. I met her at the beach."

"That's good because I've met a boy."

"You have. What's his name?"

"Ralph."

"Ralph, huh? What's he like?"

"He's furry. Scratches me a lot. Easily amused by string."

"Sounds like your kind of guy."

"He is the cutest kitten. You would absolutely love him."

Jordan proceeded to tell Kendall about his apartment, Stan, his swearing-in (she demanded to see a copy of the video as soon as possible), and his assignment to Compton. He left out the ride-along so his letter would not be redundant.

"So when are you moving here K? I'm sure we can find an apartment that allows pets."

"As soon as you put a rock on my finger that makes me walk lopsided."

"What would you prefer? Granite? Marble? Sandstone?"

"I think someone needs to have a little time on his own first."

"What are you talking about K? You know you're the one for me."

"I do know that. I'm just not sure you do."

"That is absolutely not true."

There was a silent pause, and then Kendall broke it with "You know, I gotta get going. Jennifer and Kirsten will be here any minute. We're going to watch the Bears preseason game at The Goal Post."

"I'll let you go then. Have fun doll. I love you."

Jordan hung up the phone and turned the stereo up a few decibels. Then he leaned back into Stan's soft, squishy leather couch and fell asleep thinking Kendall thoughts and listening to Eric Clapton Unplugged.

The door opened and Stan slithered in. He tip toed to the kitchen, then up to the couch. He knew exactly what to do. He sucked in a deep breath of L.A. smogxygen. Then IT came out, roaring from the center of his chest:

"O-o-o-o-oh-h Sa-a-a-y Ca-a-a-n You Se-e-e-e-e-!

By the dawn's ear-ly li-I-ight!

What so pro-o-o-udly we-e-e-e-e ha-a-a-ail"

Then came the water.

Jordan screamed "Jesus Christ!"

"Merlin, get the tranquilizer gun. The beast has awoken!"

When he got over it, Jordan smiled at his best friend in a way that said, "Touche." The tradition lived.

"Stow, I hope you don't mind the models and actresses who will be at the party I'm taking you to. I'm sure they will be excited to diverge from their usual diet of producers and directors and add a Deputy District Attorney to their list of sexual conquests."

"What time is it?"

"It's time to get showered, shaved, and slightly intoxicated."

Stan mixed a mighty batch of Myer's and tonics in a martini shaker at the wet bar, then poured them into crystal double old-fashioned glasses. After squeezing in the limes, he sipped his and handed the other to his roommate.

"How's work going Stan-man?"

"Oh, you know, typical BS. But wait 'till you see what I have planned for us tonight."

Jordan was intrigued. When Stan talked something up, it was usually not empty hype. After enjoying their drinks for a few minutes, they took turns. While Jordan showered, Stan shaved. Then vice-versa. Jordan was ready first, nothing new there. He finished his twelve ounces of mostly rum on the balcony. A bouncy blonde jogger with movie star looks breezed by on the street below. It seemed that every girl Jordan saw in L.A. was in amazing physical shape. And he decided that he was ready to meet some of them. He was feeling his oats tonight.

When the roommates reached the street, Stan was dressed down in holey blue jeans, a white T-shirt, and a black and red vest that he bought at Aardvarks' on Melrose. Jordan donned a pair of Banana Republic jeans, a blue denim shirt, and his favorite old blazer he bought at a second hand store on 'M' Street in Georgetown. When they turned the corner and entered the alley, Stan quickened his pace. He walked over to a white Ferrari Mondial convertible parallel parked between two trash dumpsters. He removed a key from his pocket. And, unbelievably, he opened the door with it!

"Hop in Stow. We got a party to go to. Wanna drive?" Stan's eyebrow raised as if to say, "not bad, eh?"

He stared at Stan-man and smiled a smile that seemed to connect his ears, exposing the dimple on his left cheek.

"Don't be too impressed Stow, it's not mine."

"Where'd you steal it?"

"I borrowed it from a friend. You'll meet him tonight. I wanted our first night out to be extraordinary. Besides, where we're going, we'll need this car."

Thankful that his father taught him to drive a stick, Jordan slid down onto the driver seat's hard black leather and fired up all 350 horses. Stan showed him how to take off the parking brake and turn on the lights. He gave him a brief lecture on the gear box. Jordan grabbed the ball atop the long, slender, chrome gear shift and popped her into first. He gave her some gas and, inadvertently, peeled out of the alley. The roommates were off to Bel Air.

Twelve

The wrinkles on Loni's forehead came from a combination of the thousand sunny days that she lounged on the beaches of Hermosa and Manhattan during her teenage surfer-girl heyday in the early 1950's, gravity, and the stress of carrying on the business after her husband Donny died of lung cancer in 1978. Grey and black salt and pepper hair scraggled down to her shoulders. Skinny as a rail she was. Inside as tough and leathery as her skin intimated. And she was always eager to tell you exactly what she thought in a manner as subtle as a cruise missile. Tonight she wore a black T-shirt with yellow letters that read, "SADDAM HUSSEIN STILL HAS A JOB. DO YOU?"

Loni worked her way down the bar with a wet rag, mopping up puddles of beer and liquor, the casualties of their owners' alcohol-induced coordination lapses. When she got to JJ, she reached underneath the bar and grabbed a carton of Pepperidge Farm cheddar fish and filled up the plastic bowl that abutted the detective's Jack and Coke.

"Only the best for my friends," she said.

JJ was hundreds of miles deep in thought. He popped his head over a newspaper he was no longer reading and acknowledged Loni because he knew she had said something. He had been searching the Orange County edition of the *Los Angeles Times* but could not find even the smallest story on the discovery of Alejandro Sandoval's body in Yorba Linda. He wasn't surprised. There were more important things that the readership needed to be informed of, like the fact that Arsenio Hall was being sued by his Beverly Hills neighbors who were trying to stop him from building a tennis court. That was pressing news to Angelinos and those residing safely behind the Orange Curtain.

He set the paper down and flirted with his cocktail, contemplating the day's revelations. His original theory still ruled. The Kansas Street Crips, all 15 of them, were on his unofficial most-wanted list. But, despite a second day of investigation, half of which was spent driving the streets, his suspects had not surfaced. The significance of their sudden unavailability was not lost on him.

"Hey detective! What happened to your Dodgers today?" demanded Mary O'Neil, a 48-year-old Irish redhead with a habit of passing out before last call at the Aftershock. She was already up to her ears in the bag, and JJ figured she had about one and a half vodka tonics to go.

"Didn't see the ball game Mary. But then I work during the weekday."

"It's Saturday you idiot!"

JJ forgot. And he felt bad for coming down hard on Mary, one of his few real friends in the world. She was only trying to relieve a lonely part of her that the vodka couldn't reach.

"Loni, another vodka tonic for Mary. Make it the good stuff this time."

Loni filled the order as soon as she finished arguing with Buddy Cox, another Aftershock regular and a washed-up, obese, bald car salesman in his early 50's who made Willie Lowman look like Lee Iacocca. The debate this time was over who first recorded the song "Suspicious Minds," Elvis Presley or Patsy Kline. The spark of the quarrel resonated from the only jukebox in Long Beach that still played vinyl.

Finally, Loni ended it with "May the King have mercy on your soul" and walked over to give the good stuff to Mary. But before she could deliver the order, it was apparent that JJ miscalculated. Mary was face down in her bowl of cheddar fish. JJ took the Stoli and tonic from Loni.

"Do you know why I became a cop Loni?"

"Because you like to get into the movies for free?"

"No. Because I wanted to help my people."

"What people?"

"Latinos."

"I have news for you; we're *all* your people."

"I know that, but you don't understand what I'm saying."

JJ was staring past Loni, and she knew there was something seriously wrong.

"It's Alex." JJ was feeling the first half of his third drink. "You know, I always wanted Rachel to give me a son. I needed a son, but she didn't stay around long enough."

"What happened to Alex?"

"He's dead."

Despite mingling with the masses in her bar for decades and eavesdropping on innumerable conversations, the bartender did not know what to say. JJ had told her about Alex. He told her that the boy was a sign that all hope was not lost in the neighborhood where he grew up. He told her that he was going to save this boy. At a loss, Loni did what all bartenders do in this situation. It's in their genes.

When she was done pouring and stirring, she set the fresh Jack and Coke next to the detective.

"Loni, I'm in pain."

"Honey, tell me what I can do to help you." This was about as sensitive and emotionally aware as Loni Krager had been since Donny's death.

"You can't do anything. I . . .I, um . . .I am responsible for Alex's death."

"Hey, you can't blame yourself for that. You didn't kill him."

"The truth is. . . I did."

"How?"

"I set him up. First I can't protect his mother, and now . . ."

JJ took a slug of his drink and never finished his sentence. Loni didn't press him. Instead she reached across the bar and placed her hand on the shoulder of the cynical detective who, despite his twenty years face-to-face with crime, death, and diseases of the soul, and his resulting loss of respect for the entire human race, had managed to become wet in the eyes for the second time in two days.

The loud THUD jolted Loni and JJ back to their environs, and their semi-embrace ended abruptly. JJ helped a half-conscious Mary O'Neil off of the floor.

"I'll drive her home Loni."

As JJ walked out with Mary on his shoulder like the casualty of war that she was, Loni yelled out to him over Loretta Lynn's "Stand By Your Man" blaring at the jukebox's loudest setting.

"It ain't your fault! It's just God's will!"

Thirteen

"Make a left here."

Jordan complied with Stan's direction, and he raced the Ferrari, which he noticed only had four thousand miles on it, up the narrow, winding street, past mansion after mansion, most of them camouflaged in trees and bushes and protected by steel gates and high fences. The Alpine stereo competed with the high-pitched whine of the engine, as Stan introduced Jordan to his favorite new musical discovery, "The Beautiful South." The music reminded Jordan of "The Smiths" except without the morose lyrics that make you want to take your own life. Stan was always into new music and loved to get his friends into it as well.

"It's this driveway coming up on the left."

Jordan turned into the driveway and stopped at the guard booth. A huge man with a body builder chest waived to Stan and opened the gate. They followed the incline until a beautiful white-washed, Spanish architected 15 bedroom Bel Air standard, complete with tennis court, pool, jacuzzi, and decks galore, greeted them with style. There were about 12 cars in a parking area that was chiseled out of the canyon. Jordan parked the white aphrodisiac on wheels between a black Lexus and a green Jag. There were three girls dancing by the pool, and Stan pointed them out. All three looked like swimsuit models, but they were a ways away and the light was low. The loud music coming from a speaker on the second floor balcony was unintelligible, but it was clear that it was dance music, because the bass was practically shaking off the terracotta shingles.

Stan reached down under the seat and pulled out a pint of Seagram 7, a whiskey that Jordan and Stan had traditionally drunk since they had their first together on Jordan's 16th birthday because it was the only drink in Stan's house. It was a classic. Stan fish-kissed the mouth of the bottle and downed a hefty shot.

"Whose gonna drive tonight Stan-man?"

"Don't worry, we can crash at Rhory's if neither of us can drive. Hey, do ya remember graduation, Stow, when we drove around in the limo and got toasted on Segrams. That was one of the best days of my life."

"Yeah, Stan-man, we kinda did it all together."

"No, my friend, we didn't do it all. Our work here is not yet done. Here, polish this off."

"Agh!" Jordan complained, after he tipped back the last of the Segrams.

The roommates walked, side by side, towards the pool gate, the back way into the affair. The music was thumping, the words were understandable at this distance, and they called out, "It's time to party, it's time to Jam!" Jordan Stowic did not need to be reminded. Jordan and Stan walked slowly past the pool, swapping flirtatious glances with the three females who appeared even more voluptuous up close and a pint of Segrams later.

A dark complected man in his mid-thirties with black slicked-back Pat Riley hair and draped in a crème-colored Armani suit stood by the doorway. "Good evening Stanley. Good of you to make my soiree."

"Rhory, I'd like you to meet my best friend from Michigan. This is Jordan Stowic. Jordan, this is Rhory Callum, my friend and colleague from the Crime lab."

"Good to know ya Rhory."

"My pleasure. Stanley's told me quite a bit of your childhood in Michigan. Sounds like you boys had loads of fun. Growing up in Michigan, you must've had to use your imagination."

"It's really not that hard to have fun there. There's ice fishing, tractor pulls, cow tipping. Not to mention log rolling and pie eating."

Rhory let out a pretend laugh.

There was an obvious tension between Rhory and Jordan. Their personalities mixed like Pepsi and eggnog. But then, Jordan was not good around fake, condescending people. Seeing this, Stan ushered Jordan inside to get a drink as soon as one of the girls by the pool called out for Rhory.

"Sorry about Rhory, he's a little bit like sandpaper. But this party is gonna be worth it."

"Rhory lives here?"

"Sure does."

"Not too shabby of a pad for someone who tests dope for the government. How does he afford this?"

"He made his money the old fashioned way, he inherited it."

"Kinda like you, Stan-man."

Stan's expression changed for the worse.

Jordan couldn't believe what had come out of his mouth. It was as if some of Rhory's personality had rubbed off on him.

"Sorry Stan. I didn't mean to say that. I don't know why I did."

"It's alright Stow."

"You know, we haven't talked about it since I've been out. Do you still have trouble thinking about him?"

There was a long pause. They moved up in the line for cocktails. A small crowd gathered around the piano where Rhory sat down to play. The volume of the dance music made it impossible to hear Rhory attempt to show off his thousands of dollars of piano lessons. Finally, Stan spoke.

"Of course I still have trouble. It's been ten months, but I feel like the funeral was last week. I have dreams. I keep hearing the doctor tell me 'Your father had very bad complications.' I keep asking him about it, but he never admits that my Dad's dead. And I keep waking up thinking there's still a chance. But there's no chance."

Jordan put his arm around Stan, whose eyes were red.

"Two double Seven and Sevens," said Jordan to the bartender dressed in a tux.

"Let's just have fun tonight Stow, I want to see you enjoy our first night out together."

"I'm already enjoying it," said Jordan as he reached and clanked Stan's glass, then tipped back the potent blended whiskey.

Stan led Jordan over to the piano, where the mostly female crowd was attempting to hear Rhory's one-man show.

"Hi Jennifer, how's my favorite casting-assistant?"

"Stanley sweetie, how are you?" They kissed.

She was a pretty, petite girl with short sandy-brown hair, well into her twenties, and Jordan couldn't help taking an extended look at her purple bra which was barely veiled by a sheer black blouse, her breasts handily filling in what Jordan estimated to be a 36 C. He knew bra sizes since he had become an expert in the field through countless visits to Victoria's Secret with Kendall, and late night lingerie orders by telephone for Valentine's and other special occasions.

"Excuse us for a minute Stow," said Stan, and he walked with Jennifer out onto the deck surrounding the pool.

Jordan turned to find the bar for his second cocktail.

"I'll have another double, please" said Jordan as he sat down at the bar stool. The guy sitting next to him introduced himself.

"I'm David Stillwell. Are you a friend of Rhory's?"

"Friend of a friend, actually."

"To be perfectly honest, I think he's a real asshole. I'm sorry that he's your friend's friend."

Jordan could tell by the free-flowing comments and his slurred speech, that David Stillwell had drunk his share of the still. And didn't hold it well.

"I just came here for the free booze and the blow. What do you do for a living?"

"I'm an attorney."

"No shit, so am I! Personal injury is my game. You ever heard of Rollie Sparks?"

"No, but I've only been out in L.A. for a few days."

"Maybe you've see the commercials. My favorite is the one where a woman is crossing the street with a baby in her arms, and all you hear is a screech of tires, then you hear the announcer, who sounds like James Earl Jones, go: 'If you're the victim of an accident, don't let the wheels of justice run you over, call Rollie Sparks and you'll get what's coming to you.' And then a giant bag of money lands on the woman and her baby as they're lying in this hospital in full body casts. It's great! And aren't my parents proud."

"I take it you're a little cynical about handling PI cases?"

"Fuck it! It pays the bills and keeps me supplied."

"You know, it's never too late to try something new."

"Hey Maurice!" he called to the bartender, "how 'bout some more of ol' Columbia?"

The bartender walked back and calmly told him that he'd had his share and that Rhory had instructed that he be cut off.

"Come on, just one more line."

Jordan was beginning to get very uncomfortable.

Then David Stillwell rolled a 100 dollar bill, and, in front of everyone at the party, including Deputy District Attorney Jordan Stowic, took the plastic baggy from his own pocket, poured a little powder on the bar, formed it with his fingernail, and snorted a line of cocaine.

Jordan immediately stood up knowing he had to leave. Besides the fact that drugs were never his scene, he had his job to think about. As he walked out onto the deck he envisioned the police surrounding the place and arresting everyone at the party including him. He strolled out onto the deck, down the stairs towards the pool, and a woman's eyes watched him intently.

From the overview of the pool, Jordan could see an entwined mass of flesh kissing and laughing in the deep end. Stan and Jennifer were both as bare as their first birthday, so Jordan had to be as tactful as possible. He walked to about 10 feet from the pool and announced, "Stan, I gotta take off."

Stan swam over to the edge of the pool, towards Jordan, and asked, "What's wrong pal, still jet lagged?"

"I'll tell you about it tomorrow, but I just gotta go."

"Well, just take the Ferrari. Jennifer will drive me home. By the way, she's pretty hot, huh?"

"Smokin' hot" Jordan assured Stan, as he took the keys from Stan's short pockets then walked down the hill towards the cars, wishing that this wasn't the kind of party that it was.

As Jordan bent down to put the key in the driver's side door, a woman put her hand on his shoulder.

"Would you mind dropping me off?" she asked.

A startled Jordan Stowic spun his head around to face her. Her velvet black hair fell to her waist. He knew her from somewhere. It was the girl from the plane! Jordan's heart raced.

"Hi."

"Did I startle you? I didn't mean to."

"Not at all."

"I've been watching you all night," she said.

"I've seen you before, haven't I? You were on my plane from Chicago."

"I'm flattered that you remember. Can I get in?"

Jordan thought about it for about a half of a second, smiled and said, "Absolutely."

He walked around and opened the door for her. He started the engine, turned up the radio and punched the accelerator. They sped down the narrow winding roads of Bel Air. He drove much faster than someone with no place in particular to go. He pushed the sports car to its limits around the hair pin turns. It excited him that he didn't even have her name.

Fourteen

JJ walked up two flights of stairs to his third floor apartment and surprised himself with the energy he had left over. He knew he was partly fueled by the Jack Daniels. He surveyed the refrigerator, taking no action based on what he saw, and flipped on the TV to catch the last half of the Tonight Show. He picked up the phone during the first commercial and checked his messages.

"You have...THREE...messages," the female computerized voice announced without emotion. The voice reminded him of his second wife, Ariola. He thought about her and dismissed their one-year marriage with a single sigh. The first message was from his old partner, Blair Davis. Davis was calling to find out how the Snow case was going. He and JJ worked in O.S.S. together for 10 years, then Davis took a promotion to Sergeant and moved to Malibu. He was a good man. A family man. The idea of a safe desk and more money appealed to him more than the adrenalin of the streets. Before he moved he joked that he would be the only black guy in Malibu that wasn't a professional athlete or entertainer. In the message Blair told JJ "Call me back if you want my thoughts. Don't forget I'm the one who solved all our cases." The second message was the special assistant to the D.A., Steve Salsman. He said "Mr. Salsman would appreciate if you kept him abreast of the investigation and alerted him as soon as a suspect is located." JJ threw a middle finger in the air as the special assistant spoke. Then came the third message.

"Yo JJ, this G-Dog, I got somethin' you might be interested in. I couldn't say nothin' in front of my little homeboy. Hit me up. My pager's still 310-603-G-D-O-G. Don't be saying nothin' to no one I called."

JJ immediately called and punched in his number when he heard the tone. He sat and waited. And waited. He watched the rest of the tonight show, the late night talk show after that, and fell asleep during the re-broadcast of the President's last speech. He dreamt of Rachel. The theme of the dream was the same. They were together, they were making love, but he could feel her slipping away.

Fifteen

Out of the rear view mirror, he could see her jet black hair blowing in a straight line behind her, like Grace Kelly's scarf in *To Catch a Thief*. Her bright blue eyes were trained on him, not the road. He enjoyed the attention from her quite a bit. They hadn't said a word since they left the party. Yet they had no trouble communicating. Occasionally, when he was not working the gear box, Jordan would reach down and put his right hand on her left thigh, and give it a light squeeze to return her touches. Or he would caress the soft hand that rested on his knee. She would just smile. Without words they were talking. The eroticism was deafening.

Jordan led the convertible Ferrari down Sunset Boulevard, through Westwood, through Beverly Hills and West Los Angles, onto the 10 freeway West. Something told him to go to the beach. The engine whined, the music blared, and they teased each other into frenzy. When they got off the 10, they were in Santa Monica, and Jordan pulled off the Pacific Coast Highway into the giant public parking lot. The waves were crashing onto the boundless beach, several football fields in width. There were a few couples scattered on the sand, wrapped in blankets, kissing in the darkness.

When he shut the car off, he glanced over at her.

"Is this ok?" he asked.

"I thought you were gonna drop me home?" she teased.

"Didn't you say you wanted me to take you to the ocean?"

She grabbed him and gently pressed her lips into his. Jordan did not resist. She stopped suddenly and ran out of the car onto the beach towards the surf, kicking off her sandals as she ran. Jordan followed her moon-drenched silhouette, a perfect female form covered in black silk, from blouse to skirt. Her bare legs were beautiful and her skin was dark tan. Jordan caught up, tackled her gingerly and wrapped her in his jacket.

He kissed her twice, then said, "Is this weird? I don't even know who you are."

"I'm your wildest fantasy, Mr. Stowic."

"How did you know my name?"

"I told you, I've been watching you all night."

"Well, I've been watching you since you followed me on my plane from Chicago."

"How do I know you didn't follow me?"

"Who was the one who followed me from the party? I didn't even know you were there."

"Who was the one who drove me to the beach so he could take advantage of me?"

"Guilty."

"Then I sentence you to fuck me on this beach right now."

In the morning, Jordan was feeling the alcohol he had drunk. He and his headache were lingering on the edge of consciousness. He looked next to him and saw her back. It was a small, beautiful model with thin petite arms attached. Staring at her, he felt embarrassed about what had happened so quickly. He didn't even know her well enough to be staring at her back. Then came a knock at the bedroom door.

"Stow, are you up?" It was Stan.

Jordan didn't answer, he just watched her as she turned over towards him. Her eyes opened slowly. Those bright blue eyes! Even with last night's makeup she was stunning.

"Jordan, it's Sweetie on the hotline," said Stan through the cracked door.

Oh shit. He had to talk to Kendall.

The woman in his bed surprised him by hoarsely commenting, "You'd better take it."

Jordan got up, purposely keeping his back towards her, and covered himself in his terry robe.

"Hi K." he said solemnly.

"What's wrong?"

"K, we have to have a talk."

"About what?"

"About us. About me."

"Are you seeing someone else? Just tell me. Because if you are I- "

"No, I'm not exactly seeing anyone else. But last night I met someone and...."

There was a damaging pause. Kendall began crying softly. Jordan would have rather have been kicked in the teeth.

"K, I just need some time, I-"

"Take all the time you want. It's over."

Before Jordan could imagine his next line, he heard her slam the receiver down. He felt horrible. But lying was not Jordan Stowic's style. His policy of truth had gotten him into many a tough spot, but he always believed in that policy. As he walked back to his room he believed that he had made the right decision. For now Kendall Wright was free. No one was holding her back with promises that would not be delivered.

Stan stopped him in the hallway and began talking in an urgent, hush tone.

"Who was that amazing woman who just walked into the bathroom?"

"That's a good question Stan-man."

"Hey, sorry about not screening the call, I had no idea you-"

"It's ok, you didn't know."

"Well? Tell me about her."

"Her name is Courtney. That's about all I remember from last night. She was on my plane from Chicago, and she just found me as I was leaving the party and asked for a ride."

"This is great news pal," said Stan, congratulating him with a pat on his behind.

"I don't think Kendall sees it that way."

"It's only natural Stow; you guys will find each other again if it's meant to-"

She strutted out from the bathroom wearing only Jordan's blue oxford cloth shirt. Stan chose not to finish his thought, instead opting for a hard stare.

"Stan, this is Courtney. Courtney, Stan."

"It's nice to meet you Courtney. Can I get you anything, coffee, juice, whiskey?"

"No, actually I have to get going. I have to be at work by ten."

"On a Sunday?" Stan asked.

"I work for an accounting firm, and I plan to make partner before I go gray."

For the next several minutes she got dressed in Jordan's room while Jordan sat on the balcony drinking a diet Coke, wondering about this girl. Didn't she tell him last night that she worked for an investment firm?

Sixteen

Monday morning came, and JJ knew it would be a very hard day. In fact, he didn't even go to the Aftershock last night to save himself the Jack withdrawal which he couldn't afford to contend with today. Alex's viewing was scheduled for 9:30 a.m. The funeral would follow.

JJ spent the early morning speaking to the crime scene technician who investigated Alex's car and the surrounding area, and the coroner who performed the autopsy on the body. They both wondered why the hell an L.A. Sheriff's Deputy was bothering them. JJ told them he was working on a joint investigation with Sheriff Blade and the O.C.S.O. They bought it.

JJ pulled up to the Hershel Funeral Home on Compton Boulevard ten minutes after nine. He wanted to get there early to console Alex's only surviving relative in the United States, his Aunt Rosie. She was inside the office, along with her husband Ruffo and the director of the funeral home. She was signing and initialing several documents and obtaining copies of Alex's death certificate. Taking care of the details, something she'd always been good at. Rosie was the first of the Sandoval family to come to California from Mexico. She arranged for jobs and an apartment for herself, Maria and their father. This all in advance of their short trek from Tecate to L.A.

She stood up and hugged JJ as soon as she finished her business.

"JJ. Thank you."

"Rosie, Alex was…" He stared away when he knew he couldn't get through the thought.

"I wish Ri-ri was here. I need her right now." Ri-ri was Maria. Her sister and Alex's murdered mother.

Rosie's overdone makeup was running around her eyes as the faucet opened yet again.

JJ handed her his handkerchief to relieve the expended tissue she clutched. To her the scene was far too familiar and recent. Just yesterday, it seemed, she was burying Ri-ri. Now she was burying Ri-ri's son.

"Tell me one thing. Just tell me this one thing, *please*. Why? Why Alejandro?"

Rosie watched JJ intensely, expecting him to provide a profound answer appropriate for the moment that could comfort her soul. Ruffo looked away. The owner walked out of the office, having heard this question many times and knowing there was no good answer.

"Rosie, there is too much anger out there. Not enough love."

That was the best JJ Ramirez could do. He walked out into the main room and saw the casket. It was burgundy oak with beveled edging. And it was closed; despite the fact the Sandovals were Catholic. She had honored her sister's wishes for a closed casket. And Rosie knew that her sister would have wanted the same for her son.

JJ stared deep into the burgundy oak and he remembered Alex and his mother.

The moon was full on the clearest, most balmy night that Compton saw that summer.

"JJ, do you want something else?"

"No thank you sweetheart."

Maria was clearing the table, and ever so polite. And she looked great in her knee-length, white, cotton dress, with her lovely dark hair and tanned complexion in stunning contrast. JJ knew he wasn't in love with her. But he loved her. And more than anything, he admired her. She had overcome much adversity.

Alex was pensive. He had to go meet his homies on the corner to go up to the carnival. There would be girls there. There would also be rivals to fight with. He didn't want to keep his homies waiting. He needed them for survival. But lately he had come to need something else. Or, rather, he had begun to fill a void. He wished he had another hour so he could spend it with JJ. He turned and faced his mentor who was now reclining on the couch, fiddling with the T.V. remote.

"Why are you a cop?" he asked.

"There are some things you just know, deep in your soul. You know that's who you are. You know that you could be no one else."

JJ knew he had his audience interested in his thoughts, so he took advantage of the moment.

"Kansas Street is never going to make you a man. That comes from inside. The inside of a man."

"It's fucked up homes." Alex looked into the kitchen to make sure that his mom wasn't listening. He saw her doing dishes. She wouldn't hear.

"I know a lot of the things we do for our neighborhood is wrong. Ya know, stealin' and hurtin' other people and shit. But we do it for each other and that's all that matters to us."

"Alex, ya gotta understand one thing. I've been in your same shoes. I had the same pressures on me when I was a Pueblo. But you have to resist it. Be true to yourself."

The Pueblo gang was a large Hispanic gang flourishing in Compton between 1955-1965. Their fights were mostly with fists at parties, parks and high school athletic contests, scarcely resembling the brutal drive-by shootings of the day.

"Sometimes, I just want to get out of it. Ya know last week Grumpy smacked his mom with the handle of his tre-eight. The old lady needed five stitches on her head."

"What does that make you think of Grumpy?"

"He's one messed-up individual homes. I don't ever wanna be like him."

"You never will be Alex. You got your mom and you got me. Don't tell her this, but one of these days, we might make it an official family. Would you like that mejo?"

"That would be cool, homes."

"You think *homes*?" JJ said mockingly.

Alex reached over and messed up JJ's perfect, gray coiffure.

JJ leaped off the couch and tackled Alex, and they wrestled on the floor, trading laughter.

The hand on JJ's shoulder brought him back to the funeral home. It was Blair Davis.

"I'm really sorry about Sniper."

"Alex. His name was Alex."

"Yeah, I know. I'm sorry. Alex was a good kid."

"You know old buddy, I could use you on this investigation. Too bad ya had to go retire in Malibu. How do you like your desk? Getting any pencil calluses?"

Blair knew JJ was irritated with him for leaving, but forgave his sarcasm because of the moment, and because he knew sarcasm came with the territory with JJ Ramirez. Except when he talked about Alex and Maria.

"Malibu is ok. A little slow, but you're not gonna get me to say I miss cruisin' the streets with you. Well, maybe a little."

"You really like playing Sergeant?"

"I'm the watch commander. I sit on my butt, sign off on reports, and order everyone around, meanwhile making good money waiting out my retirement without risking my ass in the field. Yeah, I guess you could say I like it."

"But you could've waited until after we closed out Snow."

"Man, why do ya have to throw that shit in my face every time I see you? I had to go. I didn't wanna lose this opportunity. I needed it for my sanity, not to mention Angie and our kids. You know what college tuition costs these days?"

"Have you had any more thoughts about where I should take the investigation now?"

"No new thoughts partner. I still think it was Kansas Street. Not Alex necessarily, but his homies. It had to be. Two of the victims were Playboys. Arch rivals. Typical gang m.o."

"Here, look at this." JJ pulled out a copy of the Sheriff reports on Alex's murder and handed them to Blair.

"What's this?"

"Alex's case. I'm handling it."

"Are you crazy, that's not in the county. What's your jurisdiction?"

"Richard Blade, Sheriff of Orange County. That's my jurisdiction."

"Damn it, JJ." Blair was very surprised. "Who's your partner on it, anyway." Blair began skimming through, page by page.

"You're talkin' to him."

Blair looked up and glared at JJ.

"This is really stupid. You should let Orange County handle it. You do want to keep that pension you've been busting your ass for over the last two decades, don't you?"

"Don't worry about it. Besides, it's part of Snow. If I find the persons who shot Alex, I'll be able to close out Leticia Snow and company. And that will get the press and the D.A. off my back. Not to mention a little piece of mind and some sleep."

"Bad idea. But I'm still here for you J," said Blair, his voice drenched in resignation.

"When you get a chance, just look over these reports and give me your thoughts. Right now, I think Alex was killed by his own homies because he was gonna snitch them off on Snow."

"You really think he was gonna give them up?"

"Pretty sure. But I still have a lot of work to do before I can make the arrests."

"You'll get there JJ, you always do. You didn't become LA's second best gang homicide detective for nothin'."

JJ sneered at his old partner, as Blair continued, "Well, maybe your partner had something to do with it."

Before JJ could jab at Blair again for deserting him in the middle of one of their biggest cases, he heard the door open and turned to see two people walk up to the casket and kneel down. They were friends of Rosie's. JJ walked over to them and, when they were through with their prayers, introduced himself and shared kind words about Alex.

JJ waited patiently for the guests of honor to arrive. He hated to mix cop business with personal business, but he had to talk to them. And, just before 10:30, he was pleased to see them filing into the funeral home. They were clad from head to toe in Kansas Street Crip blue. It paralleled the symbolism and revelry of a military burial. One by one, Sniper's homies walked up to the casket and placed a single blue carnation on top. By the time they were done, JJ counted 15 carnations. All of the living, unincarcerated members of the Kansas Street Crips were present and accounted for.

JJ excused himself from Rosie's friends and walked over towards the back two rows of seats where the gang had congregated. The detective approached Juan Angel Hernandez, a.k.a. Q-ball, a tall, thin, Hispanic 20 year-old boy with dark black hair shaved to his scalp, complemented by a thin goatee. He was the self-appointed leader of KSC. He held the title ever since Trigger-G went to state prison in 1991 for carjacking.

"Hey Q, where you been homey?"

Q-ball recognized JJ. He didn't like his tone. Especially not in front of his homeboys.

"Yo homes, show some respect, our little homey was blasted. This is a very sad day for us all."

"C'mon Q, don't bullshit a bullshitter, I know you guys couldn't be happier to get Sniper out of the way. You were afraid he was gonna i.d. you for those Playboys you capped."

"Man, if you wasn't a cop, I'd lay into you right now, in honor of my little homey."

"Threaten me one more time and I'll take you downtown."

"Go for it homes. Take us all. We're gettin' used to the food. We just spent five days up in Frisco jail eatin' slop and fendin' off fags 'cause them cops up there don't like us. They claimed some bullshit about us disturbin' the peace."

JJ grabbed the gangster's white t-shirt in his strong cop grasp, and pulled Q-ball to within inches of his face.

"Don't fuck with me shithead, I've had a bad few days."

Q-ball stared into JJ's intense dark brown eyes, unflinchingly, as his homeboys and the others at the funeral home watched the spectacle.

It was obvious to JJ he was not going to get anywhere with Q- ball, at least not in front of this audience. He let go. JJ started walking outside and motioned toward Q-ball, who followed reluctantly.

Once outside, JJ felt the late morning sun warming up the earth, foreshadowing the afternoon heat to come.

"When did you get to San Francisco?"

"Man, I don't know. I think it was Tuesday or Wednesday. I don't remember."

"All of you?"

"Yeah."

"Why did you go up there?"

"A concert, man, why do you give a fuck?"

"Because I think you killed Sniper."

"Why would I do that, he's our own homeboy."

"Because you killed five people, including a little girl named Leticia Snow. You know she would have been five years old today. Does that make you feel like a man you little bitch?" JJ was lying about her birthday for effect.

"That's bullshit man, and you know it. We didn't kill anyone. And anyways, there's a truce on. The 'Eme sais we don't do no drive-byes 'else we get green-lighted." Q-ball was referring to an edict of the Mexican Mafia, or 'Eme, a powerful prison gang that, remarkably, controls many of the gangs on the streets of Southern California from within the confines of prisons throughout the state.

"Then you and your homies don't mind coming downtown to talk to me."

"We ain't' doin' nothin' cop 'less you got a warrant."

"As soon as Alex is buried I'm takin' all you motherfuckers downtown, and there is not a god damn thing you can do about it you little murdering fuck."

"Whatever homes." Q-ball walked back inside to his homies, shaking his head and rolling his eyes at his homeboys who watched intently.

"See what kind of attitude that cop has after I blast him," he said so only his homies could hear.

JJ envisioned the court clerk reading the jury's decision on the penalty phase of Alex's murderers' trial. "We the jury find that the defendants shall suffer the penalty of death." This vision sustained him.

Seventeen

New to Southern California and on menacing turf, Jordan was thankful that the Compton courthouse was unmistakable, rising like a phoenix above all of the other buildings within a seven mile radius. And, like the mythical bird of the Arabian Desert, it came up from the ashes of a city that used to be something much more.

Jordan had no trouble navigating the back roads after getting off the 91 Freeway. It reminded him of driving though Chicago, using the Hancock Tower as a reference point. The Courthouse was a ten-story, white brick building with distinctive satellite dishes on the rooftop, along with a helicopter landing pad.

He parked on the second floor of the concrete parking structure for the courthouse, parking as close as he could to the stairwell. He walked down the stairs, briefcase in hand, and out onto a vast open area covered in more concrete.

There were matching trash receptacles in the same color concrete, generously smeared with red, blue and black graffiti, courtesy of local street gangs.

Traversing the concrete park, he arrived at the door to the courthouse. First-day adrenaline seemed to replace the blood in his veins. He whipped out his wallet and flashed his D.A. identification to the Marshal, as he was told to do, avoiding the time consuming line of people seeking metal detector approval. The Deputy D.A. was waived through.

It was a five-minute wait amongst the crowd in the lobby. Jordan learned that the object was to jockey for a position to sardine into an elevator with attorneys, court staff and defendants, a handful of the latter having neglected basic hygiene like showers and deodorant.

Jordan got off on the 7th floor and saw the glass doors with the words "Office of the District Attorney, County of Los Angeles,

Steven A. Salsman, District Attorney," written in black letters on the glass above the doors. Below it, there was a smaller name and title: "James D. Connelly, Head Deputy." He walked through and was met by a friendly receptionist named Yolanda, a.k.a., "Yoli."

She was a short and a slightly overweight forty-something black woman who greeted him with a disarming "Good morning baby, you must be the new D.A." Jordan would later learn that he and everyone Yoli addressed was "baby."

"Hi, I'm Jordan Stowic ." They shook hands.

"I'm Yolanda. Call me 'Yoli,' everyone does, baby. If you need anything, just let me know."

"Ok, I will thank you. Where do I find James Connelly?"

"The big boss is down the hall to the left. I'll buzz you in baby."

Jordan opened the security door when he heard the "click," and entered the inner sanctum of the Compton office of the L.A. County District Attorney. He followed her directions and maintained a slight smile as he walked, thinking about Yoli and how she called a complete stranger "baby." What term of endearment did she reserve for her closest friends? He knew he would really enjoy Yoli.

Jordan walked into the outer office area and saw Mr. Connelly's secretary, Sumi. She was a tiny Asian woman in her 50's, and she was on the phone. It sounded like she was ordering office supplies. She told the person to whom she speaking to hold on.

"Are you Jordan?"

"Yes. Jordan Stowic. Nice to meet you." He presented his hand and she shook it, knocking her pencil holder slightly.

"Mr. Connelly is expecting you, go on in."

"Thank you."

Jordan walked in and saw James Connelly reclined in a large brown leather chair, also on the phone. He acknowledged Jordan by raising his right hand, then motioning for Jordan to have a seat.

While he waited, he took notice of the items adorning Connelly's office.

On a shelf, along with the California Penal Code, was a baseball cap with the inscription, "Sheriff's Homicide. Our Day Begins When Your Day Ends." There was a framed courtroom artist's sketch of younger man resembling Connelly arguing to a jury. And a framed newspaper article headlined "Manson Convicted!" Jordan knew that Connelly had convicted his share of bad guys, both infamous and insignificant.

Jim Connelly was a prosecutor's prosecutor, from his looks to his political philosophy. A life-long Republican, he stood 6' 1", his hair thinning, resembling a grayish-black wave breaking to the left. His face was thin, matching his frame. The deep crows' feet around his eyes could have been partly caused by the high-profile cases he took on during his 28 years as a Deputy District Attorney. He'd have plenty of practical tips to give Jordan, but they'd pale in comparison to the war stories that would capture the imagination of the new Deputy D.A.

He hung up the phone. "You must be my new deputy."

"Yes sir. I'm Jordan Stowic. Good to meet you Mr. Connelly."

"Call me Jim. You're one of us now. Here in Compton we're like a family. We have to be. This whole damn area is a powder keg and we're the only thing keeping it from going off. That keeps us close. So tell me about yourself Jordan, where are you from?"

"I grew up mostly in Michigan, but I went to school in Chicago at Northwestern, then in D.C. at Georgetown Law."

"How'd you end up out here?"

"Recruited, actually. I was contemplating the Manhattan D.A.'s Office, but the pay they offered was not enough to live on since I'm not a Kennedy. And this is the largest single prosecutor's office in the world. I figured I'd get the most experience here."

"I'm glad to hear you say you want experience. Because my philosophy for young D.A.s can be summed up in three words: trials, trials, trials. That's how you learn. You get your butt whipped a few times, you figure out how the game is played, and then you kick everyone else's."

"I can't wait to have my first jury trial. I had a few trials in law school when I was in the criminal justice clinic, but they were only bench trials."

"Jordan, my first trial was way back when we had jury trials for traffic tickets. Way before your time. It was a speeding charge. The defense was simply, 'this is no big deal, everyone does it.' So, in my final argument to the jury, I took my copy of the vehicle code, held it up to the jury and said, 'ladies and gentleman, you can find the defendant guilty because he was speeding, or you can find that speeding is no big deal. And if you find that speeding is no big deal we might as well have no speeding law.' I then proceeded to rip up the vehicle code, page by page, and tossed it into a trash can next to counsel table. Then I sat down. They returned a guilty verdict in five minutes."

"That sounds like a lot of fun. Even in a small case, I bet you get pumped up arguing to the jury."

"Ah, yes, the 24-eyed monster. What a rush it is. But do you know what the greatest thrill is?"

Jordan shook his head "no."

"The last 30 seconds of trial. The jury is back with its verdict, sitting quietly in the box. Everyone knows they've reached their decision, but only they know what it is. You're anxious. The defendant, who has the most at stake, is much more so. His attorney, people in the audience, victims, their family members, defendant's family, all resting uncomfortably on the same pins and needles. The jury foreperson hands the verdict form to the bailiff. The bailiff then walks across the courtroom and gives it to the judge, who reads it to himself. You, of course, are watching the judge's expression for a reaction. The judge could announce the verdict, but doesn't. He keeps the jury's secret. He hands the single piece of paper, which holds the key to the defendant's future and the jury's judgment on your hard work to the clerk. The clerk reads the verdict aloud, but not without first squeezing every last drop of drama from the moment with a long preamble: 'in the matter of the People versus Smith, we the jury in the above-entitled cause of action hereby find the defendant . . .' and then you know. That is the longest half of a minute that God ever made. You can truly figure out what kind of physical shape you're in during those 30 seconds when your heart is attempting to jump out of your chest."

"That's a test I'm looking forward to. I've done the mental preparation, now it's time to do the real thing."

"Well, Jordan, looks like you'll be doing the real thing in about 25 minutes. Here's the file. The charge is possession of a loaded handgun. You'll be picking a jury this morning. Take the elevator to the 4th floor, to Division 12. Judge Young. Debbie Drake will be your supervising D.A.; she'll show you the ropes. I'll pop in to check on you later. Good luck."

He took the file from Jim Connelly with his left hand and shook hands with his right. Jordan Stowic was about to become a trial lawyer.

Eighteen

Mass was abbreviated and ended abruptly after communion was distributed. When the time had come to carry the casket into the gray Cadillac hearse waiting outside, Rosie rebuffed Q-ball's request that his homeboys be the pallbearers. She knew what had led to the death of her sister and nephew. "Bitch," he muttered as he walked away from her. JJ, Ruffo, and two of Rosie's friend's husbands carried Alex's body to the hearse. Then they were off to Forrest Lawn Cemetery.

As he drove East on the San Bernardino freeway, JJ felt like he had missed an opportunity to say something about Alex. But he knew why he couldn't address the crowd at St. Mathias Catholic Church. More than half of the audience were the bastards that killed Alex! JJ marveled at his self-restraint for not unholstering his 9 millimeter and ending the problem right there. He pictured the clerk reading the jury's death sentence. He would do this right.

When he got to the Forrest Lawn parking lot, he waited for the others and thought about how he would handle the questioning of the 15 prime suspects. He could arrest them all for suspicion of murder and question them downtown, in custody. But that could be disastrous if he got confessions and then some judge ruled that the arrests were illegal. The confessions would never come in at the trial. They were "fruits" of the illegal arrest. Detective Ramirez was sure he had the right suspects, but was just as certain that he didn't have probable cause to satisfy even the most pro law enforcement magistrate. He would have to get them to come downtown voluntarily.

Father Rojilio Castillo said a few words about Alex in Spanish, and then read from a bible. The crane lowered Alex's casket into a cement encasement at the bottom of freshly excavated earth. The sun was burning at 93 degrees, and there was not a dry forehead in the small crowd. Rosie was crying furiously, squeezing her husband's hand. JJ was withholding any outward sadness. He could not show any weakness in front of the 15 killers who surrounded him. The gang members stood there, respectfully silent. Father Castillo blessed everyone. JJ kissed Rosie on the cheek, and she grabbed him and hugged him bearishly for several seconds.

"If you need anything, Rosie, please call me."

"Gracias, JJ. You are too kind."

JJ walked at a quickened pace to catch up to the homeboys who had already made tracks towards their cars, and he wiped Rosie's tears from his face onto his shirt sleeve. JJ grabbed Q-ball by the shoulders and turned him around. The others stopped.

"Hey cop, you all-a-sudden got a warrant to arrest me?"

"Look, you and the homies have a choice. You can all be cuffed and taken down to county jail in a big black and white bus where you'll wait in county until I can question you one by one. Or you can agree to drive your own cars down to the station and we can talk like men. And when we're done talking, you're all free to go home."

Q-ball thought about it for a few seconds and said to his homeboys, "We'll go. We 'aint got nothin' to hide 'cause we 'aint gonna smoke our own homeboy."

All fifteen of them, ranging from 14 to 22 in age, acquiesced. JJ was very surprised, and slightly alarmed at how easy this was. As the crowd in blue walked to the cars they came in, a '78 Monte Carlo, an '82 Honda prelude, and an '86 Ford pickup, there were cries of "fuck this cop!" and "this is bullshit!" But, in the end, they all obeyed their leader.

The three carloads of gangbangers followed the detective West on the 10 Freeway, to the Hollywood Freeway North, exiting on Hill Street. Then to the underground parking structure under the Sheriff's Station on Temple.

JJ interviewed the primary suspects, one by one in the interview room, with video tape rolling. Detective Bracey helped him by interviewing 7 of the Kansas Street Crips himself. The Officers were interested in the Crips' whereabouts over the last four days, especially Thursday morning. JJ lent Bracey his tape recorder

to document his interviews. JJ expected to find the usual inconsistencies, lies and incriminating answers. He would be very disappointed.

Nineteen

The clerk, the bailiff, the reporter, the Spanish interpreter and the public defender watched as the young attorney made his way past the rows of mostly seamy people waiting to have their cases called, and through the swinging door, up to counsel table, where he set his briefcase down with a gentle thump.

Sheila the clerk pushed a button under her desk twice. Two buzzes meant all the players were present and the judge could come out of chambers and call his morning calendar of cases. Sheila was a heavy white woman with thick, wavy orange hair, sporting oversized, pink Gloria Vanderbilt designer eye wear. She had been Judge Young's clerk for 15 years, just over half of the years that the judge had been on the bench. She called Jordan up to her cubical, which abutted the judge's bench on the left side.

"Good morning. You're our new D.A.?"

"Yes. I'm going to be working with Debbie Drake. She'll be supervising me because this is my first day. Have you seen Debbie?"

"Debbie's on vacation this week. She went to Cancun with her fiancé. Looks like you're on your own."

"I'd better call my office."

"You can use Dave's phone, dial 3305," Sheila said, pointing to the bailiff's desk. "But first, I'd appreciate it if you could write down your name."

Sheila needed Jordan's name so she could write it on every docket showing who represented the People on each case. Just as Jordan scribbled his name down, a short, frail man in all black ascended into his daily throne and Dave belted out, in baritone, "Division 12 of the Compton Municipal Court is now in session, Judge Young presiding, come forth and ye shall be heard, God save this honorable court and the State of California."

Jordan was hoping that God would save him first. What was he supposed to do next? Jordan felt betrayed by the supervisor he'd never met who was apparently sipping margaritas and frolicking in the Mexican Caribbean. He wondered why Connelly didn't know she was gone. Maybe this was some kind of test.

Judge Young began calling the calendar to see who was there. If not for the microphone, his soft, cracking voice would have been inaudible. "People of the State of California versus Jose Rodriguez. Hearing no response, bench warrant is issued, fifteen thousand dollars."

Joe Nataka, the Deputy Public Defender (the P.D. for short), was a forty-something Asian-looking man (Jordan would later find out he was from Hawaii) who bore a strong resemblance to Pat Morita from the Karate Kid movies.

Joe saw that Jordan was at a loss. He told him in a whisper: "These are your files. When the judge calls the case, just write down what happens. If the defendant isn't here, write 'b.w.' for bench warrant, if the defendant pleads guilty, write 'p.g.', and write 'c.j.' for county jail. Keep track of the next date if the defendant will be coming back for trial or pretrial conference. Write 'p.t.' for pretrial hearing and 'j.t.' for jury trial. When he gets off the bench we'll talk about this morning's trial."

Jordan suddenly felt great relief and appreciation for his unlikely mentor from the dark side. Now God could save the Court and California if he had time.

As the judge rattled off names, Jordan organized his files, lining up the stack of cases labeled "District Attorney's File" in alphabetical order, writing the name of the defendant on top in black pen so he could see the 50 or so names at a glance. He kept separated to the right the jury trial file Mr. Connelly had given him. He was getting things under control . . . until the judge asked him a question.

Jose Rodriguez had shown up, and wanted to plead guilty to beating on his wife, a misdemeanor spousal battery.

"What do the People think the appropriate sentence would be in this case?"

Jordan began skimming over the file fiercely, trying to digest all of the facts, as well as the defendant's rap sheet. Joe Nataka handed him a copy of Debbie Drake's plea offer sheet. He directed Jordan to the standard People's requested sentence for spousal battery.

"Your honor, the People request fifteen days in the county jail and an order not to harm the victim in this case. We would also request . . ."

Jordan whispered to Joe, "What's three s.p. mean?"

"Three years summary probation" Joe shot back.

"Yes, and three years of summary probation, your honor."

"Very well. Mr. Rodriguez, do you waive and give up all of your constitutional rights in order to enter a plea of guilty to committing a battery on your wife?"

The judge took the plea and gave the sentence Jordan had requested.

Jordan thought Joe was awesome. Perhaps later he would have Jordan balancing on one foot at the edge of counsel table, advising him: "wax on, wax off."

Twenty

"Bracey, what'd ya come up with?"

"This is weird JJ. Everyone has the same silly story, with a few variations which don't seem particularly significant."

"Let me guess, they went to go see the Ice Cube concert in Oakland on Wednesday night, got hooked up for fighting at the concert with some Oakland blood set, stayed in jail until Friday afternoon when they visited Juan Arrellano's cousin in San Francisco for the weekend and drove back late Sunday night, at which time they found out their homey was shot?"

"Either these little scum balls are telling the truth or they're all really stupid liars. They have to know how easy it is for us to verify their story about being arrested."

"That's exactly what we have to do right now Bracey. I'm gonna get a hold of Oakland P.D., and if you could get fresh prints on all these guys before we cut 'em loose, I don't know how good the ones we got in our files are."

"I'll use the inkless system."

Detective Bracey was referring to the latest in fingerprinting technology- a computerized inkless system called "Ten Printer." It takes a photograph of a person's fingerprints like a copy machine, then instantly projects the print onto a monitor. Once the cops get a print they like, they can save the image or print out a copy on paper. This eliminates bad prints incapable of comparison. More importantly, the print can be sent to another agency for comparison to prints that agency had procured, or to AFIS, which is the national Automated Fingerprint Identification System, to match with any prints in the database. This allows police officers to positively identify the criminal record; name and numerous a.k.a.s that often accompany the ten fingers they happen to have in their custody.

The senior detective disappeared into his office and searched for the number of his contact at Oakland P.D. Meanwhile, Bracey went into the booking area and wheeled out the Ten Printer. It stood about five feet tall and resembled a metal filing cabinet. Bracey turned on the computer, reaching well around to the back for the on/off switch. He walked out into the crowded lobby, where the 15 gang members waited impatiently to be told they could go home.

"Hey One Time, you done jackin' us up yet?" Q-ball's understudy named Stranger inquired. 'One Time' was what gang members often said to alert each other of the presence of police during the commission of a crime.

"I just need to get your prints, and you can all go back to Kansas Street and smoke the chronic or whatever you gangsters are into."

"This is bullshit. If we wasn't innocent, I wouldn't put up with this."

This line from Q-ball prompted Bracey to respond, "If you couldn't sue me, I'd beat you into a pulp with my nightstick."

Like JJ, Detective Bracey had gotten more than his fill of the shootings, the drug dealing, the turf wars and the innocent victims left in the wake of street gangs. He had no compassion left, except for the victims. He even vented from time to time, causing his personnel file to get weighted-down with several complaints alleging excessive force.

"Let's just get this shit over with. We got places to go," complained Q-ball.

Detective Bracey aimed the Polaroid camera at each of the 15 and snapped instant photos which he would pair with each set of fingerprints.

He called them into the booking area, two at a time. He had already pulled out the keyboard and glass finger pad. He pressed each finger firmly onto the glass until he liked each print. Then he pressed the save button to freeze the image and save it on the computer's memory. When he was through he knocked on JJ's door and entered, talking, "I got the prints. Did you get a hold of Oakland – oh, sorry."

JJ covered the phone with his hand, "Bracey, just leave the prints with me and I'll finish this off. I got Oakland P.D. on the line right now."

"No problem JJ."

JJ continued, "Sorry about that Sal. Anyway, you were tellin' me about your promotion."

JJ traded small talk with Sergeant Sal Manetti of Oakland P.D., an acquaintance JJ made during a recent state-wide gang seminar in San Diego. They had exchanged business cards so they could share gang information if the future warranted. JJ cut Sal off just as he began talking about the house he and his wife were renovating on Bay Street.

"The reason I'm calling is because I need you to check on some arrests your guys made last Wednesday night. It was a rap concert."

"Oh yeah, Ice Tea concert. Big gang brawl. Our boys scooped up about 40 gang bangers."

"I think it was Ice Cube."

"Ice Cube, Ice Tea, ice coffee, whatever."

"You guys print them?"

"Of course. We also have field identification cards with their pictures, gang and moniker."

"You use the inkless computer system at all?"

"That's all we use now. No more bad prints."

"I'll tell you what; I'm going to transmit 15 sets of prints, could you find out if they match any of the gangsters your boys hooked up at the concert on Wednesday?"

"No problem, JJ. I'll have an answer this afternoon. The number is 616-442-2213."

"I owe you one, Sal."

JJ hung up the phone and transmitted the prints to the computer at the Oakland P.D. via the phone lines. Then he took the elevator down to his car. He pulled up along the sidewalk where an Indian man was selling hot dogs from a silver cart topped by a yellow and red umbrella. JJ paid for two hot dogs, chips and a Coke. He'd eat a nutritious lunch as he drove the 91 Freeway to the murder scene.

Twenty-One

The newest D.A. in division 12 had done just fine with the morning calendar, thanks to the help of his opponent, the champion of the underdog, Deputy Public Defender Joe Nataka. Jordan was glad they hadn't had time to start the trial in the morning because he still hadn't become completely familiar with the file. And he had to figure out what he was going to say to the jury in his opening statement in the case of People v. Dewayne Simms. He counted on using the lunch break to do that.

When he got back up to the 7th floor, he saw Jim Connelly walking out with two other D.A.s.

"Jordan, how does Mexican food sound?"

"It sounds great," said Jordan, knowing that it was bad form to refuse a boss's offer of lunch on the first day, though he preferred using his time to prep for trial.

"Just let me drop off these files."

Jordan went back to his desk and dropped off the morning's files but kept his trial file, which consisted of a chronology page, a criminal complaint, one police report and the defendant's rap sheet. He wanted to sneak a peak over lunch.

Four D.D.A.s piled into Jim Connelly's white Saturn and headed out from V.I.P. parking under the courthouse onto Compton Boulevard.

"How'd the morning go Jordan?"

"I think it went well Jim."

"Is Debbie helping you out?"

"Debbie's out this week Jim. Didn't you know that?" The D.D.A. speaking was Bob Eckert, a felony trial attorney and third in command in the Compton office.

"I didn't know that. How'd you make it through the morning Jordan?"

"Oh, I did alright. I think everyone in my courtroom was taking it easy on the new guy."

"I like that Jordan. You didn't even call me once to ask for help. You must be a very resourceful person. Did you start that gun trial?"

"Not yet."

"Remember, if you need any help with the trial, just call me. And if I'm not around call Mia."

"What are you talking about Jim? According to you, I still require a supervisor." Mia Fisher was making a sarcastic reference to Jim's recent criticism of her special circumstance death penalty trial that ended in a hung jury, and for which she received a lengthy lecture in Connelly's office about how he would have argued the case.

Connelly got her and smiled. He turned left on Long Beach Boulevard, then made a quick right on Rosecrans Avenue, heading towards one of the worst areas in Compton and one of the best Mexican restaurants in L.A. County. As they pulled into the parking lot behind "El Diablo," just across from the Compton Drive-In, Bob Eckert said, "We filed another 187 last week that happened at the drive-in. It drums up so much business for our county coroner; he should probably open up a satellite office next to the concession stand."

Connelly parallel parked on a side street bordering El Diablo because there were no more spaces in the small parking lot in back.

"Does everyone have their guns loaded and easily accessible?" Mia said, looking to see if Jordan would bite.

As he got out of the car, Jordan said, "You know I lent my gun to Dwayne Simms, the defendant on my trial. He told me they have a shooting range back in the lock-up."

The three D.A.s were amused. They liked their young colleague so far. He had spunk.

When they were seated, Bob Eckert told Jordan, "I recommend the lunch special, you get a salad, two tacos or a burrito, rice and beans for a dollar ninety-nine. Can't beat it."

"Sounds good to me," Jordan agreed.

"Four specials and four margaritas," said Jim Connelly to the young Mexican girl toting a pencil and a pad of paper.

"You want salt?" she asked.

Everyone but Jordan said 'yes.'

He was surprised his conservative boss was ordering drinks at lunch, but felt obligated to go along with what he concluded was the first day lunch ritual. He would later learn that no special occasion was required to prompt a liquid lunch, so long as it was an official day of the week, like Monday.

As they clanked oversize margarita glasses, Connelly offered a generic welcoming toast to the new D.D.A., and Jordan imagined Debbie Drake holding her margarita poolside in Cancun. He secretly toasted her for being on vacation. He knew he was making a good impression.

Twenty-Two

JJ went well out of his way down the 710 Freeway to where it hits the 91 in Compton. He then tested the time it took to get from Compton to Yorba Linda. Traffic was light, relatively speaking, and he estimated 40 minutes until he got to the exit at Weir Canyon. He winded around the exit ramp, back over the freeway, and onto Yorba Linda Boulevard, passing a tasteful wooden sign with a carving of a man on horseback that read: "Yorba Linda- Land of Gracious Living." When he got to the first traffic light at La Palma Avenue, there was an arrow pointing to the left for the Nixon Library. JJ turned right and passed by another of a zillion Southern California strip malls, than left on Via de Lomas Road, up, up, and up the Canyon, ears popping, temperature cooling, to the top. The road ended. JJ got out of the car and eyed his surroundings, memorizing the scene, searching for anything, an idea, a thought, a perspective, a clue. Nothing hit him. A metal sign was planted in the ground 25 yards from where the pale blue hearse was discovered by the jogger. It announced a real estate development called "Yorba Canyon Estates" that would soon devour this pristine earth.

A warm breeze tossed the dry yellow canyon grass, and smoggy sunshine brought beads of sweat to the detective's brow. He trudged through the grass to the edge of the canyon. The prodigious view challenged his neck muscles to stretch right to left, in order to take it all in. He breathed in its beauty, then turned down towards his car, noticing a beer can and a generic store receipt in the grass. JJ imagined the debris was left by the local high school quarterback who drove the head cheerleader there in his father's Lexus to unclasp her bra and get down her pants. Nonetheless, he carefully picked these items up with a couple of sticks he found in the grass, knowing that a good detective doesn't overlook anything.

Twenty-Three

Jordan searched the hallway outside Division 12. "Excuse me; are you Officer Blunt or Officer Cudahy?"

"No" said a young, smartly dressed black man wearing spectacles, showing a slight contempt for the disturbance. He went back to reading Rolling Stone on the cement hallway bench. Dave the bailiff poked his head out.

"Jordan, we need you, the judge wants to start picking the jury."

"Be right in Dave."

Jordan had confirmed with the L.A. County Sheriff's Court liaison this morning that the two Deputy Sheriffs needed for their testimony had received subpoenas and would be in court. They were not. Jordan was experiencing what can be the most thankless, painful, petty, and utterly annoying part of being a prosecutor- getting your witnesses' bodies in court. Like trying to build pyramids with a construction crew on crutches. Or, rather, cliff diving into the ocean only to be met by a sandbar. The sandbar being the irate judge who chews you out because you don't have your act together, or, worse yet, dismisses your case. Jordan would go on to experience witness problems many times as a Deputy District Attorney, a man of the people, for the people, by the people, and totally dependent on the people, for without people he could not proceed. People, people, people- give him people or give him a big fat dismissal!

Jordan went into the courtroom and told the judge that his officers hadn't shown up yet, but that they were expected momentarily. The judge demanded of the bailiff, "Get us a batch of thirty" and Dave got on the phone with the jury coordinator who said she would direct the potential jurors up to division 12. When they filed into the courtroom and took seats on the left side only, as choreographed by

Dave, Jordan's heart raced. He was in trial. His first one. The thought that struck him: "I have no witnesses!" Maybe he could call the man in the hall as his first witness, ask him lots of background questions, and by the time anyone figured out he had absolutely nothing to do with the case, his cops would show up. Or perhaps he could drill the hallway man on the latest climbers up the R & B chart. Jordan took his seat.

"Good afternoon ladies and gentleman. Welcome to Division 12. My name is Judge Young, and you are all potential jurors in a criminal trial, the case of People versus Dewayne Simms."

Joe turned and whispered to Jordan, "Don't worry, Young takes at least three hours to pick a jury. Your officers won't hit the stand until tomorrow."

Jordan's heart subsided and a collected cool returned. He acknowledged Joe with a thankful nod. Wax on, wax off.

Twenty-Four

The Hewlett-Packard laser printer documented the young scientist's analysis. He had formed the opinion that the contents of the baggie submitted by the arresting officer contained "25.8 grams of a powdery substance containing cocaine." He signed and dated the lab receipt, the size of half of a standard piece of paper. After two years of study and two more doing experiments for a paycheck instead of a grade, he could test dope in his sleep. It was time to send the evidence back to the arresting agency now that it was tested and processed. He placed the baggie into the manila envelope and sealed it with yellow tape that read "Los Angeles County Crime lab - Analyzed evidence." Then he initialed the tape and the envelope, and stapled a signed copy of his analysis to the envelope. All were formalities to document the chain of custody for the lawyers and the judge.

He took two envelopes and walked down a rat maze hallway that led into a room which was used mostly for storing office furniture and antiquated equipment, but which also contained a water cooler. As he walked, he felt strangely self-conscious. He entered the room and set the envelopes down on a brown filing cabinet. A hand squeezed his left shoulder and he wheeled around in surprise.

"Shit! Don't fucking scare me like that Hotchie."

"I'm sorry, my friend," said Hotchie, in his strong Pakistani accent, the kind that fueled stand-up comedians' routines about 7-Eleven cashiers. "I am making a run right now, my friend, where do you need this to go?"

"This one goes back to the Firestone Sheriff's station," he said, handing one envelope to Hotchie. "And you know where this one goes."

"Yes, of course, sir. Can I borrow your car again sir?"

"You took the bus again today?"

"My car had more problems, and once again it is in my cousin's shop for repairs."

Hotchie caught the keys when they were thrown to him.

"Just make sure the important package gets there."

"You can count on me Stanley."

Twenty-Five

The veteran gang detective was relieved to find a stack of fax paper waiting for him in his office in-box. The results were back and JJ knew it was due to the diligent efforts of his contact at Oakland P.D. A latent fingerprint expert, at Sergeant Manetti's urgent request, had compared the fingerprints of the Oakland arrestees and the post-funeral detainees. JJ went into his office, shut the door and creaked back into his chair. Twelve of the fifteen sets of prints matched the subjects taken into custody by the Oakland P.D. on Wednesday at 2010 hours. As for the other three, JJ figured, they were probably not arrested because they were juveniles. He knew that many cops, especially if they weren't dealing with a felony, won't incur the paperwork avalanche precipitated by a juvenile arrest.

JJ's mind raced. They weren't bullshitting him. They *couldn't* have killed their homeboy! JJ's head suddenly hurt from bouncing off the solid concrete wall that his investigation ran into.

Twenty-Six

Judge Young had gone through his introductory remarks to juries 243 times since he was sworn in as a judge in November of 1973. And the 244th one was one of his quickest. He then had the clerk pull 18 names at random from a brown metal box with a handle on it for turning. Dave seated them, twelve in the jury box and six more chairs in front of the box, comprising the so called "six-pack." The judge directed them, one by one, to answer some generic questions: tell us your name, city you live in, occupation, marital status, spouse's occupation, whether you've been on a jury before, and, if so, whether you were able to reach a verdict. As each participant answered, some nervously, the judge would ask follow up questions and make ice-breaking jokes whenever possible, e.g., "Miss Graylord, you say you work for Nordstrom's? If you see my wife, tell her to come home, we miss her."

Jordan kept meticulous track of each person's answer on a sheet with 18 boxes, scribbling on post-its, anticipating the use of his 10 peremptory strikes. So long as you have a reason not related to race or gender, he learned in trial advocacy class, you could kick anyone off your jury. The young DDA placed a "plus" or "minus" sign in the upper left corner of the post-it when he decided to keep or kick each potential juror. He decided as a matter of course to kick jurors 4 and 15. They were both engineers. He remembered reading in his trial training manual that engineers are too analytical and overanalyze the evidence, bringing about unreasonable verdicts. Then he passed. Joe Nataka kicked off one Asian grocery store owner who had been robbed on ten separate occasions. Both sides accepted the panel and two alternates. The remaining people were dismissed back to the jury room to await re-assignment to another case.

Judge Young smiled at the 14 men and women of diverse ethnicities that comprised the jury on the Simms matter and said, "Ladies and gentlemen, you are about to hear the opening statements of the attorneys. You are instructed that what the attorneys say is not evidence and the opening remarks are intended only as roadmaps of what the attorneys believe the evidence will prove."

"Mr. Stowic, do you wish to address the jury on behalf of the People of California?"

Jordan swallowed. "Yes your honor."

As he stood up he heard the sound of one of the double doors opening and turned slightly to see Jim Connelly take a seat in the courtroom. Now he really was nervous.

"Good afternoon ladies and gentlemen," he began. His mouth suddenly became dryer than Death Valley, and his hands trembled slightly. He was petrified as he tried not to think about Connelly watching his every move, sizing him up, guessing if he had a "rising star" on his hands. He began concentrating on the facts of the case as he spoke, thinking about the fact that Dewayne Simms was found on June 8, 1992, with a loaded .38 caliber revolver; and according to his rap sheet, he had a prior conviction for burglary and battery of a police officer. This was a bad guy who was no good for his community, and it was Jordan's job to persuade the jury to hold him accountable for his actions. Jordan faced the jury, leaning against counsel table, hands in pockets, telling them in a slightly uptight tone that he would "prove the defendant guilty beyond any doubt," and that "after you hear all the evidence in the case, you'll agree that the defendant was unlawfully possessing a loaded firearm. Thank you." Then he sat down.

Joe Nataka calmly stood up and stated to the judge, "Your honor, the defense reserves its opening statement until the conclusion of the People's case." The judge dismissed the jury for the day, reminding them not to discuss the case among themselves or with anyone else, and ordered everyone back for 8:30 the next morning.

Jordan glanced back, expecting to see an unimpressed Jim Connelly, but Jim had gone. Jordan thought he'd better get back to the office and make a call to the court liaison to ensure that he had witnesses to call to the stand at 8:30. As he rode the elevator back up to the 7th floor, he smiled at the young female bailiff that shared the ride. Despite being somewhat disappointed in his first performance, he was glad that he had survived. Jordan knew he had started down the road to becoming a flesh and blood trial lawyer. And he knew he had it in him to be among the very best.

Twenty-Seven

The conversation at the Aftershock drifted from the possible retrial of the officers in the Rodney King beating to Ross Perot's chances of being a successful 42nd President if elected in November.

Buddy Cox was squaring off: "Perot is a salesman like me. Why, that little fella could sell Playboy magazines to Elton John! If he gets a chance, you better believe he'll straighten out those politicians in Washington."

"He's a nut. He's a miniature Hitler without the stash!" Loni corrected, as she poured a generous helping of Glennfeddich for Buddy's tab.

"Loni, I usually agree with you," he lied, "but this time you're dead wrong. Perot's gonna pay off the deficit, you'll see."

"Yeah, maybe if that little freak sells his computer company and gives us the proceeds."

Loni presented his fresh drink with a slide that avoided his napkin covered with cheddar goldfish.

She tired of the topic, so she changed it.

"You seen Mary?"

"She had A.A. tonight, I think."

Loni stared at him incredulously.

"Buddy, you're making about as much sense as your little freak candidate."

"Yeah, she's had A.A. An *awful* lot of *alcohol!*"

Buddy snorted laughter through his long, untrimmed nose hairs and Loni gave him the reaction of a Buckingham Palace guard.

"You should take your act on the road, Buddy. Then you should lay there until someone drives over you."

"Why don't you just admit you want me Loni, and we'll get rid of all this sexual tension." Buddy was getting bolder by the sip.

"The only tension I see is between the palm of your hand and your genitalia." Loni called 'em as she saw 'em.

"Someday, Loni. Someday you'll come clean and fess up. I know sexual tension. I didn't just fall off a turnip truck. I been around."

"I think you fell off. Then, I think it backed over your head."

"That makes two references in one night to me being run over. Is it just me or am I starting to notice some negative vibes from my sassy little Loni?"

Loni smirked off the salesman's buzzed flirtations and went out to service the only occupied booth. There sat a young Mexican couple gazing into each others eyes with a lover's awe that made Loni miss her dead husband.

"What kind of Champagne joo got?" the male Mexican inquired.

"We don't got any. If you want Champagne, try our Beverly Hills location."

"Ok, give us two shots of tequila, El Presidente Gold if joo got it."

"Got Cuervo."

"Ok."

Suddenly, Jimmy Buffet filled the airwaves, one of his many crowd pleasers. Buddy Cox stood by the jukebox smiling drunkenly at Loni as Jimmy belted out the lyrics to "Why don't we get drunk and screw?"

Loni laughed for the first time that night, clearly laughing *at* the pathetic salesman, not with him.

Then JJ walked in with Mary O'Neil in tow.

"Look what the cat dragged in," said Buddy.

"This cop picked me up for drunk and disorderly," Mary slurred, and headed for the ladies room.

JJ took his stool two chairs away from Buddy, and Loni promptly created a Jack and Coke to greet him.

"Where'd you find her?" Loni asked.

"She was routing around in the trash out back looking for cans," JJ replied, taking in a mouthful of his bubbling brown elixir.

"This is getting to be a habit for her, at least towards the end of the month."

"Yeah," JJ concurred, "But she'll be a new woman once she gets next month's government relief check."

"So how're you holdin' up JJ?"

"I'm doin' alright."

"Have you figured out who killed your young friend?"

JJ didn't answer.

"You remember Rachel?"

"Huh?"

"You know, my first wife."

"You mean that cold-hearted man-eater who chewed out your heart and fed it to her dog?

"I loved her Loni."

"I know you did. But what's she got to do with anything."

"Well, she used to tell me that when I went cold on a case I should erase all of my assumptions and start from scratch."

"You, the great gang detective, are cold?"

"Freezing."

"Is there anything I can do?"

"Keep pouring, Loni. Just keep pouring."

"Did that advice work, what you said, Rachel's advice?"

"Not really. Usually the cases got solved when there is some break that you don't expect, like a witness comes forward or something."

"Maybe someone will come forward."

"Maybe. I feel like this is the case I've been working all my life to prepare for. It's like a test or something."

"Who do you think killed Alex?"

"Honestly, I don't know. Some gangsters I guess."

Mary burst out through the women's rest room door like Wyatt Earp into a saloon, and swaggered over to attempt to sit between Buddy and JJ.

"Give me a . . ." Her eyelids kissed. Her head bobbed.

"Timber!" Buddy squealed. JJ reached and grabbed the unconscious drunk before she hit the floor.

Instinctively Loni and Buddy checked their watches. Eight-thirty. "She's out a little early tonight," said Loni.

"Must have been drinking the good stuff," Buddy added.

Twenty-Eight

When Jordan got home he went right to the blinking answering machine, expecting a call from Kendall. It was bittersweet when Courtney's raspy voice made its message machine debut. "Jordan, this is Courtney. I've been thinking about you a lot. Let's have dinner tonight. There's a place called 'The Shelter.' It's a restaurant and a dance club that plays alternative music. You'll love it. Call me when you get in. I probably shouldn't tell you this, but I think you're amazing. Bye."

He wanted to call Kendall and see how her day was. How she was doing. Did she like her new cat Ralph? Was her job going well? And, more importantly, how was she feeling? Was she ok with everything? Jordan knew he couldn't call. He had to leave Kendall her pride. In his head he stepped into her shoes and declared, "I wouldn't wanna talk to me." So he brought the cordless phone into the bedroom and picked up a *Newsweek* magazine on which Courtney had scribbled her number during a rare free moment in their lust fest. And, guiltily, he dialed.

"Hey. This is Courtney. I'm not here right now, but leave a message and I'll get back to you. And if this is Jordan, the Shelter is located on Beverly Boulevard between Normandie and Vermont. It's the building with the little white lights. Let's make it 8 o'clock. I can't wait to see you. Ciao." B-e-e-e-e-e-e-e-e-p.

Jordan's head was spinning. For Jordan, as with most healthy Gen-X males, the sure thing was a cold shower. The thrill of the hunt was everything. He had already gone in for the kill with Courtney. But she wasn't the average kill. The confidence in her voice. The fact that she hadn't even seen the need to confirm their plans. She just *assumed* he would get the message and show up. She had him right where he wanted.

After showering and knockin' off his seven o'clock shadow (which followed a short internal debate as to whether he looked more attractive with a slight beard), Jordan got dressed in front of a full length mirror and allowed himself to enjoy the feeling of first date anticipation, despite his ambivalence about Kendall, the girl he'd loved for several years. Then he searched the apartment for a map of L.A. He remembered Stan had told him that there was one in the kitchen drawer. He found an unfamiliar book entitled "Thomas Brothers Guide" and opened it to find page after page of maps detailing every square foot of roadway in Los Angeles County. After figuring out how to get to the Shelter, Jordan dropped a note to Stan on the kitchen table and headed out.

He unsnapped, unzipped and folded down the Jeep's khaki soft top, then slipped one of his favorite CDs into the disc player. As he drove north on La Cienaga, the wind twirled his brown hair and he adjusted up the treble on the car stereo which cranked out The Housemartins' "The People Who Grinned Themselves to Death."

The air was a perfect 70 degrees. He was learning to depend on the perfect weather and wondered how he was ever able to live without it. There was no longing for the suffocating humidity of a D.C. summer or the frozen bluster of a Chicago winter.

The scenery changed as he drove towards the darkened Hills, as if to say "welcome to West Hollywood." There were men walking together, clad in leather jackets and tight jeans, and all-male night clubs pumping out house music and disco. And there were sidewalk café tables full of men talking, laughing, touching each other. Jordan saw very few women. It reminded him of an exaggerated version of DuPont Circle, a prominently gay area of Washington, D.C., affectionately referred to by homophobes and others as "The Fruit Loop."

He took a right and headed east on Beverly Boulevard, passing by the CBS Studio, towards a distant downtown L.A. skyline. The traffic was unusually light as he zoomed through green light after green light, finally spotting The Shelter on his left hand side. He was parking his car in a dimly lit lot behind the building when a short Hispanic man with a long mustache and sporting the signature red valet parker vest approached and commandeered his Jeep. "You can't pick up your dry cleaning in this town without valet parking," Stan had told him. Stan was right.

Jordan walked around to the front which was illuminated by small white Christmas lights around the awning. The Shelter was far too cool for a sign. The young DDA walked inside, showing his Michigan driver's license to the large thuggish bouncer who shot a quick glance at the i.d. and said "enjoy your evening sir," with an unexpected elegance. Then Jordan entered one of the two main rooms that made up The Shelter.

The rectangular room had a long aluminum bar with a mirror lining the wall behind it, reflecting images of the two attractive wannabee actors that tended to the bar and to their own agendas, raking in tips on the overpriced drinks as they hoped to be noticed by someone important.

"Have you seen my commercial?" asked the blonde bartender with a surfer haircut, speaking to a young girl of questionable legal drinking age who sat watching him with flirtatious eyes.

He uncapped four Amstel Lights in record time as she sought clarification. "You mean the Bud Light commercial where you're on the horse?"

"Yeah, that's it."

"Haven't you done anything more recent?"

"Not really. I'm in-between agents right now. I had to fire my last one. He was a total asshole. So things are a little slow 'till I find another one."

"Here," she said, reaching into her purse and removing a card, "call my agent, she's wonderful."

Jordan ordered a Bombay Sapphire and tonic and scanned the room with negative results. He tipped the would-be Harrison Ford a dollar and took back five in change from his ten. Then he followed the sound of the music, which he recognized as an extended mix of

New Order's "Bizarre Love Triangle," into the adjoining room, parting a dark purple velvet curtain that blocked his entrance. This room was much larger, and it contained a dance floor, currently sprinkled with three woman dressed in all black, two with pierced noses, sharing the floor but dancing alone. Two velvet couches, a coffee table, and several overstuffed chairs with ottomans abutted the dance floor. Off to the side there were people dining on linen tablecloths, and the formal contrast added to the psychedelic feel of the room. Jordan noticed that his white shirt glowed in harmony with the tablecloths due to the black light shining from the tracks above his head. Still no sign of her.

Jordan decided to get a table. He had to practically scream his name to the maître d', since the music had suddenly jumped several decibels. He recognized the theme from Sesame Street, set to an industrial, synthesized, thumping dance beat. The couches all but cleared and the dance floor overflowed.

"Are you Jordan?" asked the maître d'.

"Yes."

"Follow me."

He led Jordan to a hidden alcove behind the dance floor, pulling back a red velvet curtain. Jordan surveyed the three who sat around the table. Courtney, Stan and Stan's girl from the other night, Jennifer.

"Hi Stow. I think you know everyone here," said Stan, giving the signature handshake to his best friend.

"I've missed you," Courtney whispered in Jordan's ear, just before kissing him squarely, gently on the lips.

"Stow, you remember Jennifer from Rhory's party."

"I'm not sure. She looks different with her clothes on."

Jennifer giggled, hinting embarrassment.

"How was your first day, Mr. Deputy District Attorney?" his roommate asked him.

"It was a blast."

Jordan had trouble keeping his eyes off Courtney, who wore a pair of tight faded jeans with rips that teasingly exposed well-tanned portions of her upper thighs. On top she wore only a black vest with paisleys embroidered in lace. There was no sign of a bra, and she was rather efficient at filling out the vest.

"Would you boys please excuse us," Courtney said, as she and Jennifer left the best friends for the rest room.

"Stan-Man, I didn't know Courtney and Jennifer were friends."

"Yeah, they know each other through Rhory. Wow, we're dating friends again. It's like high school when you were dating Jenny Jacobs and I was with Melinda Robertson. God, those were some of the best times, don't you think?"

"I do, Stan-Man. But I also realize that the good old days are right now. And if you don't acknowledge that, they pass by too quickly."

"Sounds like your Mom talking."

"It is. But she's right."

"I agree Stow. And I've always maintained that Mrs. Stowic was the real genius in your family." Stan downed the remainder of a vodka martini.

"Speaking of the present, I love my job," Jordan volunteered.

"Tell me about it. How'd it go today?"

"Well, I walked into my boss's office this morning and told him how I couldn't wait to start doing trials, and he handed me a file and said, 'go to it.'"

"No shit? You mean you started your first trial today?"

Jordan nodded confidently.

"What's the charge? Robbery? Rape? Murder?"

"C'mon Stan-Man, you know they're not gonna give me a felony for my first trial. That won't happen until after a year or two doing misdemeanors. It's a gun possession case. I have to say, though, it's a lot harder than I thought. I was nervous as hell talking to the jury today. And my boss had to walk in as I started to give my opening statement."

"Wouldn't that be weird if you got assigned a dope case that I handled, and you had to call me to the stand?"

"I have to check that out Stan-man, you know it might be a conflict of interest or something, the prosecutor being best friends with his chemist."

"I can't wait until you call me to the stand and say, 'Mr. Reid, in your expert analysis, did you form an opinion as to whether the content of People's exhibit #1 contains any controlled substance?' Then I say, 'Yes, I've tested the exhibit and found that it contains approximately two liters of a gooey substance that I determined to be human semen.'"

"You'd better not fuck with me or I'll prosecute you for possession of an illegally small penis."

Stan laughed contagiously, and Jordan collaborated.

The waitress brought Stan a fresh martini, and he held his hand straight out in a clenched fist to challenge Jordan to a non-Olympic event. Jordan accepted the challenge by extending his fist to meet Stan's. And the athletes moved their fists up and down, counting: "One...two...three." Jordan's fist broke to a flat position and Stan's stayed clenched.

"Paper covers rock, so drink motherfucker!" Jordan demanded, and Stan hit his mostly vodka.

When the girls returned, they pulled the men onto the dance floor to embrace a song by The Smiths called "Bigmouth Strikes Again." They continued dancing through a repertoire of funky dance songs by Soul to Soul, Arrested Development and others, switching partners several times, and all dancing together.

The night enveloped Jordan Stowic, much like the summer nights cruising the Michigan suburbs in his father's company car with Stan, Melinda and Jenny. The combination of best friends and beautiful girls was a potent one indeed. And if you added the excitement of an incredible new job in a great city and fanned it with the buzz of the Bombay gin, you found Jordan Stowic intoxicated by a lethally fun mixture. "These are truly the good old days," Jordan thought, as he danced and spun, surrendering history to the moment.

Twenty-Nine

Areola's anniversary gift signaled him to the first of many of the morning's javas. He pealed himself off the 'Sanford and Son' couch to respond. The phone cut him off before he got there.

"Detective Ramirez," he managed to say, several octaves below normal due to the early hour and his fragile state of hungoverness. The words, "Please hold for Mr. Salsman" echoed in his head, slamming around like a winning racquetball shot. He recognized her high, whiny voice. Since the Snow case had begun haunting him, he had spoken to the D.A.'s secretary several times. As he waited on the line, he poured a cup of coffee and sipped it, wishing it cooler so he could guzzle.

"Detective Ramirez, this is Steve Salsman. If you don't mind, I would like an update on the investigation. I have your boss here in my office and we've got you on speaker phone, so you're going to have to speak up."

Shit, JJ thought, an ambush. He felt his cloudy head instantly sobering.

"I assume you gentlemen are interested in the Leticia Snow murders?"

"Of course," Sheriff Collins said. "What do you got JJ?"

"Well, I'm pursuing a couple leads right now that look promising," he lied. He just wasn't prepared to deal with confrontation of this magnitude.

"Who are our suspects?" Salsman queried.

"Members of an enemy gang of the Southside Playboys."

"How many gangsters have you narrowed it down to?" asked Chief Collins.

"Two or three." The whopper got bigger.

"As I told Steve, I consider you the best gang detective in the nation. I know you practically invented the genre."

"Thanks boss."

"But you have to do better. You must understand," he continued, in a deadly serious tone, "there are pressures on us. The Times keeps running follow-up articles. They're calling it the Roosevelt High *massacre*. The public is outraged. Who the hell wants to live in L.A. when some little thugs can blow away four adults and a little kid with an Uzi and law enforcement can't do a damn thing about it?"

"Not to mention the fact that me and the Sheriff here are up for re-election in November," Salsman added, cutting to the heart of the matter.

"I have no goddamn leads! The only thing you two political assholes care about are your fucking polls! You wouldn't know law enforcement if it bit your dicks off! Screw you both!" JJ would love to have said. Instead, he chose a safer alternative.

"Sheriff, I'll get back to you in a day or two when I get closer to an arrest." He valued his pension and had come too far in the Department to be relegated to drawing chalk marks on car tires to enforce 2-hour parking ordinances.

"If you need any support, another detective to fill in for Detective Davis, or anything, just let me know."

"Thanks, I will. Goodbye gentlemen."

After he hung up, JJ knew it was time for a break in the case. Apparently, it wasn't going to find him, so he would have to find it. He searched through his Rolodex of confidential informants until he found G-Dog's pager number.

Thirty

He drove East on Olympic Boulevard and thought about last night. His smile hid the struggle between his mind and body, the latter punishing him for settling for a paltry two and a half hours of sleep. He had quite the evening, he concluded, thinking with a hazy memory of the 2 a.m. closing down of The Shelter, heading out to Santa Monica beach, the couples splitting up, surf breaking, moon illuminating, her tanned and sandy body firm and fiery to the touch, blanket half- covering them, they had each other, later meeting up with Stan and Jennifer, early morning breakfast at Patrick's Roadhouse on the Pacific Coast Highway, driving back to her car at nightclub's back lot, finally a slow, gentle, moist kiss from Courtney, adding the exclamation mark.

Mind changing gears with the Wrangler, he contemplated his jury trial. He knew all the facts and they were simple: when the police pulled up to Dewayne Simms and shined their flashlights on him, they saw him put a shiny metal object behind a telephone pole. The officers walked over and found the gun just where they had seen Dewayne put it. It couldn't get any easier than this. Though he didn't know it yet, Jordan was a natural at the art of overestimating the strength of his evidence.

He parked in the four-level parking structure, close to the guard booth in anticipation of a potential break-in (this was Compton, after all), and walked across the concrete meadow, badging the guard to enter the courthouse via the back door. The crowd was intense this Tuesday a.m., and potential jurors comprised much of the human onslaught, shifting en masse towards the open "up" elevator. Jordan was able to squeeze on, riding the "local" to the 7th floor. He glanced at his watch as he exited, then dashed down the hallway to his tiny windowless office which he shared with a DDA named

Tony who was on vacation. The long running joke in the Compton D.A.'s Office was that the top prosecutors got the windowless offices because it minimized the chances of their being shot by errant Compton gunfire. The less senior DDAs had to fend for their lives in window offices. But it was just a joke. The big shots wanted their windows. But there had, in fact, been several occasions over the years when judges, prosecutors and public defenders in the courthouse had arrived to work to find a hole in their window and a bullet in their respective chambers and offices.

Jordan grabbed his stack of 20 or so files (his "calendar") as well as his file on Dewayne Simms, and headed out for the elevator. "Morning baby," Yoli said, as they passed in the hallway. "Good morning Yoli," he answered. When he stepped out of the elevator onto the 6th floor, he was relieved to see two uniformed Sheriff's Deputies waiting outside Division 12. Jordan walked up to them and glanced at their small rectangular tin name tags. "Blunt" and "Cudahy" he was happy to read.

"Hi, I'm Jordan Stowic, the Deputy D.A. on this trial."

"Is this gonna take all morning, or what?" Blunt said, living up to his name.

"Well, to be perfectly honest officer, I'm kinda new at this. This is my first trial so I'm not really sure."

"That's *deputy* son," Blunt said, "I'm a Deputy Sheriff, and this is my day off."

"Sorry. Listen, have you guys had a chance to look over your police reports?"

"Yeah, no problem," said Cudahy, "we talked about it on the way over, we remember this punk. He was with some girl, his girlfriend I think."

Dave came outside and Jordan knew why.

"Jordan, the Judge is on the bench and the jury is in the box. He wants to start now."

"No problem Dave, be right in. Which of you found the gun?"

"I did," Cudahy said.

"Ok, I'll call you first, then Blunt," Jordan told them.

As the Deputy D.A. walked into the courtroom, he noticed in his peripheral 13 sets of eyes following his movement.

"Good morning your honor, ladies and gentlemen of the jury, counsel," Jordan said pleasantly before sitting down, in an effort make reparations for his tardiness. He cleared off counsel table and placed the Simms file next to a blank legal pad.

Then Judge Young let him have it in front of the twelve he was trying to sell the case of People v. Simms.

"Counsel, do you know what time it is?"

"Yes, your honor."

"When this court says we will resume at eight-thirty, this court means *eight-thirty*, not eight-thirty-five or eight-forty. Is that clear?"

"Yes. Sorry your honor."

"The People may call their first witness."

"Thank you your honor. The People call Officer Cudahy." Jordan had a hard time remembering that they were "deputies."

Joe Nataka, who had remained silent during the Judge's reproof, stood up and stated, "Your honor, there is a defense motion to exclude witnesses."

"That motion is granted. Mr. Stowic, do the People have any witnesses in the courtroom?"

Before Jordan could respond, Deputy Blunt got up from the back row and adjourned to the hallway.

"No, your honor," said Jordan as he scanned the courtroom.

The clerk stood up and addressed Deputy Cudahy, who now stood facing her, his right hand raised in conformity with pre-testimony etiquette.

"Do you promise that your testimony in the cause now pending before this court shall be the truth, the whole truth and nothing but the truth, so help you God?"

"Yes."

"You may be seated. Please state your name and spell your last name for the record."

Ronald Cudahy. C-U-D-A-H-Y.

"Thank you," the clerk said, as she sat back down at her desk to resume her tedious work on a mound of court files.

The national anthem was over. Now it was time to play ball.

"You may proceed Mr. Stowic," said Judge Young.

Jordan stood up, "Thank you, your honor."

"Officer Cudahy, what is your current occupation and assignment?"

"Deputy Sheriff currently assigned to patrol in the city of Carson."

"On June 8th of this year at approximately ten o'clock, p.m., were you on duty?"

"Yes."

"And were you patrolling in the area of Carson Boulevard and Maple in the City of Carson, County of Los Angeles?"

"Yes."

"And did you arrest someone you see in court today."

"Well, actually my partner arrested him."

"What is your partner's name?"

"Deputy Dennis Blunt."

"Could you please identify the person who was arrested?"

"Yes, that man right there sitting next to the defense attorney," he said, pointing to Dewayne.

"Your honor, may the record reflect that the witness has identified the defendant?"

"The record may so reflect."

"And why was the defendant arrested?"

"Well, we saw him first sitting on the sidewalk next to his girl-friend–"

"Objection your honor, non-responsive," Joe Nataka interjected.

"Sustained," answered the Judge. "Deputy, please just try to answer the question you were asked. *Why* was the defendant arrested?"

"He was arrested because he was in possession of a loaded .38 caliber revolver."

"And, Deputy Cudahy, how did you come to discover that the defendant had the gun?" Jordan took back the questioning.

"Well, as we drove eastbound on Carson Boulevard, we observed the defendant sitting on the sidewalk near a telephone pole. He was seated next to a female black who we believed was the defendant's girlfriend. We illuminated the defendant and saw him place a shiny object behind the telephone pole."

"And, at some point did you retrieve that object?"

"Yes."

"And what did you retrieve?"

"I went to the location where I saw the defendant reach and drop the metal object and found a loaded .38 caliber revolver."

As he finished his answer, the Deputy held up a manila envelope which Jordan did not realize he had with him.

"Did you bring the gun with you to court today Officer?"

"Yes," said the Deputy as he pulled the gun out of the manila envelope.

"Your honor may I approach?"

"Counsel approach the bench!" demanded the Judge, angrily.

"Mr. Stowic, did you have that gun checked by my bailiff before you brought it into my courtroom?"

"No your honor, I-" Jordan was cut off before he could explain that he didn't even know the cop had brought the evidence.

"I didn't think so. In the future, before you play with a gun in this courtroom and endanger the lives of everyone in it, you had better allow my bailiff to secure it, do you understand me?"

"Yes. Sorry your honor."

Dave knew he had to correct Jordan's faux pas, so he affixed a plastic ring onto the revolver so that the chamber could not close, rendering the gun inoperable. As Dave walked back to his desk he whispered to the clerk in passing, "two strikes for the D.A." in reference to Jordan's violating two of Judge Young's biggest pet peeves, tardiness and unsecured guns in the courtroom. As to the latter peeve, Jordan hadn't heard the infamous story of Judge Young presiding over a trial during his first year on the bench, where a defense attorney pulled the trigger on a gun during his closing argument. Luckily, when it went off he had it pointing up and the bullet only wounded the concrete ceiling overhead. But his honor was reprimanded by the presiding judge and the story was the talk of the courthouse for some time after.

"Proceed," said Judge Young when both sides returned to counsel table.

Jordan approached with the gun and showed it to the Deputy.

"Is this the gun you found behind the telephone pole?"

"Yes."

"And how do you know it's the same gun?"

"I scratched my initials into the barrel here," said the Deputy, pointing to his initials on the gun.

"Was the gun loaded?"

"Yes, there were six bullets in the chamber."

"What did you do after you found the gun?"

"My partner arrested the defendant and put him in the back of our patrol car."

"What happened to the girl the defendant was with?"

"Since she had no involvement in the offense to our knowledge, we let her go. I believe she was seventeen years old."

Jordan thought about asking the Deputy whether the defendant had made any statements, but he remembered that the defendant had invoked his right to remain silent. Jordan knew if that fact came out it would cause a mistrial because, as his Criminal Procedure professor at Georgetown put it, "invocation of rights by the defendant at arrest plus commenting by the prosecutor at trial equals reversible error on appeal."

So Jordan ended with, "No further questions."

He felt good about his direct examination of the Deputy, except for the public and private rebuking by the judge. Now it was the defense's turn with the People's witness. As soon as Joe stopped scribbling on a page of yellow paper, he began. He was still sitting down.

"Deputy, you say that you saw a shiny metal object in my client's possession?"

"Yes."

"Was this object in his hand?"

"Yes, when I first saw it."

"Which hand?"

Now Joe stood up.

The Deputy paused briefly, and then stated: "I believe his right."

"Deputy, when you saw the shiny object for the first time, how far were you from my client?"

"I would say about, oh, forty feet."

"And would it be fair to say that it was dark outside."

"Yes."

"And there's only one streetlight at the corner of Carson and Maple, isn't that true?"

"I- um- I- I don't recall. But that sounds right."

"And isn't it also true that the street light is on the northeast corner?"

"I believe so."

"And you were at the opposite part of the intersection, the southwest portion?"

"Yes."

After that question, Jordan realized that Joe had something important that he didn't have- firsthand knowledge of the crime scene. He now wished desperately that he had gone there.

"How did you see my client in the darkness? Did you use a flashlight?"

"Yes. I illuminated your client with my mag flashlight."

"And at that point, you saw only that he had a shiny object?"

"Yes."

"You didn't know what the object was at the time, did you?"

"Well, from my training I thought it was probably a-"

"Objection" Joe interrupted the witness, "Non-responsive."

"Sustained." said the Judge, "The witness will be ordered to answer the question as asked, Deputy, did you know it was a gun at the time you first saw it?"

"No."

"And when you saw my client, he was sitting next to a female?"

"Yes."

"How far apart was my client from the female?"

"They were right next to each other."

"Touching?"

"Yes."

"Had my client done anything illegal or suspicious before you shined your flashlight on him?"

"No."

"What about the female?"

"No."

"And who was driving your patrol car?"

The deputy paused and said, "I believe it was my partner."

"Did you ever take fingerprints from the gun?"

"No."

"Nothing further."

"Mr. Stowic?" the judge said.

Jordan figured he should ask a few questions on re-direct to repair any possible damage to his case.

"Deputy, could you tell the jury whether or not there was enough light for you to see the defendant's face."

"Yes, there was."

"And, are you sure that it was the defendant who had the shiny object, and not the female?"

"Yes, I am."

"And when you went to retrieve the object did you find the gun in the exact place where you saw the defendant put it?"

"Yes."

"Be careful counsel," Judge Young interjected, "don't lead your witness."

"Sorry your honor. Let me ask you this Deputy, did you see any other shiny objects in the area where you found the gun?"

"No."

"Nothing further."

"Mr. Nataka?"

"No additional questions, your honor."

"May this Deputy be excused?" queried the judge.

"Yes" both counsel responded.

"The People may call their next witness."

"The People call Deputy Blunt," Jordan stated confidently.

One of the courtroom's double doors opened, and the Deputy strutted in like he owned the place, took the oath with a smirk on his face and sat in the witness chair with that same smirk. His khaki and green shirt was stretched to a tortuous tautness across his chest, showcasing his buffed out cop pecs, and his shiny bald head featured a large bump, completing the Cro-Magnon man persona. The dark terminator sunglasses which he respectfully removed when he was comfortable in the witness chair dealt his demeanor the critical blow. It was at this moment that Jordan realized that it wasn't just Blunt's attitude that he didn't like. This guy gave off cowboy cop vibes worse than Dirty Harry, and he wished he could just thank the Deputy for coming, give him a parting gift of a year's supply of Rice-A-Roni, and let him go back to the station. By comparison, Deputy Cudahy had the credibility of Abraham Lincoln on truth serum.

Jordan decided that he would make it quick. "Deputy, directing your attention to June 8, 1992, were you on duty that day?"

"Yes. We were on duty."

And so it went, through roughly the same story as Deputy Cudahy, albeit with a healthy dose of cynicism, unprofessional facial gestures, and the occasional editorializing which was promptly and successfully objected to by Joe Nataka.

Then came cross-examination.

"So who was driving the patrol car?" asked Joe.

"My partner was."

"And which direction were you heading on Carson?"

"We were heading westbound."

"And how far from my client were you when you spotted my client with the shiny object?"

"We drove right up to your boy. About ten feet I'd say."

"And was there a street light directly overhead?"

"I believe so, yes."

"And did you recover the gun?"

"No, my partner did."

"Thank you, nothing further."

Jordan was surprised at the short cross-examination of the Deputy. He asked one final question which he believed would cinch his case.

"Officer, are you 100% certain that the defendant is the one with the shiny object that you later learned was this gun?"

"No doubt in my mind," said Deputy Blunt before he was excused.

"Your honor, at this time the People would like to introduce People's exhibit number one, the handgun."

"Any objection Mr. Nataka?"

"No, your honor."

"People's one will be received without objection. Do the People rest?"

"Yes, your honor," said Jordan, believing that, despite the lingering bad vibes from Deputy Blunt's poor performance, nothing had permeated his air tight case.

The judge asked, "Mr. Nataka does the defense wish to give its opening statement at this time?"

"No thank you, your honor. The defense will waive opening and move to its case. We have one witness. The defense calls Dewayne Simms."

Jordan's heart suddenly raced like it was on the thoroughbred track at Del Mar. He had never cross-examined an actual defendant before. It was supposed to be a prosecutor's crowning glory. But what could he ask him to make him break down and confess in a shower of tears? He started jotting down ideas as Dewayne was sworn in.

"Now Dewayne," Joe started, "you heard the Deputy Sheriffs testify about what they saw on June the 8th, didn't you?"

"Yeah," said the defendant.

"Did you have this gun?" Joe Nataka held up People's exhibit number 1.

"No. Loose Lucy had it."

"Who is Loose Lucy?"

"She's this girl who hangs out in my neighborhood. Or at least she used to. She's a ho."

"When you say that she's a ho, you mean--"

"She sell her body."

The judge interrupted. "Mr. Simms, please wait for the lawyer to finish his question before you answer. It makes it very difficult for the court reporter to accurately record what is said."

"Yes, your honor."

Joe began again. "Did she show you the gun?"

"No, but she told me she was strapped cause she got jacked fo' her money."

"What were you doing when the police car pulled up?"

"See, me and Lucy, we was kickin' it ya know, and all a sudden this patrol car drives up, and these Deputies, those guys who testified, jack us up with they flashlights and say 'I know you got somethin', what you got?'"

"And then what happened Dewayne?"

"Well, see, we was just talkin', ya know, I's tryin' to tell her to cut out this ho stuff, cause, I don't know, guess I kinda liked this girl, ya know, even though I know she a ho."

"Dwayne, what happened after the Deputies pulled up and shined their flashlights on you?"

"Well, you know, they patted us down for guns and rock, you know. I didn't even know Lucy ditched the tray-eight."

"Dewayne, when you say tray-eight, are you talking about the gun?"

"Yeah. The gun."

"Dewayne, what happened after they patted you down?"

"Well, the one cop, not the one who's bald, the other one, he started looking around with his flashlight and picks up this gun. Lucy says, 'Oh shit!' That's what she says."

"What happened next Dewayne?"

"Well, the bald one asks Lucy how old she is, and she tell him she's seventeen. And that bald guy looks at me and says 'I'm gettin' you for this gun nigger.'"

"And then what happened Dewayne?"

"Then they put us in the back of the patrol car and drove Lucy to her Auntie's house and booked my a– booked me."

"Dewayne, are you right handed or left?"

"Left."

"No further questions."

With four questions scribbled onto his white legal pad, Jordan stood up and stared into the big brown eyes of Dewayne Simms. Dewayne was looking back at him, staring right through him, as if there was no question he could be asked that would matter, as if this entire trial were irrelevant, a necessary evil that he had learned to endure. He'd just as soon get it over with so he could serve his thirty or sixty days and get back to his friends, his girlfriend, his family and his hood. Back home, that is, until he gets caught again and the cycle is renewed.

"Good morning Mr. Simms."

"What?" the defendant replied, as if Jordan had addressed him in Portuguese.

"Good morning."

"Oh. Good morning."

"Now, Mr. Simms, you said the gun belonged to Lucy, is that true?"

"Um-hum."

"Is that 'Yes'?" the judge interposed.

"Yes," said the defendant.

Jordan asked, "When did she tell you she had the gun?"

"I didn't know she had the gun until they found it behind the pole."

"But, Mr. Simms," Jordan said as he approached the defendant, moving in for effect, "Didn't you just testify that Lucy had told you she had the gun because she had been jacked?"

Dewayne looked both puzzled and slightly nervous, "Naw, man, she told me about it later, gettin' jacked an' all."

"But, Mr. Simms, do you remember when your lawyer asked you if you saw the gun, and you said you didn't see it, but Lucy told you she was strapped?"

"Yeah."

"So you *did* know she had the gun before the police found it?"

"Man, I just told ya, I didn't know nothin' 'bout no gun 'till the cops go, 'look what we got here' and pulled out the gun behind the pole."

Jordan paused to let the jury absorb the defendant's anger and moved onto establishing the lack of motive on the part of the Deputies to lie about seeing him with the gun.

"Mr. Simms, prior to the night you were arrested for the gun, had you ever seen these two police officers before?"

"No."

"You never had any contact with them prior to that?"

"No."

"So, as far as you know, they didn't know your name or anything at all about you?"

"That's right."

"So," Jordan turned to face the jury to signal that he was asking an important question, "Can you think of any reason why these officers would single you out and lie about seeing you with the gun in order to convict you?"

The defendant paused, and to Jordan's dismay, said, "Yeah man, I can. See, you're not from my neighborhood. You probably from the valley or somethin', but in my 'hood the cops jack you up and they don't need no reason at all."

Jordan was aghast to see the reactions of two of the jurors. They were nodding in agreement! He had made the mistake he had been taught not to make in trial advocacy class. It's called asking one question too many. In the law school example, a defendant was charged with literally biting off the nose of a guy in a brutal bar fight. On cross-examination of the prosecution's star eye-witness, the defendant's attorney got the witness to admit that he never actually saw the defendant bite the victim's nose off. But then, instead of sitting down and saying, "No further questions," he asked the one question too many. "So then, sir, if you didn't see my client bite the victim's nose off, how is it that you can be so sure that my client did so?" "I saw him spit it out of his mouth." End of lesson. But Jordan had forgotten.

"Thank you," Jordan interrupted, before Dewayne could do further damage, "I have no further questions your honor."

"No questions," said Joe Nataka.

The judge dismissed the jury and counsel for a ten minute break before instruction and argument. Jordan went back up to the 7th floor to get the standard jury instructions which Judge Young would read to the jury, and then he returned to Division 12. No one was back yet, so Jordan jotted down the main points he would make in closing argument. He knew that since the prosecution has the burden of proof, he would argue twice. He would give the initial argument, the defense would argue, and then he would get a chance to rebut the defense. He believed he could close this deal.

Thirty-One

The receiver was in his hand, but a ring came before JJ could punch up an outside line. Blair.

"JJ, my brother from another mother, how's the case goin'? You gettin' anywhere without you're old partner making you look good?"

"Does the phrase 'dead in the water' help you?"

"Man, that's too bad. Any idea where to look for the nine millimeter that killed Snip- I mean Alex?"

"Better chance of recovering the second gun fired from the grassy knoll. What's happening in Malibu today? I heard on the surf report that you got a low tide and one to two foot waves. Life's a beach."

"Nah, man, it's not so bad here. As I told you at the funeral, it's good work. You feelin' a little better since I saw you?"

"Actually, I feel about a thousand times worse. And I really didn't think that was possible."

"We'll, I looked over those reports and it just seems like the same ol' shit to me. Kansas Street takes out a couple Playboys and then smokes one of their own who's gonna give them up. Sorry to say, I don't have any different theories for ya. But listen, Angie would like you to come over for dinner one of these nights, she misses you."

JJ started laughing loudly, something he hadn't done much of late. "Bullshit! You know damn well the woman hates my guts. She can't stand when we get together and talk like cops."

"Well, she did tell me to invite you. And, besides, I kinda miss hanging out with ya."

"It hasn't been long enough for you to miss me."

"It's a dinner invitation. Say 'yes.'"

"Tell Ange 'thanks' and that I miss her too, but I just don't have the time to socialize these days."

"Ok, that's cool. But give me a call when you change your mind, 'cause I know you will. Anything else going on with you?"

"Don't you have to go wax your surfboard or something?"

"I'll let you go J; you're obviously in one of your moods."

"Absolutely true. If I were locked up, they'd remove the bed sheets for my own safety."

"If I didn't know you better I'd be worried about you."

"Don't worry about me, just go off and judge your thong bikini contest, or whatever you do there, and I'll handle the real crime."

"Bye J," said Blair with his trademark amused chuckle.

JJ just hung up.

He would have smiled as he set down the receiver, but something bothered him about the call. Blair seemed oddly content with JJ's ass in a sling and his investigation going nowhere. He chalked it up to Blair's ego. He always had one no smaller than a Macy's Parade float.

Thirty-Two

"Ladies and Gentlemen of the jury," Jordan began shakily, feeling nauseated in the pit of his stomach, "you've heard all the evidence. Now it's time to decide whether Mr. Simms is guilty of the crime of possession of a loaded firearm in public."

He continued nervously, hands gripping the podium, feeling the pressure that follows every Deputy D.A. into his first closing argument. There's really nothing quite like it. Except maybe when a seventh grade boy asks the most popular girl in junior high to go to the dance with him. But then he has the convenient option of having somebody else ask her or using a note as his proxy. A jury trial requires direct communication, not to mention persuasion. But with your first trial you settle for survival. The persuasion part comes later in your trial stats.

Jordan proceeded to review the evidence with the jury, pointing to the officer's testimony which he labeled, "credible," and the defendant's testimony which he told them they should "disregard." He also explained the standard of reasonable doubt as he had learned in training, and told them "reasonable doubt does not mean beyond all doubt." He gave the example from the training manual, stating: "You have all heard of the country of China. You've read about it in books, seen pictures on television, and talked to people who have been there. But most of you probably haven't been there yourselves. It's possible that China doesn't exist at all. But you know from all of the evidence you are aware of that China does exist beyond a reasonable doubt."

Jordan hadn't learned what experienced prosecutors know. A lot of what is learned in training class should stay there. Most good prosecutors concentrate on the evidence of guilt. They leave the issue of reasonable doubt to the defense to emphasize. The right message to impart to the jury is he did it or he didn't, there's no in-between. And I, for one, am damn sure he did it.

After reminding the jury that he'd speak with them again after Mr. Nataka addresses them, he sat down, releasing a faint sigh of relief.

"Ladies and Gentleman," Joe Nataka began after positioning himself within a couple of feet of the jury rail, "Clarence Darrow, a great lawyer in our country's history, would always say when someone made a mistake, 'hell that's why they make erasers.'"

Joe had started his arguments with this line many times, and the jury warmed up to him right on schedule. Quite a contrast from the stiff and nervous DDA.

"And in this case, the police made a mistake. It's your constitutional duty to correct it. You're the erasers."

At that point, Joe Nataka went on a 20 minute mission, pointing out what he called, "major holes" in the People's case.

"For starters, the Deputies don't have a good recollection of what they saw. Deputy Cudahy said they were driving East on Carson, and Deputy Blunt thought they were going West."

Jordan was being educated on the importance of small details and why every prosecutor should be skeptical when cops tell them cavalierly not to worry, they looked over their reports, and they remember what happened.

Joe harped on the fact that Cudahy said they were 40 feet from the defendant when he put the gun behind the pole and Blunt said it was only 10 feet. Furthermore, he argued, "Blunt was obviously trying to help the People's case when he said he remembered there was a street light overhead, when Deputy Cudahy admitted it was several feet away on the other corner."

Then Joe Nataka asked a rhetorical question that he knew would stir up the jury: "If the Police really thought my client had the gun, why didn't they take fingerprints?" He continued, "But most importantly, the Deputies said my client handled the gun with his right hand. But you know from his testimony that he is left handed. There is no reason he would have used his right hand to hide the gun, if he actually *had* the gun."

His conclusion dealt Jordan's case a knockout blow. Deftly, Joe tapped into the jury's emotions regarding the Rodney King case. In August of 1992, it was almost mandatory for an L.A. public defender arguing a police credibility case.

"Folks, these days you just have to read the paper or turn on the television to know that there are bad cops out there, officers that don't always act lawfully. It's your job to make sure the police are kept in line. You and I know what really happened out there. The police even admit that my client and his friend weren't doing anything illegal. Yet these cops came up to them and shined flashlights in their eyes and treated them like common criminals with no justification. They were looking for a reason to arrest my client. They found the gun on Lucy, a juvenile who would have been too much trouble to arrest, so they decided to pin the gun on my client, a black man.

"But, fortunately..." Joe paused and used the measured silence to look into every juror's eyes. "That's why they make erasers. You are the system's only way to correct this mistake. All my client and I ask is that you do your duty."

Joe sat down and Dwayne glanced at him with a sincere smile emanating gratitude. It was Jordan's turn again, and the courtroom door opened. Jim Connelly came through it and gracefully took a seat in back; luckily, Jordan didn't notice him. He was too absorbed in responding to the defense arguments. Since he was old enough to form his own opinions, Jordan loved to argue with anyone willing or unwilling. And Joe Nataka's transparent attempt to sway the jury by alluding to the Rodney King case fired him up.

Jordan began by walking right up to the jury box with no notes in hand. Then he spoke with a confidence and ease that shocked the twelve jurors and two alternates. "This is not the same prosecutor. What'd they do with that other guy?" the jurors must have asked themselves.

Jordan started by making an unlikely reference.

"I don't know if any of you watch Saturday Night Live, but if you do, then you've seen the subliminal message guy. He drops words into his sentences that are totally unrelated to anything in order to make the person he's talking to do whatever he wants them to do. And somehow, without knowing it, and for no good reason, they do what he wants. With all due respect to the defense counsel, who has, quite frankly, done an excellent job representing Mr. Simms, this is exactly what Mr. Nataka is trying to do to you in his closing argument. Let's not beat around the bush, he wants you to think of the Rodney King officers and say, 'If we can't trust those officers, we can't trust any officers.'"

"But ladies and gentlemen, do society a favor, don't buy the fear and ignorance he's trying to sell you. Don't get me wrong, there are certainly bad police officers. And they deserve to be prosecuted. Police officers are just people. And, of course, there are both good and bad people. But not all people are bad. And not all police officers are bad. In fact most of them are not like Officer Powell or Officer Koon. They are men and women who, even though they have wives and husbands and children they love and who depend upon them, they work out on our streets twenty four hours a day, seven days a week, willing to risk their lives to make ours safer."

"Some of you are probably thinking, that Deputy Blunt, not my kind of guy. And, I hate to have to say this in open court, but I would agree. Sometimes when you deal with criminals for a living, you get a little cynical, a little hardened. However, you are not here to decide who is nicer, or who you'd invite to your house for a Labor Day barbeque. You're here to decide if the law has been violated. Did Dwayne Simms have the gun?"

"Some of you may be thinking, 'I wasn't there, how do I know who's telling the truth?' Mr. Simms said Lucy had the gun, and the police say that he had it. Therefore, I can't decide, so I have a doubt. But that's not the way to analyze it. If you took this courthouse and its twelve floors and turned it upside down, you would see alibis, lies, and excuses from defendants come flowing out like a tidal wave. It's your job to decide the facts of this case."

"When you do that, ask yourself this: with all the crime in Los Angeles and all the cases these Sheriff Deputies have to go to court on, do you think they need to drive around and invent crime where it doesn't exist? And you heard Mr. Simms himself say that he never saw these Officers before. They don't know him from Adam. So, even if they were going to invent a crime, why would they choose *him*? Oh, I know what Mr. Nataka wants you to believe, Mr. Simms is black and these deputies are white, so they had it out for him. He wants you to think every white cop lies about black defendants."

"The Constitution says that you have to presume the defendant, Mr. Simms, is innocent at the start of the trial. And that is fair. Given the risks these officers willingly take for you and the community, you owe it to them not to presume, as Mr. Nataka does, that they are liars and cheats. You certainly have no evidence that they were doing anything that night other than trying to keep loaded firearms off the streets. You should acknowledge it for what it is, it's a service. A service for you and me. One they perform every minute of every hour of every day. And we, as taxpayers pay them to do exactly what they did on the night of June 8, 1992."

"So decide who, between the defendant and the two Sheriff Deputies, has the bigger motive to lie. And decide if you would have rushed the gun to the fingerprint lab if you clearly saw it in the hands of the defendant. How would you explain your request for fingerprints? Would you say, 'I saw the suspect with the gun, but maybe I was hallucinating so I want you to test it for fingerprints at public expense?' I doubt it. Ladies and Gentlemen, don't be persuaded by the subliminal messages of Mr. Nataka. Decide the case based on the evidence and your common sense and you'll find that Mr. Simms did have the gun. He is guilty of the crime as charged. Thank you."

Judge Young gave some final instructions to the jury about selecting a foreperson, and told them to push the buzzer once if they had a question, twice if they arrived at a verdict. Then, after the clerk swore Dave the bailiff to take charge of the jury, Dave showed 12 jurors to the deliberation room. The alternate juror would wait in the hallway. The judge quickly headed for chambers to phone a colleague to inform him he could not play an afternoon nine holes of golf in Downey. At least not until the jury came back with their decision. Jordan gathered all of his case files and headed for the door. He was stopped by the outstretched hand of Jim Connelly. He set down his files to shake hands with his boss.

"Jordan, I have to say that in all my years as a D.A. that was the best I've seen anyone do for their first closing argument."

"Thanks Mr. Connelly, I appreciate that."

"Jim, Jordan, Jim. And I'm not saying it to blow sunshine up your behind; I'm saying it because I think you're gonna be a hell of a trial attorney. Someday when you're one of the best, I'm going to say that I watched Jordan Stowic deliver his first argument."

Thirty-Three

The detective entered his call back number, with area code, followed by the numbers 9-1-1. He was desperate for a lead. He leaned back in the creaky wood chair and stared at the ceiling. A crack ran through it near the far wall by the door. JJ believed it arrived with the last major earthquake to rock Southern California, known unaffectionately to So- Cali's as "The Lander's Quake." Ten minutes went by. JJ was in deep meditation when his phone rang.

"JJ man, this G-Dog."

"How you been G?" JJ asked, to put G-Dog at ease before his imminent cut to the chase.

"Chillin' like a villain blood."

"What's so important that you called me the other day?"

"Shit blood, I can't be sayin' shit on the phone. 'Specially 'cause you at the station and all."

"I don't get you G, what are you talking about?"

"This is weird shit, it's like you guys are in it now. I don't want some fool listenin' in where you are, then puttin' the word out an' cappin' my black ass."

"Now you're talkin' crazy G. What are you trying to tell me?"

"Not on the phone. Meet me at the Chinese pizza place on Compton."

"Right now?"

"Naw man, I gotta take care a some personal shit first, let's say 'round three."

"Three o'clock G. I'll be there. Be cool."

"Later fuzz."

JJ had cultivated his connection with G-Dog for the last two years. Now he would see the payoff. The planned afternoon meeting revived JJ. So much so that he felt he could go down to the roach coach on Temple for a hot dog with everything and he could enjoy it. His investigation was like a glider catching a gust of wind. G- Dog was about to give someone up. Why else would this gangbanger be so damn nervous?

Thirty-Four

Jordan had three yellow messages in his DDA mail slot. None were from Kendall. His heart sank. But reading the one from Courtney was like a swig of whiskey downed by a wounded Confederate soldier to ease the pain. "Call me A.S.A.P. about tonight. Miss you like crazy. Beach party tonight." the secretary faithfully recorded. Accurate phone messages from secretaries at the D.A.'s office were like comets, every so many decades one came your way. Before he called Courtney, he returned Stan's message.

"Scientific Services, may I help you?" said a scratchy and sexy Demi Moore voice.

"Stan Reid please."

"He's out of the office right now, may I take a message?"

"No, that's alright, I'll try him later."

Jordan's intercom rang and, after studying the various buttons on his phone, he found the right one. It was Connelly's secretary, Sumi. "Mr. Connelly would like to see you in his office."

"Ok, I'll be right there," Jordan said cheerfully.

He followed the long corridor around to Jim's office. When he finally got there he realized that he had taken the longest possible route, like a rat choosing the long way to the cheese.

"Mr. Connelly, you wanted to see me?"

Jim Connelly was reclined in his leather chair, reading about his fellow lawyers in *The Daily Journal*, the bible of every L.A. attorney.

"Pull up a chair Jordan."

He descended into a surprisingly comfortable wooden chair.

"The jury's still out on my trial. I guess that's not a good sign."

"Relax. They've only been out for two hours. Most likely they won't return with a verdict until at least tomorrow."

"But isn't it true that juries that take longer are more likely to acquit or hang than juries that come back quickly?"

"Quite frankly, Jordan, It'd be easier to come up with an alternative fuel than predict what the twenty-four eyed monster is going to do in that jury room. I've had cases where the jury came back in twenty minutes not guilty. And I've had cases where they've deliberated for two weeks and came back guilty on all twenty-seven counts. The only rule of thumb with juries is that there are no rules of thumb. But that's what makes them interesting conversation at cocktail parties. Not to mention making millionaires out of the top jury consultants."

"I guess there's nothing more I can do anyway so I shouldn't stress about it."

"You're absolutely right. And believe me, when you go back to that courtroom to hear the verdict, you'll have plenty of stress. Now, on to other things. The reason I called you in here. As I told you, I'm very impressed with your handling of that trial. Regardless of what the jury may decide, I've made up my mind that you've got star potential. Therefore, I'm going to do something a little unusual for a rookie. I'm assigning you a felony trial."

Connelly handed Jordan a file that didn't look like the misdemeanor files Jordan had been carrying to court. It was a legal size manila file with the felony case number and the defendant's last name written across the top. It read,

"TA088124 Cisneros, Alfredo." The box on the outside reserved for the charges contained the handwritten notation, "211 PC," which was short for California Penal Code, Section 211, the state law that made robbery a crime punishable by ten years in prison.

"Mia Fisher is going out of town next week and won't be able to handle the case. She tells me the defense attorney won't agree to a continuance and so it's going to go to trial."

Jordan was flattered by Jim's confidence in him, but a little unnerved about not gradually working up to felony trials, as most DDAs did. A felony trial meant Superior Court instead of Municipal Court, and the stakes were much higher. Instead of six months in the county jail, the defendant faced ten years in state prison.

"Of course I suspect you're going to be a little nervous. But after what I saw you do today, I know you're up to the task. And who knows where you'll go if you do a good job with this one. Here in Compton we get a lot of murders, maybe you'll get one of those soon."

"Jim," Jordan addressed him for the first time as if they were old college buddies, "thank you."

"Don't mention it. Just make me proud. Now, let me brief you on the facts of the case. This is a robbery of a homeless man by a gang member. It happened near some railroad tracks where the victim lives. The defendant came up to our victim and flashed a handgun. The victim gave up his cigarettes and his money – only three bucks. Apparently the homeless guy was fed up with getting jacked by these gang members all the time, so he actually called the cops and filed a report. It's not the crime of the century, but it could be a tough case. The hardest part, according to Mia, is just getting your victim into court. Take a look at where the guy lives."

Connelly took back the file and turned to the witness list in the back, then handed it to Jordan, who read the address out loud, "third bush South of the Atlantic Bridge in Compton."

"An up-and-coming neighborhood with low property taxes," Connelly said, with not a little sarcasm.

"True. And all he has to do is make sure his house stays watered and gets plenty of sunlight."

Jim laughed heartily at that one. Then the new DDA thanked him again and returned to his pathetic excuse for an office where he began combing through his felony file, giving great mental weight to every detail. Jordan had learned from his first trial how critical it was to master every fact, however minute. He thought the name "Southside Playboys" was a funny name for a dangerous street gang. From his movie education, he believed all gang members were either Bloods or Crips.

It was just before 3:00 p.m. when Jordan's office telephone rang. It was the clerk from Division 12. The jury had a verdict.

Thirty-Five

In his white Caprice JJ made good time down the 101 Freeway to the 5 to the 710 to the 91, exiting at Alameda Street in Compton. North, past Alex and Maria's block to Compton Boulevard, then right.

Several streets away he could see what was unmistakably a crime scene. He was alarmed to count six Compton P.D. patrol units. He saw a voracious crowd of forty or so people, separated from the object of their morbid edacity by yellow tape strung neatly between tall, skinny orange pylons. Most of them had hoped to see the body, unaware it had already been taken to Martin Luther King, Jr. Hospital by paramedics who made desperate attempts at resuscitation. When he reached the patrol officer stopping cars from entering the area, he held his badge out of the window and was waived into the strip mall parking lot in front of Kim's Pizza. Le Lan Kim was sitting in the passenger seat of a patrol car being questioned by a familiar looking Compton detective. JJ introduced himself to the watch commander in charge of the crime scene, Lieutenant Caldwell.

"I'm Rodriguez with Sheriff's O.S.S."

"Looks like we may have another body for you guys."

The Compton Police Department, because of their inferior resources, including their lack of a crime lab, contracted all homicide investigations to the Los Angeles Sheriff's Department. The Compton P.D. handled all non-murder investigations.

"What happened?"

"Some Piru got shot up by another gangbanger. What else is new?"

"Who was it?" JJ asked, sure that he already knew.

"Kids name was-"

"Ronald Thomas."

"Yeah. Did you already get filled in?"

"No. I just – what is the victim's condition?"

"Didn't look too good when the paramedics took him out of here. The kid was unconscious but they told me he was still breathing. It looked like a gunshot wound to the stomach."

"Any witnesses?"

"Just the owner of the restaurant, says he didn't see anything. His name is-"

"Yeah, I know Mr. Kim. Where's the victim, MLK?"

"Think so. Hey, how did you happen to get here so quickly, I didn't call anyone from Sheriff's Homicide. We don't even know if the kid's checking out yet."

"I was in the area, but now I gotta get going. Thanks Lieutenant."

"Sure."

He breezed in his Caprice toward MLK hospital, where the United States army trains its surgeons because of the unparalleled experience the facility offers in the treatment of gunshot victims. He drove very fast. He could feel the hope draining out of him with the passing of every second. This prompted him to yell into the windshield, "Dammit, don't you fucking die on me, you son of a bitch!"

As G-Dog lay dying at King Hospital, a final flame flickered anemically on JJ's candelabra of leads that might have afforded him direction out of the punishing darkness.

Thirty-Six

He felt his heart pumping briskly, picking up speed as the judge spoke, "Ladies and gentlemen of the jury, it's my understanding that you have reached a verdict?"

The foreman answered "yes" and Dave the bailiff collected the verdict form, which he handed to the judge. Judge Young scanned it and handed it to the clerk. She stood, adjusted her pink designer frames with one hand, then began reading. An eternity had passed in less than 30 seconds.

"In the matter of the People of the State of California versus Dwayne Simms, we the jury in the above-entitled cause find the defendant, Dwayne Simms, Not Guilty of the crime of possession of a loaded weapon in violation of Section 12031(a) of the California Penal Code."

The words "not guilty" were like an elbow to the stomach that had so many times stolen his breath in basketball games. He took in two full lungs of air and tried not to show his disappointment as his honor asked whether either side wished the jury to be polled individually to ensure that the verdict was unanimous.

"No, your honor," said Joe Nataka, and his client leaned back in his chair and smiled.

"No thank you, your honor," said the Deputy D.A.

Thirty-Seven

By 4:45 p.m., the Aftershock had filled up with workers from the McDonnell-Douglass plant, a pair of local drunks and a sharply-dressed, out of place, forty-something professional. The latter looked like an attorney with his colorful suspenders and pricy tie. He sipped a vodka martini and stared straight ahead, purposely ignoring his surroundings, well aware that he was slumming it.

Happy hour was in full force and effect as Loni hurriedly poured dollar drafts of Budweiser and Miller. Jimmy Buffet rocked the house with "Cheeseburger in Paradise." Buddy Cox jealously guarded his space at the bar, saving a seat to his right. He told himself, "You never know who might walk in here and want to sit next to me." He hoped it would be a loose, middle-aged blond, perhaps recently divorced, dying for some action. The truth be known, Buddy Cox hadn't been laid in over four years. And, to paraphrase Woody Allen, he was tired of having sex with someone he loved. Ever optimistic about his chances to score based on absolutely no good reason, he thought this might be his night.

Thirty-Eight

JJ waited impatiently at MLK Hospital for G-Dog to come out of surgery and regain consciousness. G-dog's Auntie was waiting with him. She told JJ that "Ronnie" was really a good boy who got into trouble when he hung around the wrong people. JJ would retire wealthy if only he had a dollar for every parent or Auntie that expounded that victim of circumstances theory. It was something he never bought. JJ's theory was simple: no rules or discipline in the home as a child resulted in no respect for family or for the law.

A physician's assistant eventually came out and interrupted a national news story on President Bush's latest campaign faux pas which was barely audible from a minuscule television with the tiniest speaker bolted high up in the corner of the waiting room. G-Dog's Auntie was awoken from her cat nap. The P.A. informed them that G-Dog was in critical condition due to the tremendous amount of blood that was lost and that there were complications from the damage the bullet had done to his organs. He would not be in any condition to talk until the following morning. JJ left his card with the Auntie and the P.A. and asked for a call when G-Dog could see visitors.

It took forever getting to the Aftershock with the 710 clogged like the artery of an obese Fatburger addict in need of a bypass. Choosing "real food" over health food, JJ enjoyed his occasional Fatburger burger, though he never went as crazy as some, opting out of the "heart attack burger" which featured two half-pound beef patties with everything plus three slices of bacon, topped by an egg, sunny side up. As he edged forward by simply letting his foot off the brake, his frustration made him want to trounce his gas peddle and plow into the back of the oil truck that spewed black smoke directly into his car's ventilation system. He could go up in a glorious blaze of disgrace and end the permanent headache of the two cases that owned him. Instead, he drifted away and pondered. He kept listening to G-Dog's phone conversation on the tape recorder of his mind. "It's like you guys are in it now." He remembered G-Dog's paranoia about someone at the station listening in and "putting the word out." The consternation made his head hurt worse. God he needed a drink!

Thirty-Nine

Before his drive home, Jordan put down the top and removed the doors on his Wrangler. He put them in the back seat then drove radio-free down Olympic Boulevard towards his new West L.A. home. In silence he contemplated the comments of the members of the jury that handed him defeat in his first trial. "These are the kind of cops that just harass you for being out on the street" a twenty-something black male juror explained. "I just didn't buy their story. I've seen cops like them before," said another. Jordan was learning a lesson about some of the Compton jury pool. They grew up in the area, and their eyes were bloodshot from the blinding flashlights of the Stevie Ladds and Grant Pundersons. Tired of being suspects in their own backyard, they wanted only to be citizens, equal to and respected by the police whose salaries they paid. What they failed to comprehend is that their own police had a tough time distinguishing suspect from citizen.

Several jurors were bothered by the fact that Dwayne was left handed. "Why would he use his right hand to hide the gun?" they challenged the dumbfounded prosecutor. "I've been robbed twice, so I don't blame Lucy for having the gun," confided another.

As bad as it was to start his career as a trial lawyer with a loss, Jordan took heart in the fact that the person who mattered most, to wit, his boss Jim Connelly, was sufficiently impressed with him to give him a felony robbery case for his second trial. Jordan had a habit of dwelling on the positives and overlooking their counterparts. And so, after deciding that this was really a good day for him, a necessary learning experience, he replaced the removable face on his Sony car CD player and turned it up to the fourth level. Courtney's message of a beach party excited him, though in an emotional conflict of interest, he simultaneously missed Kendall.

"It's happy. . . hour again, I think I might be happy if I wasn't out with them!" screamed the Housemartins, from all four speakers.

Forty

The dark skinned Pakistani-American removed the rubber band and counted a stack of bills. He handed the black teenage boy the envelope he had removed from the trunk of his car. "This shit better be pure," the envelope's recipient demanded.

"Young man, you should be glad we do business with you. Our product is pure. And it is also endless."

"This is probably shit I sold before." The young man smiled as he fidgeted with his .25 semi-automatic handgun, cocking and uncocking.

"And you will probably sell it yet again," the Pakistani said.

They left the bathroom of the burger joint one at a time, going their separate ways. One of them home to his wife and children, after making a quick deposit at the bank. The other back to work in his sales territory, after picking up a 40 ounce Olde English malt liquor. If you threw a rock in Compton or South Central Los Angeles, you were bound to hit a hamburger joint or liquor store. Donut shops and check cashing businesses made a strong showing as the third and fourth most likely businesses to be struck by that rock.

Forty-One

A red Porsche 911 Cabriolet convertible was circumspectly parked in the tiny garage meant for Stan's Impala. Jordan took a generous look to closely inspect the object of every 25-year-old male's desire before heading up the stairs past the Judas painting. As Jordan unlocked the apartment door, he heard the stereo maxed out, and had to go turn it down to call out for the Man. In towel, Stan exited the bathroom exclaiming, "Did ya catch my new wheels?"

"Are you serious?"

"Well, I figured the County is never gonna pay me enough to buy one, so I used my Dad's money."

"Are you sure that was smart, I mean, did your Dad leave you enough?"

"Relax," Stan interrupted, "he had a lot of stock from my Grandfather in Iowa that I never knew about."

"That's cool, man. It's your money."

"Look, let's just enjoy life. It's too short not too."

"Good point. That's a great car. I know you've always wanted one."

"That's right. You remember that scene in *Against All Odds* where Jeff Bridges races James Woods in his Porsche 911?"

"Yeah. What did James Woods drive? Lotus?"

"Ferrari I think. Maybe I'll get you one for your birthday Stow and you can play James Woods."

"As long as I get Rachel Ward."

"I can't afford her too. So how did your day go Stow?"

"Well, my jury came back not guilty."

"Sorry to hear it buddy. You should've had a dope case with me as your expert- then you would definitely have convicted the guilty son-of-a-bitch."

"Maybe the jury was right, maybe the guy wasn't guilty."

"C'mon Stow, everybody is guilty of something. If he didn't do this crime, he did something else."

"The good news is my boss watched my closing argument and was impressed enough to give me my first felony trial."

"No shit?"

"Yeah. It's a robbery."

"Then we gotta go out and celebrate tonight. I got a call from Jennifer, and she and Courtney invited some of their friends to El Matador for a cook out on the beach. We'll leave in about 20. What do you think?"

The phone rang and Jordan grabbed it.

"Hi there."

"I'm fine. How are you?"

"Good."

It was Kendall.

"Hold on. Stan-man," he whispered "why don't you just go, I want to talk to Kendall for a little while, I really need to-"

"I know. I'll leave you directions."

The conversation lasted for several minutes. Before ever picking up her telephone, Kendall had struggled mightily to keep her promise. She never wanted to speak to Jordan again. But she soon lost to her true feelings.

Jordan felt emotionally recharged, connecting again with his other best friend. It was apparent, however, that they were still more distant than the 2,000 miles between L.A. and Chicago. He told her about his trial, about Stan's new car, and everything new in his life not relating to Courtney. Then she asked an unfortunate question which he answered with his characteristic veracity.

"Well, I'm not really sure how I feel about this girl. All I know is that I still love you."

Uncertainty about his feelings towards the other woman was not exactly what Kendall Wright was looking for, and she promptly and firmly introduced her receiver to the base of her telephone, leaving him to converse with a dial tone. He would have called her back if he was ready to give her the answer he knew she needed. Instead he moved on, into his Jeep, off to the beach party.

When he passed Pepperdine University on his right, he thought he went too far. Fortunately it was still light outside, enabling him to catch sight a small brown sign for El Matador State Beach. The night was waiting for him, offering him everything he'd hoped to find in his new California social life. Except the girl he knew he loved.

Forty-Two

"What are you doing?" screamed the boozy and still optimistic Buddy Cox.

"If the girl of your dreams walks in here tonight, not only will I move, but I'll buy both of you a bottle of Dom Perignon."

JJ wouldn't have humored the drunken salesman had he not been in possession of the only remaining barstool.

As he sat and belted down his Jack, hold the Coke, he ignored Buddy and contemplated his remaining moves. He had reached an all time low in his detective career. He was running out of options. He reminded himself that G-Dog was still alive, although perilously so. He had seen the results of gunshot wounds to the stomach before in suspects and an ex-partner. There was a good possibility that, even if G-Dog was lucky enough to survive, he would be married to a colostomy bag for the rest of his life. If not so lucky, he wouldn't see the morning.

JJ took a mental note that he needed to get the report from the firearms analyst regarding the caliber of bullet used to kill Alex. However, without any murder weapon to compare to the bullet, it was doubtful that the report would mean very much. Of course, a future traffic stop of a gang banger and search of the car . . . you never know.

The Jack Daniels kept flowing, and he drifted back to Rachel. Every woman who walked into the bar was her. Hair that smelled like fresh summer daisies. Brown eyes that shined brighter than the sun, warming the heart of every creature who fell into their line of sight. A smile that was deafening, proclaiming the beauty and wonder of life. He wondered what the hell had happened to their love. He tortured himself well into the night. As if he needed more torture.

Forty-Three

"Good mornin' baby."

"It sure is Yoli. I'm really getting used to this never-ending sunshine."

"What baby, don't they have sun where you come from?"

"Michigan has its occasional sunny day hidden somewhere between Easter and Labor Day. The rest of the time, the predominant theme is gray."

Yoli watched as Jordan glanced in his messageless box and walked toward Jim's office, the only one with its lights on. He walked past it to his own, less impressive work space. On Jordan's desk was a piece of stationary "From the Desk of James Connelly" informing Jordan that another DDA was covering his misdemeanor calendar in Judge Young's courtroom. Jim wanted Jordan to concentrate on preparing the robbery case which was scheduled to go to trial in a few days. Jordan got to work early for this very reason. Fortunately for his morning productivity, Courtney wasn't feeling well the night before, so they ended the El Matador beach party at a reasonable hour.

Jordan spent 20 minutes sipping his Diet Coke and reading the *Los Angeles Times* while he completed his transition out of REM phase. He thought he might have dreamed about Kendall last night but wasn't sure.

He opened the file of People of the State of California v. Alfredo Cisneros and read the reports inside. It was your standard robbery of a transient. The homeless in urban cities across America tend to make excellent victims for criminals of both the elected and unelected types.

What was interesting about this particular homeless man was that, according to the police reports, he wasn't exactly homeless. For the past seven years he had lived in the third bush south of the Atlantic Street Bridge in Compton. The bushman's name was Raymond

LNU (last name unknown). Though an inhabited shrub would not make the greatest "Better Homes" cover, at least Jordan had a shot locating his victim for trial. When he searched the file further, to his dismay, he failed to find a copy of a subpoena indicating that Raymond had been served for the trial. He called over to the court liaison. Strike two, the Officer assigned was on vacation for the next two weeks. It looked as if Mia was right, the hardest part of the trial would be getting the witness to court.

Jordan obtained a blank subpoena from a secretary in the steno pool and filled it in with pen. She also gave him the office's copy of the Thomas Guide. He photocopied the pages showing the bushman's neighborhood. The DA training manual clearly stated that DDAs are never to go into the field without a police officer or District Attorney investigator with them. At 9:30 a.m., Jordan set out to find his witness, notwithstanding said manual.

Forty-Four

When he opened his eyes, he didn't recognize the woman near his bed. That was his first thought. The second was that he didn't recognize the room, though it had a nicer view than any in which he'd ever awoken. When it hit him what had happened, he propped his neck up slightly and began screaming bloody murder- "Motherfucker! Motherfucker! Stupid Motherfucker!" The nurse who went running for assistance didn't know he was referring to himself.

"Ronnie?" said the familiar, calming voice of G-Dog's Auntie. "Thank you baby Jesus," she said, when she realized her nephew was awake.

At 10:00 a.m. JJ hit his snooze alarm yet again. Except it wasn't the alarm that was ringing.

"Hello?"

"He's awake? Great. I'm on my way. Thank you."

After the evening JJ spent riding a river of Jack Daniels, he was equally grateful that, along with his informant, *he* made it though the night.

Forty-Five

The August sun heated her brow and tiny beads of sweat began to form there. There was no breeze this morning. The small, salvaged radio resting on the ground next to her broadcast the latest on the situation in Bosnia. That bursts of static concealed portions of the announcer's baritone sentences was irrelevant since she lacked understanding. A fly flew by her left peripheral view, sounding to her to buzz in sync with the static, then landed on her wrinkled thigh. She sat suspended by the multi-colored plastic weaves in her fragile metal lawn chair which were fraying at the edges from supporting her hefty frame. Sipping from a can of Hawaiian Punch satisfied her, though the beverage had long gone warm. Soon she would get out of the direct sunlight and take shelter from the day's most dangerous rays.

Jordan veered off the busy street down a dirt path until he was blocked by a rusty chain dangling between posts. This was as close to the Atlantic Bridge as he could get. He climbed down from the Jeep and headed on foot through the dry yellow grass, carrying his suit jacket in his hand. He found railroad tracks and followed them, staying on the East side of a giant concrete aqueduct known as the L.A. River. Remarkably, there was no water in sight. He decided that this "river" was a classic example of bad naming. Must have been the same guy who named that tropical island in the Arctic Ocean Greenland.

He consulted the police report to remind himself of the address. Third bush south of the Atlantic bridge. He kept walking. Dust lingering in the air from a recent train's passing triggered a sneeze. A quarter of a mile down the tracks he saw what he believed to be the first bush. On closer inspection he debated whether it was actually a tree, since it appeared to have tree-like branches. No mailboxes with names on them, no neighbors to consult, he moved on.

He thought he might be on the wrong side of the bone-dry river and contemplated walking down the bank of the concrete, across and up the other side. He declined when he saw no signs of plant life over there. Then, in the distance, he spotted three large bushes. He felt certain he was entering the bushman's neighborhood.

Raymond was caretaker to Ramona first, husband second. He "adopted" her a decade ago in Houston. He left his job with a major oil company and hit the streets to become a full-fledged homeless boozer. He first saw her pale blue eyes looking back at him in a battered woman's shelter which he started frequenting for its Sunday morning distribution of leftovers. A permanent resident of the shelter, she would help pass out the food, usually sandwiches and cookies. And she communicated to Raymond with those pale eyes. God how Raymond loved her at first sight! So quiet, so unassuming, so gentle. Those eyes saw too many years of relentless corporal punishment. They were at the same time empty and desperate. They seemed to be searching for something that he could provide. It did not bother him that she was physically unable to speak. Convinced that saving her was the only thing that would save himself, he married her and moved her out to California where they could live in the kind of sunshine he knew as a boy in Hawaii.

Life with Ramona was perfect. Simple. Peaceful. Uncomplicated. Not like his days as an engineer working on the Alaskan pipeline. Or those spent in corporate offices in Houston. Those bosses and deadlines were no more. He retired in an unusual but comfortable style. The railroad company had been kind enough to permit him and his wife to live on its property for the last seven years. Though the couple did not possess a deed, they had all the legal rights of land ownership, without the drawbacks. Mortgage payments, insurance, taxes, assessments, water, electricity, trash, cable, you name it, not their concern. When they needed to wash, or rather, when they *decided* to, they would travel five minutes by foot to the AM/PM gas station on Gage Avenue and use the facilities there. The owner was gracious enough to let them use his shower and his phone, and even scribbled down a rare telephone message when one came their way. When one did, it was usually from Raymond's mother in Hawaii, though a police officer had left a message once. Raymond was such a genuinely kind person. As the gas station's proprietor could attest, it was next to impossible to turn a deaf ear towards any of Raymond's meager requests. And Raymond repaid him with manual labor whenever a task presented itself.

Ramona was an excellent listener and friend, her eyes telling him everything he needed to know. She was satisfied with the barest necessities supplied by Raymond's government relief check. It made him feel incredibly special that he could satisfy her with such paltry provisions. Could it be she really loved him? So it appeared. What warmth and wholeness she brought him! No need for another drink. Ever.

His perfect life with Ramona had its moments. These temporary deviations from perfection were usually inflicted by some external force. Raymond dealt with an occasional stray transient who wandered onto his property or into his bush looking to steal something to trade for a bottle or a rock or some heroin. He had even been robbed by gang members who came to his neighborhood with spray paint cans to leave their marks on the cement walls of the river below him. The gas station proprietor persuaded Raymond to report a recent robbery to the police in an effort to slow the proliferation of gang crime in the neighborhood. Still, his life, until very recently, had remained simple and perfect.

Two years back Raymond won the California Lottery. He had matched all six numbers and was entitled to 4.5 million dollars. But he lost the ticket. He never told Ramona about it. He truly believed that God was watching out for him, knowing that the exorbitant wealth would end their perfect existence. He harbored no regrets. His kind and genuine disposition persisted. Raymond never played the lottery again.

Transients, gang members and lost fortunes aside, the only other concern was a winter rain shower. But it was August. The rain would not come until January. A peaceful and simple life, indeed, with only one catch. Over the last couple weeks, Raymond's life had been complicated by a secret he carried with him. One too dangerous even to share with his best friend Ramona.

Ramona watched the stranger's approach intently. His suit and tie told her that he was from the railroad company. She had seen people like him before come to inspect the tracks. He was younger than the men sent before him. And he was missing his equipment which he surely would go back for later.

Jordan saw an obese woman dressed in cutoff jean shorts and a tank top sitting in a lawn chair watching him. He got close enough to speak, but before he could do so his eyes were diverted to a most amazing sight. An extraordinary gray-green bush stood at least ten feet high and thirty feet in diameter. Blankets and towels were woven through its branches. The earth around its roots was dug out in places, and a dirty patchwork quilt hung down above the carved out area, blocking entrance into the home. It was an awesome shelter, clearly a collaboration of nature and nurture, and Jordan's admiration was increased by the knowledge that it had withstood seven years of the elements, albeit Southern California elements. All around the woman there were items ripe for the garbage: empty plastic two-liter bottles, Spaghetti O's can, tipped over and dilapidated shopping cart, empty Kleenex box, Ralph's brand charcoal bag.

"Hello there," he said to the woman who couldn't speak.

"My name is Jordan Stowic and I'm from the District Attorney's Office."

Her pale blue eyes stared into his and she nodded her understanding and smiled an embarrassed smile.

"Do you speak English?" he asked.

She nodded 'yes.'

For the next 20 seconds, they just smiled at each other awkwardly; as Jordan was about to make another vain attempt to communicate, he saw Raymond lift up the patchwork quilt and climb out from the bush like a rabbit from its hole.

Raymond, like his wife, noticed the suit and smiled. Railroad people.

"Welcome to our humble home. My name is Raymond, please call me Ray. This is my wife Ramona. She can hear you but she can't speak."

Jordan shook Ray's hand and introduced himself. Before he could announce his purpose, Ray disappeared back into the rabbit hole under the hulking bush and returned with two more lawn chairs. He unfolded them and the men now sat with Ramona in the morning sun.

"Would you like something to drink?"

"No thank you Ray," said the young prosecutor, fully believing that he would go back inside the bush and produce a cold Miller Genuine Draft if he had so requested. This was truly an amazing place, and Ray was no ordinary homeless man.

"I am a Deputy District Attorney," he began, getting down to business and producing a subpoena, "and you are a witness on a very important case that I am handling."

Raymond's wide smile instantly disappeared as if his face were an Etch-A-Sketch that had been shaken hard. Both hands which rested on the metal of his lawn chair began to shake visibly. Ramona's eyes stared at him with wifely concern, and one of her eyebrows rose high as if to ask what was wrong.

"Are you ok?" Asked Jordan.

Raymond's olive Hawaiian skin was turning white.

"How did you find out I was there?" he asked, too softly for Jordan to be sure of anything except that he was being asked a question.

"What?"

"How did you know I was there?" he said, just loud enough to be audible.

"I'm sorry, I don't understand," said Jordan.

"How did you know I was there?" He barked, scaring Ramona, who had only heard his voice take this tone when someone was trying to steal from them.

It was clear to Raymond that his perfect world was in jeopardy.

Forty-Six

When G-Dog opened his eyes from a shallow, pain-plagued sleep, he saw eyes that once looked into his with the admiration and respect of a school kid worshiping his favorite teacher. But now they stared him down, cold and black. These were eyes meant for the mentor who had betrayed the trust of his now disillusioned pupil.

He heard his Auntie say from an unknown location, "Ronnie, you got a visitor. That ok with you, sweat pea?"

"Yeah, Auntie. It's cool." G-Dog just couldn't believe the 16-year-old protégée would do him any harm.

The heavy door shut with an alarming crash. The younger man was wearing his red leather high tops, enormous jeans, and a soiled white T-shirt that smelled of marijuana. He had lost his Cardinal's baseball cap last night running away from a Compton patrol officer who tried to stop him or "jack him up," as Lil' T would put it.

"Yo homey, look what our own homeboys done to me," the patient said sternly, as if he were giving a lecture from his hospital bed.

Lil' T did not respond. He simply looked at G-Dog incredulously. He showed him none of the compassion a gunshot victim deserved. Instead he offered the same facial expression he had given to a cluck-head begging for a free rock of cocaine.

"You stupid ass fool, you brought this on yo' self."

Lil' T had never disrespected G-Dog before and this 'dis' surprised him more than getting shot by one of his homies at the Pizza place. G-Dog had to put the little wannabe in his place.

"That ain't no way to be talkin' to an O.G. You better motha' fuckin' watch out, 'cause I be happy to cap you ass when I get the fuck outa here!"

"Dummy, you the one got capped. Homeboys know you trippin'. Turnin' into a damn snitch! They told me to tell you, long as you learned yo lesson and don't say shit about where we gettin' supplied from, you and yo Auntie and little nephew ain't gotta die. Otherwise . ." Lil'T paused for effect. "Otherwise, she-e-e-it. You know what time it is."

G-Dog denied that he would ever rat out his homeboys. Then he looked back at the young Blood gang member and shook his head in disbelief. It was as if Lil'T was turning into a Crab. It was all fucked up. Clearly, Lil'T was coming into his own in the gang. But G-Dog was sure that the balls T displayed came not from between his legs but from the fact that G-Dog lay in a hospital bed with a bullet hole in his stomach. But he was also well aware that his 8th Street Piru Bloods would not hesitate to make good on Lil'T's threat. The question he had most wanted to ask Lil'T he never did. "How the fuck did the homies know I was gonna talk to the detective?"

Another visitor came and went. When JJ was finished with the fruitless questioning, both interrogator and witness had pounding headaches. The latter from the combination of fear and physical pain; the former from sheer frustration. No, G-Dog hadn't seen the person who shot him. Nope, he didn't have any idea why he was shot. Must've been an enemy gang. What was the reason he had scheduled the meeting with the detective? Oh, he just wanted to tell him that he heard a bunch of rumors that the Kansas Street Crips were responsible for the Roosevelt High drive-by. But why the need for the face-to-face? No reason in particular. And what the hell did he mean when he told the detective, "It's like you guys are in it?" Doesn't know. Doesn't remember saying that. Bullshit. Bullshit! Up to his knees. JJ knew it was all bullshit. G-Dog knew JJ knew. And, despite calm reasoning, promises to re-locate family, temper tantrums, threats of life imprisonment, and every other weapon of persuasion the Detective fired from his arsenal, the stalemate remained.

In his white Caprice going South on the Harbor Freeway, unsure of his destination but desperate to get there, he wanted his car walls to come together like the broken trash compactor in his apartment no longer could. Crush him. Mash his aching head into applesauce.

He would feel much better then. JJ had experienced witnesses piss-ing backwards before, but it was never this painful. He needed time to think. He needed to sort it out. He needed a lead. HE NEEDED A DRINK! The Aftershock. But it was still morning. He hadn't resorted to getting looped before lunchtime since Rachel devas-tated him. The depth of the depression that had descended on him matched the Rachel depression, but it was different. Rachel was a cutting, slicing, piercing bolt that tore right through his heart. This was more like a dense black cloud that began to smother his soul. He needed a way out. At the very least, some temporary relief. The Af-tershock. Unfortunately, the Detective was unaware of events trans-piring in another part of the County that would have provided the antidote he needed.

Forty-Seven

The young prosecutor's mouth was wide open during most of the old Hawaiian's story. Talk of murder fascinated him and was what lured him into the intriguing area of criminal law, which any lawyer experiencing a moment of true candor would tell you is the *only* truly compelling specialty in the profession. Ramona's pale blue eyes watched her husband with grave concern. As Raymond spoke, he shook like the branches of his bush being bullied by a gusty Santa Ana. As Raymond told the story, he *relived* it.

It was a warm August night only weeks ago. Like every other night but for the fact that humidity gave slight weight to the air around him. He had just spoken to his mother in Honolulu at the borrowed AM/PM gas station telephone. She complained for the umpteenth time of her rent being raised because of tourists from the mainland. He reassured her yet again that he'd return to visit soon and check into it for her. With kind sentiments from home, he set off on his bi-weekly walk around the neighborhood across the street from the mini-mart, just inside the city limits of Compton. This, his sole act to repel the arthritis that invaded his 60-year-old knees like a conquering army.

He started across the football field, not feeling up to lapping the entire schoolyard. In mid-field, his attention was drawn to a mother and daughter. As the young black woman pushed her sweet little girl, the infant glided up and down, up and down, giggling each time the swing reached its peak and gravity overtook her feather weight, propelling her downward, her pigtails switching directions like wind socks in a tennis match. A sight drenched by the light of God. One not seen enough and one that reassured Raymond of the endurance of the American family, albeit narrowed down a bit. He kept walking. Crossing under a large elm he saw the navy blue unmarked cop car stop in front of three Hispanic gang members on the sidewalk. Raymond instinctively stopped and waited for a confrontation. Hopefully, a quiet one that would take three more cholos off the streets and ensure that the moment between mother and daughter remained pristine, untainted by the ugliness of intimidation and violence. He told himself that the cholos should stop their angry search for self esteem and belonging and put their energy into something positive.

The middle-aged man in a blazer and tie got out of the car and spoke with the three cholos. The conversation ended pleasantly, as if the man had told a joke. The cholos started walking into the park towards the swings. What happened next blew Raymond's mind a thousand times over. The cop went to his trunk and removed a huge rifle. He propped the heavy-looking gun on his right shoulder and aimed it in the direction of the unsuspecting three. From under the dim flickering yellow streetlight, he opened fire. Twenty thunder bolts in quick succession. Boom!

He saw one cholo go down when he heard the grisly scream of a mother witnessing the most hideous sight imaginable. He jerked his neck to see. The little girl had fallen off the swing. Her tiny hands reached out for Mommy who could only watch helplessly as the biggest little love of her life died before her eyes, unaware of the blood shooting out from her own neck. Raymond stood frozen under the elm, as if a spectator with front row seats to a surreal Super Bowl of bloody carnage. The mother's last word was a gurgled attempt at what Raymond assumed was her baby's name. When all five were lifeless, it occurred to him. Run! He tottered briskly along the tree line, limping on both knees, praying he would not be seen by the killer. He was convinced the cop didn't see or hear him under the darkness of the now eerie elm. When he ran out of park, he recoiled at the sight of the killer's car lights. Tail lights. Going in the opposite direction. Thank God.

When Raymond was through telling the horrific tale, he felt like a porter relieving himself of a back-breaking load. He no longer shook, but the crinkled skin under his left eye was twitching with life. He felt renewed by the fact that he had exposed this immensely disturbing secret to the light of official authority, though he was still quite afraid of the potential of retaliation from the monster in the unmarked car with the big rifle. He hoped to soon receive the answer to *why* these people and the little girl had to die.

Jordan finally spoke. "Did you report this to the police?"

"You're from the police aren't you?"

"I'm a Deputy District Attorney."

"District Attorney?"

"Yes."

"You came to talk to me about these terrible murders?"

During the bloodcurdling tale, Jordan had temporarily forgotten why he had come to the bushman's neighborhood.

Forty-Eight

The Aftershock's morning roster varied from the night's starting line-up of O'Neil, Cox and Ramirez. Mary O'Neil was either sleeping off a hangover or looking for cans to turn into money to turn into vodka. Buddy Cox was invariably throwing his weight into a high pressure sale of one of his tired automobiles, always the priciest one on the lot the customer might, with sturdy convincing, believe he could afford. Lacking the wherewithal to walk away, the poor soul just might agree to take it off the lot, thus taking Buddy Cox out of his face. "The technique" Buddy called it. Normal people called it harassment. No one could ever say the man lacked persistence. But they could say a lot of other things.

Morning crowds were always an unpredictable mix. This particular one included two die hard smokers from the McDonnell-Douglas plant taking unauthorized breaks to replenish their blood with nicotine. They ordered coffee. Loni suggested they simply drive out to the San Fernando Valley and breathe the air there to save money on cigarettes. An unfamiliar man and woman meandered in and took a table. Though they both had the touchstones of marriage on their respective ring fingers, Loni suspected that they were not husband and wife. They were far too enamored with each other to have undergone nuptials and the day-to-day that goes along with. When it came to average everyday people, Loni could qualify as an expert in any court of law. And nine times out of ten her feel for people was right.

There was a dirty man there too. He was homeless with a long gray pony-tail tucked partially into the hood on his filth-splotched gray sweatshirt. That he was sitting at the bar savoring a scotch on the rocks and not leaning against a building with a brown bagged bottle of Night Train was due to the charity of one caring soul who believed his plea for "something to eat." Having received a windfall of $20, he succumbed to the desire to pamper himself. Loni had given him a double shot for the price of a single. She recognized the special occasion.

Her eyes caught the tortured eyes the Detective's, just after he pulled up a stool.

"Mornin' Officer. To what do I owe this displeasure?"

"Loni, I'll talk to you after you give me a double shot of Jack, hold the Coke."

"Sorry. We don't serve your kind here. Try the bar down the street, they have a special today for alcoholic cops trying to loose their jobs and ruin their lives."

"Shit. Things are so out of control."

"What's out of control?"

"They're just so goddamn out of control. Even in my darkest moments with Rachel, I've been able to maintain some semblance of control and keep it together. Through logic I could figure things out, and then feel better. But now, I am so screwed, Loni. Can I just tell ya?"

"Tell me."

"I don't have any more leads. Bottom line, I'm fucked. It's like I helped bring about the murder of the only son I've ever known. I couldn't protect his mom either, the only other woman I ever loved, besides you know who."

"You mean the woman who took out a contract on your heart?"

"It's just a stone now. Am I depressing you? I'm depressing the hell out of myself."

"I'm sorry things aren't going your way right now. But the only way to get control is to get a grip on your situation."

Loni touched his shoulder with her hand and squeezed it several times.

"What's the point anymore?"

"The point is you always figure things out eventually."

JJ ignored her and continued. "Besides, I grew up in Compton. I became educated. Then a homicide detective. I've succeeded. So why continue the struggle?"

Only something big could bring down the curtain on JJ's disconsolate theater. But something big was out there.

Forty-Nine

Jordan waited in Connelly's office as his boss finalized plans with his wife for their trip to Rancho Mirage to celebrate their 20th wedding anniversary. He made kissing noises into the receiver before disconnecting her. This made Jordan feel like Mrs. Kravitz from "Bewitched." Perhaps he shouldn't have been the third person listening to this exchange.

"Did you find your robbery victim?" Connelly asked.

Jordan told him an abbreviated version of the story the bushman relayed.

"Did he say where these 5 people were shot?"

"I think he was saying it was a high school or junior high football field."

"Holy Shit!"

"What is it?"

"Jordan, haven't you been reading the papers?"

"Actually, I really haven't had time since I got here. At Georgetown I used to get a subscription to the Post but–"

"Hang on Jordan."

His boss dialed Sheriff's Homicide and asked to speak to the Lieutenant. Lieutenant Flores, after realizing he was speaking to the Head Deputy D.A. of the Compton Office, gave out the information.

On the other end of the line: "Yeah that's Detective JJ Ramirez's case. He's working it by himself until he's assigned a new partner. His other partner just got transferred."

"I have a Deputy D.A. in my office who may have stumbled onto an eyewitness. Of course, he may have found someone who believes the government implanted a metal plate in his brain to keep him from disclosing the location of Jim Morrison and Elvis Presley. At this point, we don't know. The guy is a homeless guy who lives in a bush near the Atlantic Bridge in Compton."

"Well, I'm sure Detective Ramirez would be happy to follow up on any lead. I heard he's not exactly up to his eyeballs in eye wits."

"You know the funny thing about this guy's story?"

"What's that?"

"He says it was a cop who shot all those people."

"A cop? No shit? Well, you know us cops, always happy to violate someone's civil rights. When we get a chance to kill innocent civilians, we're really excited!"

Connelly laughed politely and hung up after Lt. Flores told him he'd page the investigating officer, Detective Ramirez, to the D.A.'s Office.

"Jordan, why don't you go about your business preparing your trial and I'll let you know if this Detective calls back."

Fifty

Afternoon already. The smokers were long gone. The cheaters left in separate cars an hour ago. The pony-tailed man remained, though his financial reserves ran dry two drinks ago. Seven consecutive Jack Daniels on the rocks slowed the synapses in the Detective's brain. Loni couldn't watch this, so she concentrated on the afternoon news, which broadcast the latest tally of murder victims in Los Angeles. It was closing in on the yearly record, and 1992 was just past the halfway mark. JJ had been the reluctant benefactor of the dirty transient. He bought him additional scotches on the promise that neither would try to engage the other in conversation. "You got it bub" sealed their contract.

His pager began to pulsate, but JJ didn't feel it, his waist area numbed from the torrent of whiskey and self-pity coursing through his bloodstream.

"Hey bub."

The Detective tuned out his new homeless friend as he swirled the remnants of Jack #7 in the glass he grasped solidly in his right hand.

"Hey bub!"

"I told you, if you want to keep your glass full, you gotta play by the rules. No conversating."

"Just wanna tell ya that gadget on your belt is doin' something funny."

Now he felt it.

"Oh. Thank you."

"How 'bout another round?" the man requested.

"Sure. Loni, hook up J.P. Getty here."

Loni disconnected herself from the daily report of murders, mutilation, misfortune and mayhem we all feel so necessary to our daily routine. She poured the scotch.

"What about you?" she asked JJ, "Another double shot of wallowing on the rocks with a twist of self-doubt?"

"How about just handing me the phone?"

JJ answered the page. It was his Lieutenant.

Flores apologized for not paging him right away, but conveyed his belief that the DA's witness was probably more of a crackpot than a crack in the Snow case. JJ didn't stay on the phone to hear the Lieutenant give any more insight on a witness he knew nothing about. He called the D.A.'s Office. Jim Connelly's secretary Sumi debated whether she should answer, it being after 4:30 and she not wanting to create any new precedents in County government overtime. Her conscience won out; after all, it was only 4:35 p.m.

"Mr. Connelly's Office."

"This is Detective Ramirez from the Sheriff's Department. Is Mr. Connelly available?"

"I'm sorry, you just missed him," she dutifully lied for her boss, who took off promptly at three for Rancho Mirage.

"Do you know if he'll be in tomorrow morning?"

"No, Mr. Connelly is off the rest of the week; he'll be in on Monday morning. I'd be happy to leave a message."

JJ left his callback number. He was no longer in the mood to wallow. He left the Aftershock, heading North on the 710 to the 405 North towards Santa Monica. He wished his head were clearer when he popped in on his old partner.

Driving up the Pacific Coast Highway approaching Malibu, Claxon's Fish House flew by on his left, reminding him of several sunsets he and Rachel critiqued over steamed clams and ice cold beers. As he experienced these memories, he knew he was overly emotional, as he had a multitude of feelings inside him that included frustration, hate, self-pity, remorse, and longing. He rolled down the windows of the Caprice, hoping a brisk salt-sea breeze would clear out the cobwebs and cool the emotions. The air felt unusually warm and heavy, and it seemed only to intensify what he felt.

When he got to the Sheriff's substation in Malibu, he parked in a spot conspicuously marked "Reserved- Watch Commander." He was not surprised when the young female Deputy working the reception area informed him that Blair had taken off for the afternoon to go mountain biking. She surprised him, however, when she added that Blair was only working three or four days a week on a new part-time work program intended to save the County money.

No partner to inspire him, he headed back, resisting the urge to stop at Claxon's for a drink. With all the emotions, one more Jack and Coke would surely nudge him off the edge. He'd end up dialing a number he had long ago written on the back of the HMO card he carried in his wallet. He was not ready either to talk to Rachel or to learn she had moved completely out of reach. Thick dark clouds from the ocean pushed inland. All alone, he drove south.

Fifty-One

One of the bags Jordan carried knocked the Judas painting off center as he traversed the stairs to the second floor apartment. Inside he looked and listened, but there was no sign of The Man. Jordan grabbed a heavily perspiring bottle of Coors Light from one of the plastic grocery bags and twisted off the cap. After refreshing himself with the less-than-frosty brew, he unpacked the supplies, letting the strange day sink in. The bushman's story had really affected him. Who could take so many lives, innocent lives, so coldly? So brutally. Let alone a cop. Maybe the bushman was wrong about that part. But somebody killed those people. He paged through the day's *Los Angeles Times* but found no reference to the investigation of the five people killed at the high school. Plenty of other tragedies though.

The phone rang. Jordan's mom calling to see how he was making out. He told her he was a little overwhelmed by Los Angeles and his job, but that he loved it. He didn't like being so far from home. She asked about Stanley, and Jordan told her he was still having a hard time with his father's death, but enjoying his newfound wealth. She was surprised that Mr. Reid had money to leave his son. She had heard the money was all spent on hospital costs. Towards the end of the conversation, Jordan confessed that he and Kendall were no longer boyfriend-girlfriend. Though she adored Kendall, his Mother resisted an urge to try to sell Jordan on making up with her. She would only repeat her oft stated advice: "With real love, you can't force it and you can't deny it."

After exchanging 'I love you's' and receiving a promise of a visit by Mary Jane Stowic, he was about to say "Goodbye" when his call waiting beeped in. Kendall. "I'll call you back, Mom."

"That's alright sweetheart, I'll call you on Sunday." Click.

"Hello, I'm calling because I have temporarily lost my mind and I'm waiting for the guys with a big net to arrive and take me to my padded cell."

"K?"

"Yes, it's me."

"I'm really glad you called. And don't worry; you'd look cute in a white jacket with lots of buckles."

"You don't think I'm a danger to myself and others?"

"Only when you are driving. Actually, you are kinda nuts for caring about me; I haven't exactly been your Cary Grant these days."

"More like my Freddie Kruger."

"Your own personal nightmare. What else could a girl want?"

"Michael Meyers, maybe."

"How about some honesty. Honestly, K, I miss you."

"You don't have to say that 'cause I called."

"You're right, I don't miss you. I just miss your cooking. I've always had a thing for blackened waffles."

"They're a delicacy in some countries."

"How have you been K?"

Jordan got filled in, filled her in, including the bushman's story, and kept on talking, calling her back after 30 minutes to even out the phone bills. It was clear to them both that some things never change.

Fifty-Two

It was well after 5:30 p.m. at 2020 Beverly Boulevard in the City of Los Angeles, a bland, two-story concrete building on a hilly street, otherwise known as the Los Angeles County Sheriff's Crime Laboratory. A young criminalist in the narcotics section stayed late yet again to, as he put it to his supervisor who had already gone home, "get ahead in the game." The supervisor was impressed with his last hire before the freeze went into effect. Stanley Reid was the go-getter in his section. After he finished the work that was due tomorrow, he completed some other tests and reports that were not needed until next week. He didn't want to arouse suspicion about his late evenings. Then he started on his extra-curricular activity that would get him well ahead in the game financially.

Earlier in the day he had surveyed the narcotics safe for cocaine to cut. Although it was much easier to cut powder cocaine than rock, there was not enough powder there today to make the work worthwhile. He had decided, instead, to cut several large rocks of cocaine. Since purity was virtually never tested, nobody would miss what he took. Only weight and whether or not the substance contained cocaine mattered in court. On nights like this when he stayed late, he would bring plenty of a white powdery substance called "procaine." Available to the general public, procaine was an excellent and inexpensive cutting agent that could restore the original weight to the cocaine Stan left behind in the safe.

Hotchie came into Stan's office and assured him nobody was around, then left to take up his lookout position in the hallway with his broom, dustpan and gray plastic trash can on wheels. Stan locked himself in his office with a Bunsen burner, a scale, a pan with a little water, a jar, procaine and the rocks. He weighed the original product, then placed it in the jar and put the jar into the pan. He melted

173

it down on the Bunsen burner, cut it with the procaine, and then re-hardened it, completing the "rocking" process. The rocks he put back into the safe now contained mostly procaine, but maintained their original weight. Those he took for himself were pure Columbian profit.

Stan no longer contemplated the laws and ethics he shattered each time he fired up the Bunsen late in the day. Nor had he continued to consider the victims, like the impoverished women enslaved by his product, or their babies born addicts.

Instead he did like Rhory, the criminalist who had enlisted him. He focused on the money.

"Those stupid crackheads are gonna get dope anyway," Rhory argued to Stan convincingly. "Why should the Columbians and the gangbangers be the ones that get rich? We deserve it more than they do." And that's exactly the thing that hooked Stanley Reid. He *deserved* it. Life had dealt him too many hands without even a pair of twos. It was time for him to get his.

In addition to the money, Stan found he enjoyed the excitement that came with his work for the operation. He knew there were others besides Rhory and Hotchie who took part, but he was never told who they were. He only knew that there was a guy referred to as the "street liaison," a man people feared.

Stan completed the melting and rocking processes several times, satisfied that his evening was going to be prosperous for himself and his co-conspirators. There were two other criminalists in other parts of the building staying late to perform forensic tests. Each was oblivious to the operation. A woman in the firearms identification section worked on a time-consuming gun shot residue test to determine whether a suspect had fired or had held a recently-fired weapon. A different kind of test was being conducted on the floor above Stan by a second criminalist. It would be the result of this test that would change Stanley Reid's life forever.

Fifty-Three

Out on the balcony, recharged by both the confirmation of self that Kendall always provided, along with his pure love for her, he reclined and began rereading *On the Road*. Jordan loved the way Kerouac invented his own dictionary to suit his descriptive stream of consciousness. He dreamed of someday writing like Kerouac. Jordan related to the story of best friendship. Dean Moriarty was Stanley Reid. Instead of traveling across the country in the back of strangers' pickup trucks with cheap wine and transients, they had their apartment in L.A.

The bushman's tale, what to do about the 2,000 miles between him and Kendall, and the Courtney situation- all on the back burner. As Sal Paradise, he sat, pausing to glance out at the Hollywood sign and hit his beer between chapters. At the moment, life was good.

When he heard the volume of his 10,000 Maniacs CD reach the "call the cops!" decibel level, he knew his roommate was home. The Tag Heuer watch his mom bought him a few birthdays back indicated that it was just after eight. Stan opened the screen door and came onto the balcony.

"What're you up to L.A.D.A. dude?"

"Just a coldie and a good read. What about you? How's the drug business?"

"What? Oh, work is work. I've been trying to impress my boss at the lab. Gotta get an 'exceeds expectations' on my promotability evaluation, which is coming up at the end of the month. He gets a hard-on when he sees me staying late."

"Sounds like you got your stuff together best friend."

"Well, someone's gotta keep a roof over your head. And as long as you're living under my roof, you will live by my rules. No more reading. Time to go out and party our asses off. I talked to Jennifer today, and she said she and Corney wanna meet us at the Shelter, late night. Jennifer hasn't even seen my new wheels yet. I may have to ask you and Courtney to take a cab home so we can christen the Porsche."

"Stan-man, that's tempting, but I'm not really up for seeing them tonight."

"You mean you're not really up for seeing *her* tonight. Jennifer told me you've been blowing Courtney off. Didn't return her calls. What's up with that? You missing the Chicago princess?"

"It's kinda complicated actually. I talked to Kendall tonight and I miss her more than you used to miss Melinda Roberson when she didn't come to your basketball games."

"Wow. That sounds pretty serious. But Stow, you know you can't hold on to her right now. You gotta enjoy your life. She's so far away; she might as well live in Tibet. Until she moves out here.. .carpe babiem, buddy."

"What?"

"Carpe babiem. Seize the babes!"

"You know what I'm really up for tonight?"

"You want to go through all your pictures of you and Kendall and narrate them for me?"

"No. I want to go to the bar with my best friend. Just he and I, a couple of beers, some quality conversation. That's what I feel like right now. What do you say?"

"Would you be too upset if this bar you are proposing contained multiple tables covered with green felt on which people knocked balls around with sticks?"

"Actually Stan-Man, I would insist on it."

"Then I know just the place."

Fifty-Four

Don Kartes became a fingerprint expert because he was asked to. Or, rather, begged to. He had worked for 15 years in the firearms identification unit. His real love was guns. And he was one of the best firearms experts in Southern California. Five years ago, the administration was pressed to staff a position in the fingerprint unit amidst a hiring freeze. Don was chosen because they knew he would make the transition easily, given his intelligence and unyielding drive toward perfection. They chose correctly. It didn't take him long to get to the top of the game. For over four years, he was the latent print guru of Los Angeles County, quickly becoming supervisor of the unit.

His daughter was turning six today, but he was still at work because of some backed up requests, including one from a gang detective named Ramirez. On the "date needed" section of the request form, it stated "yesterday." Don was told it was related to the Snow murders, a media case, which meant he actually would have to try to get it done yesterday.

There were two items booked by Detective Ramirez, each individually packaged in a zip-lock baggie. There was a Rolling Rock beer can and a store receipt which didn't have any information on it save the amounts involved in the sale. Don knew the chances of finding a usable print on any one item is not very good; on a single, small piece of paper, there was almost no chance. He believed that, if he was going to get a print, it would come off the beer can. He sprayed the can, heated it up, and waited for a print to develop. Nothing. Next item. He'd never found a print on paper before, but read about the FBI finding usable prints on envelopes containing mail bombs. This gave him some hope. He wished the receipt was of thicker paper, which might increase his chances. He picked it up with a tool resembling extra-long tweezers and dipped it into a beaker filled with a chemical called ninhydrin. Then he delicately placed the receipt into the humifier. The heat and moisture of the humifier caused the ninhydrin to react chemically. Any prints on the paper would then become visible to the naked eye. A few minutes passed. Again, nothing. Don made notes on a pad of paper which would eventually become his final report. Just as he was jotting down his negative findings, something surprised him. He glanced at the paper under the humifier and saw a feint image of what he guessed might be a thumb, smack dab in the center of the small rectangle of paper. "Bingo," he said out loud. As he watched the latent print evolve, he hoped it didn't belong to some passerby who touched the receipt before the police got there, or a rookie cop who collected the evidence like they do on bad T.V. police dramas. He hoped that Detective Ramirez had just gotten lucky.

Fifty-Five

Stan steered his red 911 Cabriolet, top down, into the small, over-crowded parking lot next to Barney's, causing not a few people to stare. A male couple strolling down La Cienega towards a romantic dinner were among the admirers. Stan knew Pedro the valet by name, and gave him a $5 bill for his troubles. Inside, Barney's was packed. Jordan and Stan waited at the bar with a pitcher of beer until a table opened up. Not a linen tablecloth in the house, Barney's ambience consisted of a few fast food chain tables surrounding a like number of pool tables. The waiters and waitresses dressed 50's to match the stuff on the wall, and beer and chili cheese fries were the order of the day. The *Los Angeles Times* review taped to the wall dubbed Barney's the "hippest dive" in Hollywood.

Jordan told Stan about his day. Stan was very interested in what the bushman had told him and asked many questions.

"It sounds like you have your first high profile case on your hands."

"It's not exactly my case. In my case this guy was a robbery victim. But that trial isn't going to start as scheduled. I got a message today that the defense attorney is engaged in a long trial and will be getting a continuance."

"Don't worry, there's plenty of crime in this town, you'll probably have ten trials before the robbery case goes to trial."

"Meanwhile, I've got to get hold of the investigating officer and get him in touch with this man from the bush."

The hostess mumbled "Stan, your table's ready" over a fuzzy intercom.

Stan followed her and Jordan to the table before excusing himself.

"I forgot to call Jennifer to cancel. Be right back." Jordan noticed Stan's mood become serious. He figured he must really be worried about pissing off his gorgeous and not-so-shy girlfriend.

A few minutes passed before Stan returned. After speaking with his boss, Rhory, Stan felt better. Rhory assured him that he was just getting paranoid. Nothing to worry about. Carefree returned to Stan's face.

"So Stow, you seemed like you needed to talk about something, so let's do. What's the topic?"

"I'll take love life for 200 Alex."

"All right, let me start by asking you this: do you love anybody?"

"I love one girl. The other one is a lot of fun, and only a freeway away. By the way, to get to Santa Monica, which exit do you take from 10?"

"Stow, if you're gonna be an Angelino, you're gonna have to learn the proper way to address our holy freeways. Always use the word 'the' in front of the number. So, in your case, you would take *the* 10 and exit on 3rd Street."

"Don't you mean exit on *the* Third Street."

"No, because Third Street is not a freeway."

"Oh. This is a weird city Stan-Man. And I love it here."

"Enough of that bullshit Stow, what's going on with the Chicago princess?"

"Well, I talked to her tonight. She called."

"The girl's determined, you gotta give it to her."

"It felt great to talk to her."

"Do you think you just want her because she isn't here right now? In other words, if she were also living off *the* 10, would you get off on her exit or take *the* 10 to *the* 405 to go to Courtney's?"

"That's a good question. But an easy one. Let me elaborate."

And so their conversation went, just as it did so many times before, each the other's sounding board and anchor in sanity and what is right. Jordan once wrote a poem about their friendship. In it, they drove down the same road of life together, though in different cars. Whenever one wanted to confer about life's scenery or ask for a direction, he needed only check with the other. In the poem, Jordan didn't see the fork in the road.

Fifty-Six

The fingerprint guru was on a roll, and not about to stop. After photographing the latent print that appeared on the receipt, he called his daughter to wish her a happy birthday. He told her he wouldn't be coming home until after she was asleep. He promised to wake her up and kiss her goodnight. What placated her was his promise to take her to Disneyland tomorrow night to make it up to her. The excitement in her voice erased his guilt. His wife was a tougher customer.

"Don, I should've known better than to marry a type 'A' personality." She told him, with a tone of pure resentment. "Just don't let it happen again this month."

"It won't honey," he promised, as he had done before.

A perfectionist workaholic, Don Kartes was the atypical County employee.

After developing and enlarging the black and white photograph of the print, he sat down in front of two computer screens which were only inches apart. He scanned the photograph, and it appeared in green on the screen to his left. He took a specially measured piece of tracing paper and placed it over the screen. Then, like a careful kindergartner, he traced the image. He was surprised how many points of comparison he had. This was a clean print. If the finger was in the system, he'd find it. After tracing the print, he shrunk it down on the copier to

2" x 2" and placed it on a card. He scanned the image from the card and it appeared on the screen to his right. It was this computer and its attached modem that would tap into the national system.

The name of the system that provides this invaluable function is "A.F.I.S." which stands for Automated Fingerprint Identification

System. It is a nation-wide computer base that includes all people arrested throughout the country on felony charges. California's data base is called "Cal. I.D.," and consists of two data bases, one in Sacramento, and another in Los Angeles. If Don pushed the transmit key, the small image from the card would travel via the phone lines to the national computer in Washington, the California Department of Justice computer in Sacramento, and the Los Angeles County data base in the building. The Los Angeles data base includes all people arrested in Los Angles County for *any* offense, including misdemeanors. It also contains the fingerprints of all law enforcement officers, including Deputy Sheriffs, L.A.P.D. Officers, Deputy District Attorneys, and criminalists. This is to eliminate law enforcement personnel prints from the possible matches when looking for a suspect from a crime scene.

When the image from the receipt was properly imputed, Don hit the transmit key. He punched it like a Vegas gambler throwing dice onto a high stakes craps table. "Keyboard disabled" appeared on the screen, indicating that the print was on its way over the phone lines. Thirty seconds passed like thirty minutes. Suddenly, "Inquiry Successful" flashed on the screen.

"Got him!" he yelled to the office walls.

Elated, he wished that he could continue the investigation beyond this small but important part. Don had entertained the idea of becoming a police officer several years ago. His wife exercised her veto power, knowing that she would probably have to file for divorce on the ground of abandonment if he threw himself into cop work.

He leaned back in his chair and waited for the match to appear.

"Stanley Alan Reid, Application for Employment, Los Angeles County Sheriff, Scientific Services Bureau" it read. Below this was a date of birth and an address in West Los Angeles.

He didn't know this person, but the name rang a vague bell.

"Damn!" He screamed in defeat, slamming his hand down on the desk, which caused the computer screen to jiggle.

Though he had Detective Ramirez's pager number, he wasn't going to bother him at this hour for bad news. Dejected, he left for home believing he had wasted precious time with his daughter on her birthday that he'd never recapture.

Another contaminated crime scene, he thought. When are people going to learn not to touch? A fellow criminalist should have known better.

Fifty-Seven

Long Beach. He awoke early, thankful he did not stop at Claxon's or head back to the Aftershock. The sun seeped in through the tiny apartment's slit windows. It was 6:30 a.m. Reinvigorated by the possibility of a witness, he moved briskly. His shower took less than three minutes. He didn't need to hold his head under the hot water to message out the previous evening's demons, and the sound of the water smashing to the fiberglass below his feet did not aggravate any condition. After shaving, he put on jeans, a t-shirt and his green windbreaker with 'Sheriff' written in large yellow letters across the back. The only other thing he did before he headed down to his company car was splash himself with Old Spice cologne. He felt like smelling good when he made all of his unplanned appointments. Early morning is the detective's best friend. Burglars, robbers, rapists, child molesters, killers, gangbangers, you name it, are night people. Up all night burgling, robbing, raping, molesting, killing and banging. And they need their sleep. Most don't open their beady little eyes before noon.

He blew across Compton like cool, sharp winds rarely do. Opening gates, banging on metal doors, fending off angry dogs, pepper spraying one, he rung in the morning looking for answers. He woke up Kansas Street Crips, Southside Playboys, cluckheads, crack whores, and even paid a visit to G-Dog, who still wasn't talking. It was before 8:30, so he knew it was too early to visit the D.A.'s Office. He drove around looking for his last resort, Lucky. He found the hype sleeping under a blanket in a vacant lot by the railroad tracks on Alameda. JJ carefully lifted his cover, trying not to inadvertently prick himself with a hidden heroin needle. Eliciting some semi-coherent but utterly useless sentence fragments from Lucky, still under the influence of his last fix, he moved on, without any more information than when he began his blitzkrieg. Yet, this morning, he was undaunted.

Fifty-Eight

Down the 710 instead of the 110, south to the 91 to the Alameda exit, Jordan found a faster, more direct route to the courthouse. It cut off several uncomfortable blocks during which, as he viewed the people standing in vacant lots and outside boarded up and burned-out buildings, his reflection in the rear view mirror worried him. A white, upper class, educated young man, he perceived himself an outsider and a target. He had been a minority a few times before, like when he went grocery shopping at the Safeway in Washington, D.C. It was more comfortable there. He felt danger here.

Parking, grabbing briefcase, crossing concrete square towards employee entrance, the smell of fresh-cut morning grass lingering, he walked. It was 8:30. The crowd was light, as Fridays usually were. Monday mornings looked like a1980's 'Who' concert by comparison. Ascending to floor seven, exiting, "Mornin' Baby" and "T.G.I.F. Yoli" exchanged, he checked his mail slot. Jordan pulled out a copy of the morning's *Los Angeles Times*. Nothing in the front page section about the Snow murders. In the 'Metro' section he read an interview with the Auntie of Leticia Snow and sister of the slain mother. In it she committed to quitting her job to start a support group for Los Angeles families that have lost loved ones in drive-bys. She told the interviewer she would call her organization "D.B.F." to stand for "Drive Bye Families." She was careful to spell 'bye' for the reporter. Adamantly, she pledged to not let the killing of Leticia and Katherine be in vain. They died for a reason. The cliché struck Jordan hard, and he saw it a desperate attempt, invariably made by those who experience senseless tragedy, to find meaning in the world and its events. He believed people die in vain every day. While Jordan agreed that we should learn lessons from the deaths of others whenever possible, he did not presume the existence of a grand plan. Reading on, he moved past the cliché. He was struck by the emotion that drenched each answer given. Missing was the posturing and the bullshit that annoyed him in most interviews. This woman experienced a great loss. She was pissed at the world. But she was going to do as Jordan was doing. She was going to try to change it.

Fridays were notorious skip days for the D.A.'s, P.D.'s, Judges and staff who occupied the Compton courthouse. But Jim Connelly's secretary was logged onto her computer by 8:30 a.m. sharp, dutifully preparing the jury trial statistics that would be sent downtown when August ran out of court days. So far, it had been a good month for the People, give or take a few 'not guilty's.' As Head Deputy of Compton, Connelly's reputation downtown depended not only on guilty verdicts, but on the volume of trials. Too few trials and some Assistant D.A. to Salsman would be on Jim's ass, accusing him of "giving away the courthouse" with an overabundance of plea bargains. If it happened too often, the transfer would come. Jim's predecessor had been "offered" the Deputy-in-Charge position of the Lancaster branch office. Given that Lancaster was at the northern end of Los Angeles County, it was the equivalent of a Cold War KGB agent being banished to Siberia. Head Deputies in the Office were keenly aware of the potential of receiving "highway therapy" and the accompanying loss in status that would befall them if they did not fall in line.

Instead of calling, JJ decided to go to the D.A.'s Office. He knew the way to Jim Connelly's Office. Though he had been told that Connelly wasn't going to be back until Monday, he hoped that he could find out something from someone. He waited to talk to the secretary, trying to place her face. In front of him was a young man that JJ instantly made for a first year Deputy D.A. He had the look. Naiveté in a new suit, powered by an over anxiousness to fight crime. He liked the eagerness, but didn't appreciate the unearned cockiness which likely came with the package. He preferred dealing with the veterans in the Office, the dinosaurs, the battle-hardened warriors. Since he'd been handling homicides, he became accustomed to them. Uncharacteristically for JJ, he caught himself checking out the young man's clothing. Black and White glen plaid suit, crisp white shirt, black leather suspenders and fancy tie, probably Armani. "Fashion plate," thought JJ, though his standard for fashion was nothing recognized by any GQ writer, living or dead.

It was just before nine, and Jordan was in his boss's office turning in a form which detailed his trial results. Not guilty. The two words were difficult to write on the form. Jordan wasn't used to losing. He made some small talk with Sumi then placed the single sheet into the metal bin on her desk. He turned and bumped into a man in a green police raid jacket. The man's hair seemed a shade blacker than jet, tempered by sprinkles of gray.

"Oh, excuse me."

"My fault," said JJ.

"May I help you?" asked Sumi.

"Sumi, good morning."

"Good morning."

"Remember me? JJ Ramirez, O.S.S. I saw you a lot when you worked downtown in complaints."

"That's right. It's been a long time. How have you been?"

"I've been alright. I think I'll be doing better if you can help me find the prosecutor who found a witness on my Snow murder investigation. Jim called about it yesterday."

Walking away, Jordan caught the words 'Snow murder' and back tracked.

"Are you the investigating officer on the Snow murder case?"

JJ turned around to face the rookie DDA. "Yes. Are you the DA who found a witness?"

"I am. Hi, I'm Jordan Stowic." He presented his hand. "I have a robbery victim who is also a witness on your case."

JJ smiled through the handshake, feeling very good about this. Suddenly, fresh-out-of-law-school DDAs were his favorite kind.

In Jordan's office, the barren walls painted a yellowish crème, peeling in several places; Jordan relayed a brief version of the bushman's story. The authenticity hit JJ right away. Leticia Snow was on the swing when she was murdered. One of the facts withheld from public in order to confirm an authentic witness like Raymond.

"Do you have a last name on Raymond?"

"Sorry, no."

"Where does he live?"

"Well, that's the weird thing. He doesn't really have an address, per se."

"He's a street person?"

"Not exactly. Do you know where the Atlantic Street Bridge crosses the L.A. River? He lives in a bush there."

"Are you talking about Compton or unincorporated L.A. County?"

"I'm not sure. Listen; do you want me to show you? I was just over there."

"I'm parked right outside on Acacia. Let's go."

Fifty-Nine

A cloud of dust struggled through the thick air, kicked up by the jolting stop of the Caprice. "This is where I parked last time," Jordan confessed, despite the blatant 'Private Property- Trespassers Will Be Prosecuted' sign posted at the entrance to the dirt road. JJ was in a great mood today, and was enjoying that he was clicking with his new DDA friend who may have found the break he was looking for. He produced a pen and note pad, pretending it to be a traffic ticket book.

"You parked here? You realize I am going to have to issue you a ticket, don't you? Spell your name for me please."

"S-A-L-S-M-A-N. Jordan Salsman. I think you know my Dad."

"Yes I do. When you see him, please tell him to stop losing all the big, high-profile cases."

"I've told him that. But he said he would have won them if only we had a competent Sheriff's Department. What do you think he meant by that?"

JJ laughed. He was feeling looser than he had since Alex's death.

"Ok Boy Friday, show me where Mr. Caruso's tree house is."

Jordan led JJ in the direction of the fully furnished shrubbery and hope filled the air, mixed with smog, and then the smell of rotting fish. The L.A. River was drier than graveyard dirt, and the gray weeds that lined the concrete embankment waived in windy intervals, impatient for rainfall.

Following the railway, they neared the bushman's habitat. The fishy smell grew more intense. Fifty feet from the incredible houseplant, Jordan stopped in his tracks. His nose crinkled from the shock of the unusually pungent odor. JJ's didn't. Wrinkle lines overtook his forehead. He'd smelled this scent many times before. It was the scent of death. Hopefully, a stray dog or cat or some kind of animal, decomposing in the heat.

As they closed in, Jordan asked, "What are we smelling?"

The detective recognized the chrome revolver resting in the dirt by the right hand of the sheet-paper white male corpse. It was clearly a .357 Smith and Wesson. JJ performed the mandatory pulse check on the wrists of the two corpses, checking the man's then the woman's. Both had bullet wounds to their heads. The young DDA kept his distance, watching the detective survey the grisly scene.

"Jordan, come over here."

Apart from the funeral home viewings of two grandparents and a boy from his high school who died in a car accident under the influence of too much peach Schnapps, Jordan hadn't lots of experience with dead bodies.

"Is this man your robbery victim?" JJ asked, with a slightly hopeful tone, as if there could be another man living in a bush further down the tracks who was alive and well, ready to give him the answers he needed.

Jordan walked up to the feet of Raymond, which were almost touching the feet of Ramona.

"Man," said Jordan, shaking his head in disbelief, "I just talked to them yesterday."

"Breath through your mouth son," JJ advised, seeing that Jordan was turning green.

JJ made an inspection of the scene without contaminating it, noticing that the serial number on the Smith and Wesson revolver had been filed off. Nothing unusual about that, since many handguns bought and sold on the street were stolen, their identifying marks removed several owners ago.

"What happened to them?" Asked Jordan.

"Looks like a murder-suicide initiated by your witness."

He wasn't the experienced detective, and maybe he had read too many murder mysteries, but Jordan disagreed.

"I don't think so. You should have seen this guy yesterday. Once he told me what he saw at the high school, he seemed so relieved. He was eager to help us get the killer. Why would he kill himself and his wife the next day?"

"Oh, yeah, I guess you would expect more from a man who makes his home in vegetation." JJ was pissed. Saying not another word, Jordan walked upwind of the bodies to avoid breathing in any more death.

JJ walked back to his car and called in the bodies. He stayed next to his unmarked and met the other officers, whom he walked to the crime scene.

There were two patrol units and the homicide detectives on call. The officers taking over the crime scene were his colleagues, Detective Sue Colby and her partner, Detective Paul Munday. At the crime scene, JJ saw that on Raymond's wrists there were thin abrasions, consistent with suspects whom he had seen handcuffed too tightly. He saw a similar but more feint mark on Ramona's left wrist. For some reason, he kept these observations to himself.

JJ stayed at the scene until he believed that there were no suicides by the bush. The wrist marks from possible handcuffs, Raymond coincidently witnessing the five murders in a case that evaded JJ, and, most importantly, the additional physical evidence he noticed. He recognized tattooing (gun powder burns in the skin) around both Raymond's and Ramona's head wounds. He had seen several sets of dead husbands and wives before. Classic murder-suicides. And each time, the husband had shot the wife at a distance of at least a foot and a half or more before turning the gun on himself. As any coroner can tell you, at a foot and a half, you no longer have tattooing. Finally, there was the gut feeling of a Deputy D.A. fresh out of law school. Surprisingly, he did not resist letting Jordan's opinion be the pebble that tipped the scales. It appeared that someone had handcuffed them both and shot them at point blank range. A double-murder. But JJ hadn't the time to investigate another murder case, so he called out for Jordan, who was sitting on a large rock by the railroad tracks, looking away from but still attempting to make sense of the gruesome scenery.

"Counselor, time to get you back to court."

"Yeah, I should probably get going." Jordan was still dazed by their discovery, and the hours that passed did not bring him out of his zone.

In the Caprice, hauling ass back to Compton courthouse, a vibrating pager took JJ's eyes off the road. He dialed in the page on his cell phone. Someone at the crime lab answered.

"Latent prints. Kartes."

Sixty

"Rhory, why the fuck are we here?" asked the young criminalist.

"We needed to confer. And this is one of my favorite spots."

The Malibu surf crashed again.

"I was in the middle of something I have to get out of the way so I can cut up some profit for us tonight. I got major car payments to worry about."

"It's important Stanley."

"It fucking better be."

"Stanley, aren't *we* getting quite the attitude. Might I direct your attention to your sad and pathetic existence before I brought you into the operation? Or if that doesn't catch your eye, maybe you'd like the street liaison to visit you?"

"You don't have to threaten me. Just talk."

"Looks like we've got a problem. Your hometown buddy has a big mouth."

"I called you last night. You said everything was fine."

"It's not. He stumbled across something he shouldn't have. It puts us all in jeopardy."

"What the hell are you talking about?"

"Your friend from Michigan found a witness who can implicate us. Fortunately, that witness is no longer a threat. But your friend may be."

"Jordan didn't see anything. He can't testify to what somebody told him. That's hearsay, and you know it!"

"Loose ends," said Rhory, shaking his head. "The street liaison advises me that we cannot tolerate them. And I agree."

The gravity of the situation became even more apparent when Rhory forced a black Sig Sauer, 9mm, semi-automatic into the reluctant hand of Stanley Reid.

Sixty-One

"Don, this is JJ Ramirez returning your page."

"How are you JJ?"

"Not too good. What do you have for me?"

"Nothing really. Good news and bad news, I guess. The good news is I found a comparable print on that paper receipt you submitted on the Snow case."

JJ had to submit the evidence found at Alex's murder scene under the Snow case name and number. He couldn't very well let it be known that the L.A. County Sheriff's Crime Lab was working on a case from another jurisdiction.

"The bad news is that the print came back to one of our criminalists. I checked him out, a relatively new guy. Must've been absent the week they taught him not to touch anything at a crime scene. Name's Stanley Reid. Reid has always worked in our chemical analysis unit, so I'm not really clear what he was doing at your murder scene. Unless of course he was filling in for firearms or lab techs."

"That's probably what it was," JJ lied. "That's too bad. But thank you for getting back to me so quickly." JJ knew that nobody from the Los Angeles County Sheriff's Crime Lab would have been at the Yorba Linda canyon crime scene, which is part of Orange County, let alone a forensic chemist like Reid. While he trusted Kartes, he felt the need to jealously guard every potential break in his case. Of course, Stan Reid could've happened by the area anytime before or after Alex was killed.

"One more thing, Don."

"Sure."

"Do you have a home address for this guy?"

"You know where to find him at our lab. Why the heck do you need his home address?" thought Don Kartes. But he obliged the

194

Detective anyway, figuring he probably had to cover his ass because of the case's high profile nature.

"Hold on, I have it here on the printout. Yes, that's 1105 Wooster Avenue, apartment number two, Los Angeles."

Jordan stared out the window as burned-out, riot-ravaged Compton whizzed by. He was oblivious to the information being supplied on the other end of the Detective's cell phone.

JJ memorized the address and thanked Don Kartes. He wouldn't have been as confident that he might have a real lead if not for the words of the now hospitalized Blood gang member: "It's like you guys are in it now."

A pile of smashed black plastic and wires, out of which protruded something resembling a horn, was all that remained in the spot where Jordan's Jeep Wrangler was once docked. It was, after all, 7:30 p.m. at the Compton Courthouse parking structure, a cement menace famous for hosting mangled and disappearing autos, crimes which sometimes occurred right under the noses of the underpaid rent-a-cops posted at the entrance and on the 3rd floor where jurors parked.

"Where are you?" JJ asked, as his Caprice scraped bottom on the uneven entrance ramp.

"I thought I parked right over there next to the stairs."

The first floor was abandoned. JJ drove Jordan through the entire parking structure to make sure that he hadn't misplaced his car, and then returned to inspect the debris.

"You have a car alarm?"

"Yeah, and as you can see, I had the really good kind."

"Too bad the guy who borrowed your car didn't know that."

Jordan smiled and shook his head, trying to keep his sense of humor, despite the theft of his law school graduation present, the car he'd always wanted. He picked up the remains of the alarm, carefully, with two fingers.

"What are you going to do with that?" JJ asked.

"Give it to the police for fingerprinting," Jordan answered.

"Good luck," JJ said, not trying to hide his amusement. "It's hard enough to get Compton P.D. to print a murder weapon."

Jordan walked to a metal trash can and deposited the evidence, taking the detective's cue.

"I'll give you a ride home," JJ surprised himself by offering, given his desire to get rid of the DDA and start pursuing his new lead. But he felt that discovering two murdered people and then having his car stolen was more than anyone deserved in a single day. Having to hitchhike in Compton might just be too much for his young friend.

"Don't I have to report this?" asked Jordan.

"I'll call it in for you. I'll tell Compton P.D. to call you at home for your info. No sense in wasting your time standing here waiting for them to send someone. Especially at this hour. Unless of course you want to get to know some of the parking structure people a little more personally."

"No, that's ok. Besides, it would be pretty embarrassing for the guy who stole my Jeep, should he decide to return to the scene of his crime."

"That's very considerate of you. Where to, Jordan?"

"Do you know where Robertson hits Olympic?"

"No problem. I was going that way anyway."

"Oh, do you live in West Los Angeles or Beverly Hills?" Jordan asked.

"Neither. I grew up in Compton. Then I moved down to Long Beach to be closer to a friend of mine who owns a bar there. Of course, some shit happened in-between that's too long and boring to go into."

"Why are you going towards my neck of the woods?"

"Just a little errand," said JJ, being polite, yet evasive enough to dissuade the DDA from any more questions. He was guarding his clues like a parent guards presents on Christmas Eve. If someone else knew about his lead, he reasoned, the lead could vanish.

As they exited the 10 Freeway, the air was crystal clear, unusual for a warm August night, and the Hollywood Hills came into perfect view before JJ turned right on Wooster from northbound Robertson Boulevard.

JJ didn't miss the coincidence.

"What's the address?" he inquired.

"1105 Wooster," said Jordan.

This was getting quite surreal for JJ, and the muscles in his neck began to tense up as they did when he made an arrest of a wanted felon.

"Right here is fine, JJ."

"You live upstairs?"

"Yeah, apartment number two, second floor. I live with my best friend from my hometown in Michigan. He's also in law enforcement, sort of."

Jordan reached into the back of the detective car, locating his briefcase, while the detective noticed that there were no lights on in the upstairs of the building.

"Would I know him?" he asked through his window to Jordan, who was now standing and offering his hand for a thank you shake.

"Actually, you might. He's a criminalist from your crime lab. His name's Stan Reid."

"Can't say it rings a bell," JJ lied.

"Anyway. Thanks for the ride Detective."

"No problem. And don't worry about your car, I'll phone it in and a Compton P.D. detective will call you at work sometime. Don't hold your breath though. You got insurance, right?"

"Yes. I think it's under my Dad's insurance."

"You'll be ok. And I'll let you know about the investigation on your robbery victim and his wife."

"You're probably a lot more upset about it than anyone," Jordan said. "You were counting on Raymond to testify on your murder case."

"That's alright. You never know when an investigation might go in another direction. I'm not giving up."

"Well, good luck. Thanks again."

When JJ began to drive off, he had already figured out how he was going to get into Stanley Reid's apartment later in the evening.

Sixty-Two

The answering machine was blinking, and the little red light beamed off the walls in the darkened apartment. Jordan locked the door behind him and flipped on the machine.

"Jordan, it's me. I miss you. It's been two days and it feels like two years. Let's go clubbing tonight. Better yet, let's have a midnight picnic. I hear the beach is beautiful at night. Call me."

Clearly the most forward Courtney had been about her feelings, Jordan thought, while surprising himself by feeling nothing. He wouldn't call her tonight.

The second message was for his roommate.

"Hi Stanley, its Hotchie. Call me at the lab as soon as it is feasible. Thank you very much."

JJ had dinner at the Fat Burger on La Cienega. He ordered a double Fatburger with cheese and bacon to go. He would need his strength for later. He would worry about his arteries some other day. He went to the office to pass a few hours before he would return to the Wooster Street apartment to confront Reid.

Stan hadn't done coke in a few years and not since his acting days at San Diego State. The lines he did tonight clouded his mind much more than eased it. The cocaine was supposed to intensify his brain's natural happy chemical, dopamine, leaving him feeling euphoric and invincible. Instead, he felt jumpy and zoned out. In an amped-up haze he walked up the stairs, past the Judas painting, clutching the gun shakily. The firearm seemed to grow heavier as he neared the door. The blue steel felt cold in his left hand, and a chill traveled from the gun, up his arm, to the center of his chest. He stood outside the door waiting for something, he didn't know what. He imagined his heart encased in ice, several inches thick. He shivered. He had to go inside and do it before his whole body was immobilized. He unlocked the door and entered. On the couch was his best friend, lulled to sleep on a commercial during the Tonight Show. Jordan was still in his suit. Stan noticed his tie. That god damned *tie!*

Stan tried to remember Rhory's plan but his brain was not cooperating. Instead he began to see a scene. Himself running out of the junior high auditorium embarrassed. Standing alone, sobbing loudly, every expulsion of breath visible in the frozen winter air. He was just literally laughed out of the school where the awards banquet was being held. Instead of celebrating his basketball achievements, he was being ridiculed by his fellow 7th graders for his dress. They were jealous of his abilities and needed to put him down. That god damned tie! His Dad made him wear it. His life was going downhill at an early age. Suddenly, he was not alone.

"Dude, I think that tie's pretty classy," said a vaguely familiar voice. "In fact, I think those idiots are just pissed because they only know how to wear clip-ons."

"Look. I don't really want to talk about it," said a 12-year-old Stanley Reid, turning away so he could wipe the tears that leaked down his face.

"It's ok bud. I've been there. But you just gotta not care what people like that think. Besides, you can kick all of our asses on the court, and they even know it."

The young Stan turned back to Jordan and managed a smile. Then, the first of many handshakes.

He came back to the present when he saw and felt the gun in his hand. Stan pushed the magazine release and examined the clip. It contained 12 full metal jacket cartridges. He jammed the clip back in, causing a loud click that should have woken Jordan. When it didn't, he bent his left arm toward the target, aimed the gun unsteadily and squeezed off a single shot. The sound was louder than Stan had imagined, more of a cannon than a gun. "My God, what have I done?" Stan thought, as he began to go numb.

JJ had seen the suspect return home. He was about to execute his plan to get into the apartment by pretending to need more information about Jordan's stolen car, when he heard a gunshot. "Shit!" he said out of his open car window.

He prudently called in his location and requested LAPD Wilshire Division Patrol to respond. He went in with his Beretta nine millimeter drawn.

Jordan had just met Kendall's train at Washington's Union Station. He was in his second year at Georgetown Law Center. She walked gracefully down the ramp from the passenger car and he watched in excited anticipation. He blew her a kiss as she got closer. She returned it, almost causing the duffle bag to slide off her petite shoulder. In his mind he was going over the plan for the evening. They would start off at the Plutocrat with cold Rolling Rocks, catching up, and then head off to a cute new Italian restaurant on Pennsylvania Avenue that would later become their favorite. As she was inches from him, he heard a loud metal bang that sounded like two trains colliding on the platform. When he awoke he saw blood. Lots of it. On the floor was his best friend, Stan the Man.

"Jesus Christ! Stan!"

Stan was unconscious. Jordan saw a gun lying on the ground.

The door came flying open with force that cracked the frame and broke off the bottom hinge. The detective drew down on the two young men.

"Down on the ground, spread your hands out!" he screamed. Jordan complied. Stan still didn't move.

"Is there anyone else in this apartment?"

"No," said Jordan, "My friend needs help now!"

After clearing and securing the Sig, then frisking Jordan, JJ checked Stan's pulse with a panicked urgency, hoping that he was not about to see yet another lead disappear.

Jordan got up, ignoring the Detective's orders, and went to the phone.

Before hanging up, he told the 911 operator: "Please hurry! He's my best friend."

Sixty-Three

Jordan awoke on a gray waiting room couch. The first two minutes coming to he thanked God for his being alive, as he often did. Awake to face another day on earth, the tribute belonged to the force that created him. That, along with prayers at bedside most nights, comprised the only remaining vestiges of religion practiced by Jordan Stowic. It was more important to him to live out the idea of goodness. Suddenly, it registered to Jordan that he had spent the night at Cedars Sinai. "Stan!" he screamed within the confines of his head. He sprang up, then calmed and slowed a bit when he remembered that the physician in the ER had stated the ultimate life and death cliché just before Jordan retired for the night to the waiting room. "Your friend was lucky," Doctor Marsellee declared. "The bullet really just grazed his skull." Jordan had to laugh out loud as he made his way to the emergency reception desk. Ever since the car accident, that lucky bastard's aim had been off. Maybe he missed on purpose. Jordan contemplated the work cut out for him. He had never spoken to anyone who had unsuccessfully attempted suicide, let alone his best friend. He would delve into the *why* and get to the bottom of it. But first things first.

"I want to see Stanley Reid," Jordan proclaimed in a hoarse 8 a.m. voice.

"I'm sorry, to see Mr. Reid, you have to be cleared by the police."

"Who are you talking about? Stanley Reid. R-E-I-D."

"I know who he is, sir. But I have to follow the orders of the Sheriff's Department. In fact, the Detective in charge is right over there."

Jordan followed the pointing finger of the receptionist and saw JJ in the corner of an adjacent waiting room, paging through some document, clutching a steaming Styrofoam cup in his left hand. He walked over to the cop.

202 · R. Michael Bullotta

"JJ is Stanley Reid in the custody of the police or is the reception-ist over there stealing stuff from the medicine closet with the good drugs?"

JJ took his eyes away from the firearms report before he could read the criminalist's conclusion as to the caliber of the bullets recov-ered from Alex's lifeless body.

"Jordan, your friend's just being held for questioning. He's not necessarily a suspect." JJ was lying.

"What do you mean, 'not necessarily?'?" Jordan asked, as if cross-examining Dwayne Simms.

After mellowing out the protective DDA by providing the dis-information that Stan Reid merely needed to be questioned about his work at the crime lab because it might be relevant to a homi-cide investigation, JJ settled back into a waiting room chair to fin-ish reading the firearms report. It stated that two of the expended bullets recovered from Alex's body could be conclusively said to be nine millimeter projectiles. The other two bullets were too dam-aged to say with certainty what their caliber was, but they had the same general rifling characteristics as the other two, indicating that a single gun was used. JJ then re-examined the property report from Alex's murder scene. As he did so, a light went off in his head. He had been such a fucking idiot! Why hadn't this occurred to him sooner? The thing that had given him a weird feeling a few days ago when he read the same report at the Sheriff's station in Santa Ana was one simple fact. There were no casings recovered. NO CAS-INGS! None recovered from the scene. No expended or live bullets either. That fact by itself was unremarkable. What was so disturbing and inexplicable was how Lieutenant Flores knew that 9mm bullets killed Alex at a time when the only evidence of that was still lodged in the boy's chest!

The long hallway smelled of the antiseptic that shined its hard white floors. Jordan walked with a swiveling head until he located room 432 and saw Stan's last name written on one of the two plastic name plates posted outside the door. The oxygen tubes resting under each of Stan's nostrils and the i.v. attached to his forearm belied the doctor's declaration that all was well. "If he was ok, why does he need to be hooked up to all of this?" Jordan thought. Must be precautionary, the result of the successes of litigious legal weasels, creatures he knew he would never devolve into. Jordan looked at Stan, who lay slumbering, his lungs heaving in and out, rocking his long, thin torso. Jordan stared and contemplated. What was Stan thinking when he pulled the trigger last night? Why do it in front of him? It must have been the classic cry for help. He didn't really want to kill himself. But a cry for help with what? He seemed so happy. His job was going well. His girlfriend was smokin' hot. He just bought a red Porsche 911 convertible for Christ's sake. *Why?*

Jordan hadn't called his family last night because Stan was pronounced ok, and he thought his best friend would not want them to know. For the same reasons, he had not called Kendall. And since Stan's father's death, Stan had no close family left to notify in case of emergency. Jordan was it.

Sixty-Four

The nurse came out and signaled the detective as she had been told to do. The patient was awake. JJ walked briskly to Stanley Reid's room with his note pad in his hand. In the pocket of his green raid jacket was concealed a micro-cassette recorder which he would secretly activate when he reached for his pen, if and when Reid began making useful statements.

"Excuse me Jordan; I need to talk to your buddy for a minute if you don't mind."

Jordan Stowic, who had only been allowed five minutes with his best friend, didn't really know what to think. Stan told him it was an accident. He had the gun because the lab was located in a rough area of Korea town, and he often had to transport narcotics. Stan said he didn't mention the gun to Jordan because he didn't have a permit and didn't want to involve him in what was technically a misdemeanor. He said he was trying to remove the clip and unload the gun when it went off. He wasn't thinking about his finger touching the trigger because he thought the safety was on.

"Stan, you up to talking to the Detective here?"

"Sure, I'm fine Stow." But Stanley Reid didn't look fine. He became whiter, like a human chameleon, practically blending in with the white hospital bed sheets to avoid detection. Confrontation was imminent.

Sixty-Five

The air-conditioner at the Sheriff's crime lab was laboring under an especially warm August morning sun. The narcotics section, not in one of the renovated areas of the building and still relying on the old cooling system, began to feel uncomfortably hot. The place was deserted as was par for Saturdays, except for the cleaning crew.

The Pakistani man felt his underarms perspiring as he dropped the specially marked manila envelopes into his mobile trash can, wheeling it to the service elevator where he would take the product to his awaiting pickup truck, then out to the streets for distribution. He had seen another janitor here this morning, so he felt even more uptight than usual. The elevator opened and he recoiled when he saw the tanned man with slick-backed hair.

"Oh! You scared me sir."

"Hotchie, you've got to stop being so jumpy. Control. That's what's making us so rich. We are in control."

"I will work on that sir. What are you doing here this morning? Do you not trust me to pick up the envelopes and get them to the purchaser?"

"Hotchie, if I didn't trust you, you wouldn't be here."

"I know sir. Thank you."

"Did you find a purchaser for the envelopes?"

"Yes, or course. Eighth Street Piru Bloods."

"Are you sure they can handle such a big buy?"

"Oh, yes sir, I have sold even larger envelopes to my contact there before."

"Ok. Good luck then. And remember, the word is 'control.'"

"I will remember. Thank you for your faith in me sir."

When the elevator doors kissed, and his underling was out of sight, he sighed a nervous sigh. When he gave the pep talk to Hotchie, he could have been giving it to himself. Rhory was concerned that things were getting out of control. He needed to reassert himself. The phone number for the man he required was in his electronic organizer which Rhory usually carried with him, but had inadvertently left at his office. There was a problem that needed to be addressed. Stanley Reid had let him down badly. There was a living witness. A witness who also happened to be a prosecutor! The witness needed to be disposed of. And Stanley would have to pay for his disloyalty. Control would be gained once again. In his office he located his organizer and quickly found the man's contact numbers. The man had consistently handled problems and kept the organization on track. He was a master at gaining control. The man was known as the street liaison.

Sixty-Six

With the prosecutor out of the room, JJ commenced questioning by discussing what Stan called 'the accident.' Stan attempted to repeat, with as much consistency as he could muster, the story he had told Jordan. JJ had Stan show him how the accidental discharge occurred, using JJ's unloaded service weapon.

"Why did you point the gun at your head when you were removing the magazine?" JJ asked.

"Just careless. I was tired and I guess I wasn't really thinking."

JJ had known fellow officers (even one firearms expert) who accidently shot themselves. The scenario was plausible, but it was time to confront him with the fingerprint.

"I know where you live, obviously, in West L.A. Tell me, do you spend much time in Orange County?"

"Why do you ask?"

"I'm a detective, I'm curious about things, so humor me."

This was getting weird, and Stan could feel himself stiffening up with worry. His mouth became dry and he took a sip from a plastic cup of water by his bedside.

"OK. Once in awhile I go to the beach in Huntington. I have a buddy that used to live in the rebuilt downtown area there. And, except for Disneyland, which I think is Orange County, that's it."

"Ever been to Yorba Linda?"

"Not that I remember, no. I've heard of it, you know, Nixon's library is there, that's about it. Couldn't even tell you where it is."

"Stan, I guess I should just cut to the chase here. I'm investigating a murder that occurred in Yorba Linda. I found your fingerprints at the crime scene. I need you to tell me what you were doing there."

To Stan, the Detective was now talking in slow motion, his lips painstakingly moving to accommodate each syllable. Upon hearing the word 'murder' his heart began racing. He was short of breath, so he instinctively started inhaling on lighting-quick intervals. The feeling in his brain was so dizzying that he had missed the word 'fingerprint.'

It appeared to JJ that Stan was hyperventilating, so he pushed the nurse call button.

"I don't know anything about any murder in Yorba Linda." Stan managed to get out while sucking in air like the room contained the last stash of oxygen on earth.

"I know you were there, your fingerprints were at the scene. Surely a criminalist like yourself can appreciate the power of finger-"

"Fingerprints?" Stan interrupted. His arms visibly trembled as he sat back in his bed in order to regain control.

The nurse came into the room and the interrogation stopped. After helping Stan control his breathing and regain his composure somewhat, she said, "Detective, Mr. Reid needs to rest now. I'd appreciate it if you would let him do that."

JJ smiled and nodded to her. "I was just about done anyway." He looked deeply into the frightened hazel eyes of Stanley Reid and added, "For right now." JJ had a dozen more questions for the suspect, but happily left the room with the knowledge that he had latched on to a guilty man.

Sixty-Seven

Rhory clicked out of his telephone conversation and reclined in a cushy deck chair positioned so that he could survey his multi-million dollar Bel Air view. He looked over and past his glistening swimming pool and his neglected tennis court, focusing on a smoggy Century City skyline. Now that he had spoken to the street liaison and everything would be taken care of, the smog that settled on the top of the skyline seemed more like a decoration than an obstruction. Rhory was in control again. Additional deaths annoyed him a little, but the success of the operation, the money, his life as he knew it, demanded no less. Too bad. He had grown a little attached, at least for Rhory Callum, to Stanley. He enjoyed the sense of accomplishment he felt when he initially won Stanley over. Stanley had resisted, clinging to the ideas that his parents (like Rhory's own parents) had programmed into him. But eventually Stanley learned to embrace the life that drug trafficking provided. It was quite a shame that Stanley had to betray him in the end over some old friend. The beauty of the plan, though, was that it was so appealing, there would be many more willing to do their parts to receive a generous cut of the endless profit.

Selling drugs was the only life Rhory had known since his parents had cut him off from their millions fifteen years earlier. He wanted to but couldn't go back to them. If only Rhory's father would trust him again. Maybe even understand him. He could share in his success and welcome Rhory back. But that wasn't going to happen. The end of his father's love Rhory could trace to the death of his 12-year-old brother David. In a freak occurrence, Rhory and his younger brother were pretending to box on the deck of their Scottsdale, Arizona home. When Rhory connected, David went backwards and over the railing, splitting his scull on the concrete 20 feet below. Given his son's overly aggressive and sometimes violent personality, Rhory's father didn't believe it was a complete accident. His mother had few original thoughts over the years and didn't find one on this topic. Rhory was banished at age 18. The only thing he remembered from his last conversation with his father was his father telling him how lucky he was that the Arizona state's attorney chose not to prosecute him for murder.

He checked his $25,000 gold Rolex. It was almost noon. He needed to meet someone and have lunch. A women outside of his business who would satisfy certain needs. First, a line to get him in the mood.

Sixty-Eight

JJ shot east to downtown, checking into the office on a Saturday, something this detective did with some frequency. On his desk he relieved himself of a heavy evidence envelope containing the 9mm Sig Sauer that Stanley Reid used to almost blow his brains out. JJ saw five messages from Friday afternoon. One from the D.A., Salsman, requesting an update on the Snow investigation, and one from Sheriff Collins, with no elaboration, though none was necessary. They were on his ass to produce, but JJ didn't mind as much now, since he was back in the game.

He dialed the phone, though not to return any of his messages. A woman answered, clearly annoyed when she realized that it was a business call for her husband. She debated hanging up, knowing her plans with her husband would be ruined if she did not. Don Kartes came on the line. JJ figured him to be the only criminalist he could easily coax to work on a Saturday with no overtime.

"Don, its JJ from O.S.S."

"JJ, what can I do for you?"

"Listen, I hate to bother you on the weekend, but I need something on the Snow case that can't wait."

"Do you have a question about the print I made?"

"No, actually, I need you to do a test fire comparison for me. Are you busy today?"

"Well, I was going to take my daughter to the zoo. I missed her birthday on Thursday, so I've been making it up to her. Last night I took her to Disneyland."

"I understand if you can't do it, but, quite frankly Don, you're the only person I know who cares enough about his work to come in on a weekend."

JJ knew how to play Don Kartes.

"Yes, I guess you and I have that in common. My wife thinks it's a sickness.

JJ laughed genuinely and added, "Sounds like my ex. "

"You do realize it's been a while since I've done any firearms testing."

"Don, you were the best. Probably still are. If anyone can get back up on the horse-"

"Enough, enough!" Don interrupted, "Stop kissing my butt. I'll meet you at the lab at 1:30."

Before leaving, JJ left a message for Flores on his home answering machine and also paged him to JJ's cell phone. He had a single burning question for the Lieutenant.

Sixty-Nine

Jordan was on the payphone in the waiting room when the nurse approached him.

"Your friend Stan would like to see you," he said.

"OK. Thank you."

"K, I have to go, Stan wants me."

Jordan had filled Kendall in. He related Stan's story. Kendall was just happy Stan was alright.

"I know he'll bounce back, he always does," she said. Kendall was a glass half-full, 20% chance of no showers at all, kind of gal, which is why she and Jordan were on the same page most times.

"Give Stan a kiss from me," she said.

"I will, doll. You know I'm always looking for an excuse."

"A kiss to you too sweetie," she added, though gentle laughter.

"I love you cupcake," he ended, feeling better about her than he had since things had changed between them.

Jordan entered Stan's room. In the bed against a window, Stan was sitting up, his poise regained.

"You rang?"

"Stow, we have to talk. There's some messed up shit happening that I don't even understand."

"What's going on? What did the detective want to talk to you about?"

"A murder."

"What's the deal? Did you have some information on a murder that you helped to investigate?"

"No." Stan paused for several seconds, staring at his friend until Jordan's face stretched with concern. Stan finally said, "You're not gonna believe this."

"What?"

"They think I had something to do with committing a murder."

"As in, like, you *killed* somebody?"

Stan only shrugged and turned his palms toward the ceiling, as if he were meditating.

"Get the fuck out of here! Why would they think that?"

"He said they have evidence."

"What evidence?" Jordan scowled.

"A fingerprint . . . *my* fingerprint."

"Where? Where did they find your fingerprint?"

"At the scene, I guess."

Jordan sat down in a chair at the foot of the bed and took in a gigantic breath.

"And you don't know what this is about?"

"No, I honestly don't. I give you my word."

The phrase, 'I give you my word,' evolved over the years since 7th grade, as a way to separate out the put-ons and the bullshit. It was a sin against their friendship to give your word to a lie. Your word was your bond and your bond was everything.

"OK," said Jordan, preparing a game plan. "Don't say anything to anyone until you get an attorney. Obviously, I can't represent you, but I can try to find you the best lawyer in L.A."

"Yeah, maybe we can hire the lawyers that got off the Rodney King cops."

"This isn't funny pal. I don't know how this is happening, but someone somewhere is making a big mistake, and we have to deal with this."

"Thanks Stow. I can't tell you what it means that you're here for me."

Stan extended his hand and they did their signature shake.

"Always will be. They got the wrong guy. I mean, besides doin' some drugs during your thespian psychedelic phase in San Diego, you haven't even committed an infraction."

"I didn't kill anybody," Stan said, resolutely.

Seventy

Before heading down Beverly Boulevard to the crime lab, JJ drove up the Pasadena Freeway to Dodger Stadium to pick up three box seat tickets behind home plate. When he got to the crime lab, Don Kartes was already there, sitting with perfect posture, refreshing himself on lab guidelines for firearms comparisons.

"Here, make it up to your daughter for missing the zoo," said JJ, handing Don the tickets. "And if your wife likes baseball, maybe she'll even forgive you your sickness."

"You didn't have to do that. You know I don't mind coming in."

"That's exactly why I wanted to do it," said JJ.

"Well then, thank you. So, what do we got here?"

"We have four coroner bullets, two of which are probably adequate for comparison, and we got a gun," JJ said, handing Don Kartes two envelopes sealed with red evidence tape.

Don used a scissors to cut open the envelope across the red tape, and he removed the black gun.

"Sig Sauer. The bad guys are getting better taste. Must have been a drug dealer or someone with some dough-ray-me, huh?"

"Probably."

"Ok, let me get some 9mm cartridges and we'll squeeze off a few rounds for comparison."

While JJ waited for Don to finish the test fire, he made a call. The watch commander had some disappointing news. Lieutenant Flores was on a week off, vacationing at his fishing cabin at Lundy Lake in the Sierra Nevada Mountains. Though Flores' cabin was stocked with all of the essentials for fly fishing, including a beer fridge, it purposely lacked a telephone, making it an authentic escape. JJ left an urgent message on Flores' voicemail; in the unlikely event he'd check it on vacation.

Twenty minutes passed before Don came back in the room and said, "Five lands and grooves with a right twist. Matching firing pin impressions. Detective, you've got your murder weapon."

Seventy-One

Jordan spent the rest of the morning at the apartment trying to contact criminal defense attorneys for Stan. It was Saturday, and none of the lawyers the California State Bar referral operator suggested answered their telephones. He had left messages for all of them and waited phone-side nursing a glass of cranberry juice. The phone finally rang.

"Hello?"

"Yes, hello. My name is Robbie Black, attorney at law. I understand you're looking to hire a defense attorney."

"I am. Thanks for calling. My name is Jordan Stowic."

"Let me tell you a little about myself. I have twenty years experience practicing criminal law in Los Angeles County. I spent my first five years with the D.A.'s Office and the last fifteen doing criminal defense. I win most of my cases. The others end in hung juries, which usually mean a favorable plea bargain offer by the prosecutor."

"Sounds great. Can we meet in person so I can explain the situation?"

"Sure. Let's see, my calendar is open today. The only thing is that my office is being painted this weekend. How about we meet somewhere, say, Claxon's Fish House. It's near El Matador Beach is in Malibu. Do you know it?"

"Yeah, I've passed it on the way to the beach."

"Well then, I'll meet you at Claxon's at, say, 12:30, if that works for you."

"That's fine. I'll see you there Mr. Black."

"Look forward to meeting you Jordan," he said, before ending with "bring your checkbook."

Seventy-Two

On the ride to the hospital to formally arrest Stan Reid, JJ's elation over finding the murder weapon gave way to feelings of extreme anger towards his suspect. This was the bastard who killed his adopted son! JJ wanted to beat the living hell out of him, and then string him up by his balls in public, only to be flogged to a slow, excruciating death. But a thought nagged him. Where was the motive? Why the hell would a dope analyst working at the crime lab want to kill a gang banger who was about to snitch on his homeboys? The evidence against Reid had mounted mightily – fingerprints at the crime scene and possession of the murder weapon – but the motive hole in the case was large enough to drive a semi through.

Seventy-Three

Jordan's hair blew wildly as he drove 70 miles per hour up the Pacific Coast Highway, top down, in Stan's red Cabriolet. He wanted to be on time for his meeting with the attorney who, hopefully, could help straighten out the mess that had enveloped his best friend. He drove past the Malibu civic center, then up the hills and canyons past Pepperdine University and The Colony (an exclusive, gated, beach-front neighborhood of the stars).

He failed to notice the large, dark American car approaching him on his right side until he heard and felt a loud crash and looked in its direction. He had been rammed hard! The Porsche crossed over into the southbound lanes and into oncoming traffic. A convertible BMW swerved to miss him, and Jordan wheeled hard to the right to prevent the Porsche from smashing head-on into the guard rail, the only thing between him and a rocky shoreline death 300 feet below. The Porsche spun out of control and smacked the guard rail anyway, sending it spinning back into the southbound lane. As he spun in the convertible, Jordan was sure that the car would eventually flip over and he would be decapitated. But it didn't. And he wasn't.

The car came to a dead stop with Jordan facing South in the southbound lane. Cars began slowly passing him on either side. He had the presence of mind to activate his hazard lights, and then he drove the wounded sports car to the shoulder. The door would not open, so he climbed out of the 911. He examined the damage on the right side of the car where he was sideswiped. He saw dark blue paint transfer there. He looked at the other side where he hit the guard rail and noticed that the left rear tire had blown. He walked to the guard rail and peered over the precipice. A close call indeed. He thanked God and didn't even care that the idiot driver who caused the accident was nowhere to be seen.

Seventy-Four

Sheriff Collins was debating which club would best extricate his ball from the fairway bunker while maximizing his distance on hole 14 of the Los Padrinos course in Downey when his caddy handed him his cell phone. Ramirez.

"JJ. Good news I hope."

This was one arrest that JJ would run by the brass before any wrists were cuffed. The Sheriff was uncomfortable with the identity and occupation of the suspect, and asked the obvious question. "Why the hell would Reid be involved in murdering your Snow witness?" JJ didn't have the motive. He could only promise he'd find it. The Sheriff agreed that there was too much evidence *not* to arrest Reid. What he might say after he was read his rights might fill in the gaps. The go-ahead was given.

JJ brought Detective Bracey and two patrol deputies with him to Cedars Sinai to arrest Reid. The floor nurse in charge explained to JJ that doctors would be releasing the patient from the hospital in the morning. JJ told her that Reid was now under formal arrest and in Sheriff's custody. A deputy would be stationed outside of Reid's hospital room. When the doctors gave the ok to release Reid, he would be taken to the Sheriff's Station for booking, then to the Los Angeles County Jail. With notifications and ass covering out of the way, it was time to arrest Alex's killer.

Seventy-Five

Jordan called Kendall from the emergency room waiting area of a small, Catholic hospital in Malibu canyons where the Adrian Dominca sisters worked; he had some time while he waited for the radiologist's take on several precautionary x-rays.

"Hey there, cupcake. I'm calling you from the hospital."

"Hi sweetie. How is Stan doing?"

"Well, actually, not all that well. But I'm at a different hospital. I'm alright, but I had a car accident."

"Are you hurt?"

"No, just a little sore. I wanted to get x-rays to be safe."

"What happened?"

"Well, I was driving to meet a criminal defense attorney to arrange for representation for Stan, when, all of the sudden –"

"Wait," she interrupted, "why does Stan need a criminal defense attorney?"

"God, it's crazy K, but Stan is being investigated for murder."

"No way. The only things he's ever killed are his own brain cells."

"I know. So, anyway, I'm driving through the winding canyons on the PCH when, out of nowhere, this car changes lanes and doesn't see me. I almost go flying off the cliff."

"Oh my God! Are you sure you are ok?"

"I'm fine. I can't say the same for the car."

"Who cares. You have insurance on your Jeep."

"It wasn't my Jeep. My Jeep was stolen. It was Stan's new Porsche."

"That's right. I forgot your Jeep was stolen. Stan has a Porsche?"

"Yeah. I thought I told you about it when we talked last. Maybe not. Kinda hard to keep up, isn't it?"

"Did the other guy in your accident get hurt?"

"I don't know. He hit and ran."

221

"Back to Stan, who are they saying he murdered?"

"I don't have any details because Stan doesn't know anything about it. K, here comes the radiologist to tell me I'm ok. I'll call you back."

"I'm coming out there."

"No, please don't K. Not yet. I have some things I have to focus on right now to help Stan."

"Ok. But promise me you will be safe."

"Always."

"And just say the word and I'm on a plane."

"I know."

Jordan received a clean bill from the radiologist, and then returned to the pay phone to call Robbie Black. An unfamiliar voice answered.

"Yes, may I speak to Robbie Black please?"

"Sorry, Mr. Black is out of the country for the next two weeks."

"That's impossible, I just spoke with him today, and we were supposed to meet in Malibu at 1:30."

"I don't know about that. This is just an answering service and I'm telling you what's on my screen. Mr. Black is supposed to be in Belize between August 18th and September 1st. I can give you the number of an attorney who is filling in for Mr. Black in his absence if you'd like."

"That's ok. Thanks anyway." Jordan hung up the payphone slowly, with a puzzled look. Did the person with whom he spoke say he was attorney Robbie Black or did Jordan just assume that was who it was? No, Jordan checked his list of attorneys with the name Robert Black circled and saw that he had written the notation 'Robbie' which is how the attorney referred to himself.

Perhaps it was the combined effect of the multitude of events that had hit him in rapid succession – discovering the dead bodies of the bushman and his wife, his Jeep being stolen, Stan shooting himself and then becoming the subject of a murder investigation – or maybe it was lingering shock from almost dying on the cliffs below the PCH; whatever the cause, Jordan's mind succumbed to a solitary, seemingly irrational thought. That car was *trying* to kill him!

Seventy-Six

It was a rare sight for a Blood like G-Dog to be seen walking on 43rd Street with an enemy from Four-Tray Gangster Crips. Released only hours earlier from MLK, he was taking a chance by kicking it with his cousin Q-tip. His cousin was a member of a rival gang and G-Dog was strolling through that rival's territory. Q-tip was aptly named for the spongy Afro that adorned his melon.

G-Dog had gone to some lengths to minimize the risks he was taking. The red laces he removed from his black leather high tops. And his black and red Nike warm up he traded for a pair of baggy blue jeans and a white t-shirt. Of course, the red tear tattoo under his eye remained.

It was a beautiful late-August Saturday afternoon. There were two small children playing in the street with a red playground ball, and a tall, wiry lady in her 30's sitting on her porch drinking a 22-ounce Pepsi, waiting for her curlers to work their magic. When the young men got close enough to the heavy female letter carrier, Q-tip flashed G-Dog the butt of his cheap, Lorcin .380 handgun that had been previously concealed in his waistband. G-Dog responded by lifting up his t-shirt to reveal that he too was strapped. A Smith & Wesson .22 revolver.

G-Dog's heart began to go to full sprint as he pulled his duce-duce completely out of his pants and said, "Yo cuz, this is it."

Enthusiastically, as if he had just accepted a challenge to a pickup game of hoops, Q-tip said, "Let's do her."

"Don't even reach for your mace, beee-atch!" G-Dog commanded.

The postal carrier spun around to the greeting of gun barrels pointed at her head and chest.

G-Dog continued, "If you don't want us to pop a cap in your big black ass, you'll give us your bag, along with your mother-fuckin' Arrow key."

223

She didn't hesitate for even a second. She handed over her brown leather mail bag, which had the mail pre-sorted by address. The cousins hoped that the pouch contained a jackpot of county checks, cash, and credit cards.

"Don't fuck with us bitch," Q-tip added, to put his personal stamp on the jacking.

She tried at first to remove the Arrow key from the ring that included her mail truck key and several other work keys, but her shaky hands betrayed her. Sensing G-Dog's impatience, she handed over the entire bunch.

The skinny woman in curlers saw the robbery from her porch, picked up her Pepsi, and went inside. She telephoned a neighbor to tell her what was going on. She didn't dare phone the police. She wanted absolutely no part of her neighborhood gang. She was well aware of the rules. You just don't snitch on gang members. It was bad for your health.

The children playing with the ball ran behind a large king palm and watched. This wasn't their first robbery either.

Tom O'Hare was a Los Angels Police Department patrol lifer. He had worked Newton Division patrol for ten of his last 14 years, never getting the bug to try for detective. He wouldn't trade the streets for a desk and his blues for a blazer and tie. Officer Tom, as he was known to the citizens of his patrol zone, was well-liked. Not only by the law-abiding citizens, but even among the gang bangers, pimps, hos, hypes, drunks, crackheads and homeless. He called most of them by their first names. And the well-liked Officer Tom always worked alone.

The community police officer turned left on 43rd from Hodge Avenue, saw the 211 in progress, and sprung out of his black and white just after it screamed to a stop. The suspects looked at Officer Tom with large eyes. They saw his gun pointed in their direction, tossed theirs, and ran like hell.

Officer Tom recognized one of the boys and knew where to find him, so he gave chase to the other boy. He thought he lost the unfamiliar kid when he saw old Benny Thomas on his stoop holding a brown bag covering cheap wine. With a dirty automobile mechanic's fingernail, Benny pointed to the back yard of his neighbor and winked at Officer Tom. Benny was certain that he had just bought himself a favor that he could redeem when future circumstances warranted.

When G-Dog saw the cop looking at him crouching behind the bush, trying to make invisible, he stood up and surrendered. He knew that, with his stomach freshly bandaged and tender, he would never make it over a fence that blocked his escape.

"Fuck!" yelled the captured prey.

All G-Dog had wanted to do was make some money so he could move out of his neighborhood where he was a pariah, and put some space between him and his treacherous 8th Street Pirus. He needed to escape his snitch jacket. His plan had ended as badly as it could have.

After cuffing and searching G-Dog, Officer Tom brought him to where the mail carrier was waiting with another patrol officer. A show-up was conducted. "Yeah, that's one of 'em. He's the main guy that did all the talking. Yeah, that's my Arrow key. It opens all the mail depositories in South Central."

On the way to Newton Station, Officer Tom began reciting from memory the Miranda warnings. G-Dog interrupted with, "Yeah, cop, I know my fucking rights. Did I jack that bitch? Whadda you think, Sherlock? The bitch said I did it, you found the fucking key in my pocket, don't even waste my time with this bullshit."

Officer Tom made a mental note of the volunteered confession for inclusion in his arrest report. All G-Dog could do now was worry about where he was going. County Jail. The worst place in the world. For a snitch like him, it could be a death sentence.

Seventy-Seven

"You are in a world of trouble, Stan Reid," JJ said, before announcing to him that he was under arrest for the murder of Alejandro Sandoval.

"Who?"

JJ didn't repeat Alex's name. He removed a card from his wallet and began reading Stan his Miranda rights. He made sure he got every word right. "You have the right to remain silent. Anything you say can and will be used against you in a court of law. You have the right to an attorney and to have him present before and during any questioning. If you cannot afford an attorney, one will be appointed for you without any cost to you."

Before JJ could confirm that Stan understood his rights, the arrestee interjected, indignant, "Excuse me, I have no idea who this Alejandro Santos is. I can tell you that I didn't kill anybody. But I'm not going to say anything else to you without my attorney."

Detective Bracey studied JJ's face for a reaction. Stone. JJ stated glibly, "Your choice. But you might be able to help yourself by talking. I'd sure like to know why you killed this young boy. I have some other questions too, like, in addition to leaving your fingerprints at the scene, you shot yourself with the same gun you used to kill Alejandro. What was that all about? And it's Sandoval, Alejandro Sandoval."

Stan reiterated that he wanted a lawyer. Then JJ and Bracey ceased interrogating Stan, as the Fifth Amendment to the United States Constitution required them to do. A Deputy Sheriff was posted outside Stan's hospital room, and the hospital staff was given strict instructions about what could and could not enter Stan's room. For instance, razors for shaving were prohibited. An electric shaver would be provided.

Stan's head swirled with questions. "Are they on to me and the operation? If so, why are they trying to trick me into admitting to some murder I didn't do? I know I was never at any murder scene, so my prints couldn't have been found there. But the murder weapon. Rhory. Stan used his hospital room phone.

"Rhory?"

"Stanley."

"What the hell is going on? The cops are saying that the gun you gave me was used to kill someone."

"Where are you Stanley?"

"In the hospital, but that's not important. Tell me where you got that gun that you gave me."

"I'm afraid I don't know what gun you're talking about Stanley. I never gave you a gun."

"What? Don't play dumb with me. Look, I'm sorry I couldn't do what you asked me to do. But that was insane. You can't ask someone to hurt their best friend. I just –"

"Whoa, stop right there. I never asked you to hurt anyone. Stanley, you've obviously received heavy medication in the hospital, because you are making absolutely no sense."

"Frustrated by his denials, Stan lost it. "Fuck you! You pompous, greasy-haired pile of shit! You're the one that's gonna go down the hardest for all of this. I didn't kill anybody, and you know it! But I can't say the same for you."

"Stanley, really. Let's speak again when you are well. Have a speedy recovery, and I'll see you when you return to work."

In a private waiting room, the two detectives had converged on a small radio receiver. The heard every word of the conversation from Stan's end of the telephone. They intentionally allowed the telephone to remain in the prisoner's room in the hope that he would place such a call. Bracey had planted a small transmitter on the underside of the bed frame while JJ was diverting Reid with accusations. Unfortunately, JJ did not have time to obtain a court-ordered wiretap that would have allowed the officers to listen in to both ends of the call.

"What do you think JJ?" Bracey asked, deferential to JJ's multiple decades of experience.

"Reid's dirty up to his eyeballs. I'm not sure what his role was, or why he'd be involved in Alex's murder. We gotta find out more about this Rhory character, as well as Reid. Do me a favor Brace, call my friend Suzie at Pacific Bell. See if you can get the number Reid dialed for Rhory. I'm going to have an overdue chat with Reid's best friend, the rookie Deputy D.A."

"I'm on it," said Bracey, enjoying his emersion into the thrill of the chase. Indeed, it was that very thrill that drew Bracey into the Academy and a life of mediocre pay, horrible hours and ridiculous risks to life and limb.

JJ made his way toward his car in the Cedars Sinai lot when he recognized the brazen, two-space parking style, then the profile of his old partner.

"Sergeant Davis, to what do I owe the pleasure of your cameo?"

"Guilt, I guess," said Blair. "I heard from the guys at OSS that you had a suspect in custody on Sniper's murder. Apparently someone who was on our team, a criminalist from the lab. Guy tried to off himself. Is all that true?"

"What's the matter? Getting a little bored arresting celebrity stalkers?"

"Well partner, at least you're not bitter. No, truth be told, my Saturday golf league fell through because they're holding a club tournament today."

"C'mon partner," JJ teased, "they don't allow brothers on the golf courses in Malibu."

"That may be. Of course, your people *are* allowed, so long as they're holding rakes or leaf blowers."

JJ smiled and said, "Touché," then presented his hand to his ex-partner for a solid embrace.

"I hear this Reid fellow's prints were found at the scene of Alex's murder."

"True. But it gets better. The gun Reid used to shoot himself is our murder weapon."

"Do you know why one of our chemists would want to kill Alex?"

"No. I feel that it has to fit in with Snow, but I have no clue how."

"Bizarre. What next?"

"I'm off to conduct a witness interview. Care to join me?"

"Why not. You drive."

Then the former partners and current buddies got into the same car, like old times, with JJ behind the wheel, as if nothing had changed.

Seventy-Eight

Once home, Jordan called Stan's hospital room. Stan told him of the latest development. He ended his brief description of his arrest with, "Looks like I'm gonna need that lawyer sooner rather than later."

"Unbelievable," said Jordan.

"I was told that I will be released from the hospital tomorrow morning and taken to jail for murder. How was *your* day?"

"I don't even want to add to your stress."

"Not possible."

"Ok, here goes. I was released from the hospital myself today."

"Are you ok?"

"Fine. Your Porsche, that's another story."

"Damn, Stow, the car doesn't matter. What happened?"

Jordan relayed the facts of the ill-fated drive up the PCH to meet the supposed attorney, being cut off, crashing into the guardrail, spinning in circles.

"What happened to the other guy that hit you?"

"He never stopped. But here's the weirdest thing. I called the attorney to explain that I had been in an accident and wanted to reschedule the meeting. But his answering service said that the attorney is out of the country and has *been* out of the country."

From Stan's end of the phone there was dead silence.

"Stan? You still with me?"

"I'm here. I'm just thinking."

"What?"

"I'm thinking that you and I need to have a talk. As soon as possible. Get over to the hospital."

"What is it?"

"Just get over here. And promise me one thing."

"What?"

"Until you and I talk, don't trust anyone, no matter who they are."

"Secret Agent Reid, would you care to elaborate, or shall I just wait for the encoded message to appear on my spy ring?"

"I'm not kidding. You need to come over here right now."

"Alright, just let me shower and change. I'll be over."

"No. Now."

"Alright. I'll call a cab."

"Stow, be safe. And don't trust *anyone*. I love you buddy."

Seventy-Nine

When Stan hung up, he stared at the ceiling. He felt a pain in the back of his throat, a pain he hadn't felt in many years. It was a warning that a dam was about to burst. And then it did. He was instantly awash in emotion. He began to cry. At first, the sobbing was barely audible. It soon grew intense, with sporadic noisy outbursts that tracked the breaths of his desperate lungs. It lasted a solid ten minutes. And it felt really good. A much needed catharsis. When he was through crying, he sat in his hospital bed with watery eyes and a clear head. Clearer than it had been since before his father's death. It occurred to him that he had never really cried over his dad. He had kept too much in for too long. Maybe he believed that if he didn't allow himself to *feel* the loss of his father, his only blood family on this earth, the loss would not be real. He felt it now. He felt other things too. He could see how far he had fallen. From making some money on the side for himself, money he deserved, money that his father never left him, to the point of endangering the life of his best friend in the world. Endangering? Hell, who was *he* kidding? He entered a room with a loaded gun and orders to *kill* his only remaining family. He was consoled by the fact that he didn't go through with it. He could never hurt Jordan. In fact, he could never hurt anyone, at least not directly. It wasn't in him. He was, however, acutely aware that, by putting that destructive white powder on the street, he was contributing to the pain of others. He hated who he had become. But now, in late August of 1992, on the eve of being jailed for murder, as he sat up in a hospital bed, he decided it was over. He would be himself again.

He watched the second hand make its torturous journey around the dial, spending quality time with each of the large numbers on the wall clock. Now, impervious to whatever would be his fate, he was anxious for Jordan's arrival. "Just get here," he kept repeating, as mantra, sometimes out loud. He had to tell his best friend everything so that Jordan could be protected from what was out there. His best friend's safety was critical if Stan were ever to return to the person he was.

Eighty

Jordan answered the knock at the door, expecting a cab driver but instead finding two cops.

"Jordan, we need to talk to you about your friend Stan Reid," JJ opened.

"Detective Ramirez, I've known Stan my whole life. He didn't kill anyone. You've got the wrong guy. So I don't think we have anything to talk about."

Blair intervened: "Son, we just want to ask you a few questions. If your friend is innocent like you say, he should have nothing to hide. And neither should you."

Jordan was offended by the implication and fired back, "Listen Detective, I don't know what law school you went to, but where I went; they taught us that you need probable cause to arrest someone for murder. All you have is a fingerprint. You don't know when it was made or how it got there. You have no motive because there's no connection between Stan Reid and your victim. So I don't know how you could possibly believe that your arrest was even legal."

"Jordan," JJ reasoned, playing his familiar good cop role, "why don't you go have a beer with us and we'll talk. You're a prosecutor and we're cops. We're all on the same side here. We just want to get to the truth. And I know you do too. If your guy didn't do this, we should be able to clear him. If he did do it, I don't think you would want to keep him from justice. Would you?"

"I have no information for you. You'd just be wasting your time."

"Why don't you let us be the judges of that son," Blair said.

"Jordan," JJ began, sensing an impasse, "we have more than just your buddy's fingerprint at the murder scene. The gun he used to shoot himself was forensically matched to the gun that killed the victim, Alejandro Sandoval." JJ made the uncharacteristic move for a cop of revealing his case. It was, however, a move he felt compelled to make. Reid probably already told him about the gun match anyway.

But he hadn't. Jordan was stunned. "Are you sure it's the same gun?" he asked, in a voice now stripped of its indignation.

"The ballistics are an exact match. Rifling and firing pin impressions. There is no doubt." JJ continued, "Why don't you come have a drink with us and talk. You have my word that I will level with you about the evidence we have against your friend if you promise to tell us what you know."

Jordan thought about it for a second then agreed. He knew that he had no incriminating evidence on Stan for them to extract. All that could come out of the meeting was a net gain of information about the investigation. He might learn something useful to Stan's defense. Perhaps he could even convince the officers that Stan didn't do it. It was worth a shot.

As he drove away with the cops, he remembered Stan's emphatic warning: Don't trust anyone.

Eighty-One

He could have chosen somewhere closer, but JJ wanted home court advantage when he interrogated his witness. For his wasn't the usual witness. The witness was smart. Not just the kind of smarts that JJ possessed from the interaction of common sense and the streets, but school smart. It slightly intimidated him that his witness had a law degree. And it intimidated him even more that his witness was a goddamn Deputy District Attorney. At least he was a rookie. In any event, he thought, he had to make this good.

Blair engaged the witness in small talk about how he was finding L.A. as JJ traversed the 5 Freeway south to the 710, the road that would lead them to within an exit of the interrogation spot. As usual, Broadway, the street that abutted the Aftershock, was peppered with cars, and the spaces that teased JJ weren't generous enough for anything more than a golf cart. He decided to park in the rear alley, blocking access to a trash dumpster that, he imagined, contained countless empty cans and bottles, as well as several ounces of discarded cheddar fish that had landed on the bar floor.

The unlikely threesome entered to an anthem by the Rolling Stones. Satisfaction. As in, "I can't get no!" For the past month, those had been JJ's thoughts exactly. How ironic, he thought, since he was about to get some. The lineup at the Aftershock was standard for Saturday night: Bill and Sylvia, a husband and wife in their late 50's who lived across the street and made their weekly "night-out" appearance; Loni's attractive cousin Doreen from Bellflower, who came down to Long Beach only when she was looking for a good time, but never stooping to find it with Buddy Cox, who, tonight, sat next to her and harassed her by bragging without credibility about being recruited by an "investment company" to open his own car dealership. Buddy was ignoring Mary O'Neil who sat on his other side, yelling in his ear, emphasizing her incoherent points with a hand clutching a vodka on the rocks that kept splashing out of its glass and onto Buddy's shoulder as if it were trying to help Mary get his attention. Loni was bent under the bar tapping a fresh beer keg.

As his group walked past the bar to a corner table, Jordan perused the smoky surroundings, acknowledging the seediness, yet feeling strangely cozy there. Jordan thought about using a pay-phone to call Stan, who might be worrying by now, but decided to wait until a break in the meeting with the detectives, when he might have something to report.

When Loni straightened up, she saw the folks at the corner table and prepared a margarita rocks and a Jack and Coke. She delivered Jack to JJ and the margarita to Blair with "Hey stranger, you still drinkin' this pussy drink?" Blair laughed, grabbed the drink and said, "It's good to see you again too, Surfer Girl." Blair had dubbed Loni "Surfer Girl" after enduring many of her stories about wild things she did as a teenager growing up in the surf culture of the South Bay. The name was especially amusing to Blair because Loni was not exactly what one thinks of when contemplating a surfer girl.

"I would say it's good to see you too, but I'm still in shock that I'm starin' at your mug. Thought you'd left for good for a better crowd in Malibu. You sure you feel like slummin' tonight? You know I'm all out of those bamboo umbrellas?"

"Surfer Girl, you know you're my favorite barkeep. Cocktails just don't taste as good anywhere else."

"Yeah, that's cause you're paying triple for 'em now at your swanky restaurants. But we're trying to keep up, here at the Aftershock. Did I tell you I have a new valet service? For a dollar a toothless bum will watch your car. For two bucks or a vodka on the rocks, the lovely Mary O'Neil will wash your windows. And for a fiver, you can get a blow job from a friendly crackhead on the corner. You can't get that kinda service in Malibu."

Blair and JJ laughed at Loni's hard humor, while Jordan smiled politely at the strange exchange, wondering if coming there was such a good idea.

"Hey, who's this hot young morsel of manhood?" asked Loni, pointing with her eyes at Jordan.

"Loni," said JJ, "I want you to meet our newest friend and a recent addition to the D.A.'s office, Deputy District Attorney Jordan Stowic."

"Nice to meet you Loni," said Jordan, reaching his hand out for a shake, but being tapped by Loni's closed fist instead.

"Don't spend too much time with these guys," Loni warned. "I did, and look what happened to me." Her crinkly face smiled, and she asked, "What're ya drinkin' kid?"

"A Coke would be great," said Jordan.

"One Jack Daniels and Coke, coming up," she said, ignoring Jordan's unusual request. Not wanting to offend his hostess or his self-described "new friends," Jordan didn't correct her.

"So, Detective Ramirez" Jordan opened, staring into the Detective's dark brown eyes that looked back at him with a relaxed, almost amused quality.

"JJ, Jordan. Call me JJ. I thought we got past formalities the other day."

"Alright. Tell me, JJ, if you wouldn't mind, why are you so convinced that my best friend is a murderer?"

"Cheddar fish?" asked JJ, sliding a small wooden bowl towards Jordan in a playful, transparent attempt to deflect Jordan's question.

Eighty-Two

"Where the hell is he?" said Stan, out loud but without any audience in his hospital room. He squeezed the television remote control in his right hand in a vain attempt to release his mounting tension. The battery cover on the remote popped off, and two triple "A" batteries danced on the hard, shining floor. Stan was worried for Jordan's safety. As each minute passed, he became more convinced that his own death was imminent. Now that he disobeyed a superior in the organization, he constituted a threat. They had tried to kill Jordan two times already, and Stan knew more than Jordan. Stan could bring them all down. He got out of his bed, walked to the door, and peered out to make sure that the Sheriff's Deputy was still posted outside. Reassuringly, he was. He then asked his captor, or rather, his protector, whether 'my attorney,' as he referred to Jordan, had tried to come to talk to him. The Deputy answered in the negative, and then went back to flirting with a red-haired nurse with a dynamite figure who enjoyed his attention so much she pretended to be reviewing a file at the nurse's station after her real task had been completed.

Clad in his county-issue janitor's uniform, Hotchie made his way down the hallway, cleaning the bathrooms and emptying waste cans in room after painstaking room, making sure he spent plenty of time in each one so as not to arouse suspicion when he got to the target's room. It might take longer than anticipated to carry out the plan. He noticed the cop leaning against the nurse's desk. The cop hardly noticed him. When he was only one room away from the target's, he thought he might be in trouble, as he felt a prick in his inner thigh while bending to empty some trash. He breathed out deeply in relief when he realized that his imagined doom was merely the car key in his pocket pressing his skin. Fortunately for him, it wasn't a prick by the syringe containing the virus, which rested in a different pocket. Strangely, the $10,000 he was promised for completion of this errand was not his primary motivating force, though it was a motive. More than money, Hotchie yearned for respect, and knew he would get his boss's and that of others in the organization, upon successfully completing the errand. Hotchie checked his watch, and then his pager to make sure it was still functioning. It was getting close to the time he would be paged, and the time he would have to deliver the injection.

The telephone in Stan's hospital room rang. Rhory.

"Stanley, it's me."

"Rhory, I thought you told me to go to hell."

"Listen, I'm sorry about our previous conversation, but I had to get off my phone so the cops couldn't trace the call and find me. I also had to check with our contact at the court to make sure there was no wiretap order issued to allow your phone calls to be monitored. I did that and, fortunately, there is nobody listening to your calls, at least not legally. Stanley, you can't blame me for being safe."

"No, I guess I can't," conceded Stan.

"Listen, I've decided to get you out. I'm also going to see to it that you are paid 500 K and that you are set you up in the non-extradition country of your choice."

"And why the hell would you want to do that?"

"I would like to say that it's because I care about you and appreciate your many contributions, but that's only part of it. The other part is that I want to go on with business as usual, and I don't want you getting in the way."

"So come get me out."

"This is the problem: we don't have the manpower to do it tonight. As usual, however, we have an excellent plan. It requires that we keep you in the hospital for another night so that we can get you out tomorrow night."

"And how the hell are you going to do that?"

"Hotchie will be by, and he's going to inject you with a slight virus. Nothing more serious than a 24-hour bug. But it will give you a good fever and make your doctor keep you there a little longer. I assure you that this virus was prescribed by a physician who is extremely brilliant, and extremely loyal to the organization. You must realize that we can get you out of the hospital easier than we can free you from prison, where my contacts tell me you are heading tomorrow. We have to act soon."

"Okay, I'll go with you, I'll disappear, and I won't say anything about you or the organization. But there's one condition that's non-negotiable."

"What's that?"

"You agree that you and the organization will not hurt my friend. He knows nothing anyway."

"Stanley, I promise that if you play ball with us, I will call off the dogs. No harm will come to your friend, the D.A. You have my word."

"Then I'm with you."

"Are you with me Stanley? Are you *really* with me?"

"I'm with you," said Stan, without hesitation.

"Excellent. So just be calm and Hotchie will be there in a few minutes."

Eighty-Three

It was almost 9:30 p.m., as G-Dog settled into his new home on Bauchet Street. More specifically, Los Angeles County Jail or "County," as it is called by its inhabitants. G-Dog was chillin' and relaxing because he hadn't run into anyone he knew. Not yet. He was relieved that he didn't know his cell mate, an older black male doing 180 days for under the influence. The junkie's name was Willie. G-Dog didn't mind that Willie smelled bad, or that he expelled numerous moans and groans while detoxing. He was just glad that his cell mate wasn't someone from his neighborhood who might have gotten word that he had been talking to the cops. A snitch jacket was G-Dog's worst fear. Once the residents of County got the word, G-Dog's days were numbered, as a homemade 'shank' would find its way into him in short order.

G-Dog thought about asking for a keep-away when he was booked into County. A keep-away is a status assigned to a prisoner, usually a high-profile one or one that is cooperating with the police, so that he is segregated from the rest of the population for his own safety. But, as G-Dog knew, a keep-away can be a double-edged sword. While the keep-away's purpose is to protect the prisoner, it can expose the prisoner to more harm by drawing attention to him. It was like wearing a neon sign that read, "I'm a Snitch! Come get me!" Also, keep-aways are kept in isolation, away from the general population, something G-Dog didn't want, as he figured he might be there for awhile doing his time for jacking the letter carrier, at least until he was transferred to state prison. Instead of requesting a keep-away, G-Dog gambled that his snitch jacket would not follow him into County. This was, he soon found out, a bet that he would lose.

Eighty-Four

Stan's mind was going 100 miles an hour when he hung up with Rhory. In grave danger, he located the emergency call button and jammed it hard with his thumb. A buzzer sounded and a light flashed at the nurse's station. A scrawny, curly-haired and freckled duty nurse stood up from her desk, examined the room number associated with the emergency, then shuffled past the Deputy and the red-haired nurse, making her way towards Stan's room. When the Deputy figured out what was going on, he followed her. She opened the door and saw Stanley Reid, alone in his room, lying on his back in his bed. She, then the Deputy, took stock of the situation in the room. It was eerily quiet as they both stood there staring at Stan's lifeless body.

Stan opened his eyes slowly, painfully, and said, "Is something wrong?" The visitors paused a moment as they realized their alarm was unfounded.

"Did you need something?" the curly-haired nurse finally asked.

"No, thanks. I'm ok." he said.

"Well, you must have rolled over onto your emergency call button," said the nurse, and she picked up the cord and its attachment and draped it over the bed's cold metal railing. She and the deputy walked out of the room.

During the thirty seconds it had taken for the freckled nurse to notice Stan's call for help and then travel down the hall to his room, a myriad of conflicting thoughts cracked into each other, like pool balls on the billiard table that was Stan's nervous mind. "I hope the cop and the nurses aren't in on it, or I'm dead." Stan knew the organization was born out of conspiracies far more elaborate than that. Then, "Why the hell would Rhory call to give me a heads up if Hotchie were on his way to kill me?" Then, "Oh, I guess he just thinks I'm stupid enough to let Hotchie inject me with cyanide." Later, "Maybe the organization is willing to pay to get rid of me. They definitely have the money to do it." Then Stan remembered his fingerprints at the murder scene and his gun being identified as the murder weapon. "Life in prison," he thought, "not much worse than death by cyanide poisoning." Then, "California has the death penalty, so I might get injected either way." Finally, a rhetorical question: "Am I better off facing a murder charge while I rot in jail, or going out on a limb for my freedom?" His decision was made. Stan, like G-Dog, was taking a big chance tonight.

G-Dog was sleeping lightly on the top bunk in his cell when he heard the rattle of keys coming down the corridor. The rattle got louder, and then began to fade as a buff Hispanic Deputy Sheriff passed his cell, on his way to punch out during a shift change. In the changing room, the Deputy dialed in the combination on the lock on his metal locker that held his civilian garb and his off-duty 9 mm Beretta. Before he could get his second leg out of his green polyester pants, his radio broadcast a call for backup.

"Altercation in D block, officer needs assistance," it crackled. He quickly put on his pants and shoes, and secured his gun in the locker, then ran towards D block, a wing that contained mostly black Blood gang members and other gang members who got along with Bloods.

When he got there, two deputies stood outside a cell, looking in at the fight, waiting passively for other deputies to arrive. The rule for deputies was simple: don't get involved until you have the numbers to intervene with minimal risk to your own safety. When the buff, Hispanic deputy and another deputy arrived, the cell was unlocked, and the pummeling was halted. Though there were many punches thrown by the two combatants, only a few punches had landed. One of the two Blood gang members had a bloody nose. The other looked unscathed. None of the deputies, or the noisy onlookers for that matter, were aware that the fight was staged.

As per procedure, the injured prisoner was taken to the infirmary where he would receive an examination by a jail doctor. The other prisoner was taken off to be placed in isolation for one day as punishment for what was his part in the fight. When the buff, Hispanic deputy asked around, he was not surprised when all of the prisoners in the line-of-sight of the evening's entertainment claimed that they didn't see anything. It was pure self-preservation to so claim, as any tattle-taling was met with extreme brutality from the prison population, and was tantamount to a snitch-jacket inside the unforgiving walls of County.

The injured Blood gang member was led down the long corridor of cells in D Block in the direction of the infirmary. While passing one of the cells along the way, he reached into his pocket and removed a folded piece of paper. He subtly tossed it into the cell.

Though G-Dog enjoyed several minutes of solid sleep after the yelling and screaming from down the corridor subsided, he was shaken into consciousness by his roommate who tugged on his t-shirt and repeated, "Wake up, man." G-Dog sat up and looked down at Willie who asked, "Is you name G-Dog, Dice or T-Money?"

G-Dog rubbed his hands through his coarse black curls and said, "Who the fuck wants to know?"

"'Cause if you is, yo ass is green-lighted."

"What the fuck you talkin' bout nigger?" he said, to buy time to process what he knew his roommate was telling him.

"Look for yo' self," said Willie, handing G-dog the wrinkled list.

G-dog took it and saw a white piece of lined paper with a drawing of a traffic light. Under the traffic light, there were three names. He swallowed hard as he saw the scrap of paper for what it was. A green light list. As in, there was a green light on the people on the list. This was a list of people who were designated to be killed. And not just killed someday, but killed while in jail. There were three names, and G-Dog's was the first one. Though only a pathetic scrap of paper, it had all the power of a judge's sentence of death. "Fuck!" he screamed out loud. Willie backed away from him, contemplating his own safety concerns as the cell mate of a homeboy who was green lighted. G-dog realized that someone from his neighborhood had seen him. "I'm a fuckin' dead man," he thought. With nothing to loose, he yelled for a deputy. He needed desperately to make a phone call.

Eighty-Five

With two Jack and Cokes down the hatch, and his mind buzzing pleasantly, Jordan listened as JJ took over the conversation from Blair. Jordan hoped that JJ was going to cut to the chase.

"Jordan, in addition to the Snow murder case, which you know about, I'm investigating the murder of Alejandro Sandoval, a young man who was found shot to death. Your buddy's fingerprint was found at the murder scene, and the gun that killed this young man was his 9mm. And, while we have enough evidence to convince a jury of his guilt, it is important for me, as a detective, and as a man, to find out the whole story. And that's where you come in. I need you to tell us what you know about Stanley Reid."

Jordan took a sip of Jack and Coke number three, leaned back in his chair, and said, "Detective, I'll tell you what I know about Stan Reid. Stan's the best guy I know. I know him as well as I know myself, and I know that Stan didn't kill anyone. He doesn't have it in him to do something even close to murder."

"We all have it in us," Blair said, "given the right set of circumstances. A war, self defense, jealousy. For some people, just drugs or money will do it. Shit, JJ and I worked a case one time where a crackhead stabbed a homeless man to death for two quarters. Fifty cents. Point five-zero dollars. The victim wouldn't give it up, so our guy stuck him in the heart and took the fucking coins. Not even enough money to get him high one time."

"Stupid," JJ added, nodding as he remembered the case. "Let me ask you this Jordan; is there any reason you know of why your friend Stan would want to hurt you?"

"Of course not. No. Why do you ask?"

"Oh, I'm just asking. There are a lot of questions that I will ask, many for no good reason except that I'm curious."

"Speaking of no good reason, is this all the evidence you have on Stan?" asked Jordan, not attempting to hide the true reason he agreed to abort his plans and join the Detectives for drinks.

"Isn't that enough?" said JJ.

Before Jordan could answer, JJ's pager beep-beeped and displayed a number he recognized as a number inside County Jail. It was followed by the numbers 911*8.

"I'll be right back," said JJ, popping up quickly, jarring the already unsteady table and spilling some of Blair's full margarita.

JJ walked up to the bar. Loni, seeing JJ make a gesture as if he was talking on a telephone that was his right hand, set the phone out for him and went on her way pouring more jet fuel for Buddy Cox. Before he dialed, JJ tried to remember who number 8 was. Since prisoners are not allowed to receive calls in jail, he had taught all of his informants that if they find themselves in custody and need to speak with him, they should page him to the watch commander's number, followed by a number JJ assigned to them. JJ was psyched as he remembered that 8 was for 8th Street Pirus. And informant number 8 was G-Dog.

When Hotchie saw the nurse and the cop run into Stan's room, he tossed the needle into a waste can. Hotchie's thoughts of fleeing were overtaken by his indefatigable desire to succeed at his mission. So he waited. A few seconds later, he saw the skinny nurse return to her station, with the cop following behind her. The cop was looking around in a manner that would have made Hotchie nervous if the cop hadn't asked the nurse, "Did you see where Kristy went?" Obviously, the cop had something on his mind other than stopping the injection.

Hotchie received an approving nod from the cop just before he slipped into Stan's hospital room with a fresh blue trash bag in his hand and the needle once again in his pocket. Stan was sitting up when Hotchie entered.

"Good evening Stanley," Hotchie whispered.

"Hotchie. They always give you the best jobs, don't they?" Said Stan, with more than a hint of sarcasm.

"I am sorry, but I do not have the time to talk. Please give me your arm."

Putting on his game face, Stan pushed back the short sleeve of his white hospital gown that was printed with an indiscernible blue pattern. Stan feared these to be his last few minutes of consciousness, and felt his body begin to quiver from an epicenter deep inside of him. He could feel the left side of his face becoming numb from hyperventilation.

"Do not worry, Stanley," said Hotchie, giving the needle a light squeeze to expel any remaining air from the plastic syringe. Some of the liquid containing the bacteria squirted into the air and landed on the floor, as if it were Stan's remaining lifeblood. Hotchie grabbed a tissue and dabbed at the tiny puddle, then placed the tissue in his pocket. As instructed, he wore gloves and did not come in contact with the liquid. Then Hotchie clenched his crooked teeth and drove the needle deep into Stan's upper arm. It was too late to turn back.

Eighty-Six

It didn't take JJ long to convince the watch commander on duty at County to get G-Dog on the phone. Phrases like, "the Sheriff wants this guy in one piece," and "this inmate is going to make sure our Sheriff gets re-elected" provided ample motivation. Then, "G-Dog, what are you doing in County again?"

"Got caught in some bullshit. But you aint' interested in that. But what you is interested in, is the shit you tried to get me to say that I aint' told you yet."

"So, why do you wanna tell me now?"

"Why you think?"

"'Cause you don't want to do time on your new beef?"

"Fuck that. Aint' got no problem with bein' locked up. 'Cept the thing is . . . I'm a green-lighted mothafucker. My ass ain't worth the motha-fuckin' toilet paper I wipe it with."

When he began speaking again, his voice began to crack with emotion, conveying the tears that began to roll down the cheeks of this supposed O.G.

"They already done tried to kill me once. My own mother-fuckin' homies. My scars aint' even healed yet."

Then G-Dog lost it completely, sobbing like an infant. JJ waited a solid minute for him to find his composure, and then tried a question: "How do you know you're green lighted?"

"'Cause I got a copy of the list."

"Well, you can become a keep-away, and we can get you segregated from the general population, then we can, ah-"

"Fuck that. They can still get to me. You know that kinda protection aint' worth shit. Fact is, I'm a dead man 'less I get the fuck outa Dodge." G-Dog's tone sounded angry now.

"Ok. Then let me hear what you got for me and maybe we can work something out."

"I'll tell ya everything. But, I aint' sayin' nothing on the phone. I got enough troubles right now. Just get your ass over here."

"Alright. But, first tell me if it has to do with the little girl and the others at Roosevelt High getting killed, or my buddy Alex from Kansas Street, Sniper as you probably knew him."

"Has to do with both. Pretty sure they is connected I think."

"I knew it," said JJ loudly, but intending it only for himself.

"Listen, man, you gotta promise me you won't tell nobody about this meetin' we havin.' Especially no cops."

"Don't worry about that," said JJ, "I'll see ya in about thirty-five minutes."

JJ hung up, dropped $40 with Loni at the bar, and collected a receptive Jordan and Blair, who were engaged in a conversation about the effects of the current drought that took way too much effort and from which each was happy to escape.

JJ drove like lightening up the 710 Freeway, utilizing the carpool lane and not hesitating to cross the double lines to swerve around fellow carpoolers going under 80. After Jordan was dropped at Stan's apartment in West L.A., JJ drove back to Cedars Sinai to drop Blair at his car. As he pulled up to the unmarked cruiser, he spied a significant dent to the left side of Blair's vehicle, but didn't say anything because his mind was already at County questioning G-Dog. Blair saw JJ looking at the damage and volunteered, "Damn trustee played smash-up derby with my car. They're supposed to wash your car for you, not wreck it."

JJ gave a brief condolence about the car and thanked his old partner for sitting in on the interview. Then he continued his poor driving habits, roaring east on the 10 Freeway towards downtown and the County jail, wondering why he didn't tell Blair about the latest development. Maybe it was because this was the second time G-Dog gave a cryptic warning to him about other cops. Why so paranoid about cops? He would soon have answers.

Eighty-Seven

On the way from Beverly Hills to Bel Air, Hotchie found an alley behind a liquor store on Wilshire that looked like the perfect place to lose the evidence. He checked to see if anyone was watching, then tossed the rubber gloves and the syringe into the darkness of the open dumpster. He drove for a quarter mile before he remembered that he had additional evidence in his pocket. He found a 7-Eleven store that had the similar accommodations, and then ditched the tainted tissue.

Rhory sat in a hard black leather chair behind a large oak desk, listening to some of the latest tapes. He remarked to himself how good his operation was at recording telephone conversations. His mind drifted to one particularly accomplished telephone guru whom he employed. Courtney. A recognized "phone freaker," as she was dubbed by the FBI agents she eluded, her ability to commit massive financial fraud by manipulating telephones was nothing short of astonishing. Her unparalleled prowess in this area impressed both the pursuing federal agents and her fellow white collar criminals. In one of her more infamous scams, she hacked into the computers at Pacific Bell and re-routed calls from to the California Department of Motor Vehicles to her private cell phone. When she answered, "DMV," she dutifully jotted down the personal information from the female callers. She took that information, along with fake identification, and obtained lines of credit, opened bank accounts upon which she'd write insufficient fund checks, and stole hundreds of thousands of dollars in cash and prizes. Of course, she didn't blink at the fact that she left the credit ratings of the victims whose identities she assumed in a state of perpetual turmoil.

While Rhory snorted another line, he imagined Courtney naked, her tight little ass popping up in the air as she knelt on the carpet below his chair, her back arched, and long black hair falling onto him as she serviced her boss, as she often did. He sprinkled more cocaine on the oak desk and reached for a razor blade when an excited knock caught him off-guard. His startled hand fumbled with the blade, and the razor gently sliced into the meat of his index finger.

"Shit!" He exclaimed. "Come in, asshole!" he yelled.

Hotchie strode in with a wide, uneven smile, feeling the pride of the teacher's pet who was about to be rewarded with the privilege of banging the erasers at the end of class.

"Mission accomplished Mr. Rhory."

"Excellent, Hotchie," said Rhory, extending his hand for a firm shake.

"I knew I could count on you. And now you must be thanked properly for your hard work." After this handshake, one of the two men's lives was in mortal danger.

Eighty-Eight

He sped up the stairs, not even making eye contact with the Judas painting, finessed the deadbolt, and flicked on the lights. He grabbed the phone immediately and found the back of the electric bill on which he had previously scribbled the number for the cab company which he had stood up earlier in the evening. He had contemplated having the cops drop him off at the hospital, but knew they would prevent the necessary meeting with Stan. He would have enough trouble getting past the cop who was standing guard. He would rely on his DA identification and his bullshitting ability. Jordan even considered calling Courtney for a lift, but didn't want another person he knew involved in this mess, and figured a cab could find him quicker, as the driver wouldn't need to primp. He would be lucky if his cabbie used deodorant.

After getting a promise from the cab company that a driver would be there in ten minutes or less, Jordan called Stan's room. No answer. Jordan's mind raced. Stan sounded so serious earlier. He was clearly troubled. And what had Jordan done? Fucked around for two hours at a sleazy bar trying to get information from the cops only to come up empty. He calmed slightly when he thought that the police may have disconnected the phone now that his best friend was officially their prisoner. Stan could be undergoing some test, or just using the bathroom. Relax. But he was so serious on the phone. Stan wanted him there right away.

He stopped torturing himself when he spotted his cab pulling up to him as he stood at the corner of Wooster and Whitworth.

"Cedars Sinai hospital. I'll double your tip and pay any ticket you get if you ignore the speed limit."

"I'll do my best, dude."

His driver had well-tanned and well-wrinkled skin, partly concealed by his long, bleached-blonde hair. He was in his late thirties, and his nightly adventures in cab driving paid for his modest rent and his surf trips to wave breaks at Todas Santos, Mexico and, less frequently, the Indonesian islands of Mentawai.

"What's the rush, bud?" he said, as he lurched his head in both directions to check for cops before blowing through the stop sign at Wooster and Robertson.

"My best friend," Jordan said, surprised that his voice was cracking, "is in trouble."

Eighty-Nine

The Malibu station watch commander was driving to Bel Air to confer with his boss, when he received a page on his message pager. It read, simply, "DDA called for a cab to take ..." He pushed the green arrow to continue the message, "him to Cedars. See that he doesn't get there. R." He immediately pulled a U-turn, chambered a round into his 9mm Beretta, and headed for Wooster and Whitworth.

The attorney meeting rooms at County Jail were really eight cubicles, with thin, wooden paneling dividing each room, and a glass window separating prisoner from practicing lawyer. A deputy sat in a glass booth that towered over the cubicles in order to visually scrutinize the interaction between con and counselor.

It was almost midnight, and the deputy in the booth didn't bother to stare down at the ghost town of chairs, wood and glass that, in a mere nine hours, would spring to life with claims of innocence, demands for trials, complaints about sentences, and attempts at client control.

In one of the cubicles, the Detective was being told a story he couldn't believe. The gang member would occasionally raise his voice when he got excited during his account, then he would immediately revert to hush tones when he caught himself talking loud enough to be overheard.

He had known about the conspiracy for over a year. It involved gang members and the sale of narcotics. Nothing unusual there. But the co-conspirators included cops! And the narcotics were lawfully-seized drugs that were put back out onto the street by cops who sold them to their gang member distributors. JJ's head swirled until he had a headache. He needed to relieve the pressure by asking a million follow-up questions. Instead, he just listened.

G-Dog gave as many details as he could, leaving out his own drug dealing. The cops were selling drugs to homeboys in several different gangs throughout the County, including G-Dog's 8th Street Pirus. He didn't know exactly where the cops got the drugs, but the word was that they came from righteous drug busts. He had also heard that the Kansas Street Crips were in tight with the dirty cops. They moved a lot of dope for them, and helped them with enforcement when other gangs refused to buy from the cops or sold someone else's dope in one of the dirty cops' neighborhoods. G-Dog had a simple explanation for the Snow murders.

"Them Southside Playboy fools finally told the cops 'fuck-off!' They aint buyin' back the same dope the cops took from they homies who is in jail. They gonna sell they own shit in they own neighborhoods. Cops didn't like that. Guess the little girl and her momma just got caught up in the cross-fire. It ain't right neither. That little girl aint' did nothin' to those crooked ass cops!"

He continued, "Them cops, whoever they is, they move a lot of dope. I'm talkin' about a lot of shit. And them mothafuckers get paid. Damn, do they get paid. I heard they got mansions and drive Ferraris and shit. Nobody fucks with 'em either. Even the hardest tech-nine-packing O.G. is afraid to short 'em on they money. 'Cause they know they won't be breathin' long if they do. These cops act like they is some kinda Colombian cartel or somethin'. Everyone is afraid of 'em. My own homies is too. They found out- fuck if I know how- but they knew about our meeting at the Chinese pizza on Compton. They popped a cap in my ass 'cause they protecting theyselves. They want they money, sure, but they also scared as a motherfucker of them dirty cops."

When G-Dog finished his narrative, JJ followed up. Most were questions G-Dog couldn't answer. Who were these dirty cops? G-Dog never saw one or even heard a name. How did the cops account for the drugs when they were needed as evidence? No idea. And, finally, who killed Alex and why? G-Dog didn't know Alex and hadn't heard why he was killed. He did, however, hypothesize the obvious, and it stabbed JJ like a sharp dagger dipped in guilt: "Maybe the little homey was gonna snitch and they found out like they did with me."

Ninety

When the cab reached the corner of Robertson and Wilshire, the driver swerved into the left turn lane and stopped abruptly to wait for a green arrow. The cabby spoke, but Jordan didn't hear him, as he was focusing intently on something else.

"Dude, your friend, what happened to him? Is he real sick?"

Jordan didn't answer. He was looking out the window and staring at a car that had just stopped next to him. It was weird because the car had a green light to proceed straight ahead, yet it just sat there. He saw red paint transfer on the driver side. He was recognizing the car when he saw a flash from the open driver's window. At the same time he heard a muffled backfiring that seemed at the same time both distant and close. Pieces of glass struck his face in slow motion. He could feel his skin being cut. After a second that seemed like an hour, he overcame the surreal nature of the moment and it all registered. "We're being shot at! Get down!" he screamed, diving for the floor.

Instead of getting down, the cabby slammed the gas pedal to its limit and launched the cab into oncoming traffic, liking his odds better there. A red BMW locked its brakes and skidded ahead menacingly. "Shit!" the cabby yelled when he saw he would be broadsided before he could complete his left turn. The BMW clipped the rear tire of the cab and spun it around. Jordan tried to hold on, at the same time staying low. As the cab spun, Jordan heard another shot and more glass hit him, this time landing lightly on the back of his neck and head. The cab stopped spinning, and Jordan saw blood on his blue oxford shirt.

Ninety-One

Rhory dialed the combination to a floor safe and took out a stack of bills tautly held together by a single rubber band. He handed Hotchie his bonus of $10,000 in one-hundred dollar bills for successfully injecting Stan. Hotchie took the money and left the 18-bedroom mansion with a crooked smile on his face, proud of his success. Rhory punched in the code to the operation room, and the door unlocked. He entered and saw Courtney on the phone. She sat at a large, unremarkable table that was crowded with a computer, a monitor, a modem, and multiple telephones. Also on the table were sets of headphones, trap-and-trace displays, wiretap monitoring devices, and large-reel recording machines. There was no activity to monitor at this time.

A large, bald man with a goatee sat in the corner of the room where he fixated on a battery of video screens monitoring the grounds. The guard, Maurice, was paid well in cocaine, but was not allowed to use on the job.

"I'll tell him," she said, glancing at Rhory. Then she hung up the phone.

"That was our man. He said he got off one real good shot at close range and the target went down. He said it looked like a direct hit."

"Excellent," Rhory said, grinning widely. "Perhaps in your prior life you were a black widow, darling. Aren't you just a little sad about helping deliver your lover to the doorstep of his maker?"

"You know I didn't give a damn about him. I only slept with him because you told me to."

"Really. You seemed a bit intrigued with him."

"I'm intrigued by you. And I'm intrigued by money. You are nice enough to give me both."

"Aren't you a lucky little thing," he said, sounding as if he were teasing but meaning every word. He bear-hugged her from behind as she sat at the table, and then put his hands down her shirt, rubbing her through her smooth satin bra.

"Hey, Maurice. Coffee break."

Before the guard could shut the door behind him, Rhory had her shirt and bra completely off. It aroused him that he was making love to a black widow.

Ninety-Two

Stan had to run to the bathroom because he felt like he was going to puke his guts out. As he knelt to worship the porcelain god, he heard the phone ringing. He was too queasy to leave his post. After a few minutes without heaving, he returned to his bed. He wished he had been able to answer the call. It could have been Jordan. After another hour passed, Stan was beginning to panic. He was breathing quick, shallow breaths. Calm down. It's just the injection, he thought. He had felt fine before the lackey showed up with the needle. Then he laughed. Just the injection? The shit was probably rat poison. He told himself to hold on. Stow would be there soon. Stan would tell him everything. Jordan would know what to do. He always does.

After seeing additional blood on his tie, but realizing that all the blood was from the minor glass cuts on his face, he inched his body up and peered cautiously out the windows. No sign of the shooter's car. Jordan then put his hands on the back of the front seat and leaned up to ask the driver if he was ok.

The cabby had his seatbelt off and was curled up in a fetal position on the floor under the steering wheel. He looked like he was in shock. His hands shook slightly. Then the cabby said in a low voice, "Yeah, dude. I didn't get shot, I don't think. I'm a little freaked out, that's all. Haven't been shot at since I surfed in Costa Rica and walked across some local's private beach. It's still no fun."

Jordan set a $20 bill on the front seat and said, "Thanks for the ride. I'm going to walk to Cedars. I think you should go there too and get yourself checked out to be safe." Jordan climbed out of the back seat and walked over to the red BMW. The driver was not injured but was pissed. Despite his anger at the demise of his prized possession, he asked, "Is the asshole cab driver ok?"

"He's fine. Just a little shaken up. I'll be at the hospital if the police want to question me."

Using his hands, Jordan stopped the traffic that was winding around the battered cars, crossed the street, and ran down Wilshire Boulevard towards Cedars Sinai and Stan Man.

Out of breath from the ten-block sprint, Jordan ducked into a public restroom in the deserted waiting area of the Hospital. He washed the blood off his face and straightened his tie. Though it was almost midnight, he had to look like a Deputy D.A. on official business. He had to get in to see Stan.

Jordan showed his District Attorney credentials to the nurse and told her that he had to speak with the patient because of "public safety reasons." The nurse seemed a bit skeptical, so Jordan added, "Mr. Reed may have information that could prevent serious bodily harm that we believe is imminent." He really wasn't lying about that. She called up to the 8th floor and asked to speak to the officer guarding Stan. Then she handed the phone to Jordan.

"This is Deputy Cudahy." Jordan had just gotten lucky.

"Deputy Cudahy, this is Jordan Stowic from the D.A.'s office."

"Hey, Jordan. What are you doing here?"

"Well, I -"

"By the way," he interrupted, "Did we win our trial?"

"Actually, no. Listen, we can talk about that later. Right now I have to speak with Stan Reid. You see, I'm working with Detective Ramirez from O.S.S. Do you know him?"

"Yeah, I know JJ."

"He's investigating a murder where Stan Reid is a suspect. Stan is a good friend of mine and he doesn't feel comfortable talking to JJ. So JJ told me that it would be a good idea if I talked to him before he gets arraigned on Monday and gets an attorney appointed. Because by then his attorney won't let him say anything to anyone."

"Sounds like a good plan. Do you need me to be in there to witness the interview?"

"No, thanks. I think Stan will be more open with me if we're by ourselves. But if Stan wants to give a statement, JJ told me to page him and he'll come over."

"Alright then. Come on up to eight. Turn left off the elevator and it's room 899 at the end of the hall."

Stan sat up in his bed and sweated heavily from a high fever. The fact that he wasn't dead yet made him feel a little better. "If those bastards wanted to kill me, I'd be zipped into a plastic bag by now," he told himself. Maybe it was just a 24-hour flu.

"By the way," Cudahy said, as he led Jordan to Stan's room, "Who did your friend kill?"

"Nobody. I think we can clear up this misunderstanding if I can just talk to him."

"Ok then. I'll be right outside if you need me."

Jordan entered the room and shut the door behind him. Stan smiled and sighed with relief.

"Stow, I am so glad to see you, best friend."

"You look like shit Stan-man. Your forehead is soaked."

"Just a little fever. Guess I caught something. What about you? Looks like you hacked up your face with a dull razor?"

"Oh, it's nothing. Just got hit by some glass when the bullet struck the window of my cab on the way over here."

"What? Those motherfuckers! Are you alright?" Manifesting his concern, Stan grabbed Jordan's arm. Jordan pulled away.

"You know these people? Who are they?"

Stan didn't respond. He just stared at his friend searching his brain to find the beginning of his story. He had planned to start with his feelings about his father's death but had momentarily forgotten now that he was on the spot.

"Stow, I have to be honest with you. Since my Dad died, I've been a different person. Someone you and I never knew. I lost my father. He was my family. So I lost my family. Then I lost what I thought my Dad would leave me. He was broke and I didn't get anything. Of course it made me sick that I even wanted anything, but something inside said, 'at least you won't get screwed out of that.' But I lost out again. And, I guess I have to go back to the accident too, when -"

"I know," Jordan said. "And I'm sorry."

"When I lost my dream. I don't blame you. It's just been my life. God and fate have conspired to make damn sure that I lose everything. And over the last year, I joined the conspiracy because the only thing that I had left – the only thing that I didn't lose, I traded. I traded it away for money."

Stan began sobbing. He bent his neck and buried his head in the pillow that he clutched tightly in both hands. He couldn't continue the story. Jordan sat down on the bed and hugged him like a father.

When he could speak again, Stan said, "Can you help me get it back, Stow?"

"What?" Jordan asked.

"Can you help me get it back?" He asked again.

"Can I help you get *what* back?"

"My soul."

Ninety-Three

After Rhory was through with her, he placed a call. She put her clothes on and checked to see if there was any activity on the phones she monitored. The blank tapes were evidence that there were no new calls, so she walked down the long hallway to the kitchen for ice cream. The black widow needed her nourishment. On the telephone Rhory learned that the target of the latest hit was at Cedars Sinai hospital, though he apparently wasn't seriously injured in the attack, since he was seen running there. Rhory told the street liaison to stand by in case a follow-up visit was needed to finish the job that had begun at the intersection. He hung up and told himself that things weren't so bad. It was only a matter of time before this little fire was put out. There had been many fires extinguished before this one. And besides, he was certain that Hotchie had succeeded. The laboratory research assistant who sold Rhory the stolen bacteria warned him that, if injected, death would occur in a matter of a few hours. He was confident that Stanley Reed was breathing his last breaths. He amused himself by opening his safe and removing a green trash bag full of ones, fives, tens, and twenties, only part of the day's receipts and the result of a week's sales by members of a gang in East Los Angeles comprised of mostly young men of El Salvadorian decent. He put the cash through a money-counter, separating it into stacks of $9,000. He made six stacks and had around $2,000 left over. To-morrow his people would make deposits in different bank accounts in different names, careful not to deposit over $10,000 in any one account so as to avoid the creation of a currency transaction report to the Treasury Department which might spark a federal investigation. After he was done playing with his money, he told Maurice that he was going to bed and didn't want to be disturbed. Not unless there was an emergency.

Before he left County, JJ arranged it so that in the morning G-Dog would be transferred to a local lock-up in the City of Alhambra, a few miles east of downtown, but a completely different universe in terms of G-Dog's safety. There would be twenty or so people in the Alhambra jail, but nobody would know G-Dog. He'd probably even have his own cell. JJ drove towards Beverly Hills with his mind stuck on one track. Cops taking dope off the street and then selling it to gang bangers. Unbelievable. He had seen a lot of unbelievable shit over the years: mothers selling their babies to buy drugs, fathers killing their children because they lost visitation rights, people killing people over insurance proceeds, five dollars, two quarters, a gang sign, an insult. He thought that nothing else would surprise him. But this did.

On his way to pay Reid a late-night visit, JJ analyzed the situation. Reid worked in the lab, so he had access to all the seized dope tested in Los Angeles County. He was probably responsible for stealing dope and covering up the missing drugs. Reid could surely tell him who the dirty cops are. He wanted to strangle Reid. That piece of shit! Even if he didn't actually kill Alex, he was there when it happened. His prints were at the scene and he owned the murder weapon. All to cover up some fucking drug dealing by cops! To say JJ was pissed would have been like saying Hitler wasn't well adjusted. JJ wondered what sound Reid's long neck would make when he snapped it in two. Feeling a little out of control, he realized that he shouldn't talk to Reid alone. He eased off the accelerator pedal as he located his cell phone and punched the power button. Before he could call Blair to join him at the hospital, his cell phone rang. It was an intoxicated Lieutenant James Flores.

"JJ you son-a-va-bitch! What the hell are you doing bugging me on my one big vacation of the year? I got all your messages on my home phone, you stalker. Harassing phone calls is a misdemeanor, you know."

"So, what are you doing calling me from your vacation at this hour?"

"Cause I know you, and I know you're working. I just got your messages and they sure sounded important. Just so you know, I'm at a payphone outside the Lundy Lake Tap and Grill, and there's a honey in there who wants to take me to her place to break in a new mattress."

"Are you sure she's not big enough to break the box spring? You sound like you're wearing some pretty thick beer goggles, Jim."

"Yeah, I've tipped a few back. Not much else to do up here. The fish aint' bitin'. But I'm sure hopin' this little chickita will."

"Jim, I called you because I need to know something."

"What is it?"

"When you told me about my witness, the boy who was killed in the Santa Ana canyons, you told me he was killed with a nine millimeter, remember?"

"I'm not that drunk. I remember. So?"

"Jim, how did you learn what caliber firearm killed Alex? Did you actually get this detail from the folks at Santa Ana Sheriff's, or what?"

"I think so. No, wait. They called, but I didn't speak to the watch commander over there until I got the details from someone else."

"Who?"

"Your old partner."

"Blair?"

"I believe so. And why does this matter?"

"Did Blair get his information from someone?"

"I assume he got it from the folks at Orange County Sheriff's. What's going on?"

"It's nothing. Listen, I'm gonna let you get back to Miss Lundy Lake. I'll fill you in when you get back to town."

"Ok. I'll have you over for dinner. The way things are going, I hope you don't mind fish sticks."

"Goodbye Jim."

As he neared the hospital, JJ pondered the situation. Though he felt a bit paranoid, he decided he wouldn't call Blair to join him. He believed that it was probably a coincidence that his ex-partner and good friend added the detail of the 9mm when relating the story of Alex's murder to Lt. Flores, or perhaps he heard it from a dirty cop. Still, JJ was a smart detective who knew he would only get to the bottom of these murder cases by carefully traversing a minefield of corruption. The last thing he wanted was to stumble into a dirty cop in the dark.

Ninety-Four

In an attempt to reclaim his soul, or more accurately, purge from it months of thievery, narcotics trafficking, drug use, corruption, and general evil, Stan set his emotional baggage onto the sturdy shoulders of his best friend Jordan.

He characterized the events, even shaded them in his favor. Still, as his own story rolled from his tongue, he couldn't believe he was describing things that he had actually done.

Jordan was more incredulous. Stan-Man a corrupt crime lab chemist stealing drugs to give to cops who sold them to gangbangers? Where was Alan Funt hiding with the camera? Stan ordered to kill him? Come out Rod Serling! But as Stan spoke, corroborating facts occurred to Jordan. His Mom had heard that Stan's father's estate was broke. Someone paid for Stan's red Porsche cabriolet prior to Jordan's remodeling it on the PCH guardrail. And Stan shot himself the other night in what he was now being told was a botched suicide attempt. Something had to push Stan over the edge. Jordan thought about asking Stan if this were all an elaborate joke, but he already knew the answer. Stan wasn't talking any longer but, rather, just waiting. Waiting for a response, any response.

As Jordan looked into the hazel eyes of his best friend, Jordan's part in this bizarre play became apparent. Stan's co-conspirators wanted him out of the way. He was law enforcement and he was too close. That now seemed the only logical explanation for both the Malibu cliff episode and the intersection shooting gallery that caused the 45-minute-old dried blood on his face.

Jordan looked away from him but still didn't speak. Stan waited. Jordan needed time to absorb the dreadful reality that Stan-Man had betrayed their childhood oath to do only good and to make a difference. He thought about how he and Stan used to patrol the neighborhood after a Michigan snowstorm and shovel old ladies out of their driveways only to refuse payment, save a homemade brownie or two. Stan had just shattered all of that.

Finally, in a rhetorical explosion, he screamed, "Who the hell *are* you!"

Stan said nothing.

Jordan got up so violently, his chair upended, crashing loudly on the hard tile floor. Before he slammed the door behind him, he added, "You probably killed that guy like they said, you psycho!"

After swimming in his pool of emotion long enough, his eyes stopped dispensing their liquid regret and Stan sat up in his bed. He wondered what he should do next. Unfortunately, queasiness arrived to compliment his fever, making him both seasick and lightheaded. He could call for the nurse, but that might make him well enough to leave for jail in the morning and spoil his chances of being busted out by the organization which he despised but which was currently his only hope. Then, suddenly, he no longer felt compelled to decide a course of action. He acknowledged that his world was coming to an end. He was certain that he would never leave the hospital alive.

Ninety-Five

JJ and Jordan passed in separate elevators. The Detective, armed for the first time with the knowledge of *why* Alex had been killed, entered the room on a mission. Now that he knew the motive, he needed to confront the man whom he was now certain was his adopted son's killer. A corrupt man, a traitor to all a good career police officer espouses. JJ lost it when he entered Reid's room and saw Reid leaning back in the comfort of his bed and . . . smirking!

JJ hurled the chair that lay on the floor in an unsuccessful attempt to drain his hostility, and then grabbed Reid by both shoulders. Like a twenty-five-year-old rookie, not an early model Detective, he threw the traitor turned killer off the bed and across the room. Stan's head banged with a painful dull thud as it struck the base of a metal floor lamp. His body slid until it smacked the wall.

"That was for Alex! I hope selling dope was worth it, you dirty mother fucker!" He was yelling at the rag doll on the floor who barely moved.

When Jordan back tracked to the 8th floor of the hospital to take up his verbal tirade where he left off, he saw Deputy Cudahy running towards Stan's room. Jordan followed at an equally frantic pace.

In the room, Jordan saw the Detective walking towards his friend's contorted body on the floor. The Detective looked more than pissed. Jordan heard Stan mumble what sounded like, "Help me Stow." Jordan sensed that he had to contain the Detective and he had to do it right away. So he stepped by Cudahy and reached JJ. Jordan slid his arms between the Detective's arms and body, and tried to wrap around his neck in an attempt to apply a full nelson hold he had learned as a wrestler.

JJ slipped away, spun around, and connected with a right fist to Jordan's face that sent him wheeling back into a chair that tripped him to the ground. Jordan landed hard on his back. Deputy Cudahy, remarkably, made like a wooden Indian, studying the events unfolding, as if watching a police training video. JJ turned his attention back to Stan, fully intending to continue the pummeling. But he noticed that Stan was no longer moving. And JJ saw blood on his own hand, not realizing that it had come from Jordan's previously cut face. JJ stopped himself. Cudahy took a deep breath as if he were preparing to finally acknowledge that he was in the same room.

Someone spoke. The voice was that of the twist of bones resting against the wall. "I didn't kill Alejandro. But I can tell you who did." Stan was amazingly cooperative for someone suffering from a high fever and queasiness and who was just tossed like a little person in a midget-throwing contest.

JJ drew in air deeply, exhaled, and said, "I'll hear you out. But after that, no guarantees."

JJ helped Stan back to his bed, and Jordan, after regaining his composure, agreed not to make Cudahy file a report about how he had just been sucker punched by JJ, whom he referred to as "Officer Powell."

Cudahy resumed his guard outside the door when JJ assured him that everything was under control. Then JJ reminded Stan of his Miranda rights, and Stan proceeded to re-tell the story that had just shaken Jordan's world to its foundation. As the details came, the Detective nodded, signaling that he had already been made aware of much of what he was hearing. At the end, JJ asked his big question: Who killed Alejandro Sandoval?

"I don't know for sure," Stan said, "but there is a guy Rhory calls the street liaison. I would bet that he did it. Probably killed Sandoval because he was a threat."

Alex died because he was a threat. There was that blade to the heart again. If JJ had just told him to keep his information to himself, Alex would still be alive. JJ had to focus. Put his guilt on lay away.

"Who's the street liaison?"

"I've never seen him. But I know he's an L.A. County Sheriff. Once I overheard Rhory calling him and he asked for him by name. A short, common name like 'Smith' or 'Baker.'

JJ thought about what the looped Lieutenant had told him: Blair somehow knew that Alex was killed with a nine millimeter even before the slugs were taken from his body. And there were no casings found at the scene. But the whole thing could be chalked up to simple miscommunication. Still, JJ had to ask, even if he was afraid of the answer.

"The name wasn't 'Davis' was it?"

"That's it!" Stan returned, without hesitation. "It was Deputy Davis or Detective Davis."

JJ stopped his mind from reeling by applying reason. With a department the size of the L.A. County Sheriff's Office, there were many Davis's. It could be a lot of people. When he directed himself back to the interrogation, he noticed a look of concern on the young DDA's face.

Jordan asked, "Are we talking about Detective Davis from tonight? Your partner?"

JJ didn't answer. He didn't know.

Stan and Jordan shared nervous eye contact that acknowledged that in the room with them was possibly another dirty cop working for Rhory. Jordan abruptly stood up and headed for the door. JJ grabbed his arm before he got there and, sincerely, said: "I don't know if it's my old partner that we're talking about. It could be any Davis in the Department. There could be other dirty cops too that Stan doesn't know about. But you don't have to worry about me. I'm one of the good cops. And I'm investigating the murder of Alejandro, who was like a son to me. I'm going to bring everyone responsible to justice or I'm going down trying. You can believe that."

JJ let go of Jordan's arm. There was a long silence until Stan asked the Detective, "Do you trust me when I tell you that I didn't kill Alejandro?"

JJ's read on Stan was that he didn't have anything to do with Alex's murder. Stan became involved with the conspiracy to steal and sell drugs because he worked at the crime lab and he was a necessary component. He was in the wrong place at the wrong time with the requisite amount of greed and weak morals. JJ also believed that Stan knew nothing about the Snow murders or the killing of the bush people. He figured the conspiracy had its heavy hitters, and Stan wasn't one of them. Some of his opinion he took from the resignation in Stan's voice. It was as if he had given up on helping himself and, instead, committed to making reparations through turning on his confederates. It was significant to him that Stan had not even asked for immunity from prosecution or any kind of plea bargain for his assistance.

"Yes, Stan, I believe you didn't kill Alejandro."

Stan-Man turned toward Jordan and asked with his eyes, "What about you?"

"Well, I think you fucked up big time, but I don't think you've turned into Charlie Manson." That was the closest to "I'm with you," that Jordan could come.

With some level of trust struck, Jordan asked the question on all of their minds: "What do we do now?"

"I can take it from here," said JJ, answering Jordan but looking at Stan. "You just concentrate on getting better. I'm going to need you to testify when I wrap this thing up. To answer the question, I know exactly what I'm going to do next. I am going to the stash house you told me about. Then I am going to hit Rhory's place. But I need you to give me specifics."

Before, when recounting his knowledge of the organization and its leader, Rhory Callum, Stan had mentioned that, while Rhory kept his money and pay and owe records at his Bel Air estate, all of the drugs were kept at a stash house in Compton. Stan had gone there to deliver stolen cocaine several times.

"Of course, you'll need a search warrant," Jordan volunteered. "Unless Stan here has a key and Rhory's consent to access the locations."

"I only go over there when I am told to," Stan said, "and Rhory doesn't let me keep keys."

Jordan, making a reasonable suggestion, said, "Why don't we all get some sleep. I know I could use some. And Stan here looks tired as hell. We can re-group in the morning."

That was unacceptable to JJ. The end was in sight. After all of the disappointments, he couldn't run the risk of losing his star witness 8 hours and a cup of coffee later. "No, we act now. I'll get a warrant. I can get a telephonic one real fast. We'll hit the stash house and get the drugs. Then we will have enough for a solid search warrant on the Bel Air mansion."

Stan tried hard, but couldn't think of the name of the Street that the stash house was on, let alone the exact address. He only knew how to drive there. As Jordan correctly recalled from his Georgetown Law criminal procedure class, it is constitutionally required to have a precise description, including the address, of a house to be searched, otherwise, the search warrant would later be thrown out of court, along with the evidence seized in the search. Stan would have to take JJ to the stash house.

In light of all of the recent events, including the most recent attempt on the life and fledgling career of the Deputy D.A., JJ did not want to send Jordan home without protection. He would come along. The three men took to the stairs, eight floors down to the lobby, where they left through an emergency exit door marked with a sign making an empty threat to sound an alarm. Deputy Cudahy was instructed to continue guarding the door as if there were someone in the room that needed guarding. Nurses and doctors would be told only as necessary.

"Here we are," Stan announced, as JJ's Caprice rolled up to the stash house on Greenleaf Avenue in Compton. JJ jotted down the address and a description on a pad of paper that read: "4238 Green-leaf. Small single-family residence of white stucco with gray shingled roof and three windows facing the street."

As JJ was taking notes, Jordan took notice of the property. The house was dark inside, yet it appeared less to be sleeping than . . . waiting. Waiting to spring to life and attack. Or so said the thoughts in the young prosecutor's head. He couldn't fault himself for thinking this. Given his near death experiences, he felt more cautious than paranoid.

Dizziness forced Stan to lie back in his seat. Now it was light-headed, feverish, queasy and dizzy. "Whatever those bastards injected me with is kicking my ass," Stan said, to himself.

Once the Detective had his particulars, they were off. Before JJ reached the station, JJ used his cell phone to call one of the many contacts he had developed over the years. Lee Cox. As head of the subpoena response unit for California Cellular for the past ten years, Lee responded to JJ's requests a million times. Over time, JJ charmed her into giving him her home phone number, where she worked some days. He only had to use that number once before. A jury had been sworn and he was beginning a murder trial the next day, when the People's star witness, fearing gang retaliation, fled to San Diego. His cell records revealed the location in Pacific Beach where he was hiding out. Lee wouldn't mind helping JJ yet again. The next chance he got, he would thank her by taking her to lunch at her favorite steak house in Montebello.

When JJ called in the early morning hour, Lee was sleepy but as cooperative as always. She logged onto her work computer from home, just as she did on the mornings she telecommuted. Lee seemed to take longer than usual to check outgoing calls from Blair's cell phone. JJ tuned out the background banter of Jordan and Stan. He was driving on auto pilot. He just needed a negative answer to eliminate Blair from the top of the list of suspected dirty cops.

"Don't see any calls to the number you gave me."

JJ relaxed a little.

"Wait," Lee said, "I'm looking at incoming now. Yes, that number you gave me called the cell 14 times this month."

JJ went completely numb.

"JJ, you there?" Lee asked.

"Watch out!" screamed Jordan from the seat directly behind JJ, jarring the driver's attention back to the road before the cop car rear-ended a black Cadillac decorating the shoulder.

"Thanks," he said, cutting Lee off with the beep of his 'end' button, meaning thank you Jordan for saving my Department car, and thank you Lee for ruining my night.

Though this was more messed up than expected, JJ couldn't believe how disoriented and unfocused he felt. The more answers he got, the less anything made sense, and the more out of control he felt. For a second, he wished he could walk away from the investigation and board a sailboat with Jimmy Buffet, only to drift through the Caribbean, wasting away.

Instead, he concentrated on the task at hand. He organized his next move in his mind and found that calm returned. He would go to his office and complete the affidavit for the search warrant for the stash house. He would fax it to the judge and swear to it by telephone. The judge would fax back a signed warrant if he found that probable cause existed to justify the search. Then JJ would gather a few officers whom he could trust and hit the stash house, and, possibly, the jackpot.

Ninety-Six

The black widow was awoken and informed that there was phone activity that might interest her. Seems the Detective had called a guy from his office, presumably a fellow cop, and told him to come downtown to the station. Said he would explain why later.

Courtney took over the monitoring of the wire and sent Maurice to the kitchen to make her a cappuccino, which would ensure that she remained awake and alert. She considered waking Rhory, then thought better of it.

"Ramirez should be at his little bar with his drunken friends by now," she said with disgust to the electronic equipment in the otherwise empty room, angry at the prospect of working late into the night. As she sat and listened to the wire, time passed slowly. The silence taunted her. She had a feeling something was up. She also decided that the time had come to insist on more of a cut. She deserved something greater than all the cocaine she could breathe through her nose and a room in a mansion. She warranted a salary for her unique services. She would ask nicely. Experience taught her to be careful in her dealings with her boss. She had once seen Rhory kill a man who demanded money because he claimed that Rhory shorted him of an ounce of cocaine. In fact, she did more than witness the killing of this man. She was part of it. As the man was distracted to shake her pretty hand on a polite introduction, Rhory produced a Heckler and Koch handgun, pressed it to the back of the man's head and pulled the trigger. She remembered how the warm blood of the dead man felt on her face and neck. And it ruined a perfectly good Betsy Johnson outfit.

"Thank you, Maurice," she said, when the large man returned from his errand. She sipped the cappuccino. Maurice sat down in his chair, stared at the video monitors, and stroked his goatee. Then he removed a plastic baggy from his pocket containing a gram of cocaine. He gestured towards Courtney.

"Wanna share? Works better than coffee."

"Idiot. Don't let Rhory catch you getting high when you're working. You'll be back in Chinatown shaking down store owners for change. Or worse."

"Is that, 'no, thank you Maurice'?"

"Ok. No thank you, you big fat thug. I think I'll stay sober." She had a weird feeling about tonight.

Ninety-Seven

Jordan's mouth was moving, so Stan knew he was talking. But each word was part of the next, as if they had been put into a food processor and blended into one continuous stream of sound. Stan, drenched in sweat, saw a black crow swooping down to attack his best friend. Then it disappeared. Stan was hallucinating. He took the glass of water Jordan had given him and poured water on himself. He felt better.

"Whoa, buddy, you ok? Stan, we should get you back to the hospital."

"No, I'm fine," he lied, "I really want to help JJ. I know where they keep the drugs in that stash house. I want to go on the search. I just have the flu, I think."

"Why don't you lay down," said Jordan, getting up off the Sanford and Son couch in JJ's office, letting Stan sprawl out. Jordan walked over to JJ, who sat in his creaky wooden chair typing furiously on his computer.

"How's it going?"

"I got a hold of Bracey at home. He's gonna come in and go with us. He's a good man. We can trust him."

For the past thirty minutes, JJ had composed his affidavit, detailing the story that both the gangbanger and the corrupt chemist had told him, referring to them only as "confidential informant #1 and confidential informant #2," or "CI #1 and CI #2." His immersion into this latest endeavor helped JJ focus on the business at hand and push to the back burner of his mind betrayal by his former partner and friend. He scribbled a number on a piece of paper and handed it to Jordan.

"Do me a favor, call Judge Henman at home and give him a heads up that I'll be faxing him an affidavit for a telephonic search warrant."

279

"You want me to wake up a Superior Court judge at 1:00 in the morning, a judge that I will probably appear in front of in the near future?"

"Just do it, Mr. D.A."

"Done."

An elderly sounding woman answered, groggy, "yes?"

"May I please speak with Judge Henman?"

A long pause, and then, "Is this about a search warrant, dear?"

"Yes."

"Okay, hold on." In the background he heard her say, "Here we go again Harry. Another warrant."

Jordan told the judge he would be receiving an affidavit for a search warrant from Detective Ramirez that, under the circumstances, had to be executed right away. He told him that there had been witnesses killed and attempts on the lives of other witnesses. When giving this information, he neglected to mention that he was one of the victims of these attempts. Jordan obtained the judge's fax number and apologized for waking him.

Thirty more minutes passed. Stan was motionless on the couch with his eyes closed, like he was in the deepest stage of sleep. Bracey called on his cell phone and gave a five minute e.t.a. Jordan proof read the affidavit and gave it his approval. Then JJ declared, "Let's rock and roll."

Before faxing the affidavit, JJ called the judge and explained the case. He had only dealt with Henman on a search warrant once before, several years ago. But he knew from his experience and those of other deputies that Judge Henman didn't mind doing telephonic search warrants when the circumstances called for them. And he didn't ask a lot of questions. Tonight, however, the judge was a bit more quizzical. His interest seemed peaked by this incredible corruption scheme. He wanted to know specific details. "Who were the dirty cops?" "Who knew about the investigation?" He even wanted to know who was going to take part in the search.

Before he hung up, JJ had the judge place him under oath and swear that the affidavit he was faxing was true and correct. All that was left to do was for the judge to read the affidavit, sign the warrant, and fax it back to JJ. This search would hold up in court.

As the fax machine sprang to life, Rhory snorted a line of coke and proclaimed, "You truly are amazing, you naughty little phone freaker. You deserve to make the FBI's top ten list. Great tired old lady impression."

"Well, you made a pretty good judge," replied Courtney, "Maybe later I can get under your robe."

"Maurice, who is working tonight?"

"Just me and then Randy out at the gate."

"Call in the other guys. And get me some of those boys in the hood that we're making rich. We need to give the Los Angeles County Sheriffs Deputies a proper welcome when they visit our Compton branch office."

Ninety-Eight

2:30 a.m. and on to Compton, or the "CPT," as it was called in popular rap lyrics, like those of Compton-born D.J. Quick. JJ drove his unmarked with Stan riding shotgun. Bracey and Jordan followed in a black and white. Before leaving, JJ announced that they would only request backup if absolutely necessary, citing the corruption problem, but failing to inform the others of the phone records implicating his old partner. JJ didn't totally trust anyone anymore. When they arrived, JJ told the dispatcher of his location and stated that he and Detective Bracey were going inside to "conduct interviews." That way, at least, someone would know they were there. Hopefully, though, the information would not be repeated to the wrong pair of ears.

JJ, warrant in hand, along with Bracey, went to the front door to perform the required knock and announce. It seemed a mere formality, as the place looked dark and abandoned, just as it had earlier when they drove by to get the description for the warrant. Bracey pounded on the front door several times with the butt of his mag flashlight.

"Police, open up! We have a warrant!" Bracey stated firmly, not yelling but reaching a similar decibel level.

Nothing. He picked up the battering ram and, helped by JJ, the two smashed open the front door. Flipping the switches inside the house produced no illumination.

"Someone didn't pay their electric bill," said Bracey.

The two officers performed a brief sweep of the one-story, two bedroom house with their flashlights pointing the way, guns drawn. No one.

"It's clear," announced Bracey.

"I'll get our tour guide," said JJ.

Stan, ignoring a noticeable rash that was forming on the lower part of his left leg and a slight pain that arrived with it, felt inexplicably energized. He was ready to help JJ find any drugs that might be hidden in the stash house.

"What's in there?" asked Jordan.

"We swept the place, nobody's there. Now I need Stan to show me where the drugs are."

As the three were preparing to enter the house, Stan said, "JJ, there is a hidden compartment behind the refrigerator. It's pretty big. That's were they stored a lot of the dope."

Bracey was rummaging though the drawers in the kitchen, which by all indications had not been used in years. Not only was there dirt, but really old dirt. And cobwebs. He heard a sound. It came from the other side of the kitchen, near the refrigerator. Bracey opened the 70's model Frigid-Aire. Nothing but more dirt inside. It was unplugged. His flashlight lit up the area behind it and he noticed the outline of a door. A hidden closet with no door knob. He figured the cause of the noise he had heard to be a rat. He pushed the refrigerator away from the wall and pried open the door with the tips of his fingers.

Bracey shined his flashlight inside and didn't see anything. The space was cavernous, and much larger than the other closets he had checked. He guided the beam of light deeper inside and saw that the floor was cement, as if the area had been added on. Then he saw a pair of tennis shoes. He raised the beam and saw that legs were attached. Before he could reach for his sidearm, a light blinded him. The sound of the gunshots registered only after he was thrown onto his back by their force. So many shots. Too many, he thought, as he lay there bleeding.

JJ instinctively unholstered his Beretta when he heard the gunfire that broke out. Automatic fire. "Bracey!" he screamed, running towards the open front door.

When JJ was inside, he saw Bracey down in the kitchen. No sign of anyone else. Open window in the kitchen; that was new. JJ checked and re-checked all of the rooms, then went over to Bracey, who was already unconscious. He tore off the wounded man's shirt, exposing his protective vest that he wore over a white undershirt, now a bloody-pink. There was one deformed slug, a large caliber, stopped by the vest that exhausted itself and gave way to several other rounds that made it through and into the good cop's flesh and organs. Bracey's standard-issue Kevlar was designed to stop most common handguns firing legal ammunition, but was quite ineffective against large caliber rifle fire, like the .223 caliber rounds that had pierced him. JJ removed his own polo shirt to help the victim, and it was practically swallowed whole by the large open wound that was Bracey's chest.

Shirtless, JJ ran to the front porch and screamed: "Call for help! Officer's been shot! Needs assistance!"

Jordan had already used the radio in the black and white and called for backup, and he told this to JJ. Jordan had provided the necessary information to the dispatcher and had added, "Send officers Code 3!" He had learned this last part on his ride along and hoped it would light a fire under the reinforcements, as if the "officer shot" part wouldn't suffice.

JJ stayed with Bracey until the EMTs arrived, along with four Compton P.D. units. Ten Sheriff's vehicles coming from the Lynwood Station would arrive a couple of minutes later. Stan, who had hit the dirt when the firing started, then had disappeared from view, was running back from about a block away. He was yelling. JJ ran to him and heard him say, "I saw the guys. I recognize the car. A black Mercedes. It belongs to Rhory. I know where to find them."

"Let's go," said JJ.

Before he left, JJ recognized Detective Stoney Jackson of Compton P.D. Stoney agreed to stay with Bracey and to call his wife; JJ would follow the lead he had on the suspects. Stoney told four patrol officers in two Compton black and whites to follow JJ. Then the three cars full of good guys (one a recent convert) drove from one of the poorest parts of the County, Compton, to one of the richest, Bel Air. Yet they were chasing evil deeper into hell.

Ninety-Nine

After JJ radioed to his watch commander what had happened on Greenleaf, nobody talked in JJ's car, as it bounded North on the 110 Freeway towards a sleepy L.A. skyline, then jogged across the 10 over to the 405 Freeway North.

Stan removed his seat belt and sprawled out across the back seat of the Caprice. He suddenly felt so tired that the plastic cover installed to protect the fake leather upholstery from suspects' bodily fluids felt like a down comforter at the Marina Del Ray Ritz Carlton. He started to fall asleep, but was awakened by pain in his left leg. A very sharp one. A knife was digging in hard. He checked it and saw that it was purple and getting swollen. The rash was spreading. He kept quiet. Swallowing, a new symptom was revealed- his throat stung like hell. But he still hoped these were just side effects of an injection of an innocuous strain of flu. He was wrong. Dead wrong. In fact, his body was engaged in a life or death struggle.

Group A Streptococcus is normally a harmless bacteria that causes nothing more than strep throat. But there is a rare, aggressive form that releases lethal toxins and causes what is known as "necrotizing fasciitis," which means, literally, death of the fascia, the tissue that binds skin to muscle. In the press, this has become known as "The Flesh Eating Bacteria." While the tabloids are correct, it is a bacteria, it does not technically eat the flesh. Rather, it starves the human tissue of its most vital element-- oxygen-- killing it. It robs the tissue of its oxygen by attacking the capillaries, preventing the oxygen-carrying blood from reaching the tissue. It also enters the bloodstream and wreaks havoc on the organs.

The deadly bacteria can enter the body through the tiniest break in the skin caused by a cut, scrape or burn. Once inside the body, this form of the Streptococcus bacteria multiplies quickly, producing toxins that start a cascade of abnormal physiological events. The toxins spread in skin and fatty tissues. Once the toxins are introduced into the bloodstream, they move quickly to other parts of the body, including the organs, such as the kidneys and lungs. Immediate diagnosis and treatment is critical. In terms of survival, hours matter. Days are irrelevant. This disease is one of the few where one can literally see it spreading.

The Centers for Disease Control and Prevention estimated that, in 1992, between 2,000 and 3,000 people in the United States were killed by the same deadly bacteria that was tightening its grip on one Stanley Reid.

One Hundred

The debriefing was underway on the second floor balcony overlooking Century City. Four men, lit by candlelight, sat on rod iron chairs at a tiled table. Overhead, a heater easily tamed the cool evening breezes winding in from the Pacific.

"How did it go?" Rhory asked, as he fidgeted with the bandage on his index finger.

A large man with night black hair and a flattened nose used his disproportionately small hands to accentuate as he spoke. "Beautiful. Two bangers from Eighth Street Pirus were inside the house waiting for them. I gave one of them an AR-15. Cops go in. Sounded like our guys got off some really good shots. Don't think the cops fired much. I saw the Pirus get away on bikes. They ditched the guns in a dumpster."

Sensing a possible rebuke, he continued, "Don't worry, it's not registered and the serial number's filed down. No prints."

"Did anyone see you?"

"No one. Me and Kurt watched from a ways away in our car. And the car's not registered to you anymore."

"How do you know you weren't followed here?"

"I practiced counter surveillance driving the entire way. Kurt checked for helicopters."

Rhory smiled. He was feeling very powerful in this moment. He made life and death decisions. Someone fucked with him, they died. Stanley Reid would not live to testify against him. The detective on the case, quite probably, was dead. Anyone left standing after this round would go down in the next. He had more money than he could spend. Life couldn't get much better. But something was irritating him. His finger. His threshold for pain had never been particularly low, but the pain from the razor splice teased him into a foul mood.

On cue, Maurice handed his boss two rubber-banded stacks of 20-dollar bills, totaling $2,500 each. Rhory then tossed them at the chests of the former naval S.E.A.L. and ex strip club bouncer and said "Good job fellas. Now get the fuck out of here."

When they got off the freeway in Westwood and headed towards Bel Air, JJ switched his radio to the Compton P.D. frequency and told the two black and whites that trailed behind to kill their lights and sirens. They complied. Surprise was part of the plan. The black and whites followed JJ's unmarked through Bel Air, and Jordan provided JJ with the lefts and rights. Knowing he was close, JJ drove faster, though the road became markedly more precarious, the twists and turns past millions in real property ill-suited for the reckless driving of the overzealous Detective. Soon his rear view mirror revealed that he had lost the black and whites.

"Idiots." he said.

"It's ok," assured Jordan, " just radio them the address when we get there. Anyway, it's coming up past this turn on your left."

When they pulled up to the estate's gate, JJ did what Jordan suggested, then tuned his radio back to the Sheriff's frequency. He told the dispatcher his location. Her name was Rita, and she calmly stated a simple fact. Deputy Bracey had passed away at County U.S.C. Hospital.

It was later than 4:30 in the morning when the guard saw the car drive up and stop by the gate. Though there were no visible bubble gum lights or lettering, the vehicle was unmistakable. Randy used his walkie talkie to call Maurice.

"Cops are here," he said.

When Rhory got wind he made sure the Navy S.E.A.L. and bouncer didn't leave. Then he radioed back to the gate, "How many are there?"

"I see two." Glancing down at some photos in a book, Randy added, "One of them is Ramirez. He's trying to get a look over the gate. Now he's walking over to me."

Rhory was at the same time nervous and pleasantly excited. "Let them in. Be nice. We'll have some fun with them." Rhory got on the cell phone and called the street liaison. "I need you to come over and clean up. I'm about to make a mess."

Jordan saw the familiar red Ferrari convertible parked at the top of the hilly driveway. JJ looked, but did not see the Mercedes Stan had described as the one that drove away from the shooting at the Greenleaf stash house. The "hot pursuit" doctrine would probably not provide legal justification for their pushing past the guard and entering the property, but JJ was planning to go anyway. Though strangely placid in external demeanor, inside the Detective simmered with loss and sadness, and, mostly, a lust for revenge. Bracey was gone. It wouldn't be for naught. He felt that this is where the story would end.

"Evening officers."

Badging the hired thug at the guard house, JJ replied in a strong voice, "Detective Juan Ramirez, L.A. County Sheriff. Let me see some identification."

Jordan stood behind the Detective, and watched the large man closely as he reached for his wallet and driver's license. Stan happily obliged JJ's request to stay down in the back seat, as he had never had less energy or been more physically spent. Stan didn't know it, but he was dying.

JJ walked back to the Caprice and called in the license. It was valid with no wants or warrants. He told the thug, "I'm here to speak with the owner of the home. Mr. Rhory Callum."

"Stand by." The thug, a.k.a. Randy, engaged in a fake call to Rhory on a telephone in his booth that didn't even work.

"Mr. Callum said he'd be happy to answer any questions you have about anything." The thug, no actor, was overplaying the scene.

It seemed a little too easy, so JJ said, "We're going to wait for some other officers who want to be there during the interview. They should be here any minute."

So much for the element of surprise. Over the radio, JJ apprized the Compton officers that he would wait for them to enter the home to talk to the owner. JJ radioed Rita the dispatcher and requested an additional Sheriff unit to be sent to the mansion. She said she would do it. JJ's cop vibes told him he needed to play it safe.

When the Compton officers arrived, Randy opened the gate and let the Caprice and the two marked units inside. He directed them to the top of the steep, twisting driveway, then closed and locked the gate. He ran up the hill and led Jordan, JJ and the four uniformed Compton officers past the tennis courts, across the Spanish-paver deck that surrounded the pool, and, finally, to a large front door, which he opened for them.

The four Compton officers were: 1) Carlos Rodriguez, a veteran patrol officer of 15 years with a wife and two kids in college, 2) Morrison, a.k.a. "Morey," Thomas, a 6'6" buff, former Compton High School football star, unmarried and in his third year with the P.D., 3) Michael Coolidge, a smallish, 8th-year cop who transferred from L.A.P.D. because his wife convinced him that the agency did not promote African Americans, and 4) Donny Millens, a slender 21-year-old rookie with blond, spiky hair whose teenage days spent as a volunteer "Explorer" with Downey P.D. convinced him that when he grew up he had to be a cop in the toughest part of the county, where he was needed most.

"Mr. Callum is waiting in his study. It's the last door on the left at the end of this hallway," the thug announced, and then walked out of the house; presumably back to his guard booth.

The foyer looked much more immense than Jordan remembered it. He was overwhelmed by the long hallway with high ceilings and a floor obscenely comprised of solid Italian marble. The walls were adorned with overpriced modern art, including one huge frameless canvass covered in splashes of paint that collided violently.

"Nice place," understated Officer Thomas.

"Morey, man, you coulda had all this if your knees held out," said his partner Rodriguez, the veteran.

Cooley added, "Or if you'd just been smart and skipped U.S.C. and gone straight to the Raiders."

"No shit," concurred Millens.

Jordan heard what he thought might have been the front door locking from the outside, but he wasn't sure. The cops became quiet. JJ studied his surroundings, as he led his entourage with purpose towards the office at the end of the endless hallway. He thought about drawing his 9 millimeter, but didn't. Jordan's head throbbed from the evening's excitement and the Jack Daniels he tipped back earlier at the crummy dive bar. He noticed something that he hadn't when had been in the mansion under happier circumstances. The ceiling. He had only seen this mirrored variety once before when he was in a casino in Atlantic City.

They were finally at the hallway's end. JJ tried to open the door to the study. It was locked.

He knocked, "Mr. Callum, it's the police." Nothing. Then he tried the door across from it. Closet. The other doors. All locked.

"This is fucked up," said Millens, basing his comment on his less than vast experience, though one James Bond movie was all that was necessary for the observation.

The other officers, then Millens, removed their weapons and began walking back to the front door.

"Mr. Callum!" said JJ to the walls, "we're just here to talk to you."

Gunfire. Men hit the floor. Men were squirming on the floor.

The mirrored ceiling. "Look up!" screamed Jordan. He saw rifle barrels sticking out of the ceiling. They had fat tubes on the ends that Jordan recognized as silencers.

"Run!" JJ cried, piercing the airwaves between shots.

Jordan sprinted, but tripped over one of the fallen Compton officers. Rodriguez. He was hurt badly. Jordan saw two other officers down. More gunfire. Jordan ran towards the front door through which they had entered.

JJ, already there, yelled, "It's locked. Up the stairs!" Three of the Compton officers were no longer moving. Thomas stood over Rodriguez, administering CPR. Rodriguez wasn't breathing.

"Mother Fuckers!" he screamed, holding his radio. The radio, for some reason, was not working. Batteries were fine, but he could tune in only static.

Catching on to the source of the gunfire, Thomas fired shots into the ceiling. The rounds only ricocheted in other directions. He ran up the staircase, following behind the detective and the Deputy D.A. At the top of the stairs, JJ bent down and pulled up his pant leg, exposing an ankle holster. He removed then handed his back-up .38 to Jordan. "Take this. Shoot anyone besides us with or without a badge."

More gunfire. Officer Thomas peered down from the staircase onto his fallen comrades. Bullets riddled uniformed bodies that were now moving not of their own volition but from the force of the lead being pumped into them from above. Thomas stood, frozen, until he felt a hand on his shoulder. It was the Sheriff's Detective.

"We need you. Your family needs you. Focus." JJ grabbed the officer's hand, which clutched his service weapon, and pointed it in the direction of the stairway heading down to the first floor. JJ already had Jordan covering the other direction with his .38. Thomas regrouped and put a fresh clip of 12 rounds into his gun. He heard more gunfire that he assumed was cutting into the rag dolls that were his friends. Then he heard silence.

The windows on the second floor were locked. Worse then that, they could not be smashed open. JJ tried with Thomas's night stick. Given the thickness of the glass, trying to shoot them out would be ineffective, even dangerous. Each of the three survivors was armed but running low on ammo. They walked on, towards a light at the end of the second floor hallway. It looked like an open doorway.

One Hundred One

Randy at the guard booth detected a lull in the shooting. The previous shots were barely audible to him as he waited at the gate for the three teenage men of El Salvadoran decent. Randy used the lull to radio both the Sheriffs and the Compton P.D. dispatchers, making them believe the officers were Code 11 for East L.A., cop speak for the fact that they were leaving the last location in Bel Air and heading to East L.A. to conduct further police business. When he spoke with the Compton dispatcher, he pretended to be Sheriff's Detective Ramirez; for the Sheriff's dispatcher, he was Compton Detective Rodriguez. This so that the respective dispatchers would not notice any voice discrepancies.

When the three young men were dropped off at the guard booth, their blue Pendleton shirts, white t-shirts, baggy jeans, and shaved heads made known their gang membership. They were Soto Street Locos who hailed from homes located on the road with the same name in East Los Angeles. In addition to selling drugs, they earned money stealing cars and selling them to chop shops. At Randy's direction, the three changed from their gang attire to navy blue security guard uniforms (that was the closest to cop uniforms that Randy could get his hands on in a pinch). Then they broke into the locked cop cars, pulled out their ignition wires, and fired them up. They would drive them to a garage in East Los Angeles where they would be reduced to parts by noon the following day. The thieves were told that the cars were stolen earlier in the day just to fuck with the police. For their trouble they were given a $6,000 cash bonus to split, in addition to the cars themselves.

"Shit, man, there's a dude back there," said a cholo known as "Creep," as he was putting his street clothes into the back seat of JJ's Caprice. Randy and the other two Soto Street Locos walked over and saw a tall, slender man lying uncomfortably on the back seat. Randy removed a Glock 9mm from his waistband, and, holding the gun pointed at Stan's head with one hand, shook him with his other. Stan did not awaken.

"This dude looks fucked up," said one of the vatos.

Randy searched for a pulse on Stan's neck but could find none. Though his head was drenched with sweat, he felt ice cold. Randy knew of the death sentence handed down on Reid, and shook his head in awe of the power that the organization had to get what it wanted. He no longer entertained any doubts about whether Rhory could pull off the murder of six law enforcement personnel in his own home without detection.

"You need to dispose of this for me too," said Randy to Creep, who was the group's leader.

"No way, man. You didn't tell us we had to take care of no dead dude."

"There's another $10,000 in it for you if you take him. I'll have the money dropped off to you tomorrow."

"We aint' gonna do it for less than 50."

"I could get a guy wacked for less. I'll give you 20."

"40. My homeboys and I ain't gonna risk gettin' booked on no 187 for no chump change, man."

"30."

"35 man, and that's it."

"Deal."

Before the cholos drove away, Randy gave them the admonition of the organization. They talk, they die.

One Hundred Two

Back inside the house of horrors, things were light years beyond weird. The three frightened men continued slowly down the long upstairs hallway, towards the light of the open doorway, guns pointed, looking for a way out. They heard crackling, then voices over an intercom system. Jordan was surprised to recognize that it was he himself who was speaking. He was talking to Courtney. Then Jordan was speaking with JJ about what Raymond, the man who lived in the bush, told him he saw at the Roosevelt High schoolyard. Then Stan was speaking to Jordan. "Don't trust anyone," said Stan, shortly before hanging up. Jordan remembered this conversation as the one he had with Stan earlier in the evening, but what seemed like a week ago, preceding his near shooting death in the taxi cab. The next call was an even more recent one: JJ talking to Judge Henman about the search warrant. A voice came over the intercom. It was live. It was Judge Henman.

"Detective Ramirez. You will never appear in my courtroom again." Mad laughter. "Not a bad impression of his honor, wouldn't you agree?"

Waving his gun in all directions, Thomas demanded, "what the fuck is going on?"

JJ explained, "Its Callum. He's been intercepting our conversations. Now he's showing off. C'mon out you sick fuck! What are you afraid of?"

"Yes," the intercom voice said, "I'm such a scaredy cat, that's why I have the balls to take out five cops and a Deputy D.A. in my own home. I don't even mind that you told your dispatchers you're here."

"I agree, you are a stupid mother fucker!" said Thomas, getting in on the conversation with the unseen maniac.

The intercom voice dripped with glee as it continued, "And, Mr. Deputy D.A., I just got word that your friend Stanley is dead. So sorry. It's a shame to lose such a valued employee."

Deciding that this had to be some wacked-out dream or hallucination (who the hell slipped him the acid, he wondered), Jordan didn't acknowledge the news of Stan's death.

"Detective Ramirez, listen up, you'll like this next one."

At first JJ didn't recognize the boy on the telephone, who spoke in a hoarse, groggy voice.

"Hello?"

"Sorry to wake you buddy. This is Detective Davis. There's been a change of plans."

"What is it?" asked the boy, his normal voice returning.

"JJ and I received information that your life is in immediate danger. Your gang has put a green light out on you. Your Aunt and her kids are also in danger if you stay there. You are going to have to go into the Sheriff's witness protection program."

"Are you sure, holmes?"

"Positive. So you have to leave right now. Do you have a pen?"

"Hold on. Okay."

"This is where JJ and I are going to meet you. Take the 91 freeway east all the way until you get to -"

Yorba Linda. The set up. Suspecting Blair's involvement based on circumstantial evidence like phone bills was one thing. But hearing his voice leading this young man, JJ's surrogate son, to his death, was something else altogether.

No longer walking cautiously in step, he ran ahead of the other cop and D.A. until he reached the end of the hall. Meaning every word, he screamed "I am going to fucking kill you!"

JJ reached the light. It was the only door that was open on the second floor. Once inside the large guest room, JJ panned in every direction. Thomas and Jordan arrived in the room to see JJ spinning and pointing his gun at absolutely nothing. JJ covered Thomas while he checked the closet and Jordan covered the hallway. In the closet were only blankets that matched the comforter on the king bed.

"Men are coming!" yelled Jordan, going with the weird dream, but with more than a tinge of worry that this was, in fact, happening in real time and space. He slammed the door shut and locked it with the turn of a button on a lock that couldn't stop a 10-year-old with a wire hanger.

"How many?" asked JJ.

"Four. Five maybe," reported Jordan. Loud, hard steps in the hall-way. "With large --"

Gunfire erupted before he could say "rifles." Fragments of wood flew. JJ threw Jordan out of the way of the door and the incoming projectiles. The detective looked up at the ceiling, and this time there were no mirrors. Just a . . . skylight! It looked like normal glass with a slight tint. He fired into the dark heavens above him and, eventually, created a way out.

Thomas fired his main and backup weapons through what was turning into an open doorway. Jordan, lying on the ground, added rounds to Thomas's. The four or five men retreated. Thomas had to reload. When Jordan had fired all six bullets in his gun, he placed the useless revolver in his waistband. The men in the hallway squeezed off more rounds and moved closer again.

Thomas boosted JJ then Jordan up and through the open skylight. When it was his turn, he slid the king bed under the skylight, removed a small chair from under a desk and placed it on the bed. When he jumped onto the wobbly chair, it slipped out from under him, and he hit the wall with a thud. Standing up again, he saw a gloved hand reaching in to unlock the fragmented bedroom door. Motivation.

This time Thomas landed on the chair solidly, then, thinking high school high jump competition, sprung up, his muscular arms lurching for the hole in the ceiling. He accidentally scraped a jagged piece of tinted glass that cut his hand deeply, but still managed to get a grip on the open roof and pull himself up. His athletic feat was the most important of his life, though there were no fans applauding him this time.

The threesome moved as quickly as they could without losing to gravity, making their way across the terra cotta shingles on the slightly pitched roof. They were quite high for only being up two stories. The gargantuan height of the first floor ceilings made it more like three stories. Peering down at the driveway, alarmed, Thomas said, "Where are our cars?" "Mother fuckers took 'em," he said, answering himself.

"They didn't think we'd need them," said JJ, as he noticed that Jordan had been shot. He was bleeding pretty good. Shoulder wound. Through and through.

"Keep pressure on this if you can" JJ advised. Then, splash! Thomas was down, and was quickly out running toward the gate. Good idea. JJ led Jordan to the edge of the roof nearest the pool. At that time, he saw a Sheriff's vehicle pull up to the now open gate. Backup. Thank God! He made Jordan jump. Then he followed.

The cold pool water smacked Jordan back to reality. His feet and legs hit the bottom painfully. The water felt strange on his shoulder.

When JJ came up for air he realized that he had lost his gun. He was relieved, though, when he saw a familiar face looking down at him in the trembling water.

"Jim!" he would have told him how great it was to see him, but instead he cut to more important matters, "three Compton P.D. officers are seriously wounded by gunfire inside. There is one psycho owner and four or five gunman with fully automatic weapons in there too. The D.A. here's been shot in the shoulder."

"Everything's under control JJ," said Lieutenant Flores, reassuringly.

"There are ten deputies inside right now. Come with me."

JJ helped Jordan out of the pool. They walked with Lieutenant Flores towards his car and JJ did the math in his head. Suddenly, JJ grabbed the Lieutenant around the torso, restraining his arms. "Take his gun!" he yelled to Jordan, who complied. Once Jordan had Lieutenant Flores safely at the gunpoint of Flores' own duty weapon, JJ removed Flores's backup .22 from his boot and switched guns with Jordan.

Seconds later, Jordan felt light headed from the blood loss and collapsed, falling onto the hard cement. The .22 skipped away from him, just a bend and a grab away from Flores.

"Back away from that gun," warned JJ.

"You're making a big mistake," Flores pleaded.

"Am I? Even if you left right after I talked to you in Mammoth, you're still an hour early. You weren't on vacation. You were laying low because I was closing in on your sorry ass. There is a reason you knew too much about Alex's killing. And where are the ten deputies?"

The Lieutenant smiled and said, "There's one now."

Before he could turn around, JJ felt hard steel pressing against the back of his head.

"Morning partner," said Blair Davis, from the safer end of a .44 magnum.

He thought about trying something, but Lieutenant Flores quickly disarmed him. Then he collected the .22 that Jordan was holding before he hit the ground.

"You went too far, partner," Davis taunted.

"You fucking murderer. You're not my partner. *Your* partner's got a tail and a forked tongue."

"Congratulations JJ. You win. You're the good guy. Great job. Now what the fuck do you have to show for it? Nothing. All that matters in this lifetime is power. And, as we all know, money *is* power."

"Heads up," said Flores, when he saw who had walked out of the house and was making his way over.

Rhory Callum wore a black, silk robe and slippers, as if he had just awoken for a midnight snack. He was followed by Maurice and Kurt, who wore automatic rifles strapped around their thick frames.

"It is such an honor to finally meet JJ Ramirez, the great gang Detective," said Rhory.

"Fuck you."

"And so eloquent. You must have studied at Oxford."

"Sorry. Let me try again. Fucketh you, and fucketh thy mother. Is that better?"

"This is getting rather boring. Careful, Detective, when I get bored I usually change the channel."

"Ok, new channel. Fuck you, fuck Davis, fuck Flores, and fuck your gay body guards, but you probably already have." JJ was doing his best to offend.

"Okay, time to change the channel."

Blair Davis backed away from JJ, and Maurice moved closer, aiming his SKS automatic rifle with its silencer at JJ's head.

"Wait," said Rhory, "let me move further away, I don't want his brains on me. Though I can't imagine there's much brain matter in there."

JJ didn't have much time left to think of a way out of this. If he was going to die, he at least wanted to take Alex's killer with him. He wished he had shot Blair earlier when he had a gun.

The young D.A. lay motionless on the pavement listening to voices but not opening his eyes. Knowing he had to do something, he pushed off with his hands and sprung to his feet. He reached into his front waistband, and then grabbed the closest person to him around the neck. It was the man in the silk robe. Jordan placed the empty .38 revolver against the side of Rhory Callum's head and said, "Drop your weapons, or your fearless leader dies."

Davis still covered JJ, but now Flores and the two body guards pointed their weapons at the entangled bodies that were Rhory and Jordan.

Randy came up from the gate, though it was not as if the good guys needed another armed goon to contend with.

"Everybody relax," said Rhory, with an earful of snub-nosed gun barrel.

"Should I try to take him out boss?" asked Randy.

"No. All of you drop your guns."

"Don't do it!" commanded Flores, "The Deputy D.A. here is not gonna kill anyone."

"I'm with you Jim," said Blair, "He doesn't have the cahones."

"Oh, I'll do it," Jordan said, hoping Lee Strasberg's acting method was working for him. Not that he wouldn't do it, but it was just that he *couldn't*.

"What are you waiting for?" asked Flores. "Do it."

Rhory implored, "C'mon Jim, the organization needs me. Don't be foolish, put down your gun."

Sensing that he was becoming expendable, Rhory continued, "Randy, Maurice, and Kurt, make the officers play nice and put their guns away."

Maurice turned his huge gun on Flores. "You heard him, drop your gun."

The Lieutenant, not about to be second to the punch, shot the hired thug three times in the stomach. Falling backward, Maurice managed a trigger burst from the automatic rifle that tore through the Lieutenant's neck. Almost simultaneously, Kurt mowed down Blair Davis, aiming too low and taking out his legs, as opposed to vital organs. Randy shot and missed. On his knees, the corrupt detective Davis, the consummate marksman, put a round between the eyes of Kurt, dropping him instantly like wild game, and then emptied his clip into Randy's side-of-a-barn target of a chest.

During the melee, JJ dove for cover behind a large pineapple palm tree. Rhory struggled briefly with Jordan, who easily gave up the revolver and ran. Rhory aimed at Jordan and clicked through the entire chamber before realizing he'd been had. The DDA was about to open a door to the house in an effort to find cover, but it opened from the other side. At that moment he was face to face with the woman he'd made love to only days ago. This time she wanted to make war.

"Hi love," Courtney said, looking at him down the sight of a Russian Makarov .380.

Jordan got down on the ground on his stomach as she commanded him to do, his shoulder killing him in that position. When Rhory got there she gave him the gun and said, "You do it. This is boys' stuff." Sensing death, Jordan looked down at the ground. About to check out from this planet, all he saw was Kendall's beautiful face.

JJ picked up the .44 from the ground near Davis, who was no longer clutching the gun, but, rather, holding his bloody legs as he moaned in pain and screamed expletives at a god in whom he no longer believed. Figuring that life in prison would be a harsher punishment than a quick bullet to the brain, especially for a cop, JJ locked Davis's hands together using the dirty Sergeant's own handcuffs.

He turned and looked out over the still, bullet-ravaged bodies and saw, 75 yards away, Rhory standing over Jordan with a gun and the wrong motives. At that distance, he could not possibly hit Callum, so he yelled for him to drop his gun and shot into the air above him.

Undaunted by JJ's actions, Rhory's killing arm stretched out straight. He took aim at the back of the young Deputy District Attorney's head, the gun barrel only inches away from its target. But at that moment, he could no longer feel the gun. Rhory's hand went completely numb. With his other hand, he pulled up his black silky sleeve and exposed an unbelievable sight- a ghoulish case of gangrene that stretched from his cut finger to his elbow. And the worst part was that it appeared to be . . . moving! The gun had already fallen to the ground. Streptococcus A had claimed its second victim of the evening.

Before Courtney could do anything, Detective JJ Ramirez picked up the Makarov and was once again in control.

A little late, but nonetheless much appreciated, Officer Thomas arrived back on scene. And he brought friends. A S.W.A.T. team, two helicopters, all of the remaining Compton P.D., and most of the Pacific Division of L.A.P.D.

One Hundred Three

On the way to the hospital, the pain was more than Jordan could bear. Not the pain in his shoulder, the more serious one in his heart. His best friend was gone. No more good times, no more analyzing the hands, good and bad, dealt by life, no more Stan-Man.

Appropriately, the young D.A. was taken by ambulance to County U.S.C. Hospital. No one did gun shot wounds better than the doctors at County U.S.C. After he was stitched up, given strangers' blood and poked with needles that prevented infections, he called Kendall. He told her what had happened. And he told her that Stan was technically still just 'missing.' She was on her way to the airport until he convinced her she should come on Wednesday, as it would take him a couple of days to be interviewed by the police and get himself together. That's what he wanted, he told her. Very reluctantly, she agreed. Jordan also called his parents and assured them he was alright and that he would visit them in a couple of weeks.

As Jordan was being wheeled from a precautionary X-ray back to his room, a gurney passed him. It was being pushed by an orderly and trailed by a Deputy Sheriff. On the gurney, he saw someone he recognized. It was Stan the Man! He was alive! He was also unconscious. Jordan grabbed the arm of the Deputy. "This is my best friend, Stan Reid. My name is Jordan Stowic. I'm a Deputy D.A."

Jordan proceeded to find out that Stan was in serious condition and being taken to surgery. The cop told Jordan how he found Stan. He was on the early morning patrol in East L.A. Actually, he was on break. He heard a dog barking loudly. Given the early morning hour, he went into the alley behind the donut shop to quiet the dog. There he saw a stray German shepherd mix tugging on what was a human arm. That arm happened to be attached to a body that lay behind a trash dumpster. Thank God for Lassie!

Jordan didn't care if Stan was rescued by Lassie, a Saint Bernard, wolves, dolphins, Big Foot, or a trained seal; bottom line-- Stan lived! Jordan thanked the deputy profusely, and then spoke at length with Stan's doctor, a sharp young internist named Dr. Kenneth Lee, who made a confident diagnosis, though the first diagnosis of this kind for him. Streptococcus A. Stan was being prepped for surgery as they spoke; so that doctors could remove the infected parts of his skin which Dr. Lee called the "necrotic tissue." That, the doctor explained, was only the first part of the treatment. Stan needed to be airlifted to another hospital. He required placement inside a pressurized hyperbaric oxygen chamber, treatment County U.S.C. was not equipped to provide. Oxygen was necessary to kill the bacteria and stop its spread. Afterwards, Stan would be given a powerful antibiotic called Clindamycin, which would, hopefully, stop the bacteria's toxins from affecting any vital organs. The nearest facility was in Thousand Oaks, the Los Robles Regional Medical Center, which had a hyperbaric unit. Finishing his summary, the young doctor added glumly, "while I am confident that you're friend will survive, he will probably lose part of his body to the gangrene."

Jordan was about to fall asleep, when JJ entered his hospital room.

"How you making out counselor?"

"I'm alright," said Jordan.

"I was happy to hear that Stan's gonna make it."

"Yeah, you'll have your witness."

"Hey, I'm also glad for you. I know how close you guys are. It's just that your friend messed up big time, and, quite frankly, even if he testifies for the prosecution, he'll still have to go to jail."

"I know."

"By the way, that girl at the Bel Air house was arrested on an FBI warrant. Seems she's got quite an interesting fraud background."

"That's good news."

"Wasn't she your girlfriend?"

"No. Just a girl I went out with. There's a big difference."

"Well, young man, I hope you get better soon and get back in court. Maybe some day we'll even have another case together."

Jordan laughed at how ridiculous it seemed to suggest a repeat of the last 24 hours.

"Thank you detective. But if we ever have another case together, I will gladly let you do all the police work. I'll just stick to that court stuff."

Before JJ left the room, it was agreed that he would let Jordan know when the funerals for Bracey and the Compton officers would be. They planned on attending them together.

One Hundred Four

It had been four days since Jordan was shot and had witnessed other men die. He spent the last two hours sitting with his best friend at the Los Robles Medical Center. Listening to him cry. Joining him. They had to remove Stan's right leg. A third of his muscle in his other leg was gone. Parts of his body would be numb forever. Rehabilitation efforts would be extensive. On top of that, he would spend a year of his life in a place he'd never been and always feared to go -- County Jail. This because he accepted a plea and cooperation offer from the D.A.'s Office that required him to testify against Blair Davis, James Flores, Hotchie, and others. There would be no trial for Rhory Callum. He died when the toxic bacteria shut down his vital organs.

Stan's tears were, in fact, not shed over his lost limb. They were tears of joy. Jordan had really forgiven him. He would be there to help him get through this, just as he helped him after the car accident when they were in high school, or the tie incident in junior high. For the first time in a long time, Stan believed he would make it. It was guaranteed by a true friendship.

The traffic made it take over an hour to get from Thousand Oaks down to LAX, and Jordan worried that he'd be late. Once he parked, he sprinted through the terminal, dodging counterfeit nuns and men pretending to be blind to get handouts. When he got to where he was going, the gate agent told him the flight had landed five minutes earlier. A tap came on the shoulder. He turned around.

"Ken-Doll!" he exclaimed, kissing and squeezing the merchandise. The pain in his shoulder from the embrace was negated by the excitement of seeing her.

"How are you darling?" she asked coyly.

"A hell of a lot better now, K."

"How's Stan doing?"

"He's going to have a tough go, but I think he's in the right frame of mind."

"I can't believe how much has happened since I've seen you," she said.

"Yeah, too many things for one August."

At the baggage claim, they hugged and kissed until Jordan noticed that almost every traveler had carted off their bag. The carrousel was almost deserted.

"That one's mine." she said. A large suitcase. "That one too." A big box tied with string that probably should have been on the special carrousel with the golf bags. "Oh, and that one." A hanging clothes bag stuffed like a pregnant Thanksgiving turkey.

"You moving in sweetie, or are you just planning on holding a yard sale while you're in town?"

"Well, that brings up a good point. In fact, there's something that I would like to ask you."

"Yes?"

"Do you mind if I stay with you in L.A. for a little while?"

Smiling his answer, which was obviously "Yes," he asked, "Kendall Jane, are you asking if you can play house with me?"

"No, I just want to have sex with you everyday. You can do the dishes."

Laughing. Kissing.

"What about Joe and Barbara?"

"They can do their own dishes."

Jordan walked Kendall away from the baggage claim to a man in a hat holding a sign that read, "Kendall Wright." Jordan directed this man back to Kendall's fleet of luggage.

The limousine took them down the coast towards San Diego. Along the way, they sipped champagne and told each other their memories of their first moments of attraction to each other at Northwestern. These confessions had been made many times before, but they never got old.

At sunset, the driver finally stopped at a cliff in La Jolla, overlooking Black's Beach. He rolled down the windows so that the couple in the back could absorb the orange and crimson sky. It was at that time that Jordan inserted a tape into the tape deck. It was Harry Connick's version of Gus Kahn's "It Had to Be You." Then he put his knee to the floormat, produced an emerald cut diamond ring, and, with the surf breaking below, asked his love to marry him.

One Hundred Five

JJ spent the morning in downtown Los Angeles at the main office of the Los Angeles County District Attorney. He was an integral part of high level meetings with District Attorney Salsman and Chief Collins. The Snow case was closed out, and that was the good news. But a new Pandora's Box of police corruption was opened, and that corruption included murder and drug trafficking, among other crimes. It was decided that there would be a special task force of Deputy Sheriffs and specially-assigned Deputy D.A.s to ensure the validity of the facts on all of the previous cases handled by the dirty cops. A separate trial team would prosecute the charges against the police defendants. Salsman was pissed about a rumor that the United States Attorney's Office and the FBI were contemplating a federal filing. He hoped that they would give him first crack at the big media case. So did his re-election committee.

At the end of the meeting, JJ announced that he was taking a two-month stress leave. He was entitled to it under the Sheriff's leave policy, and Chief Collins asked only that JJ provide a number where he could be reached in an emergency. The detective told his Chief that he'd call him when he knew where he would be.

JJ took a cab from the meeting to a used car lot in West Los Angeles. He didn't even haggle before handing the happy salesman a cashier's check for the asking price of a white 1967 Corvette convertible in mint condition. JJ had tried to find red, but white was the only option on such short notice. His first stop in his new wheels was Compton, where he visited with Alex's Aunt Rosie. She had made him promise that he would stop by to see her so she could thank him in person for bringing Alex's murderer to justice.

Smelling like Aunt Rosie's perfume, he put the top down and gear-shifted his roadster from Compton to Long Beach on the 710 freeway. The wind shaped his salt and pepper hair into abstract art. It felt good.

Loni's mop was soaking up the spilled beer of the hardcore morning crew when the wrinkled face above it peered out a tiny window that rationed sunlight. She set the mop down. When he walked in, she greeted him with, "Look at Mr. Bigshot," referring to JJ's means of transportation. The detective entered the Aftershock and looked around as if it were his first time there.

"Where ya been," she asked, "You weren't picked up for having sex with a 17-year-old who looked 22, were you?"

"I've been busy."

"I know. I read the papers. I guess you solved your big case."

"Yes I did," he said, moving closer and catching her off guard with a gentle embrace.

Though the hug she said, "I'll get you a tall glass. After what you've been though, you could probably use mucho cocktails."

"Actually, I just came by to tell you that I'm going away for a while."

"What, you're a hero now, so you bought an expensive car and you're moving up to a better crowd?"

"Not at all Loni. I got some business up North. Monterey."

Catching on, Loni said, "Didn't you used to have one of them old Corvettes in red. Yeah, back when you were with old what's her name, Miss 'You'll never get over me.' And didn't she move up there to --"

"I can't fool you Loni," he said, handing her an envelope. She would later open it to find a check for $1,000 to help her pay the bills. He figured she'd miss his business over the months to come.

Loni turned down the volume on the Jukebox to listen to the roar of the Detective's 8-cylinder engine as it fired up and drove off, North to Monterey, 400 miles and one missed opportunity away.